The author's first printed sto
and on and off until the outbreak (

Abroad in many places, as a
e wrote three novels – published
publishers asked for a fourth, and in these novels two best
sellers emerged.

He wrote for newspapers and magazines and about his
lovely daughter, who sadly died at the age of seventeen years
and ten months. His beloved wife died at the age of sixty-four.

William Scott has a BA honours and others in the Arts
honours.

AND
THE GODS
LOOKED
DOWN

AND
THE GODS
LOOKED
DOWN

William Scott

Central Publishing Limited
West Yorkshire

ISBN 1 903970 21 0

**Published
by**

Central Publishing Limited
Royd Street Offices
Milnsbridge
Huddersfield
West Yorkshire
HD3 4QY

www.centralpublishing.co.uk

And The Gods Looked Down

CHAPTER ONE

1874
ORIGIN OF THE SPECIES

The failure of Mary Leach to tell George put her in an early grave. In the bustle of the wedding she had worried about scrawling her signature in the Parish Register of Bethnal Green Church, with George's father there paying everything, and her secret was lost for a time as she changed her name to Foulkes.

They went to live in an old cottage, sparsely furnished, built with others for Spitalfield's foreign silk weavers a century past and refurbished now so that the landlords could credibly raise the rent.

Bethnal Green in 1874 was not a Metropolitan Borough of London, which attracted people of taste or wealth. The poorest humanity abounded among its 80,000 inhabitants. Beggars and buskers had their regular pitches in those strangled streets of poverty, the poor seeking the widow's mite generosity of the poor, for the abodes of the wealthy elsewhere were bulwarked by long gardens, or menservants who opened doors and threatened to call the police to all beggars and buskers; the rich had untrained imaginations that kept poverty at the distance of Greek mythology.

A few years before the frugal wedding ceremony the Baroness Burdett-Couts helped the wretched populace by providing the means to build the Columbia Market, set amidst the model housing near the Gothic Hall, a valiant, public-spirited venture by a lady of great sensitivity to try to clear the slums and provide a centre where cheap food could be bought.

George Foulkes, coachman, was a lady-killer, a proud young man of twenty-four, tall and large boned, with regular features, short, stiff, waxed moustache, short sideburns, dark hair, the crown being brushed flat on either side of a clean, straight, middle parting. In his livery of grey coat with red lapels, red buttonhole flower, grey bowler and grey kid gloves, he made a smart impression sitting straight backed and aloof on the padded seat of his employer's landau, his highly polished boots against the sloping foot-rest, and the vehicle beneath him in spanking condition. Of all his staff, the employer thought most highly of George because of his proud appearance and his expertise in the care of horses.

But George was not content with his £24 per year. He planned to move from London and serve some wealthy gentry in the provinces. He found no pleasure in driving through the London streets with their horse-dirt and multitudinous crawling vehicles. The prosperous businessman his employer, went on vacation once a year down to his country abode in Sussex, using the train. George was left behind to drive the children and their Governess wherever they wished to go, an impingement on George's sensitivities, for his job was conducive enough to subservience without his having to submit to the whims and orders of a mere governess who always treated him on the same level as she would a scullery-maid. George hated snobbery and never once considered himself as the personification of it.

He hid his poverty from the outside world by pride and an appearance of respectability. His employers were always the cynosures who directed his working deeds and opinions. Their auras of importance transferred themselves to him, and their wishes, whims and idiosyncrasies were his guidelines. He dedicated himself to faithful service and in a strange way he used his subservience as an asset of superiority over his peers.

He was thankful for the Columbia Market where food was cheaper than anywhere else. It meant that he could pay Mary a reasonably low housekeeping allowance and keep his pocket lined for ale, tobacco, and women, no longer restricting himself to occasional gratuities from his employer's business friends.

At first George was not displeased with his marriage. Mary was a good, economical cook and housewife, and a placid partner. He had been incidentally fortunate that, being no beauty, she was shapely and in her best clothes could be attractive. She seemed grateful that George Foulkes had made her an honest woman and the child in her womb would be legitimate.

When the child was born that same year they christened her Ellen - Little Nell George called her for a few weeks. He derided the idea that the child was a beauty as Mary's neighbours maintained.

Three months after little Nell's birth, George saw exactly what he wanted, a Mercury advertisement which said:

WANTED, coachman, smart, aged under thirty; knowledge of horses; £28 per annum; hse inc; good refs essential; no beer; Sir Frederick Minnes, Furlongton, Lancs.

George bought six sheets of writing paper from the corner shop, took out his fine pen and black ink, and in an excellent copperplate handwriting and grammatically correct wording, applied for the post. He had been a good scholar in the rudimentary education he had received at the Catherington Church School, Horndean, Southampton. His employer and the Secretary were disappointed when he asked for a reference. Why did he want to leave? His father, a widower, had taken ill up in Lancashire, George explained, and he would have to take a post up there to be near the old man. He would never otherwise have dreamt of leaving his present employer who had been so good to him, and so forth. He received an excellent reference and posted it off with his application letter. Two weeks later he handed in his livery, the stable keys, packed everything they possessed in four suitcases, and travelled to Euston Station.

In the dusty third-class carriage of an early train, the baby asleep in Mary's arms and George sitting opposite, she was glad they were alone. With no other person there

George had no need to pretend. She actually believed that her husband was superior to her - he could write a good grammatical letter and his speech gave the false impression of a cultured person. Mary's knowledge of the world was pathetic. She had a singsong voice that lacked any Welsh music because her mother, not Welsh, was loud-mouthed and vulgar, her sexual attractions being the Welsh farmer's only reason for marrying her. Mary thought, sometimes, that a fine-looking man like George could have had any girl he wished; she was unaware that Mr Samuel Foulkes, a bricklayer, had been warned by his wife that Mary was probably pregnant and, being a good Hampshire Methodist, he had threatened George with a hiding - Samuel was having no bastards in his family!

'It'll be good to be living in fresh country air, girl,' George said, watching the green landscape through the train window. 'Away from all the smoke and dirt and traffic. Peace and quiet is what we want, girl. It'll be a great improvement - extra two pounds wages. London's a dear place to live in. I bet things are cheaper in Burnley than they are at Columbia Market.'

'Oh? D' y' think so, George?'

'Sure of it.'

Mary was cheered by the news.

'You'll have to let your family know where we are living, girl. Your father'll want to know. Tell him about Nellie. He'll be pleased – and your mother too.'

'Yes, George,' she murmured, her heart fluttering.

'Aye, girl,' he went on, his brain working hard. 'Tell them all about everything and they might send us a pound or two for Nellie. We could do with some help from your folk. My father paid our wedding expenses. We got nothing from your folks. A farmer earns more than a bricklayer.'

'It isn't a big farm,' she said in a small voice. 'It was very run-down, George - that's why they got it so cheap.'

'Even so,' he declared, 'there'll be more money from it than from a bricklayer's job.'

'Maybe, George, I don't know.'

'No maybe about it,' he answered sharply. 'I'm telling

3

you. Your family's done damn all to help us. Write and ask them to send something for the baby.'

Mary's face paled as she sat eyeing her husband. He frowned at her.

'What are you staring at? Close your mouth. You look stupid.'

'George - I - I - can't write.'

'Of course you can write. You signed the register in the vestry that time.'

'My father learnt me to write my name.'

'My God! I might have known! It was a damned sloppy signature.'

'I never went to school, George,' she told him, pathetically, expecting some sympathy.

'Never went to school? That's typical. What kind of parents have you got? If I'd have learnt how to write my name I would have gone on and learnt more. Have you no pride, girl?'

She understood now that this husband of hers had a dangerous streak of contempt for weakness in others. In that railway carriage going north, the seed of fear of her husband was sewn. Her confession of illiteracy had confirmed her inferior status.

At Crewe they had to change for the Burnley train. As they seated themselves on the platform bench, the child began to cry and Mary said it needed suckling.

'Well,' said George, with harsh emphasis, 'you don't suckle her here, girl - not while I'm with you, and that's final.'

She placed the India rubber dummy in its mouth and the child was quietened. But when the locomotive came creaking and puffing into the station, the child awoke and started to cry again, and this time it would not be soothed.

The train was crowded. A well-mannered young man gave up his seat to Mary and her child. George stood holding on to the luggage rack, his body half covering them. Little Nell wailed and wailed, to its father's fuming irritation. In desperation Mary pulled the shawl high over her left shoulder and across her body, shielding the baby's head in a tiny cavern of secrecy, and the baby began to suckle, bringing peace to the compartment. From where George stood he could hear plainly the lip-sounds of the hungry child and the embarrassment surged into his cheeks. He damned his wife for disobeying him. By God! She was not going to make a spectacle of him! The young man, standing next to him, looked away through the window. The women passengers saw everything and thought no more of such a natural act.

It was a stopping train and at the next station four people alighted, leaving two empty seats one next to Mary and the other near the window on the far side. He astonished her when he sat down in the far seat, allowing the young man to sit next to her. What had she done? Had she not nursed the child to sleep now? She removed her nipple from its mouth and covered her breast with her blouse, drawing the shawl around the baby's head.

George's profiled face across the compartment puzzled and frightened her - his thin lips were tight, his brows knotted in a black annoyance. It was fortunate that she could not read him. Everyone note - he was not acquainted with that woman opposite, that brazen peasant he had married against his will, feeding her baby in front of everyone, with three men present, too! I'll kill the bitch! He continued to glare out of the window, not once moving his head to look at her. Her family were ill-bred creatures with no concern for fine sensitivities. The disgrace she had almost brought on him! The whole disgusting exhibition sickened him. If she needed to suckle her young in public like some damned sow in a farmyard, she was not going to do it when he was with her! Why hadn't she gone into the ladies' room at Crewe? Of course, she wouldn't know what a ladies' room was. That young goggling pup gives her his seat and she has the utter stupidity to bare her breast in front of him! These women think she's a slut!

At Burnley he waited until everyone had alighted and then stood up to collect the cases. Without a word he struggled onto the platform, deposited the cases and walked off to hire a brougham to take them to Furlongton. When he returned she was on the platform waiting, her eyes fearful, her whole body rigid in cold bewilderment. A porter was loading their cases onto a trolley.

'There's a carriage outside,' he told the porter, ignoring the fact that his wife had taken it upon herself to find a porter - he wanted no scenes in public.

'Righto, sir,' said the porter, and dragged the trolley to the exit.

George gave in his tickets and pushed through the turnstile, she cringing along behind him like a lowly serf. He gave the porter three-pence and they boarded the brougham.

'What is the matter, George?' she asked. Her seemingly quaint naivety enraged him.

'What is the matter?' he rasped. 'You mean, you don't know? But why should you know? You are just a bloody slut. Are you some farm sow that you can suckle your young in front of everybody? You make a show of me again and I'll - I'll kill you, by God!'

For the rest of the journey they remained silent, the atmosphere in the small interior of the carriage ominous and black.

The mill cottage allotted to the coachman was small and furnished with necessities for kitchen living area, and sleeping places upstairs. They were utilitarian furnishings but adequate for people in their station of life. Across the road, almost opposite their front door, were the wrought-iron gates to a drive that led to the Briar House of Sir Frederick Minnes, the owner of Briar Mills.

With the business of meeting his new employer, being shown around the stables by the estate manager, and in taking stock of the horses he would be attending, George Foulkes postponed the matter of the incident in the train; but that evening he had things to say. She had put the baby in its crib upstairs and was making some cocoa.

'I'm warning you again, woman, make a show of humiliating me again in public and I'll kill you, I swear.'

'Would you have all the passengers complain about the child's crying?' she asked.

'A child crying is normal. A woman who bears her breast in public is not.'

'No one takes any notice of it, George. The child had to be fed on a long journey.'

'Not in front of men,' he snarled.

After a pause, she said wearily, 'It shan't happen again.'

'By God! It had better not. You're lucky this time. I'd give you a damned thrashing if it weren't for this new job. I'm saying no more now - but you just watch yourself.' His harshness sent a quiver of terror through her heart as she remembered her secret.

That night in bed Mary was amazed when her husband immediately turned over and went to sleep. She sighed deeply, her relief enveloping her whole body and mind. She checked the baby's crib next to the bed, closed her eyes, yawned away her distress, and contented herself with the thought that for once she was to be left alone.

*　*　*

Dear Mr and Mrs Leach,

Mary and I are glad to inform you that we have been blessed with a little girl, Nellie, who is now six months old. You will see from our address that we moved from Bethnal Green up into Lancashire. I have a better job now and this country air is good for Mary and the child.

As I am writing for Mary she has asked me to mention that with all recent expenses in moving, etc., perhaps you would like to help us by sending some money for little Nell's money-box and this will enable Mary to buy some clothes later on as she grows bigger. I might point out that my father was very generous in his help towards wedding expenses.

We hope that you are both keeping well and are prospering on your farm. Also give our love to Mary's sisters and brothers.

Your affectionate son-in-law. George Foulkes.

This secret letter elicited no response for some time and George cursed his wife's family as he waited for the anticipated postal order. It was one noontide, as George was eating his midday meal, that there came a knock at the front door. When Mary opened it, the shock of what she saw sent her reeling against the doorjamb.

'My God! Mother!' she gasped in a croaking whisper. 'Why have you done this to me? He'll kill me! He'll kill me!' She stared down at the child who held the red, plump hand of her grandmother.

'Don't be ridiculous, you silly girl!' said the red-faced woman. She pushed past her terrified daughter, dragging the child with her into the living room. George was just finishing his meal. Mary followed her mother, her body quivering in panic, her eyes glistening wide.

'Well, Mary luv, now thou't wed thee con 'ave Lizzie - she is yourn after all. Av had 'er long enough now.'

George jumped up, his thick eyebrows like two arched caterpillars, his arm knocking over his teacup.

'What's this, woman? What's this?' he shouted.

'Well, George, affectionate son-i-law,' said Mrs Leach with a cheerfully sardonic voice, 'this little lass is Mary's child, a sickly wun too, but av dun me best wil 'er an' con do no more. Thee con 'ave 'er now, Mary, luv, t' bring up as y' please.'

'What the hell!' George bellowed, staring at the terrified child.

'Now don't you start shoutin' George luv. I'm gerrin next train back at wun so I'll wish thee both good-day - an' care f' yon child as I've done, Mary, mind.'

Off she swept, her feather boa flowing with the speed of her flight, leaving behind a fuming incredulous George Foulkes and his stunned, petrified, cringing wife who had had the twofold shock of a slut - mother's inhumanity and the sight of her innocent bastard child, its staring eyes now taking in the red-faced, spluttering man before her as he unfastened the buckle of his belt.

Even before the hefty figure of Mrs Leach had ensconced her fleshy body in a hackney cab on her way to the station, George Foulkes had started. He grabbed his wife's long hair, dragged her into the kitchen and began to leather her in a fury of hate, beating her with the belt, ignoring her screams and the child's screeching, snarling as she writhed in pain, 'Whore! Whore! Whore!' with each descending lash.

He left her lying on the kitchen tiles, her face pouring with blood, her blouse torn, her skirt unfastened, her body a heaving mass of agony. He gripped the child by the ear and dragged her screeching in awful terror up the stairs and into the small back room, locking the door behind him. He stormed off to his work, watched by the neighbours who had gathered outside to wonder at the frightful din.

It was late when he came home and she could smell the ale on him even before he had closed the front door. She hobbled painfully to the oven and took out the potato hash she had made with great difficulty, sobbing the day through and knowing what the future would be.

'Get that bastard brat of yours up into that back room,' he ordered. 'If it makes so much as a murmur I'll kill it stone dead - and get yourself upstairs into that bed.'

From that time forward for Mary Foulkes, her husband's sexual assaults on her aching body were nothing less than vicious, bestial, uncontrolled rapes.

*   *   *

Despite Mary's duplicity about Lizzie, four more children were brought into the world, Mary continually suffering with awful aversion and deepest heartache her husband's sadistic gratification of his enormous carnality. He used it to punish and torture her, dominating her failing body like some alien sex monster. Annie was born in 1876, George in 1878, Maggie in 1880, and Emma in 1882. By some miraculous gift of strength at the time of each birth, Mary brought these children into her sad, sad world, without wanting to, without hope for their future, without love, without feeling, with mental torment and in dumb loathing of the man who had made her perform each animal delivery.

In the house George Foulkes showed the venomous evil of his fury. He detested the wretched, innocent Lizzie, taking a fiendish joy in thrashing her for the most trivial misdemeanours, pulling her by the ears, his habitual form of torture when he was drunk. The neighbours threatened him with the police and the Guardians, but it was no more than a threat.

Mary Foulkes died at the premature age of thirty-five, her exhausted, injured, ravished body put to rest in the Parish Church graveyard. On the day following the funeral, Lizzie, now thirteen years old, her distracted brain aching with misery, grasped Emma's hand firmly and walked down to the village pond, and stood there looking down into the depths of black water.

'What are you going to do, Lizzie?' Emma's piping voice enquired.

The child sensed the terrifying desperation in her half-sister's attitude. She saw the tears on Lizzie's cheeks and with instinctive self-preservation, tried to free herself from the restraining grip.

'I want to go home,' Emma bleated.

'What's the use?' Lizzie sobbed. 'Mama's gone! Mama's gone! We shall never see her any more. What's the use?'

She dragged the little one nearer the water and walked into it until it covered their ankles. Emma struggled and screamed. She fought and splashed and wriggled, and her piercing shrieks could be heard in the village. Lizzie forcibly dragged the shrieking child deeper into the water; and then, all against the wretched girl's expectations so early in the morning, came a high-pitched, horrified voice.

'What are you doing, Lizzie?'

Startled out of her obsessive deathwish, Lizzie turned her head. Some yards away, on the edge of the cart track, stood Mrs Cowburn, their neighbour.

'I saw you leaving home, Lizzie. Don't tell me y' were goin' t' drown y'sel' - and the little wun, too, Lizzie Leach?'

came Mrs Cowburn's dismayed question.

Lizzie released her half-sister's hand and let her misery gush forth. Emma splashed out of the water in terror and ran to Mrs Cowburn, the tears on her cheeks as she huddled against the woman's thigh, her three-and-a-half year-old understanding telling her that Lizzie had been about to destroy them both!

The older girl cried bitterly, saying nothing, standing in the water, tacitly acknowledging Mrs Cowburn's suspicions. The good neighbour's attitude softened with deepest pity. She went to the water's edge and stretched her arm to Lizzie. Slowly the poor girl moved out of the mud and Mrs Cowburn, holding Emma's small hand, put her other arm around Lizzie's shoulder and hugged her.

'There, there,' she soothed. 'Come on, little lass, we's all have t' get thee boots and stocks off an' dry 'em afore thee goes hom'.'

'Don't - don't - tell - me - me - stepfather.'

'Eh! o' course not silly. We'll tell that wun nowt. Think like this, Lizzie, this Mama's at rest nah, all peacefu' in 'er quiet grave, an' 'er poor soul is gone t' God in heaven. Y' mama's 'appy nah - away fro' that mon, thank God! Y' mun fight, Lizzie, lass - aye, y' mun fight.'

In the neighbour's cottage the boots and stockings were taken off and set to dry. The four Cowburn children doled out two dessertspoons of porridge from their breakfast for the two visitors; and none of the family asked any questions, guessing the truth, without horror or surprise, from the evidence of the wet footwear.

George Foulkes, thirty-six years old, was now seeking for a 'housekeeper.' to look after his maternally orphaned children, and there appeared on the scene a buxom wench of twenty-five generously proportioned and cheerful, capable enough and kind enough to chide George for wasting too much money on ale and causing the children to suffer. The fear of their brutish father showed in all the children's eyes and nervous gestures. Even young George as he grew up, tall, bony, hollow-cheeked, had no spirit and cowered when he heard his father's footsteps. He was beaten mercilessly on many occasions and left to cry in pain in the back bedroom.

Of all Foulkes's children, the youngest, as she grew up, began to show signs of the first opposition. They were setting out for Sunday school, Emma badly bruised from her father's fist, two blue marks across her forehead and one across her cheekbone.

'You, girl, will tell your Sunday School teacher you bruised yourself falling down the cellar steps. Is that clear?' George Foulkes told her.

'That's a lie,' Emma defied him. 'I'll tell her the truth - you punched me.' From the other side of the table he lunged to grab the child. With amazing alacrity, despite her aching body, Emma dodged away nearer to the front door.

'By God, girl, if you say that I'll kill you!'

'You won't,' Emma shouted. 'They'll hang you - and I hope they do!'

'You bitch!' he roared, making another attempt to get his hands on her. She was too quick and escaped through the open doorway and caught up with the others.

'You'd better tell her what he said,' Nellie advised. 'If you don't he'll take it out on all of us.'

'I won't tell her his lies - indeed I won't. I'll tell her the truth. He'll always be the same if you don't stand up to him.'

'You are a nuisance, you,' Nellie snapped. 'Do as he says - for peace.'

At Sunday School the elderly female looked at the child.

'Emma Foulkes, child - what have you done to yourself?'

'She fell down,' Nellie began.

'I fell down no-where,' Emma shouted. 'I have done nothing to myself - my father beat me black and blue.' Nellie whispered to Emma to say no more.

'I shan't be quiet,' Emma told her, indignantly. 'We don't come to Sunday School to tell lies. He beats us all, every day, Miss Thompson.'

'Oh, dear dear, poor child,' Miss Thompson sympathised. 'We must all pray for him.'

'Pray for HIM?' Emma squeaked her amazement. 'We

must all pray for ME!'

'Now, Emma Foulkes, that is being insolent. We must pray for your father so that he may repent and improve his ways.'

'He will never, never, never improve his ways,' Emma cried, with tears of frustration.

'Now sit down, Emma. We shall say no more. You are overwrought. We must not fill our hearts with hatred, child.' Realising the futility of saying any more to this stupid woman, Emma stamped off to her seat.

So that was the way the church helped those in need? The thought lodged itself deep into Emma's subconscious mind.

Henceforth Emma set out to defy her father, shrewdly recognising his weak spot - if the truth emerged, someone in the village would inform his employer, whose high opinion George cherished and the livelihood of George Foulkes Esquire might be jeopardised. When Emma came home a half hour after the others, her father was waiting, a knot of evil wrath inside him, his fingers itching to choke the life from his only defiant child.

'Come in, you bitch!' he ordered her in a ferocious whisper, holding the door partly open. 'I'll kill you.'

'If you touch me,' Emma shouted as loud as she could, 'I'll scream to the neighbours and they'll fetch the Guardians.'

'Come in,' George snarled through his teeth. The housekeeper appeared, knowing what was afoot.

'Just leave her alone, George. The child's had enough,' she chided.

'You mind your own business, woman,' George rasped.

'It is my business,' said the housekeeper, 'and don't you talk to me like that, George Foulkes I won't stand it. I can walk out of here any time I like.'

George glared, gave a low growl, and stalked into the house. 'Come on in, lass,' said the housekeeper, Miss Heller, originally from Cornwall. 'You'll be all right, my dear.' Emma was to remember Miss Heller later on.

Slowly the other children learned to grasp any titbit of opportunity that came their way. Mrs Cowburn's cousin needed an assistant in his porkshop in Rochley, five miles away. She told Nellie and the girl saw the passing straw in the maelstrom and grasped it eagerly. Off she went to become a counter assistant at Keats's shop, agreeing to send half her wages home each pay-day. A succession of housekeepers brought in by George Foulkes to run the house and see to the children, were sensuous ladies who were soon aware of the hate that existed between the children and their father. Miss Heller had left because of it. At ten years of age Emma saw a group of men carrying a wooden gate on which lay the body of her father. He had been kicked by one of his employer's horses. Emma stopped short, taking in the scene, and then skipped delightedly towards the men, singing, 'My father's dead! My father's dead! I'll get a new black frock!' There was no mistaking the huge joy in the child's voice as she drew near. The men stopped in their tracks as she skipped towards them.

'Did y' ever see such, lads?' one whispered. 'It fair gives me t' creeps!' Drawing level with the makeshift stretcher, Emma saw her father move.

'Oh! Oh!' she moaned. 'He isn't dead! He isn't dead! Why didn't he die?' The utter desolation and the hate on which it was built, was not lost on the men and they talked about it that evening in the Farmers Arms.

* * *

Emma grieved at the sound of their clogs as they set out early each morning, waking her up and leaving her feeling left out and insecure. They were all working at the Briar Mill, Lizzie, Annie, and George for sixty-nine hours a week, and Maggie attending halftime, with alternate weeks of morning or afternoon school. Often when Emma walked home from school alone, she thought of ways of escaping. The increased income of the household had not improved living standards for her father was drinking more and taking more women, widows and the unattached, causing rows of jealousy with his latest housekeeper, and squandering what should have been for the welfare of his family. In his mid-forties he seemed to be interested in knowing as many women as he had time for. The old women in the village joked that George's private parts had become public property, in hamlets farther afield than Furlongton, too.

Emma worked hard at school, knowing in her prematurely adult mind that even elementary education would become an asset in later life. Her mother had been illiterate, Nellie had told her, and their father had taken advantage of it that was just a situation that her father would gloat over, she thought.

One Saturday morning when her father had gone to the stables, Emma sneaked from the house and started on the five-mile journey to Rochley, determined to find Nellie and stay with her. It was a foolish notion; not only would it incite her father into a murderous rage, it would also incur the interference of the local School Board Officer.

The pork butcher's shop was on the periphery of the market square, well known for its first-class pork, pies, black puddings and many other tasty foods. The mere thought of the food gave Emma's stomach the assurance that she was doing the right thing in going to the shop. Nellie had escaped the mill by coming here and so would she.

A local inhabitant doing her shopping directed her to Keats's porkshop for all the townsfolk knew it well.

'I want to join my sister in your shop,' Emma told Mr. Keats. 'I can work hard and I am very good at reckoning.'

Mr Keats knew all about George Foulkes from his cousin, Mrs Cowburn.

'Well, little lass,' he said, 'I doesn't know what y'father'll say. I hopes he shan't find out - he might get t'Guardians on me tail.'

'You shouldn't have come,' Nellie scolded. 'You're under age - and without his permission, you silly thing. There'll be terrible trouble.'

On closing time Nellie was terrified to see her father loom up, a staggering spectre in the gaslight over the shop doorway. Emma was vulnerably placed - outside the counter, removing a tray of meat from the window. She dropped the tray onto the counter and made to escape. George Foulkes snatched her by the hair and dragged her out into the night. Emma screamed but George was too drunkenly furious to trouble himself about passers-by. He turned off the road after a time, taking hold of Emma's forearm in a blood-stemming grip as they went through the fields towards Squire's Clough.

'I'll kill you, you bitch,' George ranted. 'I'll kill you as dead as a doornail. As dead as a doornail. You'd defy me, would you? I'll kill you, I'll kill you!'

Emma was frightened. Squire's Clough was a doom-laden place, its name originating from an eighteenth century story that a farm labourer had seen the figure of the squire dragging the blood-soaked body of his young wife through the wood. The place had been haunted ever since, people said. The locals dreaded going through Squire's Clough after dark, but George Foulkes knew nothing of the legend and dragged the terrified child after him through the trees, and when she stumbled, he punched her with his bony fist. The experience lived in her memory all her life.

When the School Board Inspectors came and diligently tested the children, Emma found no problem in examination. For her arithmetic she received maximum marks; her English essay on The Evils of Drink - chosen from ten subjects, knowing herself to be an expert - received 95 marks; her reading aloud ability, amazed the two inspectors because of its lack of broad, slovenly, local dialect of which they had heard a tiresome amount.

The teacher vouchsafed the information that Emma's father was a Hampshire man. This gave the Inspectors a pleasant picture of a Hampshire gentleman insisting on his child speaking the correct southern speech and, they registered 100 marks for Emma.

The teacher's explanation did not bear analysis. If George Foulkes had such an effect on one of his children, why did Emma's kin speak with a Lancashire dialect? It was true that Emma was a favourite of hers and this made the child special;

the other Foulkes children were not as broad as the local children, but the truth was peculiar to Emma. She was the youngest and most solitary child of the family. She had grown apart from her own kin - they disapproved of her defiant attitude for their father's frustrations in dealing with his youngest often made them scapegoats. Emma's solitariness had helped her assimilate her father's southern speech. This, and her own resolution to speak and read well, had earned its reward. The inspector suggested further education for this brightest of scholars, but knowing Emma's background the teacher explained she would be going half-time to the mill soon. The inspectors were sorry for the child because of her tremendous potential, and before they departed, the chief inspector gave Emma sixpence.

Emma had understood most of the conversation she had overheard and, at least, knew that she was top pupil in the village school and assured of a good report. She would not serve a lifetime in a cotton mill, she told herself many times. She knew exactly what she would do: on the Saturday before school holidays she set off again for Rochley, running most of the way through Squire's Clough, and in about an hour reached the porkshop. Mr Keats read her excellent report and marks and the family agreed she could stay.

Emma was not tall but she had a certain attractiveness, especially when she donned a white overall and arranged her beautiful hair in ringlets, and Mr Keats believed he had found a very able and intelligent assistant.

The Sunday passed peacefully, Emma sleeping with her sister in the back room of the Keat's home. Nellie was anxious about her father. He was bound to come, she said.

'He won't come for a while,' Emma laughed. 'He won't think I've dared to come here again.'

'He will come,' Nellie said, gloomily.

Emma knew there was a certain peevish jealousy in Nellie whose frightened brain would be asking why this sister had come again to interfere in her life when everything had been moving along happily? Emma was a nuisance and should stay away.

A whole week passed before George Foulkes thought to revisit Rochley, fuming at his delay in guessing where Emma had gone. He stood at the rear of the crowded shop waiting, eaten up with impatience, his glare taking in the Keat's sons and his two daughters. By God! He'd show that cocky little bitch who was master.

George Foulkes was irritated because he knew he dared not force Emma to attend half time at the mill. Any legality would make public much of his dirty linen.

Emma's heart fluttered when she saw the fury in her father's eyes and then she relaxed, knowing that she had the backing of her eldest sister and two of the Keats boys. But at a convenient moment Nellie vanished into the safety of her employer's house and stood peering nervously through the curtains of the small connecting window. The last customer departed and George Foulkes moved forward.

'I want you, girl,' he growled.

Emma felt the big carving knife by her hand and grasped it, watched by the two boys. She was unafraid now. She tapped the blade on the counter, staring into her father's blazing eyes without flinching. She knew her fathers cowardice because of his devious tricks to avoid scandal, and it gave her courage. If she did not stab him to death she would certainly wound him if he molested her. She estimated correctly. Foulkes recognised the recklessness of a desperate child and did not advance nearer.

'You little bitch!' he snarled. Turning to glower at the boys, he threatened, 'I'll see you all suffer for this,' and stalked out quivering in anger. Emma never again entered her father's house.

The two young men laughed and hugged her.

'We were waiting f' him to do some'at little lass, but thee didn't need us,' said one boy.

Less than one year later, with honest reluctance, Mr Keats had to inform Emma that he could no longer employ her; his own daughter was now old enough to take her place. Mrs Keats had found an agreeable situation for Emma at the pleasant seaside resort of Southport where Mrs Keats's friend had a boarding house. The job was temporary but Emma would enjoy being there. She packed what belongings she had, said a sad farewell to Nellie and her saviour friends, and travelled by train to Southport. Her sadness at leaving was short-lived - what was parting from friends compared with years of hardship and cruelty? The boarding-house work was nothing more than the lowliest of chores - washing dishes all day! The staff was amazed at the child's energy, not knowing her background history, and the way she sang at her work. Emma felt happy and free, enjoyed the good, regular food, and was thankful for the respectable wage from an employer who was well informed of Emma's life of misery. Long hours were of no significance to Emma. At bedtime the kitchen table was overturned, lined with two blankets, and into this Emma slept peacefully each night. She was intrigued by the manners of her employer's two children - to their mother's call they ran immediately, stood to attention and said 'Yes, ma?' If she ever had children of her own, Emma vowed, that was the way she would bring them up. They were certainly charming kids!

After some weeks she became anxious that at season end she would be homeless. Undressing herself one night, before slipping into her table-bed, she recalled Miss Heller's words on leaving George Foulkes's house – 'This is my home address, Emma, dear. If you are ever in trouble, write to me.'

In late August Emma stayed up one night and wrote to Miss Heller's Fowey address. Two weeks passed without a reply, turning her thoughts to the dreadful possibility that once more an adult would let her down. When the boarding house closed would it be wise to return to Rochley? No. She was not wanted there, and to return to Furlongton would be a complete surrender. In the second week of September a letter arrived with a Blackburn post-mark.

Dear Emma,

It was a delightful surprise to hear from you. I am glad you managed to leave your father and get a job. The reason for the delay in replying to your letter is that it had to be sent on by Laura my eldest sister to the new address above. Maria, my other sister, and I have taken a boarding house here and we would like you to come and be our maid-of-all-work. You would be a great help and it will answer all your problems about your future, Emma, dear. We look forward to seeing you when the summer season is over. Our kind of boarding house is open throughout the year, our clients being businessmen, commercial travellers, etc. shall be delighted to see you again.

 Your most affectionate friend,

 Ruth Heller.

*   *   *

It was a newest building with eight bedrooms and three attic rooms. Emma saw immediately a tremendous amount of work for her £18 per annum - making beds, emptying chamber pots, dusting ornaments and furniture, cleaning windows and the heaviest chore of cleaning the monstrous kitchen range with its grate, hob, and water-boiler. It needed black leading, and naked steel required vigorous rubbing with emery paper to scour off superficial rust, then polishing with metal-polish. It was strenuous work for a slightly built girl and Emma envied the older girl who washed dishes and served at tables.

Yet, Emma was very grateful - there was a comfortable bed in the attic, the food was good and plentiful, and the Heller sisters were kind. She was earning money and had a secret moneybox in her locker in which she put coppers each week. In her loyalty to the two sisters she did not imagine that they might be taking full advantage of her vulnerability to exploitation. Emma was amenable, like all dependent creatures in times of wretchedness, and the sisters were paying her above the average wage for maids-of-all-work. Emma knew that without them she might have perished!

After four years of daily toil, Emma was eighteen and

within weeks of her birthday her routine existence changed dramatically - a new boarder arrived, a grocery assistant to the local branch of a huge grocery company, transferred from a Scottish branch to train for managership when the Blackburn manager retired. Andrew Douglas Ferguson, a tall, handsome, gentlemanly Scot, bedazzled Emma and left her hopelessly in love. He was to become her husband and the father of her six children. He was thirty-five years of age, Emma eighteen years and four months.

* * *

In 1895, when her stepfather was forty-five years of age, Lizzie Leach, now a young woman of twenty-two, came through the mill-gates, the hooter still sounding and the clogs of the workers making a din that smothered all conversation. Outside the gates stood Mrs Cowburn accompanied by a healthy, red-cheeked woman of about fifty, not unattractively dressed and wearing a wide, round straw hat that made her an alien figure among the weavers.

'Lizzie,' Mrs Cowburn shouted. The girl ignored her.

'Lizzie,' she shouted louder. 'Poor Lizzie's a little deaf, and no wonder.'

She pushed through the throng and managed to touch Lizzie's shoulder. She turned round startled.

'Come with me,' Mrs Cowburn enunciated with the exaggerated mouth-movements of the mill-worker. 'Your auntie has come from Derbyshire to take you away, luv. This is your Auntie Gladys.'

'Hello, Lizzie, dear,' said the stranger. Dear me, she thought, what a sad little creature! She felt a rush of terrible pity. Lizzie was in no way attractive, her nose broad like that of a Negress but without the pleasurable delicacy of features and black, shiny skin. Her eyes were sunk behind thick glasses and with a highlight of permanent fear in each. Her mouth was agape, foolishly, like someone in a daze.

Her thin, weary voice said, 'I don't know you.'

'Of course not,' Aunt Gladys laughed. 'I'm your mama's eldest sister, dear. Me and your Uncle Tom have a nice farm near Glossop. I have two boys - twenty and twenty-two. Your half-brother, George, wrote to us in Wales. Come on now, we'll collect your things before your stepfather gets home.'

'He'll kill me,' Lizzie quavered, almost tearful in her dread.

'He'll do nothin' of t' sort,' said Mrs Cowburn. 'My man'll see t' that, never fear, luv.'

Lizzie went home and packed her flimsy belongings, said a tearful farewell to Annie, George, and Maggie, and within half an hour was on the train to Derbyshire, her Aunt Gladys having made a successful rescue.

Young George, now eighteen, was in a turmoil waiting for his father to come home.

'We've no need to tell him. We'll say we know nothing about it,' said Maggie.

'I'll tell him,' said Annie.

'You would,' said Maggie, disgustedly. 'You're always telling tales. That's how you've looked after yourself, you mean thing.'

'He'll get to know so we may as well tell him,' Annie argued, sensibly.

'I'm going out to watch the cricket,' said George, donned his cap and went before his father came home.

In the stables near the house of the Minnes family residence, George Foulkes was brushing down the bay. His inside throbbed with resentment. The sudden confrontation with the estate manager had taken him unaware and he was consumed with feelings of mingled hate and fear.

'That's official' said the estate manager, summing-up. 'Services no longer required.'

'Why?' George asked in faint tones. 'What have I done?'

'Done?' bellowed the estate manager. 'Just look at yourself, man. You're a bloody wreck! Hangovers every morning, drunk every bloody night, unable to turn in on time. Where's all your pride, man? At one time you were the smartest liveryman I'd ever seen. You've ruined yourself, Foulkes, and no mistake. Just knowing horses isn't enough.

You're a bloody disgrace. Do you think the gaffer wants to be driven around by a damned, dissipated old scarecrow like you? Drink and women - they're your downfall, George Foulkes,' and no mistake. And I've no sympathy for you. Get that bay finished and bugger off home - and start looking round for another cottage within the week'

George made a last, quivering, cringing appeal.

'Where can I go? I've four kids at home. How can I find a place within a week?'

'That's your problem. And by all accounts you treated those kids worse than dogs. And serves you bloody well right for getting in this position. There's your money and there's your reference - and Sir Frederick has signed it himself, which is bloody good of him, I'd say!' The estate manager placed the two envelopes on top of the stall dividing rail and departed.

For the first time in his life George Foulkes Esquire felt the doom-hand of insecurity hard on his shoulder. He was forty-five and now had little hope of obtaining another respectable job like this. Almost twenty years he had served Minnes. As he walked slowly home down the long drive for the last time, he saw that even reducing the family's pocket-money would gain him very little. He was in a daze of trepidation. If he stayed home and lived on the kids, there'd be an everlasting feast of gossip in the village, especially when that bloody woman Cowburn heard what had happened. He couldn't stand that. Sir Frederick owned practically everything around there, God damn and curse him! George knew that if he applied for a job to any of the county squires, they would discuss him with Minnes. He must go somewhere away from the influential powers of Sir Frederick. He could then depend on the reference, a good one in the circumstances, praising his prowess with horses and generously omitting any reference to his personal attributes.

Annie told him that a Welsh aunt had taken Lizzie away. He sat and stared at her. So, that ugly little bitch had done it on him! Another damned wage lost!

'Where's she gone?' he demanded.

'We don't know, father. The woman wouldn't tell us,' Annie said.

'Where's George?'

'He's out watching cricket, father. I told him not to go till you came home.'

'You liar,' said Maggie. 'You said nothing of the sort.'

'Shut your bloody mouths,' George roared. 'I'm going out. Be in bed when I get back.'

He stalked down to the Farmers' Arms and spent all his wages. Two farmhands borrowed a barrow and brought him home at closing time. They took him upstairs and put him on his bed fully clothed. They had done it all before.

Her father was still snoring loudly when Annie started out for work next morning. She was always earlier than the others and Maggie shrewdly suggested one time that Annie walked alone because she believed that the less people knew of her doings, the less they could report to their father. 'She thinks we're all tell-tales like herself,' said Maggie. Near the mill gates Annie heard Ralph Hodge calling to her above the clink of clogs. He was hurrying towards her with his plumber's bag.

'Hey, Annie! Wait a minute, lass.'

'What is it, Ralph?'

'Thi fayther's got t'sack, hassen he?'

'Got the sack? Thar's a liar, Ralph Hodge.'

'Nay, I'm not, Annie luv. Old Minnes sacked him yesterday. He were fair drunk in t'Farmers last neet. They wheeled him hom int wheelbarrer. T'old divil spent all hees wages. Y'll have t' get art o' yon cottige, Annie luv.'

'Ralph, are y' not kidding me?'

'Nay. Eet's God's honest truth, Annie. Anyhow, there's t'whistle. I'll see thee toneet.'

Annie entered the mill yard, her quick brain digesting the information. So, the old bugger had got the sack? He'd be a parasite on them now and she was not having that. Tonight she would tell Ralph she was ready to wed. Get out while you can. She told herself. A quiet wedding and off they'd go. Mrs Hodge was a nice old soul and had promised

24

Ralph they could live there. Father wasn't so handy these days with his beatings - not since he had been out of condition. He would probably raise Cain but to hell with him! He could like it or lump it. Ralph was only little but that didn't matter. He had his own Plumbing business and that did matter. His faults would be like thistledown after her father's tantrums. Nellie, Emma, and Lizzie had all escaped. Now it was her turn. Let George and Maggie put up with the old bugger if they were daft enough. He deserved to be left alone, and then see how he'd go on! He had lost a damned good job through drink and whoring. No boss would want him now - drunken old tramp!

She would see Ralph and tell him straight that they should wed. He would jump at it. She was nineteen and the old devil might try to stop her as she was not of age like poor Lizzie. But she could run away like the others. Everybody in the village knew what an old bastard he was, and they wouldn't blame her for running away. Yes, Ralph, love, here's your bride waiting for you!

That evening they gave in their wages and received their pocket money. Their father was as amiable as they had ever known him and they wondered why. At five o'clock next morning George Foulkes packed all his belongings, left a note on the table, and sneaked out to walk to the station to catch the earliest train to Liverpool. The note said: 'Annie - I left Minnes. Gone to Liverpool for a job. Make your own way in the world now. Don't try to trace me.'

'We're free!' Maggie shrieked. George sighed deeply. At last, the leaden weight was lifted from his heart. He felt newborn.

'We have to leave this cottage,' Annie said, in dampening tones.

'I don't give a damn,' George said. 'We won't see him any more.'

'I'm getting wed,' Annie announced in triumph. 'Ralph asked me last night and I said yes straight away. He doesn't need to see father now.'

'Who's paying for the wedding?' Maggie asked.

'Ralph, of course. He knows I can't afford anything,

We're living with his ma until we have enough to buy furniture and then we'll rent a house. I'm staying at the mill for the time being. First banns will be read next Sunday.'

'You're always lucky,' Maggie said. 'Ralph's a good plumber and gets more work with all these new gadgets coming out. George, I think we had better look for lodgings somewhere.'

'After work I'll have a word with Mrs Cowburn,' said George.

'Where shall we go?' Maggie queried. She was only fifteen and a half.

'We'll see,' said George. 'Don't worry.'

For once in their lives the three young people walked together to work, their outlook marvellously changed. The world was a wonderful place!

*   *   *

No one would have believed that little Lizzie was happy. She never smiled. She worked hard for her Auntie Gladys and Uncle Tommy Barker. Although a trifle slow in learning new things, she executed her work well once conversant with the process. Barker was well pleased with the girl. She cost him nothing except her keep and an occasional sixpence from Gladys. Lizzie was not an alluring beauty and neither of his sons would ever be attracted to her. He was proud of his sons, Richard and Alan, and there was no doubt that they would be wanting to wed soon. He wanted them to marry well, into money, maybe. But he was pleased that the two boys were kind to poor Lizzie. Gladys had talked seriously to them that first night when Lizzie had gone up to bed, telling them about that horrible bugger George Foulkes.

Lizzie lived in a world devoid of higher social conditions. None of Tommy Barker's aspects of life contributed to Lizzie's uneasy thoughts. She was happier, yet viewed through her strong glasses from a distance all visitors to the farm. Mrs

26

Cowburn knew where she was and the awful possibility that the address had been passed on to her stepfather worried her. She took no comfort that she had come of age and was no longer beholden to George Foulkes.

Food, shelter, and work were all that concerned Lizzie, and for these elementals she thanked God in her small, narrow bed each night in the attic. Even the fact that she received no wage did not depress her.

Her mind was relieved of all anxiety one morning when the friendly postman handed her a letter. It had the Furlongton postmark and Lizzie's heart gave a little lurch of fear.

Dear Liz,

The old man has gone! Give three cheers! He was sacked from Minnes. He thinks he'll get a job in Liverpool as he is not known in the big city. He isn't as smart as he was and I don't think anyone will take him on as a coachman. Anyway, Liz, good riddance say I. Maggie and I are living with Mrs Cowburn for the time being. We pay her our wages and she gives us one and six each pocket money. She's a good lass. Our Annie is getting wed to Ralph Hodge, the plumber. She is keeping on at the mill. They will live with Mrs Hodge. Annie was always lucky. I hope you are getting along nicely at the farm. Maggie and me would like to hear from you - just a note will do as I know you don't like writing letters

Love from us all,

George.

When Lizzie showed her letter to the Barker family they were all delighted.

'You're safe now, Lizzie, dear,' said Gladys. 'Nothing more to worry yourself about, thanks to goodness. On Saturday we shall go into Glossop and buy you a new dress, dear, to celebrate the occasion. You must write back to George and thank him. He's a good boy is George, and very sensitive, too. Aye, it's at times like these that y' starts to believe there's a God in his heaven, indeed to goodness. You must say a little prayer tonight Lizzie, dear, and thank God for his mercy.'

That night Lizzie did say a little prayer, kneeling by her bedside in the attic, thanking the Lord for all his great mercy and forgetting her past miseries for the time being. God looked down kindly on the poor creature, marvelling at her faith and trust, and feeling slightly guilty for up to that time Lizzie had had nothing to thank him for! Well, God was in his heaven and Lizzie began to believe that he was making it up to her now.

*　　*　　*

On the Saturday morning of his desertion, George Foulkes stood by the bar drinking bitter beer by Walker's Warrington Ales. The public house was opposite old Haymarket. In his mind George was planning what he needed, to establish himself in this great city of Liverpool.

He needed a respectable job with good money and perhaps his excellent reference would do the trick. He confided in the landlord that he was looking for a job as coachman. Did he know any?

'Nah,' said the landlord, 'not round here. Yis wanna get out in the suburbs - the big houses. I've gorra copy of yesterdee's Echo if yis lud like a shufti?'

'Thanks. I would like to look through it,' said George, in his best manner. The landlord went into his living room and brought out a copy of the Liverpool Echo, well known among other outstanding features, for its many classified advertisements. George searched down the columns of small print under drivers, ostlers, grooms, liverymen, stable boys, and so forth. His eye caught the word 'Coachman: Undertakers require coachman for hearse; livery provided; grooming, stabling, etc. £30 per annum. Apply Tunstall & Kirk, 50B Byrom Street.

'Where's Byrom Street?' George enquired.

'If yis look outa the window yis'll see it. Cross over Old

Haymarket and it's ahead of yis.'

'Thanks. I'll have one of your hot pies - with a couple of pickles.'

'Right yis are, sir,' said the landlord, glad to be selling a food so early in the day.

George paid the landlord and carried a second pint of bitter and his plate with the pie and pickles on it, together with a small fork, and sat down at a table in a corner by the window. He was all alone in the bar. Well, driving a hearse wasn't what he was used to, but what was the difference? They paid better wages than Minnes. The horses would be black, two of them, or even four-in-hand. He'd look smart in his black livery. The shock of being called a dissipated old scarecrow had disturbed his self-image and he was now setting his mind to improve it.

An unshaven fellow entered the bar carrying a parcel. He went to the landlord.

'Hey, mate, would y' like t' buy dees paints off me?'

The landlord frowned. 'What kind o' paints?'

'Oil paints an' bluddy gud brushes.' He opened his parcel. The landlord eyed them.

'They're no good t,' me, mate. What would I do wit' all those tubes o' paint?'

'They're worth five bob,' said the tramp.

'Lissen, wack, they're worth nothink t' me. I doan wannem.'

These exchanges aroused George's interest. Yes, he thought, I could paint horses and sell them. Extra cash. He had had an artistic flair as a lad.

'Bring them over here,' he called.

The tramp turned, gathered up his parcel and took them across to his potential lifesaver.

'I'm interested,' said George. 'But they're not worth five bob to me. I'd waste a lot just learning.'

'Look, mate. I've bin at it years an' coulda bin a goodun 'cept f' the ould drink. I'm burstin' f' drink - all parched an' ditherin'. All y' gorra do is git y'self sum turps sum raw linseed oil - they're only cheap - sixpince a bottle - it lasts ages.'

'What do I paint on?' George asked.

'While yis a' learnin', use cardboard, mate.'

'All right,' said George, showing no enthusiasm, 'four bob.'

'Yer on, mister. Four bob.'

George paid him and the fellow hurried over to the bar. George wrapped up the oils and brushes and put them in his bag. The man returned and sat down with his pint and his plate of pie and pickled beetroot.

'Tell me more about painting,' said George.

'Well, now, mate,' said the tramp, cutting his meat pie. 'First of all, sketch out what yis wanna paint onto y' card.'

'Horses,' said George. The tramp chewed for a few seconds the hot pie in his mouth then gulped down a swig of beer.

'Right, mate - horses. Draw y' horses slightly off centre - dead centre's no good. When y've sketched it out, fill in the background – y'know - trees, hills, or mebbe a stable or somethin'. Then y' starts paintin' - usin' the ould paint weakish at first - plenty o' turps. Fill in y' horse in brown or whatever yis like - mix y' colours on a bit o' wood or card. When y' paint's dry, start paintin' the details - y'know, muscles an' lights an' shades, like. Oh, aye, yis'll soon git thee 'ang of it.'

'Thanks,' said George. 'If they were good, how much could I sell them for?'

'Well, all depends. Y'cud gerras much as ten bob. Gerrum framed o'course, nobedee'll buy 'em wid'out a frame. Make 'em y'self, mate. Bit o' timber cut up, mitred at d' corners an' y' there. I made all me own.'

'That'll cost a bit,' said George.

The tramp was wolfing down his pie and beetroot. George felt more hunger just watching him.

'I'm having another,' he said. 'Would you like another? I'll get them.'

'Mate, y' a gint, an' no mistake. I'm starvin'.'

George went back to the bar feeling expansive and gratified. Compared with these ignorant townspeople he certainly was a gentleman. His speech and intelligence was far superior. Yes, George was feeling cocksure again. He bought two more pies with pickled beetroot and two more pints of beer. He was still well in pocket with the kids' wages. He could go careful later if he failed to get that job. That job would make everything famous. After this meal he would get tidied up somewhere. He could still look smart if he took care. A barber's shop could smarten him up for a few coppers.

Half an hour later he entered a barber's shop two hundred yards away in Dale Street, as directed by the landlord.

'I'm going for a job,' he told the barber, frankly. 'Do you think you could wash and cut my hair and give me a good shave?'

'Sure thing, sir,' said the barber, 'an' a hot towel maybe? Have y' travelled far?'

'Forty miles by rail. Where would 50B Byrom Street be - this end or the far end?'

'Now then - it actually won't be far up. The numbers start from the Town Hall, y'see - so it should be twenty-five doors up on the right-hand side. Near the undertaker's I should say.

'It is the undertaker's,' George sniggered. 'That's where I'm going. Coachman wanted.'

'Oh?' said the barber. 'I doesn't get many coachmen in here. Tunstall and Kirk are reg'lar customers o' mine. So y'll be driving a carriage, then?'

'Yes, if I get the job I'll be driving the hearse.'

'Ah' the barber laughed, 'drivin' people to their graves - like my missus is doin' t' me?

'I can appreciate that joke,' George tittered. 'I had a wife like that - driving me to my grave - but she died in the attempt.'

The barber knew his trade well and made a first-class job of George's appearance, brushing down his suit and bowler with a stiff brush, adjusting his tie and fixing his moustache. George was well pleased and tipped the barber a threepenny-bit.

The reference and his appearance secured the post for

George Foulkes. Kirk was there, his partner, Tunstall, being out on a job somewhere.

'You can drive four-in-hand, I presoom,' said Kirk.

'Yes,' said George, his confidence unbesmirched by doubt.

'Sometimes we uses tandem an' sometimes pairs,' Kirk went on. He was a shrewd little man with professionally sombre appearance. 'All depends what they're payin' for the turnout. The Irish generally likes the whole kit an' caboodle. They spends more on funerals than they do on weddin's - all depends whose died on 'em, o'course. When y' gets here at eight on Monday Joe Flaherty'll give y' the lowdown on procedure. There's a job on Monday at ten-thirty. Joe'll tell y' when t' go into the house and screw down the deceased and so forth. Y' never goes in 'til the family asks y'. Joe travels with you on top - he has the ould tools for the job. The men carries out the body in the box an' once the ould box is slid in, you an' Joe waits f' the retinoo t' fill up with mourners. Then off y' goes nice an' slow to the ould church. The men takes out the box an' walks in, slow-like, an' puts it on a trestle. I stays in church, you an' the men waits outside. When I gives y' the signal, you open the ould hearse, the men comes into church an' carries out the box wit' all the mourners follerin'. Then drive off at a slow pace, no trottin' unless requested by the main bereaved.'

'I'll be glad to have Joe with me,' said George. 'I don't know Liverpool.'

'Oh, I shouldn't worry y'self. Joe'll tell yis all about it come Monday. Have yis got a place to live?'

'No, I haven't. I was going to search round this morning.'

'Well,' now, I'll tell y' what - my widowed sister takes in lodgers. I'll write the ould address on this here card. Mrs Clara Thomas, her name. Wavertree Road. Go to the ould Haymarket terminus an' pick up a tram. It's not far - a penny ride, I believe. She'll be pleased to put yis up - good food and a nice place - all comfy like.'

'Thank you,' said George, taking the card. 'See you on Monday at eight, then, at the stables round the back?'

'Aye, that's right. Good morning.'

Well, Harry Kirk thought, a good catch there - coachman for the gentry! Must tell Dick Tunstall. Smartish fella – not bad-lookin' neether. I hope we have a decent mournin' coat f' him. I'll see t' that come Monday.

Clara Thomas was about forty, red-haired, cheerful, and buxom. She read her brother's card and George's wary eye noticed her raised eyebrows and pursed lips as she read. Her exclamation of 'Um!' was full of speculation. George was still a ladies' man at forty-five, with as handsome a bearing as it was possible to salvage from his past. Clara liked him at once. She had three other boarders - a young student, an elderly shop-manager, and a middle-aged tug-master, none of whom seemed as interesting as this coachman. He was a good find.

'Come in, Mr Foulkes,' she said, warmly. 'I've just lost a lodger from the front ground. This is the room, looking on to the main road. Threequarter bed an' fully furnished as y' can see. Eight shillings a week, including two meals a day, breakfast an' late dinner. You find your own lunch - but I can provide a packed lunch for twopence a day extra. Three meals on Sundays. Sixpence a week extra f' coal-fire in the winter, an' twopence extra for a hot bath.'

'Thank you, Mrs Thomas. Do I pay in advance?'

'It's usually a week in advance, but my former gentleman paid a month in advance. Please y'self, Mr Foulkes.'

George took out a sovereign and twelve shillings and handed them over.

'Oh, thank you, Mr Foulkes,' she smiled. 'I'm sure you'll be very happy here.' She walked up the passage from the hall and George noticed how she wiggled her shapely posterior.

He unpacked and put away two shirts into a drawer, some long underpants, and a vest or two. A nice, cosy set-up, he thought, very comfortable and handy. George Foulkes had established himself in the world of the quick, the slow, and the dead!

*   *   *

The new century came in with fireworks and the ringing of many bells, and warm feelings of great optimism in Lancashire. Cotton was supreme with Lancashire mills supplying world markets. Mill owners were persons of immense wealth and they inspired lesser men to mount the wagon of initiative and invest what hundreds they could find from savings, inheritances, profits from small businesses and so forth, in workshops, looms, and the power to work them, together with partners with knowledge of the procedures of the Manchester Cotton Exchange. Between 1900 and the outbreak of the Great War many ordinary folk would be able to retire to mansions on the Fylde Coast. Those who had been careful with their resources and had enjoyed some element of luck, found themselves travelling on the select Club Train from St. Annes to Manchester, thereby joining the elite of cotton trade magnates.

But Destiny had nothing generous in its plans for people like the family of George Foulkes. Annie had continued at the mill until forced to leave for the birth of her first child in 1897. She had faithfully handed over to her mother-in-law half her wages and had saved the other half for purchasing furniture, furnishings, utensils, and equipment for the house she and Ralph had rented by the time the baby came. Maggie and George continued with stern monotony to work at the mill through the years, George spending his time at cricket in summer, football in winter, Morris dancing, and the reading of Karl Marx and Engels. Maggie was going about with a young fellow three years her senior, a carter for a local timber merchant, Jack Dickson, a quiet-spoken countryman, lean and bronzed and rugged with the great attribute of concealed strength in his wiry muscles.

Lizzie Leach, lonely bastard, continued to drudge hard for her guardians, missing the elder son, Richard, who had married a farmer's daughter and had taken a small holding ten miles north of Glossop. Lizzie never forgot Richard's kindness and good-natured friendship.

Nellie had written from Rochley to Maggie, c/o Mrs Cowburn, giving her the good news that the Keats family had, opened a second shop and had made Nellie senior assistant under the management of the elder son. Her wages had increased by three shillings per week. They had been very good to her, she wrote. A bank clerk was a regular customer at the new shop and bought pork pies for his lunch. He lived with his widowed mother and seemed to be very interested in Nellie, confiding in her his thoughts about his mother and his home.

Maggie replied, congratulating Nellie, outlining the news - father absconding, Annie's marriage, Lizzie's escape to Derbyshire, and young George's delight that the old man had gone, despite the loss of the money. Mrs Cowburn said Nellie could now stop sending her weekly amount as their father had gone. Mrs Cowburn could manage very well without it.

Annie called with her baby in its bassinet and read Nellie's letter.

'Um,' she sniggered, 'a pork-pie romance. Still, a bank clerk. She should marry him.'

Yes, young George thought, they would all be wed soon; but he was only twenty-two and had his way to make in the world. Marx's writings had made him think about his ambitions. Marx maintained that the value of a product depended on the time and amount of labour expended on it. Labour produced far more than it consumed, said Marx, and the surplus value went into the pockets of the capitalists who allowed the labourer just sufficient subsistence to enable him to produce his own kind for the future use and profit of wealthy bosses. Working people of the world must develop a class-consciousness to encourage sufficient antagonism towards their capitalist masters to instigate class war and eventually destroy the capitalist system.

George digested Marx's theories shrewdly and had his doubt. His ambition had been to purchase his own business and become an embryonic capitalist himself. Capitalism could not be overthrown, he believed, because it had the law, the armed forces, the police, the money power and all the favourable connections behind it. Workers of the World Uniting, thought George, would immediately unite the world's Establishments and that would crush the proletariat populace into depths of even more harrowing slavery. Revolution was not on, was George's opinion, and it was better that improvements in living standards be brought about by evolution which was rebellion without the R.

*   *   *

Away from them all in Liverpool, George Foulkes senior applied himself conscientiously for a time to his job, often finding that a show of good manners and respect endeared him to widows whose sons tipped him on occasions. He regretted buying the oil paints for they lay untouched in the bottom drawer of a chest in his room. During work he imagined sometimes that the paints had dried up in their tubes and the whole lot having to be thrown away.

'I'd like to do some painting, Mrs Thomas,' he said one day. 'Would you mind?'

'Why should I mind, Mr Foulkes?'

'Well, they're oil paints and they have the smell of turps and linseed oil,' he told her honestly, not wishing to spoil a growing relationship with Clara Thomas. He had done his best to impress her with his gentlemanliness and quiet respectability.

'Try them out,' she said, reasonably. 'If they smell too much I shall have to ask you to stop, shan't I?'

'Thank you,' he smiled. 'We shall have to see how they go.' She returned his smile sweetly and he knew he was on to a promising future with her.

On thick, rigid, white card he started to paint one Sunday before dinner. When they were dining, Clara Thomas smiled at him.

'I don't think you'd better carry on painting, Mr Foulkes. I can smell it from the kitchen.'

'I suggest, Clara,' said Joe, the Tugmaster, 'that Mr Foulkes use the shed in the yard.'

'Yes, Joe, he could use the shed - but what about the winter, he'll freeze?'

Why was everybody called by his first name and he was always addressed as Mr Foulkes?

'Look here,' he said, impulsively, 'why not call me George instead of Mr Foulkes all the time?'

'All right, George,' Clara laughed. 'It's much easier. What do you say, Joe?'

'Well, there's something about you, George, that earns you the title Mister.'

'Yes, I feel the same,' said the old business manager.

'It's your bearing, George.' The student, an unusually astute youth, said nothing but continued eating his meal.

'You are flattering,' George laughed, feeling superior. He knew he had a bearing.

He was about to retire for the night when he heard a slight tap on his door.

'Come in,' he called. He was removing his tie as he spoke and turned to see Clara Thomas.

'I'm sorry about your paints, George,' she began.

'Oh, don't trouble yourself, dear lady.'

'I was thinking about Joe's idea - the shed. I'll get it cleared out tomorrow.'

'That is most kind of you, Mrs Thomas.'

'Oh, George, you must call me Clara. I'm calling you George now – Clara's the least you can do. I'll get a stove in the shed for winter - and perhaps a hurricane lamp.'

'Thank you. You are kind. I've a bottle of beer in the cupboard. Would you join me?'

'That's very kind,' she beamed, and sat on the edge of his bed. 'The others have gone up.'

'I know,' he smiled. 'I heard them. They're early birds.'

'Well, Joe's usually up at four, and Harvey's away at eight. Emrys is off to college at eight-thirty.'

'Well, the night is ours, Clara. Drink this. It's good for

you.'

Half an hour later he deemed that it had all been worthwhile to play along for so many weeks as the polite, reserved gentleman with excellent manners and decorum. Clara made an alluring bedmate, provocative, warm, and shapely. She had not experienced such bliss before, George having a natural ability together with much experience. Unbeknown to the other lodgers, they enjoyed themselves beyond measure on many such occasions.

*　　*　　*

The house in Preston near the Ribble looked neat and red, with bay windows in a terrace that faced a little backwater of a street beyond which was a village green where the kids could play safely away from the main road. The street was cobbled with green grass growing between the joints, giving a peaceful, unused, rural appearance. It was an idyllic little hideaway, peaceful and pleasant, with the front window facing south and the summer sunshine streaming through white lace curtains, giving Nellies heart a burst of pride and joy.

The slippers were in the hearth ready for her dear Herbert, soon due home from the bank, and the hotpot all ready. Herbert was now a manager and they had been married a mere six months, with Nellie a happy slave girl cherishing her lord and master.

Herbert Cassells was a modest, kindly fellow, a smaller edition of G.K.Chesterton, with Nellie his Frances Blogg. He knew he was no great catch as a husband and he was thankful that this woman, Nellie Foulkes, was happy to coddle him and anticipate his every wish. He had lived with his mother, until her death and she had regulated his entire life. After her death he dreaded the future. What on earth was he do to? He was a domestic nincompoop and would have starved had he not confided in Nellie at the porkshop, her sympathy making him plunge desperately into matrimony. Herbert had not the least knowledge about cooking and there was one aspect of it that irked him – Nellie's cooking. She had been habituated at the porkshop to the many uses of fat, and she had a penchant for mashed potatoes with large blobs of butter mixed into them; roast pork glistening with crusty, fat-dripping crackling; black puddings eight months pregnant with lumps of fat; saturated fried bread with bacon and eggs swimming in a pond of fat for breakfast. There were more fatty foods that eventually made Herbert retch even at the sight of his junior clerk's oily hair at the bank.

Herbert always looked forward to Tuesdays. Hotpot was on the menu and Nellie's rice pie, too, was good. In a deep bowl, lined with pastry, Nellie placed a two-inch layer of currants and raisins, covered them with a thick layer of rice in creamy milk, then placed the lot to cook in the oven, bringing it forth with a thin yellow-brown skin flavoured with nutmeg. Herbert enjoyed two pieces of rice pie each Tuesday, ignoring as much of the pastry as he dared. He made no complaints, his restraint in mentioning fatty content always winning the battle against his strong desire to say - 'just a little less fat, my dear.'

Above these subjugated irritations of his opposition to fat-soaked foods, his life was almost as comfortable as it had been with his mother; but you couldn't have everything, he often mused. This was an imperfect world and ideal situations as rare as Kohinoor diamonds. In time his secret opposition to fat rose like bubbles to the surface in burps and gurgles of powerful wind, increasingly apparent as the years passed.

Each Autumn he arranged with the boy next door to climb the apple tree in the backyard and gather the luscious red apples, giving the boy's family a generous number in appreciation, and helping Nellie to spread out the rest upstairs on the attic floor. To combat the fatty foods he ate an apple a day when they were ready, and even ate fruit at lunch time, there being no porkshop near the Preston branch, and the fortunate placing of the fruit and vegetable market near his bank had given him this craving for fruit.

Nellie's great delight was to go out with Herbert on

Saturday afternoons to do the shopping, then to have afternoon tea at Booth's teashop in Fishergate, afterwards popping into the Theatre Royal for an evening of grand entertainment. Then they would ride down Fishergate on the open-topped tramcar to the river terminus and walk home happily, arm in arm.

Nellie gloried in this period of her life with all the happy gusto of a craving soul, her past years, in comparison, remaining in her memory as years of hard work and misery.

✳   ✳   ✳

In time the persistent tedium and morbidity of funerals aroused in George senior a fear of death as he grew older. Each time Joe and he screwed down a corpse, George imagined himself lying there, waxen and stiff. He began to dread entering houses of the dead.

'I'm sick of the bloody routine,' he told Joe. 'Let one of the others go in with you.'

'Y' can't,' said Joe. 'They doesn't get paid f' that job. We're responsible. There wus a case last year when thee found the corpse wasn't dead. The bloke saw the eyes move, be God. Th' old doc in charge wus tol' off. Yis doesn' need t'look at the ould corpse, y'know.'

'All right,' George answered wearily, 'lead the way, I suppose.' He'd damned well get another job. He wouldn't put up with it!

He was missing those old days when he had met wealthy, important people. He had gained their regard because of his bearing. Hearse driving was a distinct come-down. Tunstall and Kirk treated him with some respect, it was true, but they were socially inferior to people he had known. In fact, he himself was socially superior to all of these common lot around him. He could not analyse precisely the psychological effect of his reduction in status. His egocentricity had suffered and there was never any opportunity to impress anyone with his charm and superiority. He began to believe, suddenly, one evening, that his decline had begun when they had all started to call him

George. That had been a sorry mistake allowing them to treat him on a par with everyone else!

Everybody was talking about the events in South Africa the Battle of Spion Kop, the Relief of Ladysmith, and the Euphoria of Mafeking in May. He had been thoroughly bored and irritated throughout the weeks. It was his scepticism that now made him a complete outsider whilst the papers were full of South African heroics.

He was fifty years old. One day Clara made the first excuse about not being able to come to his room. The student and Tugmaster had left months ago and their replacements were a new student sent by the University bursar, and a railway official, Paul Endicott, a tall, good-looking fellow about forty. George suspected that Clara was in the process of transferring affections and he was right.

He had been using the shed for several summers, but there had been no oil-lamp and no light provided for the winter months. The oil paints had remained faithfully plastic and he had painted several studies of horses in their basic forms. His tardiness in learning the technique of modelling muscles and lights and shades, frustrated him. He was also irritated by the wasting of turps in washing out brushes. Clara had seen some of his work and had been in no way impressed and had walked away at times with an 'Umph!' and an unpleasant look on her face.

On a fine October Sunday afternoon, he went into the shed to start another painting. He heard in his head the discussion after lunch about the Khaki Election. All the Sunday papers had discussed it and its result - Unionists 402, Liberals 185 - a most resounding victory. One or two papers had stressed the Liberal point of view that the Unionist Government had exploited, for its own gain, the huge wave of patriotic fervour that had swamped the country, together with its assurance to the populace that they would not introduce on the domestic front any controversial measures; in consequence, a huge number of Liberal voters had been swayed across to the Unionists, giving them an open warrant to do what they would. The argument had started when George, once more, gave an opinion that placed him as the outsider.

'The Liberals were right,' he declared. 'A damned Unionist confidence trick to appeal to the country while all the silly people are raving on about the war. They won't keep their promises about the domestic issues.'

'Ridiculous!' Clara answered, sharply. 'The Unionists are the only party that can win war. They've done pretty well so far, thank you. Pity help us if the Liberals had got back!'

'I agree,' said Endicott. 'Better the devil we know than the devil we don't. Get the war won, I say, that's the main thing.'

'The war will be won no matter who got in,' George scorned. 'In any case, the success in Africa isn't all due to the Government.'

'What rubbish you talk at times, George Foulkes!' Clara sneered with the animosity of a woman who has recognised for some time that her lover has not turned out to be the marvellous gentleman she had imagined. Some of George's ardour over the months in that front room had shown a progression of very immoderate sexual indecencies that had repelled her.

The discussion had continued and even the student and old Harvey Green, the shop-manager, had turned their arguments against him. Eventually he had left in a temper, their heated remarks sending him in a boiling frustration to his studio shed.

After half an hour's work, he was suddenly disturbed by Clara opening the shed door and putting her head round.

'You can't use the shed any more after today, George,' she stated firmly.

'Oh? And why not?'

'Because Mr Endicott has a new bicycle coming tomorrow and I've agreed that he can keep it in this shed, that's why.'

'Oh, so you've agreed, have you?' George snapped. 'Well, I was here first. Why should I move? I pay my rent the same as he does. You promised me this shed and I refuse to move. I'm not interested in his damned bicycle!'

'Now don't you be awkward, George Foulkes. I've done my best to oblige you in the past.'

'All right, I shall paint in my room, woman.'

'Here, don't you woman me! You'll do what I say. You don't pay rent for this shed. And you certainly will **NOT** paint in that room - stinking the place out. Besides, you are no more an artist than I am - giving us all the impression you were some kind of artistic genius! You are pathetic!' The cutting scorn in her voice sent his pulses racing.

'How dare you! I'll get out of your bloody house - and your brother's miserable firm!'

'Right, Mr. Bloody George Foulkes - and take y' stinking paints with you!'

Clara slammed the shed door and stamped back to her kitchen. 'Arrogant bastard!' she muttered. When he had gone she would get the girls to scrub out that front ground thoroughly and then Paul Endicott could move in.

Next evening George perused the Echo and found a lodging in Dingle - front ground-floor room with bed and use of kitchen, five shillings per week. That would do him. He would have to cook his own meals, that was the drawback; but he must leave. No one was going to speak to him like that little slut Clara Thomas - and held given Kirk his notice. In Job vacancies he found an item which said, 'Wanted: driver for dray; tend horses; £35 per annum; free dinner beer. Walker's Warrington Ales, Warrington. Refs required.'

He packed his belongings and took an American type double-decker tram from South Castle Street to Dingle. He paid the rent for his new abode and early next morning took a train to the brewery at Warrington.

*   *   *

'So, y' knows all about horses?' said the interviewer, a big red-faced, stout fellow with hands like boxing gloves.

'Yes,' said George, 'I've worked with them all my life.'

'We 'as Clydesdales an' one or two Shires at Liverpool. 'ow'd y' manage them?'

'Horses are horses,' said George.

'Aye, mebbe. Well, we s'all give y' a trial f' a month. Y' starts at seven-thirty an' finishes when y've bed down y' animals. That stable in Liverpool's a picture an' it's gorra stay that way, savvy?'

'It will stay that way.'

'This reference - it's a good'un - Sir Frederick Minnes.Why did yl leave there then?'

'Erm, personal reasons,' said George, thinking furiously.

'Such as what?' the big man demanded, not being put off.

'Well,' George breathed, conjuring a voice and attitude of a gentlemanly reluctance, 'his daughter it was, really. Poor girl.'

'Oh?' The big man leaned forward. 'Tell us more.'

'Erm, she took a fancy to me' said George, with a nice show of modesty.

The big man stared open-mouthed, then spluttered,

'She - she - took - took a fancy - Ah! Ah! Ah!'

'It's true,' said George. 'Her father sent her to Switzerland.'

The man's huge stomach started to shake and the laughter bubbled from him.

'That's a damn good'un - Oh! Oh! Oh! Ah! Ah! Ah! that's a good'un!'

'He said he was sorry he had to ask me to leave.'

'Ah! Ah!Ah! I bet - I bet - I bet he were sorry. I've gotta say this - Ah! Ah! Ah! I -'ve gotta - gotta say this, George Foulkes, y' can fair tell 'em, y' can that.'

George was unnerved by the big fellow's huge, scorning guffaws. The job was escaping!

'An' what would this 'ere daughter - Ah! Ah! Ah! - This 'ere daughter do in Switzerland, eh, George? Play snowballs? Eh? Play bloody snowballs.' Again he was convulsed.

'Finishing school,' said George soberly, beginning to

44

hate the raving lunatic sitting there.

The big fellow's white-spotted red handkerchief appeared and he wiped his eyes as even his knees came up with each spasm of laughter.

'Finishin' school?' he shrieked. 'Finishin' school! So she were - she were - a bloody - a bloody schoolgirl?' Again the huge guffaws and the shaking.

What George had pictured in his lively mind did not match quite with the big man's view of his visitor - a bony, lanky fellow in threadbare clothes, with dim eyes and bags beneath them. The big man had been picturing in his mind the beautiful daughter of the gentry, her long lashes fluttering as she eyed this shabby old rake with his crooked, waxed moustache, who had probably laid more females than King Solomon.

'Be god, George Foulkes, I'll say this for y' - y' can fair spin 'em, mister. Now about this last job? Why did y' leave the funeral place?'

'I got fed-up with seeing corpses,' George told him, peevishly.

For a few seconds the man was serious wiping his nose and looking down at his papers.

'Well, George, you'll 'ave no trouble wit' --- he began to titter and then coughed - wit' schoolgirls on this 'ere job, savvy? Y' gits y'beer when y' delivers around y' dinnertime - one pint, mind. The landlord's'll give it y'. When y' gits t'Liverpool depot ask f' Arnold Todd - he'll be y' gaffer, savvy? All right then, I've got y' address. One month's trial, George. Look after those 'orses an' the depot. Give Arnold this card. Good-day.'

'Thanks, and good-day,' George muttered, the raving bloody crackpot!

He departed feeling an uneasy mixture of foolishness, anger, insecurity and very unsure of himself in not being able to beguile his listeners as he once could. As far as he could see, he had visited an asylum and was glad to get out.

*　　*　　*

Living with the Cowburns, Maggie and George Foulkes junior became part of the family and a close association developed between George and Charlotte Cowburn, who was about his own age, and they were eventually married. They were both working at the mill and were able to afford the rent for a cottage on the edge of the village. It was not much of a cottage, stone-built and damp in places, with two bedrooms, a living room and a scullery with a deep slopstone sink under a squeaky water-pump. In 1905 they presented Mr and Mrs Cowburn with a grandchild. He was christened Henry, a fine, bouncing, healthy child despite everything, and George was very happy. Charlotte was a strong, healthy girl but small in stature with a snub nose and well cared-for locks of auburn hair. She was George's delight.

Ralph Hodge had prospered in his plumbing business, now employing two youths. He was intelligent enough to keep abreast of all the latest developments in sanitary ideas, waste disposal systems and water supply. He had installed siphon water closets in town houses in most of the surrounding large towns and cities where water mains had been laid. In Furlongton he had installed similar siphons but made their wastes to issue into deep sumps in the gardens. He had included his own house, his mother's, the Cowburn's, and George and Charlotte's cottage. Annie was building up a self-esteem because of Ralph's hard-won prosperity. She felt someone of importance in the village, dressing her two children in fairly expensive clothes and travelling into Manchester for her own outfits. And then came the war.

In April of 1914 Nellie wrote to Maggie, belatedly sending her a copy of her wedding portraits. They were not displeased with Nellie's appearance at forty years of age - a fairly handsome woman when in her best clothes; but they frowned a little at the paunched, droopy-moustached figure of the bridegroom - a tall, stout-bellied fellow, pince-nez on his nose, his hair untidy and thin, giving a greyish mist where the light shone through it.

'He must be sixty if he's a day,' said Annie when Maggie showed her the picture.

'Well,' said Maggie, defiantly, 'I say good luck to her.'

She found an old bronze picture frame and put the photograph in it to stand on the well polished welsh dresser.

In the second year of the war, Lizzie Leach left the farm of her guardians and was taken on at the Dyeworks in Glossop helping to turn textiles into khaki twill for the soldiers. At forty-three, she earned more than she had ever earned in her life.

George Foulkes junior was conscripted into the army in 1916. He said a sad farewell to Charlotte and held her close. He ruffled the hair of Henry, aged eleven, and boarded the train to Preston. At Fulwood Barracks he was kitted out and provided with a Lee Enfield rifle and for six weeks he softened his new boots by marching and stamping and countermarching and bayoneting straw men and performing all the other mad things that the country needed him to do.

George had surprised the Furlongton community when he passed his medical A1. It was beyond their understanding that someone as thin as George could be fit. They did not consider that there are only two causes for unfitness - over-eating and under-eating. Since boyhood George had not fitted either of these categories - he had outlived the starvation period of his father's reign and had maintained a regular intake of plain food ever since, with no unhealthy luxuries, and these spartan conditions had brought his body to a state of lean fitness.

'A lean dog for a long race,' Arthur Cowburn observed with trite wisdom.

And George went off to France as soon as his squad had concluded its training.

CHAPTER TWO

1920

EMMA'S BROOD

A pantechnicon rumbled into Marsh Street, Kirkdale, a village named in the Domesday Book when it bordered the marshlands that swept down to the Mersey, and the driver wondered why a family should leave a comparatively respectable district like Kensington to move into this downtrodden area, and he mentioned it to his hefty mate sitting next to him.

The street was paved with irregular setts and the huge vehicle bumped and creaked over them, the horses quivering in indignation, their nostrils poised above the squalor, their equine brains hating every yard of the journey.

On the left going down was a high wall of glazed black bricks made for the London Midland and Scottish Railway Company; beyond the wall was the big crater of the sidings. On the right going down were crowded courts, their rough bricks mortar starved; groups of tatty haired children, their necks grey with dirt, the small ones digging sour soil from the gardens of their sour souled neighbours. School holidays it was, with the teachers saying prayers of thanksgiving in Saint Alexander's for the respite from the stench and stupidity of them.

On the tailboard of the van two boys lounged, one in an armchair, the other sprawled on a sofa, both articles secured with webbing. Their bodies vibrated with each rough bounce, as if crossing an endless cattle-grid, and they continually thrust themselves up to save themselves from slithering to the cobbles.

The elder, Angus, thought Kirkdale no fit place for a decent family to live in, a slum, a demi-purgatory that even Shakespeare could never praise.

Some mites stopped playing to watch the huge van rattle past, as it rolled like a tramp on the choppy waves of setts. The tiny square gardens had sections of their Victorian railings missing; there were drab woody privets, thin starveling bushes with soot-green leaves, gasping in the smokesick air from the stinking puffertrains that filled the kids' hearts with joy and their lungs with grit. The van driver shouted curses to the older kids who were daring each other to cross the street when the horses were within coffin distance of them.

A mouldy Mission hall, once filled with Christian soldiers marching onward, displayed a notice on its bleached front door, BARR'S CHARITIES, Sunday 25th July, 1920. Cocoa & Buns - 7.30 - 8.30 am. BRING OWN CUPS.

A haulage contractor's engine chugged and steamed and stank towards them and the removal man waited for it to go past, laden with barrels, before he turned the Clydesdales right into Miranda Road and within two hundred yards called Whoa outside the bay windowed supperbar for which Emma had paid £50 for the goodwill and a month's rent in advance of £1.16s.0d.

The two boys jumped down from the tailboard and stood looking at the property.

'What a bloody dump!' Angus said.

'Yer,' Malcom frowned. 'What was Ma thinking of?'

*   *   *

Emma bought two hessian bags with white tape handles for fourpence. The Mary Ellens were standing outside the fish market shouting their wares --- 'Sage or mint or parsley. D'ye want a bag?' They had big Irish ruddy faces and huge masses of hair held in a bun at the back. They wore warm pashm and wool shawls and had tattoos on their arms.

'I'll take a bit o' mint,' said Emma. 'We've mutton for Sunday.'

'Thank y' lady,' said the Mary Ellen.

'We'll have a pot o' tea and then get the fish,' Emma

told Robby. 'Oscar's second lorry hasn't come yet. I must have it fresh.'

They climbed the wooden steps up to the cafe and ordered a pot of tea and some muffins. Robby plastered his with butter and jam. There were only two fish porters there, swigging cocoa and smoking. Robby smelt the fish on their clothes and the cocoa steaming in their mugs.

'I'd like to pop into Blackler's but we haven't time,' Emma said. 'Must catch the twenty-eight car. I don't want to walk down to Haymarket for the twenty-three - my feet are the devil this morning.'

She bought one and a half stone of best hake. The man plomped them into the hessian bags.

'There yis are, ma. Pay at the office there.'

Robby felt dwarfed by the market, an enormous domed cathedral of fish with white-coated pardoners selling the ocean's indulgences for wholesale prices. At nine years old Robby hated carrying fish. The 28 tram was waiting at the terminus opposite Lime Street Station, with the conductor reversing the trolley pole by its attached rope. Emma and her son went round to the driver's platform.

'Fish for Argos Road,' Emma called.

'Yer, O.K. Missus. I'll purrit under the ould stairs f' yis.'

They were seated comfortably when the old tram started. It clumbered along the loopline onto Lime Street, past the Empire Theatre where Jack Buchanon was filling the house each night, and eventually into Byrom Street and along Scotland Road, forking left at the Rotunda where Billy Bennett was topping the bill. After fifteen minutes of pugnosed journey, Argos Road stop. Robby alighted quickly and ran round to the front, anxious in case the driver forgot the fish. His ma hobbled round after him and took one of the bags. She placed sixpence into the driver's palm.

'Thank y' driver,' she called, and the tram moaned off with its ozone smell to Litherland.

'These drivers of the twenty-eight are good if you tip them,' she said,' as they waited for a motorcycle and sidecar to pass them.

'I'd be good if you tipped me,' said Robby.
'Uh! You've had tea and muffins,' Ma said.

Every week Robby borrowed four books from the library, three for his Ma and one for himself. Emma used the quiet hours between opening times to read. She liked the novels of romanticists like Silas K. Hocking, Marie Corelli and Mrs Gaskell. She revelled in Hocking's stories of Cornwall, a place she imagined as a land of paradisiacal beauty in its narrow lanes, wild coast, tin mines, all images fed into her young mind at Miss Heller's in the Blackburn commercial hotel. The images were now re-discovered in the reverent gentleman's writings; but his religious themes made no impression on Emma's view of the church.

During warm holidays from school, after his chores, Robby sun-bathed and dreamed on the shed roof, the billowing sheets on the wash line witching him into worlds of Jim Hawkins, Captain Blood, Robinson Crusoe or Coral Island. Even in his younger days the old park in Bootle had his ranch house among the privets from where he rode off in lurching canter, holding invisible reins, covering the field's prairie perimeter, with a six-gun forefinger firing mouth explosions as he fought the Red Indians close on his and his faithful horse's heels, all in the silent hours before sunset when the parkie blew his whistle and went round locking the gates. Few saw the boy's fantasy play. It was an age of homemade entertainment for the kids, fashioned from their imaginations, sadly to be replaced in the years to come with crass, switch on and off gadgets. In that sweet sorrow time those kids lived and loved their play.

Robby's shed roof was a magic carpet to take him on dream adventures across far horizons. He lay on his stomach on the sloping roof one sunny day and started his pirate yarn. He was ten and took his style from Jeffrey Farnol, a quaint old writer, strewing his text with <u>thereupons</u>, <u>whereupons</u>, albeits, and <u>notwithstanding</u>. He filled an exercise book and the blue ink from his cheap fountain pen stained his fingers beyond the soap and water of two bath nights. The story fizzled out and the pirates were all cremated on the coal fire on one Sunday evening of deep sighs. The family said he was a dreamer, even his Ma, who confined her dreams to her reading sessions.

In the shed with its Arabian Nights roof, was an iron machine, a heavy cylindrical container resting on axles in a semicircular trough. The drum inside the cylinder had a perforated zinc lining. With a third of a hundredweight of potatoes inside, the drum was turned with a large L shaped handle, the trough kept full of water that splashed out with each turn, the rough lining scraping away the soil and skin, and after a suitable time, the potatoes gleamed white, all ready for picking. In spring the job was easier for new potatoes were unscathed and tender skinned; but in winter the diseased bits and the eyes had to be picked out with a sharp picker. When the water froze and the snow-covered yard matched the whitewashed walls, the lads brought in the tubs and worked inside behind closed doors. And all this hard labour often before school each morning, or at night by the light of a hurricane lamp.

In the living room there was an old-fashioned hearth with a coalfire and oven - like the Heller's, Emma said. Huge pans of pigs' and sheep's trotters, marrowfat peas and butterbeans stood gurgling away amid the flames like geysers in New Zealand. The oven was laden with Emma's popular pies baking slowly sold at fourpence for each steak and kidney and threepence for meat and potato. Emma invented savoury burgers of mincemeat, onions and herbs. Thick honeycomb tripe, fillets and steaks of fish, sausages in batter, and homemade fishcakes were laid out on trays in the sloping shop window, with lumps of ice in summer time. Emma dipped pieces of fish into batter and placed them into the boiling fat as the pale blue smoke rose. The fish sizzled, the batter inflated, and the infuriated fat threatened to overflow the deep pan's rim. In another big pan chipped potatoes fried to a golden brown and were ladled into a receptacle ready for serving, the fat drained off through a wire net lifting scoop. Peas and beans were kept simmering on small gas rings.

Beneath the main counter Emma kept stacks of paper

bags, boxes of mineral waters, packets of flour, large bottles of vinegar, and bars of rock salt. The youngest child, Margaret, cut newspapers to size and rubbed together the blocks of salt to fill the salt shakers. Mineral waters,' pickles, piccalilli, and pickled gherkins adorned the shop window and above the display were the words SUPPER BAR in white letters. The bright colours of the soft drinks, interspersed with vivid reds of pickled beetroot, red cabbage, and the yellow of piccalilli jars, made an attractive frieze against the window glass. Emma's shop was popular and each lunchtime and in the evenings the shop would be packed with customers.

Emma provided nourishment for slum families within their poverty level; and remembering the starvation days of her childhood, she made sure that her family was well fed, and built-up in them a sound constitution that made hospitals alien places to the children.

After midnight the lower levels of society begged for leftover scraps for a halfpenny, ends of tripe, a last cowheel, or a last meat pie. Emma gave them what they needed. These were the paupers of the poor who haunted butchers' shops for scragends or greengrocers for fades.

Andrew Douglas occasionally looked through the connecting window and saw poor children in bare feet and persuaded Emma to give away the boys' or girls' old footwear. Emma knew that the gifts would be pawned and the money boozed away by the parents. Poverty was a good teacher, she said, but adult paupers were poor scholars.

In her toddling days, Margaret loved to go out with her brothers Robby and Douglas, on outings with Ma and Dadda sitting in front of them upstairs on the tram to the Pier Head. Dadda always smoked a cigar and the aroma drifting back became a fond memory for the young ones in later years. The rattling tram moved at fifteen miles an hour, scraping lazily around bends, with friction squeaks against the metals, and when it arrived to join its assorted brethren, the family alighted and started down the wide, domed roadway that sloped on hinges to the pontoon landing stage half a mile long. The roads rose and fell with the tides and you never knew how steep they would be from hour to hour.

They boarded the chubby ferry steamer to Wallasey and the sea breezes cooled their faces and nurtured their lungs. Querulous seagulls glided to catch titbits. Robby thought of faraway places and sea rovers. The Liver Building and the shipping offices dominated until they were left small by the ferry chugging its choppy westward way. It was a peaceful Sabbath scene of anchored cargo boats mid-stream, and fortress transatlantic liners with all their siren magic, preparing for return voyages to New York. Dredgers rumbled towards the estuary, each endless chain of rusted buckets, a Jules Verne figment, going to scoop mud to make the big ships' channels. Sturdy dwarf tugs nudged large vessels into the landing stage. All was exciting and esoteric in its functioning.

The yellow bus at Wallasey took them on a circular tour of the peninsular, and then a walk down to the pier, homeward bound, licking ice cream on the way. They were happy days.

Some Sundays they took the tram to Seaforth, terminus of the Dockers' Umbrella - the world's first electric overhead railway, prototype for the New York Elevated Railway. They travelled seven miles of dockland and back for a few pence, following the riverbank to Dingle where, incomprehensibly, the little train concluded its journey at an underground station. From the train windows were fantastic sights of ships, docks, shipyards, cranes, tugboats, workshops and warehouses, some for tobacco standing where they stood in the eighteenth century. This friendly little railway had a history of passengers among whom had been G.K. Chesterton, Rudyard Kipling, King Feisal, film stars and politicians. The train had light wooden carriages with slatted seats on either side of a central aisle, and it stopped at short intervals at narrow platforms connected to ground level by iron staircases.

Andrew Ferguson always came from work to the back entrance of their home, too shy to push past loud, shawled women in the shop. As the years hastened on their way, Margaret held a vague, melancholy memory of her Dadda framed in the kitchen doorway giving her his usual greeting of:

'Where's my little ducket, then?' There was a misty conviction in her mind that her Dadda had been a tragic figure.

Three years after her birth in 1919, she learned to tie her bootlaces. She went upstairs secretly to her Dadda, lying half conscious with ptomaine poisoning from food at his work's canteen. Proudly the tiny creature entered the sick-room and raised her small foot for her father to see.

'Look, Dadda, I tied my own laces,' she told him happily.

Dadda moaned, struggling in the sad clouds of his mind to give a reassuring praise to his precious child. Shortly after this he moaned again, shivered violently beneath the bedclothes and died. He was fifty-seven years old.

*　　*　　*

The eldest child, Flora, brought up the younger ones, seeing that they were able to wash and dress themselves as soon as they were old enough. Flora was tall and strong and performed everything with huge, sweeping efficiency, even when serving customers.

Emma had photographs taken of all her children, the three elder and the three younger ones separately. She sent copies to their father's relations in Scotland, determined to make her conditions known to her late husband's family; she was now a widow with six children, regardless of whether, as they had guessed, Andrew Douglas Ferguson had been the black sheep of his family or not. Several weeks passed before a letter informed Emma that Aunt Jean in Canada, matriarch of the Ferguson's, was coming over to see the family and would call in at Emma's address on her way north. She would arrive in a fortnight's time on a Saturday.

Emma's household became an uproar of scouring and cleaning, to make a first good impression on the visitor, Emma's main object being to coax some financial assistance out of her husband's family.

Aunt Jean had an aura of graciousness about her. She was class, the kids thought, comparing her with their own kind. Aunt Jean had booked in at a hotel in Lime Street after disembarking. Emma's dread that Jean would stay overnight, vanished happily, for it was not certain that she would have had a bugless night. After Emma's paraffin and ammonia treatment of the bedroom walls, the lady would have carried that smell with her to Scotland and back to Canada, and what would that have done to arouse the family's sympathy?

'Ye bairns are verra bonny, Emma,' Jean declared, holding her china cup with small finger extended, her expensive suede gloves on her beautiful grey coat lap.

'Of course, Andrew Douglas was a verra bonny mon, there's nae doubt.'

'He used to say I was pretty,' Emma replied, claiming a half share in the comeliness. Her sister-in-law was not getting away with that.

'He married me when I was eighteen - he was thirty-five. Twenty-two years we had our life together. We had our ups and downs but he did not regret our marriage.'

'Oh, I'm puffectly certain, dear, that he never regretted his marriage', Aunt Jean soothed. 'We all have our ups and downs, Emma dear.'

Emma's declaration had missed one incident known to the older three children:

Andrew Douglas had absented himself for six years. By chance, a commercial traveller visiting Emma's shop in Kensington before the war, mentioned that he had seen Andrew Douglas in Burnley, manager of a grocer's shop. The following weekend Emma had gone off in a flurry to find her errant husband, had discovered his lodgings and had brought him home by reminding him of his responsibilities. In later life Robby understood why there were seven years between his age and that of his elder bother, Malcolm.

'Your tea is excellent,' Emma, my dear. 'I have no tasted the like in Canada these mony years. Tis unfortunate, dear, I am sorry to say so, I canna stop to see the elder bairns.'

'Aye,' Emma thought, ' bet you're sorry - I don't think.'

Emma herself was not sorry. Angus, as a farm labourer since leaving school, would come home with the manure smell on his clothes; Malcolm would arrive about ten, the assistant's job at Jackson's Hats and Boots meaning long hours for meagre reward; and the same with Flora, a cashier at the Blacklers Store.

Jean left three half-crowns for the younger ones and then departed. She had graciously stayed one hour, the pre-arranged arrival of a shining taxicab cutting short their colloquy. Her eyebrows arched when she saw the circle of grubby kids around the Cinderella's golden coach; the kids seldom saw taxis in that area.

The letter from Scotland was friendly but firm between the lines, and after that there was no further correspondence between Emma and her Scottish in-laws. And the gods looked down and knew that the humiliation had been given by Aunt Jean's report of Emma's living conditions; and the gods knew that the humiliation had not been accepted. It would take much more than that to humiliate little Emma Ferguson.

* * *

Flora was disappointed by the lack of family interest when she started to go out with Jack Volant, Coal Depot Manager of the Moss Side Coal Company, its office by the sidings in Marsh Street. Ma insisted that Flora take Margaret with them wherever they went, and the frustrated Flora always had to return early to put her young sister to bed. Emma always had in her memory her bastard sister's agonies, and how her villainous father had beaten her mother, and brought death to the tragic woman at an early age.

After long months of courting, Jack Volant being a patient, long-suffering beau, Flora reached the age of twenty-one and the couple were married. Their chaperon,

Margaret, aged six, was a bridesmaid, excited to be riding in a horse-drawn brougham to the Roman Catholic Church. The child was thrilled with her wedding hat, frock and shoes. The hat was clocheshaped in the ghastly fashion of the twenties.

Now, Emma thought, it would be a one-woman fight for survival; the hard working Flora had deserted her - and married an R.C. too! She felt desperate for several days after the wedding and never thought that her good, self-effacing daughter had used the marriage as an escape.

At the wedding, eight-year-old Douglas hid beneath a side table, concealed behind its drapes, and was sighfully glad when the do was over. Douglas bolstered his torments of shyness by tantalising his younger sister, swearing and daring, blustering and imitating the various characters they knew. One such character, Gregory, lived his life in a nadir of shyness and fear. When a big boy came near him, Gregory scraped along the red bricked wall of the playground, his arms across his chest, elbows and wrists like a praying mantis, one knee bent and pushed against the other leg. Douglas aped this cringing soul with the perfection of a born mimic and Robby's tears of mirth dripped from his eyes as he watched. Each night, while it lasted, he would urge Douglas to --- 'Go on, do Gregory again.'

Douglas also impersonated Miss Maguire, a crab embodiment of all spinster schoolmarms. The kids made a repeated rhyme about Nell Maguire peed on the fire, ending with a cat that suffered the same indignity as the fire.

Douglas's bane was the maypole, erected into a socket in the hall. Miss Jarret played Come Lasses and Lads, Take leave of your dads, on the piano, and the small boys and girls weaved in and out, making coloured patterns of the tightening ribbons. Douglas and two other boys entangled the tapes by clumping round like sick wildebeests babes. Miss Maguire's high blood pressure reached beetroot shades and her short cane swished across the bums of the clattering creatures. Douglas swore to strangle Nell Maguire with a maypole ribbon when he was twenty-one.

Standard three room always had bulbs on the window

ledges, the tops of the bulbs probably like the way the Spaniards grew their onions, Douglas believed, knowing nothing about hyacinths.

Miss Jarret's lunch was always a Jaffa orange and a large green apple. These two fruits were placed on her desk each morning. That classroom smell lingered in the pupils' minds for years - ink, chalk, orange, apple, flowers, and the stale sweaty smell of one or two kids who had been sewn into their clothes for the approach of winter. Once Douglas sat next to a boy who gave off odours of stale sweat, urine, and musty hair. Douglas caught a flea off him and never forgot it. After closing time Emma found the flea and broke its back on her thumbnail at twelve thirty a.m. At times, too, Emma spent the small hours of a Saturday combing nits out of the children's hair, further gifts from neglected children.

One Friday morning Robby was sent for from the senior class and asked to translate Douglas's essay on What I will Do Tomorrow? He had written Mi mut mat tek me to mark i et in the mormin to biy sum hak and Robby said it meant - My mother might take me to the market in the morning to buy some hake.

'Thank you,' said Miss Jarret. 'It is fortunate that someone can translate his dreadful work. I hadn't the least idea what it meant. You must tell your mother, Robert, that he is very backward and is not improving.'

Robby never did mention the incident.

Miss Jarret had a twelve-inch ruler with which she rapped the knuckles of her most troublesome pupils, Douglas among them, and she became Number Two on his murder rosta.

Those purgatory years vanished in senior school; Douglas developed late. There was never scorn from any of his classmates. They all knew Miss Jarret and Miss Maguire and had been through the millrace of their domination.

From the playground they saw the workhouse across the road. For some years after the first Great War, wounded soldiers and men who had recovered and awaited demobilisation occupied the workhouse. The kids were intrigued by the sentries, puttyed to the knees, marching up and down behind the closed wrought iron gates, Lee Enfield '303 rifles sloped, smartly clicking heels and stamping in big boots. A flag-fluttering staff car meant that the guard was called out, the gates opening, the squeak of the sergeant Guard Commander --- Slow - up ARMS! --- then the routine of presenting arms. The old workhouse was a sinister place, and the lads pitied those weary, browbeaten, khaki-clad men with their shining rifles. The place seemed to hold dark secrets of the sad past-hinted suffering and misery and the soldiers prolonged that impression, never once exciting the children, even on Empire Days, that Imperial Celebration to introduce a training that would make patriotic citizens of the Empire. Prominence had to be given, Lord Meath had said, to the proud saluting of The Flag, and all over the world where the British held sway, The Flag was saluted even when people's bellies were full of the hunger wind.

The jowler down the side of Emma's property from Miranda Road made a T junction, part of its crosspiece being a cul-de-sac behind their next door neighbours, Mr and Mrs Jones, a respectable couple, the husband having the status of an engine driver. On the far side of the Jones's was the corner public house, and when time was called, the boozy women came along the entry to the T junction to relieve themselves. Like shire mares they stood, letting go of the abundance of booze in their bulging bladders.

Working in the light of a hurricane lamp one night, the lads heard the women beyond the wall. Douglas muttered, 'Dirty old sods' --- took the hosepipe out of the trough, placed his finger over the end, and aimed the spray over the wall. There was the silence of dulled brains; then a female voice shrieked out --- 'God, Clara, it's startin' t' rain 'urry up - we'll get bleedin' drowned.'

The boys were convulsed with secret laughter. The Mary Ellens came along the short entry towards Miranda Road, Douglas expertly following them with the spray. Reaching the main road out of the spray the women paused.

'It's stopped, Clara an' a carn see a bleedin' cloud nowhere!'

'Sumtimes it rains widout clouds,' Clara suggested.

'Ow thee 'ell can it rain widout clouds, y' daft cow!'

They went off home, Clara's friend scornfully expounding the scientific theories of precipitation until their voices faded into the distant night.

The sprays continued regularly until one old dear, less drunk than the rest, discovered it was a trick and went into the shop to complain to Emma.

'Well, it's not a lavatory in that entry, you know,' Emma said, but did not pursue the matter because some of the women were customers; but she soundly rated the boys later for being Damned Devils.

Engine driver Jones found out what was happening behind his back door and informed the big Irish policeman on the beat. After closing time one night, the lads heard ... 'Hey - cum outa der, y' doity ould biddies! We'll 'ave no pissin' in d' jowler, so we won't.'

The Authorities fixed a gaslamp to the corner of the wall. The huge gasmantle gave a yellow light over the yard and entry, automatically lighting by clockwork set to lighting up times, and there was no more widdling in that particular jowler.

*   *   *

Benny's eyes were glassy with a desire to torment, like a juvenile Shylock.

'Christ was nowt. D' y' want t' know who he was?'

'I know who he was,' said Robby.

'Y' t'ink y' do - but all that there about the virgin birth is baldedash, Fergy. In doze days all d' women were virgins before their first-born kid. 'Is father wasn't God, y' know. I'll tell y', Fergy, his father was a Roman centurion - that's who 'is father was. Mary went wid a Roman centurion - that's what she did, an' it all 'ad t' be kep' quiet on account o' d' disgrace, y'see.'

Robby stopped suddenly in his tracks. He had never heard such blasphemy in his whole life! The dignity and faith of the whole of Christendom were in the balance!

With a hefty lunge, he had Benny by the neck, swung him round and kicked his legs from under him. The young tormentor was now on his back on the pavement, Robby sitting on his stomach and gripping his wrists with big, hard hands. The victim looked like Barrabus before the cross was erected. His comfortable bulk compared unfavourably with Robby's workfed body.

'Take those words back,' Robby commanded.

Benny struggled and found it futile, he was pinned to the paving stones. He relaxed all at once. The ruse failed to put Robby off his guard.

'Hey, y' strong!' Benny gasped. 'As strong as a man!'

'Don't try to softsoap me,' Robby growled. 'Say y.' sorry.'

'All right - I s'pose I'm sorry. Let me go.'

'No. Not suppose you're sorry - you've gotta be real sorry.

Robby's grip tightened.

'Ow!' Benny shrieked. 'Y' urtin' me 'ands. All right. All right. I'm sorry.'

Robby released his grip and jumped up. Benny scrambled to his feet and dusted himself down with white, chubby hands.

'Fergy, y' a bastid,' he said, moving away quickly. In two strides Robby had him again, round the throat.

'Urg! Urg!' Benny gurgled.

'Say y' sorry,' Robby snarled.

'Urg! Urg! Sorry - sorry - sorry.'

Robby released his victim. Benny rubbed his neck and wrists and felt that that had come too close to a serious breakdown of relations. But his startling anti-Christian opinion, deeply piercing sacrilege, sank like a parasite into Robby's mind.

'I thought we were friends,' Benny gasped.

'Yer - and so did I. Friends don't insult each other - or bloody shouldn't. What would you say if I told you the Old Testament was a load of cowdung?'

'All right, all right. I said I was sorry,' Benny breathed, taking out a greyish handkerchief that must have been in his pocket since the pillar of salt.

'Fergy - sorry. Shake.'

Robby accepted his friend's hand and shook it once.

'We've gotta swear not to insult each other - 'specially about religion.'

'Yer. I'll swear t' that,' Benny agreed.

'I swear,' said Robby, and they shook hands properly, solemnly, both knowing that they would keep their promise.

Back came Benny's hand on Robby's shoulder as they walked on.

'Fergy - you're different from the rest of 'em round here, an' that's why the Da likes me knockin' around wid yis.'

'Does he?' Robby laughed. 'I didn't know that. Ma thinks y' old man's a good sort. He pops in our place sometimes for a chat when he's going to a job.'

'We've an 'ell of a lot t' purrup wid, Fergy. People round 'ere are d' scum of de earth. They tell their kids t' keep away from us.'

'No. I don't think so. Ma's never said that to us.'

'That's wharra said - you're different.'

They walked on to the end of Marsh Street and stood on the corner of Miranda Road.

'Hey - I've got some old encyclopaedias that'll come in 'andy when y' swottin', Benny said. 'Y' can 'ave 'em cheap. Harmsworth's monthlies, de are. Shillin' each.'

'How many?'

'From A to Z - about thirty editions.'

Robby laughed incredulously.

'Thirty editions? At a shilling each? You must be off y' rocker! I can't afford all that money. Anyway, I bet they only cost one and three new.'

'Y' can 'ave 'em f' five bob.'

'Five bob!' Robby was amazed at the generosity, not knowing that Benny had used a pedlar's ploy by mentioning a shilling in the first place. Robby's excitement waned.

'Sorry. Can't even afford five bob.'

'Wharra bout y' ma?'

'No - she has enough on her plate.'

'All right - half a dollar for some of 'em - A to O. What say?' Robby plunged in at once.

'Right. I'll scrounge the money somehow.'

They sealed the bargain by slapping their hands together like north-country farmers.

Next day, Robby joyfully took home the stack of paper-backed encyclopaedias, having borrowed the money from his ma. Some were the worse for wear but they were a huge bargain. Benny had been generous, and with all his faults he was a good friend. But a few weeks later, opposition came from the headmaster. Robby had just been appointed House Captain.

'I advise you, Robert, to pick your friends carefully,' Captain Becket told him. Benny had been sent to Coventry for some so-called serious offence. It was forbidden for anyone to speak to Benny for one week whilst he remained isolated on a dais in the hall every break-time and for ten minutes after school. Robby had to obey the system in school, feeling guilty, but out of school he disobeyed the rule and saw his friend as usual. Benny understood his position.

Benny's father, Abe Solomons, had a glazier's shop around the corner from Emma's place. He was tall, thin, upright, with a ragged grey beard. The street Arabs in that suburb of hell chased after decent old Abe, shouting - 'Who killed Christ wid d' putty knife?'

After a while old Abe turned and slated them in his ancient tongue. There was always trouble with the Jews and Arabs.

Abe complained to Emma about his sons, a younger generation that refused to take an energetic interest in the business of glazing. They obeyed their father's orders under constraint as they grew older and more blasé. Abe believed Emma's children to be right for his own brood. They were a good influence in an environment made hostile by bigoted people. Margaret was a good friend of Rose Solomons and Angus and Malcolm with Abe's elder sons, Asher and Joseph.

*   *   *

By the time Robby and Douglas were established in Senior School, Angus had left Farmer Vose at Maghull and had become an apprentice printer. He had one thing to show for his time on the farm - a pup the farmer had given him. It was now growing into a large hound, part Alsatian and part some lower canine caste.

Angus had often wondered why farm workers were the lowest paid class in the country. It had been the only livelihood available to him on leaving school. Why Jones, the engine driver, was so highly regarded when the farm worker had no status, puzzled the lad. He knew that railways needed a strict discipline and engine drivers were probably respected because of their skill and special responsibility for thousands of lives. But it annoyed Angus that a goods porter received more than a farm worker and drivers more than cotton spinners. Rail unions were strong. The Liberal Government had reinforced them in the 1911 Trades Disputes Act and railwaymen now had the right to strike without being victimised. Railway companies had adopted a paternal attitude towards employees so that there were accompanying benefits - sick pay, retirement pensions, company housing, health and welfare services for employees and their families, libraries, social clubs, baths, and recreational centres, safe limits to the hours a driver worked, holidays and company towns like Wolverton, Swindon, and Crewe.

The wretched farm worker worked seventy hours a week, and in winter often cared for farm equipment without pay beyond board and lodging. Their union was pathetically weak and faced in 1908 the opposing might of the self-preserving National Farmers' Union, owners and employers who controlled both prices and wages. History told a sorry story that, in four years, by the outbreak of war, the farm labourer's wage had risen by only one measly shilling! Reading this in his farmers' magazine, Angus was disgusted.

The train driver broadened his mind when travelling great distances day by day. He saw a developing industrial world unknown to most agricultural workers. The availability of self-study, too, gave the railwaymen some measure of intellectual superiority over the labourer. That was why the engine driver was on a much higher social plane compared with the farm worker whose only doubtful beneficial difference lay in his healthier work and peace of mind in rural surroundings.

Angus's questioning intelligence had not helped him rise to any great heights at school. In contrast, Malcolm had been appointed School Captain when Angus had gone. Captain Becket thought highly of Malcolm, especially his endeavours on the sports field. His weekly article in the local press on School Sports had described Malcolm's efforts in the words 'When Malcom Ferguson came to the wicket, he opened his shoulders and closed his eyes and made a worthwhile 33 runs.' The boy had had some reservations about that description.

It was because Becket remembered Malcolm so well that he also made a favourite of Robby, something similar in appearance to his brother. Robby was favoured, too, by the art master, Banford, who sowed a seed of enthusiasm in Robby's mind for drawing. He gave his favourite pupil almost impossible tasks to do - drawing cutglass sugar basins, lace curtains, apples and oranges on folded newspaper; yet Robby managed them with skill and the school put his work on exhibition. Nobody attended from Miranda Road.

*   *   *

Timothy Doyle, Angus's close friend, lived behind the dairy shop on the corner -Mrs Doyle's Dairy. They had a scraggy cow in the shippen, and a horse and milk float, cow dung and manure in the yard. Milk was doled out with a small tin measure from a white ten-gallon milk mug with muslin cover. Certificates all round the walls showed the quality of dairy cows they had entered in shows. It was a tiny, clean- scrubbed dairy, feeling cool and smelling of fresh milk like a baby's skin. Timothy helped Angus with the potato washing at times and giggled at his chum's wiseacre comments - an accident at soccer, a vivid sketch of his being carried to the touchline by the trainers and all the girls running to gather round, Angus pretending to be half conscious, having his thigh massaged and imagining all those girls doing it instead, getting him in a right state, his play-acting allowing his old man to erect, as if he were all innocent, and the girls nudging and tittering, and some blushing. Angus was one of Aunt Jean's bonny bairns.

Timothy worked in the city slaughterhouse and Angus would say 'Don't tell me any more,' when Tim described the mistakes the tyros made sometimes, with the animals only half dead as they writhed on the tiles, blood gushing into the gutters, and the hard-boiled old butchers coming to pole-axe the beasts again. Tim worked in the gut department cutting away the inedible bits for disposal.

Angus's firm team played away games on Bootle park, a drab place those days, like much of the area. The grass was trodden on, the soil stone hard at the edges. There was the cricket ground, one of the few lush green sights in all that defeated world. The old iron tap, halfway along the main path, had the water spurting from a lion's mouth into a round iron bowl; you had to press the front stud in the lion's neck and hold the iron-chained cup to the lion's mouth. It was a sturdy example of late Victorian craftsmanship, and the water was nectar at half-time if you hated lemons.

Old fogies occupied the bowling greens, their clothes reeking of stale sweat and baccy smoke, living their lives waiting to die, passing time away, living from day to day with crusted pipes and trusted woods that got no nearer the jack than they did forty years ago. An iron notice said: 'eep off the gra' - typical of the place, nothing sacred, nothing safe, neglect, weariness, can't be bothered. Destructive little bastards tore out railings, broke notices, split trees, trampled grass, crushed flowers, spat phlegm, dug soil, chewed privet leaves, did their dollops in corners - ten degrees below animal standards, young, decadent, stampeding sub-cattle, fit only for Timothy Doyle's gut department.

Alf Atkins, Robby's friend, lived in Pallas Street. Ironic street names around there, a district called Classical by the post office - Iris, Argos, Hector, and even Zeus's grandson honoured in Pelops Street. They were all terraced houses in Pallas Street, their inhabitants earning a kind of respectability in good behaviour.

In the early days Robby took Margaret to school, leaning on her convenient shoulder, walking up Marsh Street, Alf Atkins talking all the time, and the poor child suffering the weight of big brother's arm, and Alf saying, 'I-'m making some more racers tonight. Are y' coming over?' Robby would agree to come and Alf would have his sharp penknife and bits of wood which he carved into cigars, scoring out a hollow for the driving seat, and sticking in drawing pin wheels. Robby painted them from Alf's watercolour box. Alf would grow up to be a mechanic, Robby imagined, and his friend's appearance - lean, sharp-eyed, with big, dextrous hands - became the prototype in Robby's mind for all engineers and mechanics of the future. Alf's was a placid home and Robby spent happy days there. Margaret never forgot Alf Atkins either.

Emma made a taboo. The kids never talked to Maggie Kelly who lived with her sister almost opposite the supper bar. The Kelly's were greengrocers on the corner of Braemar Street. Maggy, aged forty, sat in her rockingchair on warm evenings, just inside the shop doorway, a character - tall, buxom, red-haired with big Irish face, huge circular earrings and the hair in the usual bun at the back. She had a long cane, bent like the ones in schools, and she thrashed boys who thieved fruit from the crates which acted as showcases around the door. Maggy feared no one and even the biggest lads feared her. The priests liked Maggie because she gave generously to the church. Braemar Street was one of Scotch tenement houses with balconies to each floor from which chamber pots were emptied onto the heads of inexperienced rent collectors and bum bailiffs, and policemen who walked up in threes. The Ferguson children were strictly forbidden to enter Braemar Street and to them it became the locality of the damned and doomed, and they imagined kidnapping, slavery, Chinese opium dens, German spies, and torture chambers in that long street.

In the cake shop on the other corner was an oriental, slit-eyed oval-faced girl, Winnie Ray, who always smiled at customers. Angus would order in a potentate's voice – 'Get me a Winnie Ray cream slice,' and Robby would go across grumbling that Angus should get his own bloody cream slices. He would glance fearfully up Braemar Street then hurry into the shop and Winnie would show big, lovely white teeth and serve him. Angus always said they were the best cream slices he had ever tasted, as if he had been all over the world tasting cream slices. He never went his own errands.

Seven-thirty on Sunday mornings, the patter of bare webs and the occasional clink of a dropped tin mug, the shrieks of --- 'Gerrup f' Barrses! Gerrup f' Barrses!' The mission hall would open its doors and get the scruffy kids into a queue and fill their mugs with hot cocoa and give them a bun each. Mrs Barr, deceased, a Methodist lady, had left her money to charity for starvelings. That mission hall was a popular Sunday treat.

There were spies among the kids and each Monday morning St Patrick's headmaster called out the wretched traitors, reading from a list provided by the school grass. Two cane strokes for each traitor and six for regular offenders. Some thought it was worthwhile to be punished to get a mug of steaming cocoa and a bun on cold mornings. Emma was horrified when she first heard of the caning. 'If that's religion,' she said, 'they can keep it - bigoted hypocrites. Why doesn't the priest step in and stop that fellow caning them?' This question ignored the fact that priests were not always priestly, and there was always one of them to witness the punishment.

* * *

Emma put her head out of the window and called to the porter.

'When is it Furlongton?'

'Next stop but one, luv.'

'Thank you.' She sat down next to Margaret. Robby was in the corner compartment with Douglas. Robby believed that all the other passengers in that compartment thought ma was a damned nuisance. She had to keep poking her head out of the window making silly enquiries. Everybody knew the porter shouted out the station when the train steamed in. Ma said they weren't clear – 'nTREE for Aintree, and 'mSKIRK for Ormskirk. Why didn't they speak clearly? You never knew where you were on the damned train, especially on a misty morning, ma said.

Robby sank deeper into his corner, wishing the family were by themselves. There again, ma was always in too much panic to find an empty compartment. You needed an empty compartment in these trains without corridors and then you wouldn't have lots of people gawping at you, like that chap opposite, running his eyes up and down himself and Douglas, probably thinking they were two little brats spoilt by that silly woman who couldn't keep still.

And the gods looking down said, 'Same family story. Just like his grandfather - and in a train, too. And he's wrong about that chap. He's not thinking along those lines at all.'

'What did his grandfather do?' asked a young learner god.

'Oh, he disowned his own wife when she breastfed their first child on a crowded train.'

With relief they alighted at Furlongton and Emma handed in the tickets and got half back for the return journey. And the fuss that Mrs Cowburn made when they arrived! She made them tea and provided homemade cakes. She was a complete stranger to the kids.

'Aye, Emma, luv, Arthur died during t' war through an accident at mill. Minnes were good wi' me - allowing me to stay in t' cottage an' give me a pension as a kind of compensation, y' might say. Aye, luv, they wus good t'me. Mind, Arthur worked forty year for 'em.'

'Well,' you certainly deserved the best treatment, Mrs Cowburn, you certainly did.'

'Eh, I'm fair glad General Strikes o'er. What a to-do! Things mun settle down nah an' we s'all get on us feet again.'

'So they've all left and got married then?' Emma asked.

'I've not heard from a single one of them, believe it or not.'

'Aye, and all wi' kiddies too – 'cept poor Lizzie - an,' Nellie. Lizzie's gotten a small cottage at Glossop, has the lass. She's still at dye works I believe.'

'Poor Lizzie,' Emma sighed. 'She had a dreadful life with that old devil. Nearly drove her out of her mind.'

'Aye, he did an' all - an' med her deaf, 'e did. Poor lass couldn't help bein' illegitimate. An' crucified y' poor mother. Eh, I've often bin thankful I followed Lizzie and thee down tut pond, after your poor mother died.'

'Me too,' Emma laughed. We wouldn't be here now if it hadn't been for you stopping lizzie in the nick o' time.

'Aye, what a to-do! O' course, poor Lizzie lost all 'ope when y' mother went. Eh, George Foulkes 'as a lot to answer for on t' day o' judgement.'

'And how is Nellie?'

'She's in Preston, tha knows. She wed chap at bank. Older than her he were. An' Maggie wed Jack Dickson - but y' never knew Jack, did y' luv?'

'No, but we'll be seeing him no doubt.'

The children sat quietly on their chairs, Douglas uncomfortable, looking out of the window at the wrought-iron gates of the Minnes grounds, home of the local mill-owner. Robby wondered what his elders were talking about and Margaret sat on the edge of a ladder backed chair, swinging her legs.

'Tha s'all ave a bit of a bus ride, Emma, luv. I s'all gi' thee all their addresses. Maggie an' George are in Leyland, tha knows, an' Annie an' Nellie in Preston. Eh, I bet they'll be surprised t' see thee.'

What Emma did, after leaving Mrs Cowburn's cottage, she regretted for weeks to come. She took the children on a round tour of all her relatives.

Aunts, uncles and cousins added to Douglas's awful discomfort. They stayed two nights at Maggie's cottage in

Leyland then Emma remembered her promise to Flora and Angus who were managing the shop, and they arrived home in Liverpool on Sunday afternoon.

*   *   *

In December 1926 Emma received a shock letter from Dingle.

My Dear Daughter,

I am writing to you because I have not been well lately and I do not know where to turn for help. I drive a brewer's dray for Walker's Ales and in this weather it is a hard job. No man at seventy-six should be working. I do not want to go into the workhouse. I can never keep myself warm and I have been having less food lately because of the rising prices.

I spend my spare time painting horses which have been my life and I sold several pictures. My landlady has no sense of smell and she does not mind the painting. I have a front room and share the kitchen with another lodger, a tram driver.

I wrote to Annie who is now living in Preston (my letter sent on by Mrs Cowburn) and she wrote back and said that as you were already in Liverpool, you could perhaps help me in my time of need. I often think of you when driving around on cold, wet days. I think of your wonderful cook shop with all its warmth and good food as Annie described. I would love to join you for the Christmas festivities.

Your loving father

George Foulkes.

'Eh!' Emma cried. 'The damned old hypocrite! Here, read it. I could laugh if it weren't so damned wicked!'

'Why?' Robby asked, starting to read.

'Your loving father, indeed! He's never loved anyone except himself in all his wretched life. Your Auntie Annie wouldn't have him. Oh no. Palmed him off onto me. Just like her. I suppose you'd better go and see him.'

'Me? Why me? I don't know him.'

'We can't ignore his letter. He'll think we're frightened to see him - and he'll turn up here, you'll see, in any case, if we don't stop him.'

'Why should we be frightened to see him?'

'Oh, it's a long story. You'll probably find it interesting - he paints horses.'

'Yer, I've just read it,' Robby grumbled.

Robby walked to the number three tram terminus and boarded an ancient tram. It was Saturday afternoon and he could hear the roar of the 50,000 crowd from Goodison Park. Angus had refused to lend him the money to go to the match. He could have been enjoying himself in Goodison instead of jiggering along in this old tramcar to find an old man's address in Dingle and see what he was up to.

It was a terraced house of worn bricks in a straight road of old property.

As the door opened, Robby got the whiff of oil paints, and when he entered he felt the stale, unaired atmosphere of the small room. The sash window had green curtains with tassels around the edge, and stole much of the light. Round the walls were pictures of horses, all lacking artistic merit, with landscape backgrounds that were childish attempts at composition. The horses' muscles could have been painted by an intoxicated William Blake. Robby knew instinctively that none of the paintings was worth a second look and he doubted that his grandfather had ever sold any.

The old fellow was pathetically thin and far removed from the buck who had de-flowered all those young women of forty years ago. He was now on his best behaviour, making two cups of tea and offering an oaten biscuit from a rusty tin.

'There you are, lad. Drink that tea and eat your biscuit. I can tell you're Emma's lad. She were the best of the bunch, our Emma. I expect she's told you of her old father, eh?'

'Not much,' Robby murmured, sipping the insipid tea and nibbling the stale biscuit. Under the window he noticed a dark stain of damp on the green-striped wallpaper; the gas fire hissed and he smelt the gas in the warm, unventilated atmosphere. The meter had three pennies on top of it, which the old man fed into the meter to keep it going.

The old man was poking around in a drawer for something. Robby saw his, lined face, wrinkled neck, and puffy eyes with bags beneath, untidy moustache no longer waxed. This was a shabby, shambling, dissipated old man, having about him the stale, odorous decrepitude of a neglected body.

The grandfather brought out a sepia photograph of a smart young man in light derby hat. Behind the figure was a highly polished carriage with two shining horses. The subjects in the picture showed a degree of perfection.

'That's me when I was young. They were good times, lad. Horses have been my life. But it's hard these days in weather like this, cold and frosty, shivering on the high seat on the dray, depending a lot on the young fellow with me to put the barrels down the chute into the cellars.'

Robby did not know what to say to this tale of woe.

'Do you get well paid?' he asked after a while, not knowing what else to say.

'No, we don't get well paid at all. We get a free pint of beer for our dinner but the wages won't buy me enough food with the prices that keep going up.'

'Ma says the price of food isn't going up. Sugar and bread and tea are the same since the war ended.'

'No, no. They're going up. Perhaps your ma gets things cheaper being in the food trade.'

'I don't think she does. The shop stuff we get wholesale but everything else like groceries, we pay for like everyone else.'

'Oh well, we'll say nor more,' the old man said, irritated. 'I've been looking at you. You're a big lad. How old are you?'

'Eleven.'

'Hmm. I suppose you get well fed with your ma having a shop?'

'Yer. Ma's cooking is very good and she gives us sensible food.'

'Aye, I bet she does. How many of you are there?'

'Six of us. Father died in 1921 from food poisoning at the works' canteen.'

'Oh dear. That was a tragedy. How old was he?'

'Fifty-seven.'

'Eh, that was a tragedy, dying so young. I'm seventy-six, young man - you wouldn't think so, would you?'

'No,' Robby murmured faintly, thinking you look a hundred. 'She was a lass of spirit, was Emma. Aye. Not like the other. How is her business going now? I bet it's a busy concern, eh, seeing she's a good cook?'

'So so,' said Robby. 'There's a lot of work to it.'

'Aye, I bet there is. I'd like to come and see your mother. One evening next week, young man, you must come down to the stables near the brewery, and watch me tend my old Clydesdale.'

Finding out where the stables were, Robby was allowed by Emma to visit them. The place was immaculate with red stone block floor, each block chamfered like the base of a pyramid, with no expense spared. Bright, whitewashed walls with clean straw in stalls, occupied by gleaming horses. Horse trappings and harnesses hung on the walls, glistening leather and brasses. George Foulkes combed the last of the big horses and whispered gently as he worked.

'Ah, hello, young man. So your dear mother let you come then? This here is Toby, my favourite. He has a grand way with him.'

The old man continued his work, humming and whistling windily, smoothingly between monologues. Robby vaguely recalled his ma's tale of how a horse had kicked her father, and she skipping towards the men carrying her father on a gate, and she singing 'My father's dead, my father's dead. I'll get a new black frock!' Then, coming level with her father, she saw him move, and she began to cry. 'Oh, he isn't dead!' And the men looking shocked and whispering to each other. It had been a talking point in The Farmers' Arms that night. Robby wondered what could have happened to cause such an attack from a horse, the old man seemed so fond of his charges.

'Has a horse ever kicked you?' he asked.

'No, never,' George lied, and Robby did not press the matter. Once home, he gave his ma a report on the conversation. Emma laughed grimly.

'He's an old liar. He'd tell you anything to save his face. He could be cruel with them at times. He must have learnt something in his old age - or he was taking special care on account of it being a Clydesdale.'

That was all Emma said. There was no invitation for Christmas. You didn't invite the Devil to a Christmas feast, Emma said. Her father's devious quizzing of his grandson reaped nothing for him. Away in his tiny room in Dingle, eating chicken sandwiches provided by the landlady as a special Christmas treat, he cursed Emma and his other children. Not one of them had offered to take him in! It was cruel and inhuman. She was always the hard bitch, was Emma, never doing what she was told, damned well running away all the time, telling people family secrets, trying to blacken his name in the village. Aye, and this was the season of goodwill!

In January 1929 Flora called with her child in his pram. Emma showed her a note from the Dingle landlady saying the old man was ill. The brewery had paid him off with two weeks' wages, and dispensed with his services.

'He's trying to force my hand - playing on the family's sympathy because they don't know him. Well, he'll get no sympathy from me.'

Flora showed her anxiety.

'You can't leave him there to die, surely?' She had become a devout Catholic. 'If you get him here I'll come to help you with him.'

'Yes I can see that's a good Christian way of dealing with him - but you never suffered his cruelties when you were young.'

'I know it's hard to forget, ma, but you just can't leave him there, ill and all alone.'

'All right, against my better judgement - I'll send the lads for him. But once he gets better, he's not staying. He's not going to sponge on me the rest of his life. Angus will see his landlady and pay her a month's rent out of the old devil's fortnight's pay, and then he'll have to go on the parish like everyone else who've wasted their money on drink and women. You notice, none of the others have offered to do anything - damned selfish folk! Our Annie started all this - telling him our address.'

Against all expected sequence of events, the elder boys brought the old man home. The situation was reversed, Emma was boss and the old man pathetically subservient, the children thought, now that he was at the mercy of his former victim. Emma knew what he was up to, being subservient. He would go careful for a while and then you'd see, he would grasp the security of Emma's home, a wicked old convolvulus strangling her family. She was determined that he would go back to Dingle. Angus had wheedled out of him a pound note to pay the landlady, assuring Emma that her father's abode would remain vacant.

With the dithering fury of a decrepit creature, once recovered, George Foulkes was taken back by the two elder boys. They felt no regret, knowing all about him.

Back in Dingle, George Foulkes continued to paint and live out his life in meagre days, cursing Emma when he had to apply for Parish Relief. He watched the world go by bitterly until the day he died, penniless, skeletal in appearance, leaving nothing behind of his household goods but a collection of paintings of horses, half a dozen squeezed tubes of colour, and some turps. Robby used them up while they were soft and pliable.

It was almost a pauper's funeral and remarkable only in that it was attended by the dead man's most difficult child and her two eldest offspring Flora and Angus. They passed by the corpse, giving a cursory glance. His face was shrivelled like a grey potato, the body stiff and straight, its dead bones protruding. The evil in the man that it had been, emanated from it even in death, the poisons of a dried up root oozing from the corpse into the memory of Emma.

'Put the lid on,' she told the undertaker, annoyed that she had been burdened with the expenses. On the tramcar after the service she smiled at the irony of it all - victor in life and now in death she had been. None of her sisters or her brother had come, and she had written to them all!

*   *   *

CHAPTER THREE

Having an aptitude for survival, Emma married Alec Stone, about fifty, an ex- Merchant Navy man who had started his sea life on the last of the windjammers and ended it on merchant ships. A good-humoured, rough-hewn character, with Hindenburg moustache and a free and easy air about him that indicated he should never have bound himself in fetters of domesticity. Taking over from Flora, he became a willing helper in the shop and often undertook to do housework too. He did everything hugely, like most seamen, and his method of cleaning the back kitchen and scullery was to throw down buckets of water and scrub it around with a stiff yard brush, then mop it all up as had been his practice when swabbing decks. He liked his drink and ciggies and Emma had much to say when he helped himself from the shop till to pay for these pleasures.

Alec's elder brother, Joe, a coal merchant, glad that his brother would be settling down at last, had encouraged him by offering him a job delivering coal. Disappointment hit Emma hard when Joe changed his mind after the wedding, nullifying the wisdom of her marrying again.

The younger ones liked Alec from the first. They laughed at his stained moustache, his thin whisps of hair, all red and strong, and his mighty physique, marred by a paunch acquired in pubs. Douglas found a good character to mimic, and would call out 'Come on, young fella me lad let's get the ould deck swabbed down.'

Angus and Malcolm disliked Alec from the first. Without a word one day, Angus, aged twenty-one, left home, calling in at Jack Volant's office near the sidings in Marsh Street to confide his troubles.

'I'm leaving home. Can't stand it, Jack. He just walks in and takes over - no job, nothing. Merchant seaman - irresponsible, easy come, easy go. Why did ma marry again? And to a fella like that? It makes you sick. I'm going to

Auntie Maggie's in Leyland. Should be able to get a job there easy.'

Jack Volant's sallow countenance looked worried. He rubbed his nose.

'What about that printing job? You've given up a damned good trade there, Angus. Have you told them you're leaving?

'Bugger it. I'll tell 'em to send on my cards when I get there. But don't tell anyone where I've gone, Jack.

Jack assured Angus that his secret was safe with him.

The gods, looking down, muttered 'Just like his grandfather, buggering off like that because things aren't suiting him. And watch out for squalls with Jack Volant, too'

Later, when faced by Emma for running away without telling anyone where he was going, Angus said, 'I told Jack Volant! Emma had words with poor Jack, despite his insistence that he had sworn to keep Angus's secret. A solemn promise like that was wicked. It did not cross her mind that Angus's motive was to create the maximum impact in absconding, then plead innocence in the event of a serious breakdown of relationships with his ma: he was her favourite.

After Angus had gone, Jock, the dog from Maghull, became Alec's best friend, his instinct telling him that the devil-may-care mariner was kind and generous. When the supper bar was crowded, and only Emma to manage, she called the dog

'Jock, go and fetch Alec,' - and the huge hound would startle those customers who did not know the routine, by leaping over the half-sized door in the side counter and make for the pub on the corner to scratch the door and be let in by the men to sniff round their legs.

The pub on the corner was still standing, with neighbour Jones's house, when many dwellings had been razed in the blitz. It had yellow, imitation oak on the outdoor, the Bar, and the Saloon where the fat women moneylenders went, with sagging purses and bosoms, because of class distinction. Jock always ignored the Outdoor and the Saloon, knowing Alec as he did. If his master was not there, Jock would be let out and trot off to the next pub on his canine list.

'Ah, ah Here's old Jock,' Alec always said when he had been scented out; 'Here, Jock lad? Drink this up!'

The dog enjoyed lapping up the dregs of Alec's beer but the barman usually frowned, grabbed the empty glass and plunged it into hot water at once. The Bar customers were amused and none of them ever complained about the dog.

They would leave, Alec waddling off at a quick, habitual gait from his life on rolling decks, the dog to heel, proud and happy, licking the drops of beer that clung to his whiskery snout. Glass-eyed and chummy, Alec put on his apron in quick time once he reached home and began serving in the shop, Emma whispering-

'You've had too much again, y' damned devil!' and Alec, winking at the nearest female customer answering

'Y' can never have too much, luv.' Then the discussion would follow on the wickedness of drink, with Emma and her female allies who had suffered from years of besotted husbands, versus Alec, and occasionally a male ally.

Unlike regular gangs of stevedores, Alec had no tally and little chance of being taken on unless the port was particularly busy. He did work occasionally on the docks, but his wages were not a pot of gold at the rainbow's heel; yet they helped, now and then, towards the upkeep of the family, and paid outstanding debts on occasions. At times the wages were a boon to Emma when she least expected.

Malcolm left after Angus had been absent a month, to become a steward on a passenger steamer to New York. Just twenty and dressed in his issue trousers and smart jacket, he was an attractive figure, a necessary requirement when serving wealthy, fussy passengers who thought their high fares had bought them perfection.

Both elder boys affected resentment at ma's second marriage, pretending she was disloyal to the memory of their father, giving no thoughts to her needs.

She had no adult partner with whom she could share financial responsibilities. Cruelly for the little woman, the man she had married was of little use since his brother Joe had turned him down.

There were quarrels and Emma became more and more desperate because of all the work she had to do. She thought she had found a solution when she wrote to her sister Nellie, a widow since 1928. The children soon came into collision with Aunt Nellie's cooking. To Margaret's delicate stomach Nellie's fare, entirely opposite to Emma's fine foods, was indigestible, and she found the abundance of fat, turning to grease when you were a slow eater, made her refuse most cooked meals. Although Robby and Douglas also had cause to complain, they had appetites like billy goats and consumed everything, especially Nellie's hotpots, stews and rice pies.

Nellie suffered pangs of terrible heartburn, dyspepsia and wind, which she was unable to release, fortunately for everyone around. She often longed to give a healthy belch, but it never came. On a red-letter day she did enjoy the relief of some delicate farts, but such days were rare.

Her reign lasted a few short months as she and Alec were poles adrift, and they gradually evolved a passion of hate for each other. Alec had done his best with her at first to combat Nellie's hate in his usual breezy, guileless manner. Nellie departed to take up residence with one of her nieces.

During her stay, Robby took Nellie to see The Jazz Singer. Al Jolson's twang, before stars were sent for elocution lessons, was beyond Nellie's ken. Her double chinned, grim lipped profile reflected the light from the screen and showed utter incomprehension. Her - 'What's he say?' to Robby was continuous throughout the show. He did not enjoy that particular film and thought that 'talkies.' would never amount to much with This Wonderful New Dimension in Cinema History! The Jazz Singer suffered the birth pangs for all its descendants and the technician gynaecologists responsible for the premature birth, would improve the equipment in later years. Aunt Nellie did not go to the pictures much after Al Jolson had bewildered the mind out of her.

* * *

Benny Solomons was forbidden to go to matinees on Saturday Sabbaths. Robby and Douglas went to the Sun Hall for a ten-thirty start, paying two pence to get in. Robby used his remaining penny to buy monkey nuts and Douglas bought liquorice-sticks. Tom Mix and his horse Tony were favourites. The climax of each episode found Tom tied up in a burning shed, or hanging from a cliff with his gloves gradually slipping from his hands. He always remembered to whistle for Tony and the picture cut to the horse grazing in a lush island of green in a rock-strewn landscape. Tony always pricked his ears and stopped chewing. You could see the horse thinking before he set off like Pegasus then the screen blacked out to show big white letters --- CONTINUED IN THIS THEATRE NEXT WEEK. Will Tom escape from the burning shed? DON'T MISS NEXT WEEK'S THRILLING EPISODE! The boys had to go the following week to see how Tom was rescued or whether Tony could stop those gloves slipping somehow. The villains always had distinctive differences from the goodies. There would be a close-up of a Red Indian's hand, middle finger missing, holding a spear. Perhaps the villain had only one ear or wore a patch over one eye. The goodies were always doomed until next week.

Tom Mix's Stetson was sent over from America to go the rounds of British Cinemas. The kids came down after the show to the orchestra pit where the manager stood guard over the precious hat placed on a special table, and the kids were allowed to touch it before going home. In that transitory Temple of the Holy Stetson, the kids worshipped for a day.

Free passes paid for Emma's advertising of cinemas. Narrow posters from various cinemas advertised current programmes which changed every three days, and they were hung in different places on the walls where the customers could read them whilst waiting for their orders to be made up. Emma used the passes of the best cinemas, going on her night off with her lady friend. When she transferred her patronage to live theatre, the kids used the passes that their ma had relinquished.

Before his departure abroad, Malcolm accompanied Robby to the Gainsborough in Litherland, a clean, cosy place smelling of the scented disinfectant they used. The dark blue ceiling had stars picked out in tiny light bulbs. The girl who snicked the tickets always shouted down to the usher,

'Passes Lizzie!' Malcolm whistled windily, 'like his grandfathers,' and Robby's cheeks glowed with shame as the two boys followed the usher with the torch. Robby heard imaginary murmurings - 'Look at those two scrounging buggers getting in for nothing,' and he was glad to sit down in the darkness and to feel the blushes cool from his cheeks and regain pallid composure. Malcolm leaned over and whispered, 'That bloody girl with her loud mouth!

Half the gods looking down thought the boys' shyness was an inheritance from their reserved father; the other half argued that the characteristic was the vanity of grandiose feelings handed down from the old bugger Foulkes. 'Emma has no qualms about using complimentary tickets,' one of the first gods pointed out. 'She believes she is entitled to them because she has used her wall space on contract. What do you say to that?' The opposition answered, 'You can't count Emma. She beat the old sod and even had him buried.' And so the argument went on up in the gods as the two boys watched Ramon Novarro fencing it out with the villain.

When Alec used passes, taking one of the young ones, the gods looked elsewhere, knowing him well. Alec didn't give a single damn because status or shame or fine sensibilities were all strangers to Alec. If he had met Queen Mary he would have offered her a ciggie and a pint of bitter. At evening cinema on occasions, an old woman who could not read or couldn't afford glasses, pushed in next to Robby and whispered, 'Read to me, son.' Robby often sighed wearily and wondered why he always had the bad luck. All those people and these old women kept picking <u>him</u> to read!

Robby read out the captions and discovered that many of the old dears reacted to his every word as if everything that was happening was Gospel truth. He told one old woman it was only a story.

'Yis, A know, luv, but A can't help meself,' she replied.

At the matinees famous comedians made the lads double with laughter, and dangerous villains made them anxiously nibble fingernails, and for two hours they forgot the world outside. In that fancy world of darkness and comfort, no harm could come to you ~ except the catching of a flea, perhaps, from the old dear leaning over to hear your commentary. It was common those days to read captions if you were an unlucky youngster and much better educated than the Mary Ellens.

Robby often wondered why everyone in old newsreels rushed about in jerks. Lloyd George faced the camera, jerking arms and jerking one foot to the other, then, in a flash of self-conscious importance, he jerked into a carriage and the horses raced off at 70 miles per hour and 300 trots a minute into a far distance that took three seconds to get there. Silly wheels kept turning backwards as vehicles went forward, or slithered like reluctant dogs on leashes. Yes, everyone had slowed down a lot lately, as old newsreels showed, and had lost that vigour which had won the war to end war for the soldiers who jerked along French roads at one kilometre in less than two minutes, pursuing the terrible Huns who wore those treacherous spiked helmets.

*   *   *

Emma's careful saving bought her a new electric potato washer. The male species were unreliable and if she were to be let down again, she would be able to do the potatoes herself. The machine was identical to the old one except that it had been fitted to take a driving belt from an electric motor fastened to the wall. The boys were delighted. Switch on the power at the required speed and the spuds were washed in half the time. The only effort came in winter when the eyes needed to be picked out.

Emma's friend, Jane Murphy, had also made money by

working hard. She had a very prosperous hardware store in Croxteth. Her husband, Michael, was a good landscape artist and could put R.A. after his name, having exhibited his work several times some years before. Jane also had a credit drapery department where everything from aprons to men's suits were sold on weekly payments. Jane employed two girls in each department.

Robby visited Michael Murphy upstairs whilst Jane and his ma chatted over tea and cakes. The studio had a skylight and all round the walls were finished works waiting to be varnished. Emma promised vaguely one time that Robby might take lessons from Michael who was willing to charge half-price fees. His attention had been aroused by some of Robby's drawings from school. He was an eccentric but to Robby he was always interesting and kind. From a huge meerschaum pipe he puffed smoke to the skylight.

'Whole lot of claptrap talked about art,' Michael said once. 'All those bloody silly isms - cubism, dadaism, futurism, etcetera - bloody nonsense! Tongue in cheek tripe. Art dealers love isms. Give a mystical name to some'at and it'll sell for outrageous prices. And things don't get any better. An old master portrait went the other day for 5,000! Could you believe it? Gulling the public, that's what they're doing. You paint your own way, lad. Ignore all so called experts.'

'What about impressionism, then?'

'Ah, bright lad! Now Impressionism is the only ism I like. It's the free way of painting with no meticulous detail. It's the way I try to paint - fresh, lively, loose, as the artist sees it on first impression. Yes, Impressionism, O.K. For the rest, chuck 'em out of the window. Robby, I think you'll make a good artist one day. Keep at it but don't be put off by anybody. Mind you, it isn't a sound profession to be in. If you can't make yourself known, you'll never make a living from art. But you keep painting, lad. Keep painting.'

Such words of encouragement from a successful artist filled Robby's mind with the determination to exploit what talents he was supposed to have; yet on more realistic occasions he wondered whether Michael Murphy's predictions would ever come true. In these down-to-earth moments he resigned himself to the influence of his environment and told himself he was an amateur and would remain so. How could he succeed? Art equipment cost money and the family could not afford money on daydream luxuries. He did not know that Doctor Johnson had already expressed the essence of his circumstances three hundred years ago - <u>Slow rises worth by Poverty-depressed.</u>

Emma's attitude to life was basic - shelter, a bed to sleep in, food to eat, clothes to wear, and enough income to maintain these essentials in years to come. With Emma, such basics were difficult enough to ensure and left her no leeway to think of Getting On, Becoming Famous, Being Healthy, rising in Social Status, and Achieving Marvellous Things. With the tools and means at her disposal she had fashioned, almost miraculously, a worthy environment for her brood, despite all her setbacks, her hard, young life, her bitter years under her father's tyranny; yet the rising generation was dissatisfied and longed for a better life. Emma could do no more than to work hard, hope for something better, and try to mollify the rising discontent of her children; that was the lesson of her life and the unforgettable inheritance of a hated father who had given his children, wretches that they were, no firm foundation on which to build their lives. With Emma, necessity had never whispered, it had always demanded in strident tones. Her answer to her family's discontent was to pack all their belongings and move.

* * *

The children said goodbye to their friends, Robby promising to keep in touch with Benny and Alf. Timothy Doyle at the dairy had missed Angus's friendship; but the poor fellow, three months before Emma and her brood departed, contracted galloping consumption and died too young!

Sleepers Hill supper bar was within a mile of the two

main football grounds, Anfield and Goodison. It was a steepish main road with tram tracks. The children were pleased with the move to this more congenial district and the two youngest often went into the nearby park to play and climb trees without being caught by the parkie. Margaret showed something of the tomboy in her make-up. The park was a large oasis in the desert of bricks and concrete.

Searching for help, Emma found May Jones who lived near, and asked her to look after the home and the kids, and help in the shop in the evenings. Emma had known Fay as a customer in the old days in Kensington. Fay was house-proud and soon had the house in order, and Emma acknowledged that the living quarters had never been so clean. Everything that could gleam was made to dazzle.

Fay had a remarkable resemblance to a currently famous film star, Janet Gaynor. Her face was round and brown eyed, and her hair well kept and styled like the film star's. Both Fay and her mother were very keen filmgoers. Her father, a pavier, had won compensation for damage to his knee. His wife and daughter were delighted to spend the money, kept secret from the married sons and daughters. They attended matinees, went home for teas of luxuries of boiled ham, roast pork or chicken, attending the first house of one cinema, then rushing off to attend the second house of the third cinema that day. Hearing the story from Fay herself, Emma was dumbfounded. Their enthusiasm for the churned out pap of Hollywood lasted until the money had gone, and the only person to derive no benefit was the victim, the wretched Mr Jones who had stayed at home with his leg up, reading the <u>Liverpool Express</u> or staring into space, and swearing that one day he would damage the other knee, keep the compensation, and get stinking drunk every night.

Alec liked the Sleepers Hill district. There were two or three pubs that sold his favourite brews; but the faithful hound thought it all a bit of a damned nuisance having to learn and memorise a whole new routine of smells and places.

* * *

Angus arrived from Leyland unannounced, on holiday from the rubber works. He introduced two attractive girls, Gwendoline and her elder sister Harriet. The younger children recalled Aunt Jean and felt a similar sense of inferiority.

Margaret was delighted when Angus said they planned to go across the river to New Brighton and would take her with them. Emma prepared some butties of cheese and jam and they set off on the tram to the pier Head.

The girls were excited by the river and all its great liners, cargo vessels, cranes and contraptions. They boarded the New Brighton ferry and sailed through the wind across the choppy Mersey River.

About midday they decided to have lunch and Angus and Margaret sat on the sands and opened their parcel of butties. Gwendoline smiled at this quaint procedure and went off with her sister to a restaurant. When Margaret later described what had happened, Robby understood Angus's predicament - he could not afford to pay for the girls in a restaurant and, in any case, it was highly unlikely that Angus fancied dining out with two posh ladies who were comparative strangers. Both he and Angus were gauche in such niceties.

Two benign gods were watching the scene.

'When they enter the water to bathe,' said one, 'we'll make that posh girl, Gwendoline, lose her false teeth in the water. That will break the ice for Angus.' The second god pursed his lips. 'But we must let Angus find them,' he said. 'We don't want the poor girl going home without her teeth.'

After lunch Angus and party donned bathing costumes behind a screen, separately, and entered the water, the river in those days being free from pollution. With loud open-mouthed laughter, Gwendoline's top denture flew out and plunged into the sea. There was immediate panic, Gwendoline screeching and Harriet trying to quieten her. Angus searched frantically around Gwendoline's feet and with prayers of thanks, recovered his adored angel's teeth.

'Oh! It's a miracle,' Gwendoline cried. 'How on earth did you manage to spot them? You must have marvellous eyesight!'

It was pure luck. Without his glasses Angus could not have spotted an elephant on the doorstep. Tentative relations were eased from then on.

Some few weeks later, a despondent Angus returned home. Douglas moved into Robby's bed to make sleeping space for his elder brother. Lying awake that night, Robby overheard Angus sobbing and murmuring 'Gwen! Oh Gwen, why? Why?'

So, Robby surmised, Sleepers Hill, Angus's rough family, their living conditions and bluff old Alec had put Gwendoline off! The usual clever dick, blasé Angus was hard smitten, Robby thought. He would now rave and blame ma. Well, it was his own silly fault, not ma's. He should have warned ma about coming on a visit with these posh girls. What the hell did he expect? And why run after someone middle class who he could never hope to marry? It was typical of Angus with his inflated ego! (Robby had been reading about Freud in the library one day).

*　*　*

The Seamen's Hostelry in Brooklyn was a basic place for men ashore, Malcolm Ferguson and Peter Jackson being two of them. With arms outstretched they lay on their bunks, their heads resting on their hands. Peter had just described what he had seen in a dream the night before.

These two stewards from the S.S.Vestris were similar in appearance. Malcolm had always dressed as smartly as the value of his clothes would allow. At Jackson's store in Liverpool he had learnt a lot about dressing to advantage, but before he had reached the age of nineteen he had been dismissed. Mr Brookes, the manager, had warned him about arriving late to work. On the next late arrival Malcolm concocted a tale about his ma's stove bursting into flames, and how the fire brigade had made such a mess, keeping them up all night. Mr Brookes was very sympathetic. A month or so later, Emma took Douglas for a pair of shoes and Mr Brookes received her courteously.

'Sorry to hear of your terrible fire, Mrs Ferguson,' (he had not heard about Emma's remarrying). 'The firemen always do make such a mess.'

'What fire?' Emma frowned.

'Your shop fire,' Mrs Ferguson.

'We've had no fire,' Mr Brookes.

'Oh? Malcolm told me all about it - he said it was the reason for his being late again. I'd been on at him for coming late.'

'Eh! The damned devil! We've had no fire. Eh, what next? I'm very sorry he lied to you, Mr Brookes. The devil.'

'Well, I'm very disappointed. I'm sorry to say, Mrs Ferguson, that I must dismiss him. I detest dishonesty. He described the fire so well that I had no doubts about the truth of it. He's out at the Post Office at the moment; otherwise you could have had words with him. I appreciate your honesty, dear lady. He obviously doesn't take after his mother.'

'No, he doesn't. He takes after his grandfather. Well, I must say, it's very upsetting for me - and for him, the silly young fool! Sometimes he believes his lies, just like my father.'

Peter Jackson never romanced in this way. He was reliable and could never make up such detailed stories. Peter was a counterbalance to their friendship and while Malcolm was with Peter, his fabulosity was kept in check. Malcolm, too, had complete faith in Peter's psychic powers, inherited from his mother, a well-known spiritualist medium.

'So we should stay ashore, Peter?'

'Certainly. I'm not going back on the Vestris. I have some relatives in Trenton, New Jersey. We'll go there and get a job - doing what we know, waiting.'

Peter's relatives in Trenton were sceptical about his prediction and believed it to be a youthful excuse for skipping ship. But at the end of the week the news was all over the world - the S.S.Vestris, one day out from New York, caught fire and sank with many lives lost. The public enquiry took months to discover the truth about the disaster, survivors having been rescued and brought into New York. That was the reason why Malcolm was absent from England for such a long time. The family waited anxiously for news and telephoned the shipping office. After a few more days.' anxiety, the news came through to reassure the Fergusons that Malcolm Ferguson, Steward, had not signed on again after reaching New York.

Fay Jones discussed Malcolm with Robby on many occasions, saying how she loved him because he was 'real good-looking' and she'd always liked him when they were kids at Kensington. Robby, as the elder of the three younger ones, received confidences he would normally have been forbidden and he knew, even before his elder brother came home, that Fay would marry Malcolm one day.

Robby never forgot one day when his ma had gone to see her friend, Mrs Murphy, Margaret and Douglas had gone out and he and Fay were alone in the house between opening times. He was getting on for thirteen years of age and was tall and strong. As it was a warm July day, with school holidays just started, he had decided to change his clothes. He took off his shirt and vest and his knee-length trousers and was about to put on a pair of shorts when the bedroom door opened and there was Fay.

'Oh! She giggled. I'm just in time to tickle you!'

Robby was utterly confused as she came towards him. He felt the tingling of his body and then her arms had encircled him and pushed him onto the bed. 'Ooh,' Fay breathed, 'you're so like your brother!' Then madly and passionately she kissed him on the lips, the face, and the chest and then began to stroke him with soft hands. The feeling of pleasure surprised him, and he suddenly put his arms around her and held her tight, his instinctive reactions making themselves felt by the girl. Suddenly, Fay realised what she was doing. This was an illegal seduction of a young boy, despite that swollen weapon of his. She laughed and jumped up, pretending it had been a mere romp. 'Have you a handkerchief?' she asked. He took one out of his trouser pocket on the bed. She lay down beside him, kissed him again tenderly, and then began to stroke his penis until the orgasm came, with him maturely gathering what came. Quickly Fay called, 'Don't tell ANYbody,' as she rushed from the room and down the stairs.

* * *

With unemployment very high in England, the two elder brothers joined forces and decided that a credit drapery business would provide them with a livelihood. Emma doubted it and wrote immediately to Jane Murphy who had sold her hardware store and was concentrating on credit drapery. The Murphys were well off, Angus reasoned, and if Mrs Murphy could make easy money from credit drapery, they could as well, especially as they had more brains than Jane Murphy. He had overlooked a vital truth - Jane had been in business for twenty-five years and had a hefty bank balance from her two businesses. Emma waited for Jane's reply with quiet confidence knowing that Jane would counsel No! Jane's advice was very sound and Emma used her letter to put a stop to 'all this nonsense' she thought.

Dear Emma, I do not want to put a damper on your sons' scheme, but I feel I must strongly advise against it. Unemployment is high and the depression will continue. I am established, of course, after many years' work and have plenty of regular customers who have dealt with me for years. Croxteth is a very respectable area and safe for credit. am not confident about Walton or Everton. Perhaps the boys should wait for improving conditions before taking on such a precarious business.

'What does she know about Walton and Everton?' Angus scorned. 'She just doesn't want opposition.'

'Don't talk ridiculous,' Emma snapped at him. 'Jane's been established for years - before you were born. In any case, you wouldn't be in opposition - it's an entirely different area.'

'I think we should make a stab at it,' Angus said, like a wise businessman, irritating his ma, 'what d'y' say, Mal?'

'Yer,' Malcolm agreed. 'I'll try anything once!'

Emma sighed her anxieties for the next two or three days and then deciding that she could not stand in her sons' way, she began to scrape together as much money as she could, even using the younger children's National Savings which they had taken to school regularly every Monday morning.

After two or three weeks in the venture, Angus grumbled that it was no use trying to build up a business from a base like a supper bar. Why didn't ma get out? She had worked long enough. Let the family look after her now. She deserved a rest after years of hard work. Robby would be leaving school soon, and if Alec tried harder, he could get a job on the docks. Why didn't she sell the business and buy a new house on mortgage?

How reasonable and sensible and attractive it sounded. How much, indeed, would ma have liked a house of her own, and leisure to follow other ambitions! The image outshone the reality. With some anxious doubts, ma conceded defeat.

Two days after the advertisement in the *Liverpool Echo* the agent brought a prospective buyer, small, wizened George Witherup. He toured the premises, his seedy eyes missing nothing. Ma had set the goodwill at £150. Her shop was not a goldmine but she knew it was a good business.

'Um. An 'undredanfifty's an 'ell ovalot,' Witherup whined. 'Coalfired burners yon, antiquated washer. Ah doesn' theenk it's wuth it.'

'Antiquated?' Emma frowned. 'That machine, I'd have you know, is almost new.'

Giles Brown, the agent, an old drinking partner of Andrew Douglas in days gone by, had dealt with the transfer from Kirkdale. He took Emma aside.

'Look, Emma. I'm sure he'll buy if you drop a bit - say one forty?'

'No,' said Emma. 'I've built up this business and they

trust me around here. Besides, this shop's in an excellent spot. Football crowds Saturdays and Wednesdays very often, there's a good passing trade on a busy tram route. I can't take less than one fifty. We've taken a new house and need every penny!'

Witherup was unimpressed by the agent's repetition of the advantages.

'Ah'll tell thee what al do - let me have t'shop for a trial period o' two months an Ah'll gi' thee 'alf ot price now an t'other 'alf when Ah'm assoored takin's is what thee say they is.'

'Heavens, man! You've seen the books and the bills,' Emma retorted, hotly. What more do you want?'

Having taken the dire steps for her sons' sake, Emma was now keen to sell as soon as possible. She saw Witherupts lip curl.

'Books con be cucked as wheel as taties an' pies,' he sneered.

Emma was enraged and let her feelings be known.

'Mrs Stone is as straight as a die,' Giles Brown broke in. 'There's no call for insults. This is a good shop, Mr Witherup, and the area is a large residential area.'

'Wheel, Ah'm sorry then,' Witherup growled. 'If y' books is genuine, there's nowt t' worrit thee, is there?'

'I need all the money,' Emma said.

'Tha's'll 'ev eet I' full i' two munths.'

With awful foreboding and a little persuasion from Giles Brown, Emma again conceded and a week later the solicitor drew up an agreement for the two parties to sign. Clauses in the agreement stipulated that Emma would be obliged to leave an experienced person with Witherup for one week to introduce him to the customers. After that, the Witherup's would be on their own. If takings averaged a minimum of twelve pounds a week, at the end of two months Witherup would pay Emma the balance. If the business fell below this figure for three weeks or more, the money already paid would be refunded to Witherup.

A week later the removal van took all their belongings away, leaving a very reluctant Fay Jones to stay with

Witherup for a week to show him and his wife the ropes of running a supper bar.

To the children it was an unforgettable event in their lives. The new house, only recently built near Aintree in a good, clean district had three smart bedrooms, sitting-room and dining-room, washhouse, larder and cloakroom, large kitchen, and, most exciting of all, a large, pink-tiled bathroom. No more tin baths in the scullery, with water boiling in the brick built corner wash-boiler, with females coming in to catch the boys in their nudity!

It was Wednesday afternoon, four days after they had settled in. On holiday from school, Robby was looking out of his bedroom window, contentedly surveying the scene of a wide, new-laid passage between the houses, far different from the narrow jowlers he was used to.

There was the distant view of fields and trees and a farmhouse or two. The racecourse stretched away beyond his view. The sky was blue and pleasant and he felt a singing in his heart. At last they were living in a paradise, away from all the squalor and hard work. He turned his head in the other direction, idly, absently, and there, some fifty yards down the backs, a window had opened and a girl's head and shoulders appeared. She seemed to be a blonde beauty at that distance. She waved in a friendly manner. He looked up and down the passage. There was no one else in sight. He waved back and smiled. After looking and smiling again, he withdrew his head and closed the window. Almost the same procedure took place the following Saturday afternoon. Everton were playing away and he was at a loose end. This time the girl ended her miming by making a pedalling motion with her hands and pointing down. Ah, a bike ride, he guessed at once. He waved and nodded agreement and closed the window.

'I'm going for a ride,' he told his ma downstairs. She was busy on her old treadle sewing machine, finishing off some curtains. Robby waited at the back entrance with his cycle, a second-hand one he had saved up to buy. The girl came quickly, pushing a good, old-fashioned upright machine with green threaded silk over the rear wheel in the fashion of ladies' cycles at that time.

'Hello,' he greeted her. 'Shall we ride towards the racecourse?'

'Yes,' she agreed. 'I'm Maria. What's your name?'

'Robby Ferguson.'

As they rode off, side-by-side, she was all smiles each time she looked at him. She was a lovely young girl, about sixteen, he guessed. He would soon be fourteen but he was tall and she possibly took him for much older than he was.

'Why did you wave?' he grinned. 'Do you know me? I'm sorry, I don't know you.'

She was charmingly frank with him. She had immediately liked the look of him when he first rode up to the new house.

'You look awfully nice,' she blushed.

'That's very nice of you,' he said, his nerves throbbing in response.

They rode out into the countryside, an empty world, with the racecourse on their left, and they excitingly all alone. The sky was clear blue and the sun warm and friendly. She gave him a piece of Rowntree's cream chocolate and they munched it lying in the grass looking up at the heavens.

'Have you a girlfriend?'

'No.'

'I haven't a boyfriend either.'

'Haven't you?' he queried, getting up onto his elbow.

'You're nice enough to have dozens of boyfriends.'

She laughed. 'You're very flattering,' she said.

They finished their chocolate and she threw the paper behind her head.

'Why don't you kiss me,' she whispered.

Her complete frankness sent a shock of electricity into his innocent brain.

He put his leg near hers and lowered his face towards her. Immediately her arms enveloped him and their lips met.

'Open your lips,' she breathed, and her tongue searched between his lips and his whole body thrilled; and he remembered Fay Jones. Kissing like this was a new magic to him. Instinctively his hands searched her body and they lay close, kissing madly and hotly. He found the top of her stocking and touched silken flesh, all warm and thrilling. She stroked his back and then her hands descended and pressed his middle tightly towards her. He was in an ecstatic state, something he had never experienced before.

'Come out o' that field,' came a loud, snarling voice. 'You're trespassing.'

Suddenly Robby sensed that a dog was pouncing towards them. They separated quickly and then he saw the man, holding a gun, and the dog beginning to growl had almost reached them.

'Come by,' the farmer snapped at the dog. The two guilty trespassers wheeled their bicycles out of the field, watched by the old man. The dog growled suspiciously and his master said again, 'Come by.'

Before they mounted their machines, Maria said, 'The horrible old spoilsport.'

'Yer,' said Robby. 'Curse our luck!'

They rode out three times during the following few weeks, progressing in their relationship, and then, a complete, miserable mystery to the girl, the Ferguson family vanished, leaving no trace.

Every detail of those ecstatic meetings stayed with Robby for years. In later, adult years, he cursed himself for a fool for not seeking further encounters in his love affair, and speculated on how his life might have been utterly changed by continuing to see Maria. He often cringed at his self-image of those palmy days. What a damned fool he had been!

*　　*　　*

The progress of the boys' credit drapery business, eating away at Emma's money, was turning out to be a farce. The two of them were easily beguiled by cunning folk who were unable to get credit elsewhere, and they leeched onto the boys so that financial difficulties sprang up like weeds.

After paying the agent, the solicitor, outstanding bills from the shop, and the mortgage instalments for the house, Emma had £39 left out of the £75 Witherup had paid her. During the seventh week of the two-month period, she received a curt note:

Dear Madam, I am sorry to inform you that I cannot continue in this business. Turnover has averaged about £8 in the last four weeks. I must ask you, therefore, to keep to the terms of our agreement and return the money paid. I will be ready to hand back the business to you within the week. George Witherup.

Emma guessed that the solicitor had sent the letter 'That illiterate little rat couldn't have written it.' In any case, it was typed. Emma had been a very good scholar at her little school in Furlongton and knew, instinctively, what people were capable of in the literary sense.

'Oh no!' Margaret cried, followed by curses from Douglas and deep, sad sighs from Robby. He would never see Maria again!

When Angus and Malcolm came in from canvassing, they too were furious.

'You should never have signed the damned agreement,' Angus said. Alec happened to be working on the docks that day, otherwise there would have been a row. For all his faults, Alec would never hear a disparaging word against Emma without a warning shot across the bows.

'Don't you start being wise after the fact,' Emma rated her eldest son. 'You two started all this, with your big ideas - to beat Jane Murphy. You wouldn't be told. We should never have left that shop - it was our only steady livelihood. Now where are we? You've left your poor mother with only £39 to pay that little devil back. What on earth can we do?'

Emma always said 'Your poor mother' or 'His poor mother',' like that, as if talking about a third person, and Robby always felt guilty and ashamed when he heard her.

Desolated, Emma journeyed to the solicitor's office with Giles Brown.

'I'm sorry, Emma, that's how it is,' he sympathised.

'The solicitor's checked his books. Witherup hadn't your personality - the people didn't like him.'

'Who could like him?' Emma fumed. 'What in hell's name was he doing with that shop. It was a good shop. Eight pounds a week, indeed! I could strangle the damned devil!'

'I spoke to Fay Jones the other day. He certainly knew nothing about cooking. She told me he was too impatient to do things properly. He even put chips in half heated at one time. She had to take them out and wipe off the grease. He just wouldn't listen to her. He knew things would get worse. He stopped selling pies and all the other things you used to sell. Have you the money to pay him back?'

'No,' Emma moaned. 'That's the trouble. That's why I want to see that solicitor. He should have sold what I sold. How could he expect to do the same trade otherwise?'

Emma sighed miserably. 'I had thought to go into partnership with Jane Murphy - now that's all down the drain.'

The gods smiled sympathetically, knowing that Jane Murphy would never have agreed to such a partnership - a minnow feeding off whale's food.

Emma's ignorance of legal documents had defrauded her of her rights. Witherup had no legal claim on Emma. She had been persuaded to accept the dictates of a stupid agreement and the agent and solicitor were to blame. The shop's capabilities were proven by bills and books, but Giles Brown had wanted a quick sale.

Back they went to Sleepers Hill, misery in their hearts, with the older boys coming each night with precious little to show for their endeavours. The money Emma had left was paid back, followed by a bitter argument over the balance, Emma leaving nothing unsaid to the foxy little man that she thought he deserved to hear. He threatened to sue, but after Emma had told him to do so, he finally agreed to accept the balance over six months at six percent. From that time forward, Robby loathed Witherup. Each week he took £1. lls.10d to the fellow's house in Seaforth, an amount that covered both principal and interest.

*   *   *

Robby read his brilliant school reference with amazement and disbelief - second year in higher grade on leaving; mental attainment well above average; intellectual gifts; powers of steady, persistent effort; personal character scrupulously honest and truthful; a boy in whom most implicit trust could be placed; rank of prefect then House Captain; served with loyalty and affection by all his prefects and the 80 boys for whom he was responsible; most reliable boy ever known by the Headmaster, Captain J. R. Beckett etc.

Emma thought it a wonderful reference and Douglas said he hoped he would get one like it when his time came. But the reference did not shelter Robby from the ignominy of attending the dole school for three months, days of misery for him, and swore that if any job, no matter how paltry, offered itself, he would grasp it with both hands.

It was Angus who saw the small advertisement in the local press, asking for an assistant to deliver batteries. Robby went to the address shown. The shop was one offering a service of recharging wet batteries used in wireless sets, at weekly intervals for a few pence a week, and it was his job to deliver newly charged batteries and collect the flat ones, being paid the pennies at the same time. He had a box tricycle, common in those days with ice-cream vendors. He sat astride the saddle over the rear wheel, the box in front of him, handlebars attached to it. The batteries made a heavy load and took some hard pedalling. He often had the exhausting task of pushing the tricycle up steep roads and was glad that he was strong enough. There was never any relief from the weight, charged or flat, the batteries were the same. Each Saturday night he washed out the box with washing soda because of the acid leaks. For this work, including the inside job of checking chargers and removing batteries with the right specific gravity, he received ten shillings a week!

His employer was a shabby little man, kind and gentle,

with a lined sallow complexion and a small toothbrush moustache. Angus Christened him Al Saint John, light comedy film actor at that time, and Robby never knew him under any other name. Casually glancing at his employer one evening, Robby noticed the jacket he wore, riddled with small holes all round the pockets and bottom edges. Immediately he looked down at his own jacket. Yes, there they were, the holes, more insidious than moth damage, burning away his jacket.

'Shouldn't we were overalls,' he asked. Al St. John laughed.

'I've worn out three overalls already,' he said. 'You can't help it on a job like this. This is an old suit I'm wearing. Never wear a good suit, son, while you're working here.'

Robby was too ashamed to tell him that that was the only suit he had.

His ma's reaction to the acid was instant; 'Right. You'll get out of THAT job and no mistake.'

Luckily, for once, shortly after leaving that job, Robby became an apprentice French polisher.

Prior to the family moving to Aintree, Margaret had begun a term at Blackburn House, a smart school for girls. Their return to Sleepers Hill for her, especially, was like re-entering a Netherworld of doom! Shame haunted her. She lived behind a supper bar; her stepfather was nearly always out of work; every other girl in the college came from a decent, conventional home, their fathers had good jobs, their children always dressed smartly; they were people who lived in houses with front doorways through which they entered and were home immediately. Some of the girls lived in homes with gardens! Why had this life of hers, Margaret asked herself, to be dominated by the turmoil that had been ma's livelihood for years and years?

The gods agreed among themselves that this attitude was natural in a young girl.

'The child cannot think constructively,' said a wise old god. 'The truth is that poor Emma knows no other occupation that can enable her to fight her way through life

102

so cheaply.'

There was a streak of creativity in Emma's make-up. She was an excellent maker of hats. She bought old hats from jumble sales for two pence and sprigs of artificial flowers for a penny, and made very stylish models which were admired by people as new creations from the milliners. Emma never realised her ambition to become a milliner. With cooked foods response was immediate; with hats it would take months of building a reputation and an establishment in a respectable part of town where rates were high, and the milliner's raw materials having to be bought in a trade that depended on the whims and pleasures of the populace. That was why Emma's brood had to endure the turmoil of the supper bar trade.

* * *

Witherup's daughter was a girl of about twenty, timid and pale.

'Father's in hospital,' she told Robby, as he stood in the porch. He was quite unmoved.

'Oh, well, this is the final payment. Sign your name across the stamp, please. This is the book your father marked the instalments in. He handed her the book.'

'Mother's gone to the hospital,' she murmured. 'I don't know what to do.' Robby was impatiently blunt.

'You sign it,' he said. 'Count up the entries and you'll find they come to £38.4s.0d, which includes interest.' The girl stared at the book and looked anxious.

'I suppose it's all right?'

'Of course it's all right,' Robby rasped. 'Will you just sign it, please - I'm in a terrific hurry.'

Frightened by his aggressive attitude, the girl hurriedly scrawled her childish signature across the stamp. Robby grabbed it, snapped Goodday, jumped on his cycle and was off. That was bloody well that, he thought, fuming impatience at the girl's stupidity, and he consigned Witherup and all his kin to hell and back. The hate he had felt at each visit would have blunted the sharpest knife, and every week his loathing became an aura around the little man, charged with such intense resentment that even Witherup had felt uneasy. Now, Robby decided, ma can sell the bloody shop and make no mistake about it this time. But events were not as straightforward as his young black and white brain pictured them!

There was no way out for Emma but to borrow money to keep the shop going. As a guarantor for the boys' credit drapery, now waterlogged with bad debts and unpaid bills, she was penniless. They sold the debts for a nominal sum to a bad debt specialist who sent his collectors around wearing tall hats on which BAD DEBT COLLECTOR was written, and many debtors paid 6d or 1/- out of shame, shrinking, despite their incorrigible ways, from neighbours discovering their secrets.

For Emma's borrowed money there was now a Bill of Sale on all her belongings! Robby again became the payer of debts, cycling into town every Friday night to the office. The girl there was a dark beauty, always waiting for him as the last client, in the softly lit office, with its heavy velvet curtains at the back, like a place for séances. He could have loved that girl, her smile always giving him coy welcome and he thought of intriguing goings on behind that curtain. A chance remark about her father told him she was the moneylender's daughter! Still, she was always friendly and had that seductive smile. They were two fireflies passing in the night between breeding seasons.

*　　*　　*

Angus bought *Market Bargains*. It was his idea to go round the suburbs hawking toiletries - soap, baby powder, razorblades, hair cream, lotions,' etc. Robby idly picked up the paper one time and read, SOAP 1 gross, 2/6d. How could anyone afford to make soap so cheap?

'That's the wholesale price,' Angus told him, knowingly. 'That stuff would make your face raw. Let's see

- one gross, sell at 1½d each. Um. 15/6d profit. Damned good profit!'

'What's the use of selling soap if it makes everybody's face raw?' Robby asked.

'Someone's got to sell it. Why shouldn't we? said Angus.

'Say some mothers use it on their babies?' Robby quizzed.

'Ah. Now, we'll make sure they know it's not baby soap,' Angus assured him.

With the parsimonious amount they had received for their bad debts, they purchased various toiletries at ridiculously low prices, filled two cases and tramped the suburbs - far away from Sleepers Hill, Robby noticed.

He felt disenchanted with his elder brother who had thrown away an excellent printing apprenticeship, had spent all ma's and the younger ones' money on a futile credit drapery washout, and now he was selling junk around doors, with their Malcolm being led like an underling! Robby was damned that he would ever go anywhere like that with Angus. He would never be Angus's serf any more, he thought, remembering the Winnie Ray cream slices. Angus wouldn't get anything out of this latest wild-brained venture. Yes, Robby now regarded Angus as an objectionable, headstrong, unscrupulous person with a strong core of utter selfishness in his character. He had ruined his mother and them - himself, Margaret and Douglas. It was unfair and one day he would tell Angus so.

The elder brothers were counting their takings one Friday night. Robby overheard Angus say, 'One thing about it, we don't touch that district again for a year or two.'

'No, not on your Nellie,' Malcolm guffawed. 'They'd have a bloody shot-gun ready for us.'

'Why?' Robby asked.

'Because they'll have found out what the damned stuff is like,' Angus scorned. 'The trouble with you is that you've no business sense. You're just a dreamer.'

'I'd rather be a dreamer than a crook,' Robby intervened, but Angus didn't seem to hear him.

'You'll never get anywhere, you know,' he went on. 'Dreaming about being a writer for a start, and an artist. It's ridiculous. I mean, I could write stories, even poetry but they never publish anything from people like us.'

He was silent for a while, entering figures in the cashbook.

'Walking around today,' he said suddenly. 'I thought of a story.'

'Oh? What was it?' Robby was all-alert

'I was thinking about bank accounts - like the big business people have, with cheques and all that. Once we build up this business we'll use the bank system.'

'Like hell you will,' Robby thought.

'This businessman, John, has a weak heart. Half-brother George is desperate for money. John's in his office one Friday night. George goes there. If John doesn't cough up he'll kill him. He sees a machete on the wall and takes it down and goes in. John's startled at George's appearance because he looks dangerous. John tells his half-brother to calm down. Did he want to borrow some cash? How much? John says he'll write a cheque. He starts to write. George thinks this will be no good because cheques can be stopped next morning.

George lifts his machete and approaches John. John has a heart attack and falls across the desk, covering the chequebook. George is relieved that he does not now need to kill John. He cleans out all the money from the safe and leaves, wiping his fingerprints off the machete before he puts it back on the wall. He is seen by no one and he knows he has got away with the perfect crime.

Next morning the police arrest him when he's about to board the train for Dover, carrying a suitcase of notes and another of clothes. George is dumbfounded. He's charged with robbery and with causing the death of his half-brother by menaces. All the evidence is on the cheque -'¼brother here - dangerous - machete - demands money!' You could call it Paid by Cheque.'

'Brilliant!' Robby enthused. 'I could write that.'

'Mind you,' said Angus, appearing modest, 'that's a

rough outline. I haven't time to dress it up for you. You've got to get the details right.'

Every week *The Leader* magazine had one short story across its middle pages. Robby thought he could do as well as some of the writers who contributed. The trouble was he was only fifteen and could never think of a simple theme to fit 1,500 words. Here now was a suitable little plot thought up by Angus.

Charlie White, the French polisher, mentioned that his friend had an old portable typewriter and would be willing to lend it to Robby. Charlie even promised to bring it to work next morning.

'That's damned decent of you, Charlie,' said Robby, delighted by such generosity. 'I can't type but if I could borrow it for a week, I'd be grateful.'

Charlie brought the machine as promised next morning and Robby worked all day in a dream of how he would word each paragraph. He found the process of picking out separate letters painfully slow. He had his story written in longhand and typed it out very carefully. At the end of the week he could manage the machine surprisingly well. After much work, he finished the story and was delighted by the neat, black type. He bought two large envelopes, addressed one to himself, stamped it and enclosed it with his story, and with the other sent off his story to *The Leader* in Fleet Street.

He endured three slow weeks of anxious speculation. Would his 1713 words be too many? Magazine stories were always cut to the bone, he had read in a library book *Writing for The Press*. Almost every word had to count, like a sonnet.

Then his large envelope came back and Robby shivered. As his ma handed him the envelope she said, sadly, 'There you are lad. They don't want it. Don't grieve about it.' There was no encouragement there. His ambition was a waste of time to ma.

Wearily he opened the envelope with the bread-knife. Clipped to the manuscript was a short letter. Ma had gone into the kitchen. He was alone. 'Dear Sir, I like your story

Paid by Cheque. Unfortunately it is rather long. If you could reduce it by 200 or so words, I will reconsider it for publication. Arthur C. Findon, Editor.'

After a surge of excitement, Robby's first thought was secrecy - he would tell no one about this for the moment. They didn't seem interested. Malcolm and Angus were still in bed before they started their rounds, and his ma busy preparing for opening time, quite assured in her mind that nothing would ever come of his dreamy endeavours. He crept up to his bedroom and hid the story under some shirts in his chest of drawers.

He tentatively asked Charlie White if he could possibly borrow the typewriter again. If Charlie gave him his friend's address, Robby would call for it himself and save Charlie the trouble.

After work he cycled to Charlie's friend's house and borrowed the machine, saying how very grateful he was. The man was smoking and Robby decided to buy him and Charlie some cigarettes for their kindness.

Arriving home with the machine, he was met by Emma.

'You're not trying to write any more stories, surely, lad?' she greeted him. 'It's silly. You'll be so disappointed.'

'I'm just practising on the machine,' Robby told her quietly.

After his meal he went into the yard to do his chore of washing the potatoes. They were spring ones and needed no attention. Douglas joined him after a time and Robby confided in him what he had to do, showing his younger brother the Editor's letter.

'Don't tell ma or Angus,' he warned. 'I've done half a sack. Will you finish off?'

'Yer,' Douglas agreed, readily. 'Get upstairs and get on with it, and post the thing off.' At times Douglas could be loyal and co-operative. Of late Angus's persistent air of superiority had irritated him, and if the story was published it would prove that the younger half of the family was capable of accomplishing things. One in the eye for Angus, although held thought of the plot.

In the bedroom Robby went through the text, using a

pencil to cross out or insert here and there. Extracts like - The firm exported its cloth to the Middle East and African countries, he altered to - an export firm; - The machete which John's father had brought from the West Indies many years before was fastened to the wall outside the office - became - Old John's machete decorating the entrance hall. Heartlessly cutting here and there he reduced the text to 1487 words. After three nights he had typed it and posted it next day. Within the week the Editor wrote, 'Dear Mr Ferguson, Thank you for your revised script. It will be published in The Leader in four weeks' time. You will be paid the standard fee of 3 guineas.'

At first, Angus was as excited as Robby by the news; but then he remembered that he was the wise, elder brother with good business sense and experience, and a mite cynical as became a businessman.

'Three guineas for 1,500 words. Ridiculous!' Angus declared.

'It's the standard fee,' Robby retorted. 'Why should they pay us less than anyone else?'

'Ah, they can tell straight away that you're inexperienced,' said Angus, knowingly. Robby thought this statement nonsense but said no more.

A month later, as promised, the story appeared in the centrespread PAID BY CHEQUE by Angus R. Ferguson. - A story with a surprise. One by one the family read it, Robby three times that day. Having your words printed marvellously black, expertly and accurately was exhilarating and Robby knew that nothing could be more rewarding His instinctive feeling for the written word earned him the right to be an author.

'You'll have to start thinking of another plot Angus,' he enthused, picturing a future of happy co-operation between himself and his eldest brother.

'Yer. I will,' Angus promised, and went out with Malcolm on a further venture to sell junk.

That was the first and last idea Robby received from Angus. The hawking fizzled out and after a few weeks, Emma used the tablets of soap for washing down the worktops and counters. She used the baby powder for her feet after bathing. All the razorblades had been sold except three packets, Angus claimed two and Malcolm one. When the three guinea fee was received, Angus claimed his share of £1.lls 8d and gave Emma five shillings. Robby presented her with a pound note.

'Angus gave me five shillings,' she told him. 'You give me the same, son.' Soon after that Angus left home and never came back to live in Liverpool any more!

*   *   *

The workshops were contained in a large, old mansion in Upper Shaw Street. There were six steps at the front and huge windows surrounded by stonework. The hall was broad and the staircase wide and gently rising, suitable for the easy carriage of furniture. In the rear was a long yard which had once been a garden, and in it stood the sawmill, a long shed where the cabinet makers worked on their machinery for cutting, planing, and moulding the lush planks of oak, mahogany, and walnut, and occasionally teak and maple that were all used for high-class furniture.

Charlie White and he occupied the back ground floor overlooking the sawmill area. On the first floor was the master upholsterer, Harry Robins, nicknamed Hank because of his years in the USA which accounted for all his tales of adventures with lesser known gangsters. Each lunchtime Charlie and Robby took up their enamelled, tapered cans of tea, with their cup lids, and their sandwiches to Hank's room and sat on one of the settees or armchairs that waited to be trucked by car ferry across the Mersey to the company's store in Birkenhead. Hank amused them with half-truth yarns about his past.

Hank's teeth were discoloured by his daily mouthfuls of tintacks. You could see that Hank was a good sort and harmless, having been a Real Devil in his youth.

Charlie thought a lot of Hank and Robby. He could appreciate Hank's humour, and Robby often noticed his eyes gleaming behind his Harold Lloyd glasses when he listened to the old man. Charlie was small and slight but strong as you could see from the thickness of his forearm. He collected jazz records and Robby spent some happy hours at Charlie's just listening to the best American jazz players and on occasions having sessions of Ambrose, Britain's best, in their opinion.

Charlie had polished a piece of oak about six inches by four, covering it all round, and had deposited it among the remaining weeds near the sawmill, leaving it there for a year. Robby found it, rubbed off the dirt, and there it was, a shimmering, beautiful piece of oak, quite untouched by the years' weather. When Charlie polished a piece of furniture you knew it would last hundreds of years if treated properly. In those days good furniture was solid and sound, and even the inferior kind still compares favourably with today's best.

Special jobs came their way sometimes. They were dispatched off to banks, public houses, or large hotels where counters, doors, doorframes and wall panels needed re polishing. They enjoyed the variation in their workdays and the meeting with different people. At last, Robby thought, he was regarded as an expert. He would start the cleaning down with cloths and sandpapers, then the polishing to give a deep foundation on which Charlie could work to give the final, lasting deep glaze finish.

Branstead, the employer, had a Belgian bedroom suite. The two workers enjoyed a week there in Branstead's bedroom when he and his wife were on holiday, and the housekeeper giving them an excellent meal each lunchtime. They laughed at their boss's choice of bedroom pictures - photographs of erotic female posers, reproduced paintings of female nudes, and drawings of torsos with pink nippled breasts.

The art of French polishing was to apply shellac and other ingredients in cobweb thickness and delicacy, layer upon layer, smoothing surfaces after each application had dried with a fine sandpaper touched with linseed oil, until a brilliant glassy skin covered the object. It was a skilled job needing infinite care, gentle touch, and endless patience, and

111

Robby loved the work. All his subconscious predilections were for creative work.

Douglas had found an equally unique and pleasant occupation with a high-class tea merchant. He had delivered tea to special customers, some of whom were titled folk, in his junior days. One was a favourite for his mimicry – Lady Fitzarthur-Cozens who liked him and gave him generous tips. He had learnt the blends of different teas and realised that the working-class had a taste for tea that lacked imagination. Their means confined them to cheap brands. Douglas's job continued and enabled him to survive and thrive; but Robby's apprenticeship was sailing towards the rocks!

Branstead was forced to close his workshops and buy in furniture to sell. Hank was given a month's wages and urged to retire, later reopening on his own. Charlie and Robby were sent over to Birkenhead to polish the lettering over the firm's new shop – BRANSTEAD'S HIGH CLASS FURNISHERS. The proprietor had done his best to keep his men in work; but after the sign was finished, Charlie departed for pastures new. Craftsman and former apprentice parted sadly, two good friends who would never meet again! Robby almost wept, not only was he losing a fine friend, but his security too. He was retained at the shop to re-polish damaged furniture, brush out the shop each evening, and be a general handyman, to his disgust. He was alone in a trade for which he was only half trained, and he missed Charlie's expertise and advice. Each lunchtime he went up to the shop's attic where there was a fireside chair. He drank tea from his enamelled cup and ate his sandwiches in melancholy solitude. And searching through the old newspapers and debris one day, he found a novel, The Rosary, a pathetic story about a blind man and his sweetheart. The theme suited the depressive mood of the times and Robby always associated Branstead's High Class Furnishers in Birkenhead with that tearjerker book.

Robby always met Janet after work, a quiet, warm creature about seventeen, who served behind the counter of her father's confectioner's shop where Charlie and he had gone frequently to supplement their cheese sandwiches. Janet walked down to the landing stage with him, he pushing his bike and she talking of her family. She always kissed him goodnight with her soft, generous lips, and he was able to hold her shapely body close, both with hearts and bodies full of longing; and then the ferryboat would chug near the end of the pier and they would have to part. He had enjoyed her gentle company, but it all came to nothing in the end, as he believed his life would become - nothing in the end! He was sacked and joined the doleful dole queue of misery, always recalling with happiness his days with Charlie, Hank, and Janet; Hank's American stories, Charlie's record sessions, and the warm confectioner's shop that delighted him on cold hungry days.

In 1932 Alec died of pneumonia and was buried in Linacre Lane cemetery. On the day of his funeral, in the evening, Old Jock, the dog, went out and never returned. Robby imagined, sadly, that the poor, loyal, grieving animal would be out searching pubs and being told by the men. 'He's not here, Jock, old lad.' And when old Jock died of grief, he would still be searching in some faraway Dog Valhalla of Flealess Joy where there were plantations of buried bones, and kennels with ermine linings, and avenues of lamp posts, the main one leading to the Mongrel Palace where dogs like Jock were awarded The Order of Dogged Determination because he had persevered for so long to smell out his old, generous, free-and-easy mariner master, Alec, waiting somewhere with a pint pot with dregs to be licked from it!

CHAPTER 4

Angus had to labour in the rubber works, a stinking occupation that left its odour on his working clothes. Aunt Maggie did not seem to mind when he came in from work each evening. The cottage itself had an aroma like the dank crypt of a church but more friendly than the rubber smell. Angus had acquainted his aunt with conditions in Liverpool, omitting the vital information that he had thrown over an excellent apprenticeship, and had failed in two bigheaded schemes to make money, and he painted a romantic, false picture of the honest youth trying hard to make something of himself.

'Poor lad,' Maggie said. 'Things must be bad in Liverpool. Eh! I'm glad I don't live there.'

She had changed beyond recognition. She was fifty, small, wore glasses which fronted watery eyes, and moved about rapidly like her sister Emma, always having some scheme in mind to wrest an extra penny or two from life. Angus's contribution for boarding was a great help and Maggie never questioned the rightness of taking him in. Emma needed every penny her family could earn, but Maggie's thoughts did not range far enough to wonder how her younger sister was faring.

Her cottage had a long front garden and a rough field at the rear, common with the rest of the row of cottages and limited by a high wall which bounded Uncle Jack's place of work, the timber yard. By the wall stood the cottagers' privies, bucket closets that a blind man would find easily in summer months. She never once locked her front or back door. Insurance and rent men came when she was out, took the money off her old dresser, marked the books, and left change, and nothing was ever stolen, not because there was nothing worth stealing, but because in those days there were honest, civilised people in that small town.

Maggie's son, Archie, was nineteen and when Angus

came for the second time, Archie was dangerously anaemic. He drank blood. After a successful trial with the county cricket club he found his poor health forbade his becoming a professional. He had won a scholarship and was being educated for a career as an industrial research chemist. Archie was a gem found on a dung heap! Maggie's other children were two girls, the elder a doe-eyed beauty, the younger a languorous, pale-faced girl who, Angus imagined, was always on the point of going to faint.

For Robby, staying there one summer became an olfactory holiday - the pervasive warm smell of Mrs West's bake-house across the way; the sweet smell of petrol on the main road; the damp, inky smell of the old school in Union Street; the ancient stones in Maggie's kitchen and scullery, like a Norman church promising incense which he would recall in years to come when visiting a cathedral in the heart of Belgium; the fragrance of wild flowers in Maggie's front garden wilderness that had never known spade or hoe; the cabs of early buses with their bench seats, smelling of hot oil and displaying a notice DO NOT TALK TO THE DRIVER; the varnishy scent of new double-deckers, their bulb-horns squirting noise; and all these buses bearing the name LEYLAND on the front of their long bonnets - Leyland, the cradle of the famous motors, the baby that grew into a giant, making vehicles that were the Rolls Royce of heavy goods and passenger transport.

There were the scents of the countryside itself when he took walks with his cousins; travelling to Preston on Uncle Jack's timber wagon on hot days, with the smell of hot tar, the tang of timber planks, the horse and manure odours, and the aroma of Uncle Jack's pipe, all giving the ten-year-old Robby a fancy for idyllic, healthy country life.

He visited Uncle George and Aunt Charlotte during his holiday, in Water Street, its name deriving from an ancient Smithy Well. Theirs was a house redolent of furniture polish and carbolic soap. Robby remembered Uncle George as tall, thin, aged fifty-two, his cheeks hollow, his brow high and learned, his bones large and prominent. His moustache was neat and waxed tightly. He was bald on top and wore pince-nez that clipped to his large nose. Winged collar and dicky bow were favoured by George, and he resembled his father, although he would never admit it. With his walking cane in one hand, Robby beside him, they crossed the Vicar's Fields towards the farms, past the immense beech trees with gnarled roots finger-gripping the earth. George bought buttermilk for two-pence from farmers' wives and Robby drank it, not wanting to hurt his uncle's feelings by refusing. Robby hated buttermilk. Another favourite destination was Neddy Springs across many fields, with the skylark overhead and the smell of hay in their nostrils. The nectarine taste of icy water, glinting like crystal on a blazing day, was nature's gift; and the watercress all around the gushing water like food and drink in the land of milk and honey. And one day, in years to come, the spreading motor-works stole the fantasy and the rustic charm was no more.

Aunt Charlotte was still handsome, with the smallness of all Lancashire women those days, a shrewd, tough woman who always remembered Emma for the one incident that had never occurred - her drowning. Beyond the privy at the end of Aunt charlotte's garden were fields and farms, before the days of speculative builders.

Uncle George had spent long days in the trenches at the Somme and would be racked with rheumatism later in his life, and a shrapnel wound for which he received a meagre war pension. Poor, suffering Uncle George deserved better, Robby always thought, and his sisters, too. They were a generation of Foulkes that were destined by the gods to struggle and fail, to be crushed and hurt all through their years.

Angus saw Gwendoline walking home from her father's engineering works, a small business that employed a few qualified men and two apprentices. She worked in the office, accounting and corresponding. To Angus the prospect of marrying Gwen, with her back-ground of wealth and importance, was like a serf being rescued from a dungeon by a princess. –'Hello, Angus. So you've come back,' she smiled. 'How are you going on?'

'Oh,' he said, abashed, 'I'm back at the rubber. But my

aim in life is to be my own boss one day. This rubber job is just temporary.'

'Our Harriet's husband is thinking of leaving his job - he's an engineer you know - and wants to take on a coal business. Shall I have a word with him? He needs a partner.'

'That would be great Thank you.'

He walked Home with her, she thinking that he was a very shy earnest fellow a little less gauche than he had been, and although not tall, was good-looking. When they reached Gwen's home, he said farewell and she promised to see him again. Angus never remembered walking the extra five hundred yards to Auntie Maggie's cottage, for his brain buzzed with delight and hope.

He was determined to fulfil his ambition to become his own master, anything less made him restless and headstrong, and when Gwen's promised discussion with her brother-in-law, Willis Cromwell, surprisingly brought good results, Angus promised himself that he would make no mistakes this time. As an engineer Willis was ignorant on questions of business transactions.

'Well, Willis, you can leave all the business side to me,' Angus assured his future partner. 'I've been in business all my life, you know, so there's no problem there.' He would show this dreamy yokel how to run a business, Angus thought. So far, to be fair to himself, his misfortune had been the lack of necessary capital and bright ideas died without financial backing.

The gods smiled knowingly. 'There he goes again,' said an elder, 'pretending a long experience in business and he's only twenty-four.'

'Yes,' said his brother god, 'and he's made a damned mess of everything he's touched so far.'

'I can't drive,' Angus went on, as if scorning such an accomplishment. 'I've never had any inclination to drive.'

'I can do the driving,' said Willis, 'and look after the wagon and servicing and so on, if you'll sell the coal. How much can you put into the partnership?'

Angus had been anticipating this question. He fudged it for a second or two, preparing his partner.

'Not much, I'm afraid.'

'How much?'

'Well, I've saved twenty pounds since I came here.'

Willis considered this, filling his pipe slowly, staring into space.

'I'll tell you what,' he said. 'You buy the coal and deal with the buying and selling. I'll keep on the driving and mechanical side.'

They started well. Friends and relatives promised to patronise Willis's new project. Angus was pleased when, within three weeks, his share of the profits was more than he earned at the rubber works!

The first tiny irritation came when Angus began to analyse the conditions under which he was working. Willis, a tremendous bookworm, would be reading and smoking his pipe comfortably in the driving cab whilst Angus jumped up on the back platform, moved the coal to the edge, jumped down, took the sack on his back, and lugged it up the garden path. Angus's feelings became all twisted inside him after a few more weeks. He fumed to see Willis's broad, large-headed form sitting there in the cab, pipe in mouth, book in hand. Angus's grievance was acute because of his position - if you are not careful, he told himself, you will fall out with this lazy sod and ruin all your chances with Gwen. He was being treated like a Tom Noddy and that was not on!

He suggested to his partner, tentatively, that he should do more work and not sit in the cab, leaving Angus to carry all the coal, especially in wet weather. Willis's answer was quite bland,

'That was not our agreement, Angus. I said I would drive and service the vehicle and you agreed to buy and sell the coal. I can't be held responsible for driving AND delivering coal.'

Angus spent several more weeks in smouldering irritability, deciding to give up.

'I'm sorry, Willis,' he said, playing their disagreement gently. 'I'm straining my guts lugging this coal. It's damned hard work, you know.' He was quite capable of doing the work but had decided to appeal to Willis's sympathy.

'I know it's hard work, Angus,' said Willis, 'but it's better than the rubber.'

'I'm not so sure about that,' said Angus, not pleased at his partner's blackmail.

'I'll tell you what - if you deliver all, singles, I'll help delivery when there's more than one.'

This seemed reasonable and Angus agreed, thankful that he had been diplomatic in shifting his partner at last. But Willis's tackling of this new arrangement was stolid. Angus delivered the singles but when these were interspersed with five hundredweights or sometimes half a ton to one customer, Willis spent so much time on the platform, placing the sacks for Angus, that Willis ended up in delivering only one out of five or two out of ten! Added to this, in wet weather, Willis used a strong empty sack fashioned into a hood to cover head and body and he wasted time putting it on. Angus had found the hoods a nuisance and used an old jacket.

The situation was now worse for any further complaints from Angus would receive the reply that Willis WAS sharing the burden - hadn't people seen him delivering the coal?

'Willis will keep strictly to what you agreed,' Gwen told Angus. 'He's a stickler for detail. I know how you feel. He thinks he is entitled to sit in the cab - he did buy the vehicle, didn't he? You've got to be honest. And he only takes out of the business what you take out.'

'He wants me to do all the donkeywork,' said Angus. 'He could do a lot more, but he messes about, wasting time.' He began to think he had gone too far, in maligning Willis so strongly. He could see failure coming to him around the corner, meaning a return to that hellhole the rubber works.

'I know what you mean Angus,' said Gwen. 'It doesn't seem fair. But that's Willis, and you'll never change him. If you aren't happy, give it up.'

Angus gave it up.

With increasing understanding of Willis, Angus saw him as an eccentric intellectual with strange pastimes -

making copies of eighteenth century charts and maps, very intricate with names of places in minute lettering. To Angus everything Willis did was a waste of time and labour, without profit. Each new hobby irritated Angus more and he considered Willis an even worse dreamer than his brother Robby.

Willis sold the vehicle and returned to his job at the engineering works. Angus returned to the rubber works with bitterness in the depths of him. This was his fourth failure, and he began to question the reasons for his, and his family's, proclivity towards failure. Nothing ever came right for the Ferguson family! His ma had worked all her life and ended up penniless, owning nothing, according to Robby's letter from Liverpool. The whole family were menial task-doers, destined to be underlings all their lives. Well, that was not for HIM! One day he would be his own boss and to hell with anyone who tried to get in his way! Leyland was a thriving little community of 12,000 inhabitants and only 17 out of work! This was the very environment in which he knew his ambitions could be fully realised. Through the coal business he had been able to save £40.

The gods looked down and marvelled that anyone so intelligent could be so utterly stupid. 'He has saved £40,' said one god, and yet, once more, he throws a good prospect to the winds! Had he persevered with Willis, his future would have been assured. Such an idiot! He ruins himself with his colossal conceit. He could not bear to be the donkey with Willis driving him. Now he will return to being the donkey with a board of directors driving him! And they will not take out exactly what he takes out, you may be sure. For that honest agreement alone, he should have stayed with Willis.'

Angus was never aware that his huge conceit was the answer to all his derogatory thoughts about his family, not asking himself who had been responsible for his ma's failure, acknowledging that it was not Emma's fault. All the family except Angus knew this, and it confirmed their mother's bitterness about her eldest and favourite son.

*   *   *

Mrs Helman owned the huge Sparrow Drive house. She was small, skeletal, white haired. Everything about her was spotlessly clean, except her habit of wiping her nose and placing her handkerchief on the table, even at mealtimes, as if, subconsciously she was declaring her infallibility as the Goddess of Hygiene because even her nasal mucus was pure. The children had seen the habit on occasions when they had gone up from their basement accommodation with the rent.

It was a three storied building with a long yard at the back and a long garden in front. It was built high like its neighbours, and the garden path, almost as long as a cricket pitch, had to be scrubbed every day except Sunday, four times by the old woman's Maltese daily girl, and twice a week by Emma. But the Fergusons, unlike the other residents who paid higher rents, were not allowed to enter at the front but gained access into their cellar by the back gate which came out onto a narrow back entry. Young Margaret, coming home from school on winter evenings dreaded the last fifty yards. Mrs Helman pooh-poohed the idea that Margaret might be molested in that jowler.

The cellar walls of the passage, scullery, and lavatory were gleamingly whitewashed; the front living room was papered in an old brownish wallpaper, its window looking out on three steps that could raise one to the level of the front garden. In contrast to the rest, the living room was a dark hole.

Emma felt defeated, unable to manage any longer the financial strain of her business, and Robby's sacking had been the final blow. She had paid her debts honourably and was now penniless, owning a Welsh dresser and a mere few odds and ends of household items to bring with them.

The rent included electricity but after a short time there were so many whingeing complaints about the size of electricity bills, that Emma decided to keep the peace. They illuminated the cellar with two old oil lamps and candles, and on rare occasions when they had something to cook, Emma used the old-fashioned coal range. In that cellar the younger children saw ma weep bitter tears, the first time they had seen her cry.

And the gods looking down pitied her deeply, recognising her continual vulnerability to dire misfortune.

Malcolm was selling wireless sets. As with everything he tackled, he went into work with enthusiasm, occasionally bringing home a set that he would be demonstrating next morning, and the family had enjoyed the luxury of listening in.

Later he had contrived to buy a second-hand set and this they had brought with them. It gave little pleasure. Mrs Helman's continual complaints about the sound made it necessary to keep the volume so low they could hardly hear it.

Each day Malcolm started on his rounds demonstrating and trying to sell for cash or hire purchase the respectably sound sets. He and Douglas were the only breadwinners plus Robby's dole money of six shillings.

To the old woman Douglas was the demon in that hell-hole habitat. Her treatment of his ma made him loathe the old witch. He often flaked whitewash off the walls with his bicycle as he came home at night, and Mrs Helman always found out with uncanny regularity and there was a whining row next day. Douglas often called up the cellar stairs, 'Get away from that door, you shrivelled old cow! I can see you sneaking around!' He often called her an old bitch or witch or skeleton. Emma remonstrated with him and dreaded the scenes, but in quieter moments approved of his attacks.

Each night the family sneaked up the stone steps at bedtime. Emma stayed behind to check that everything was neat and tidy. On most occasions they reached their bedrooms safely without altercations. The three boys slept in one large bed in the attic, Emma and Margaret in the smallest bedroom below them. One night Robby was last to go up. On the first landing, waiting in her dressing gown, stood Mrs Helman's granddaughter, Milly. The first week they had been there Emma said that Milly was a consumptive and warned them to stay away from the girl.

'My God! You've been a long time,' she whispered, harshly. I've been waiting for you.' Completely unprepared, he was grabbed strongly by the wrist and dragged into her bedroom. She pushed him onto her bed and kissed him with an unrestrained, clinging passion that set his head throbbing with awful alarm. He could feel the nakedness of her body through the dressing gown. She released him and went to the door to close it. 'Get undressed,' she hissed.

'Like hell,' he said. Then came the screech of the whining doom.

'Milly! Whaty' doin' ? Come 'ere - fix me pillows.'

Unknown to the Ferguson's, Milly was a nymphomaniac and the grandmother knew it and always discouraged male boarders by saying that Milly was consumptive. The old woman had been listening and had recognised the scuffling from her grandchild's room. Milly said, 'Wait!' and flitted along the landing muttering 'Stupid old Cow!'

Robby rushed into the bathroom and began vigorously to wash his mouth, inside and out, his whole being terrified at the possibility of catching the dreaded T.B. germ from that very wet, passionate kiss!

Next evening Milly's voice came down the cellar steps:

'Mrs Stone, is your Robby there?' Grandma wants to see him.'

The voice was followed by high-heeled footsteps descending. Robby was up in a second, opened the front window, squeezed through, up the front steps onto the lawn and away, a startled gazelle, towards the gate on Sparrow Drive.

*   *   *

Robby pedalled around searching for work each day. When he thought of his happy, successful school days, he smiled at the irony and bitterness of it all - what use that reference from Becket? What use his apprenticeship? What use his story?

For the first time in his life he felt weak, tired and weary. The lack of good food was gradually taking its effect.

Malcolm, too, was becoming more and more despondent, despite his former disposition to regard everything with optimism in the best of all worlds. He lay awake at night on his back, staring wide-eyed at the ceiling of the cramped attic room. He remembered his days at Trenton, New Jersey, meeting wealthy, friendly people. He remembered Peter Jackson's cousin, Adele, and her family. She would have married him if he had had any prospects: a waiter in an hotel was not paid a living wage and had to depend on tips to make a decent income. He remembered the open car he had learned to drive - a Duesenburg 1928 model, a double cowl phaeton and the great trips they had had, the picnics with Adele's family, he and his shipmate, Peter, who had second sight and forecast the sinking of the S.S.Vestris. And it had come true. Yes, it had been a stroke of good fortune for them. But for what purpose? The snap shots they had had taken - ma had copies somewhere - recalled how Peter and he had looked clean-cut young fellows, neatly dressed, gentlemanly and happy, Adele's pa and uncles calling them Great Guys and the womenfolk referring to them as those Handsome English Boys. Glorious days they had been! The depression had not touched Adele's family. How life could deteriorate in a year! When he saw himself in a mirror, he saw that even the bloom of youth was fading - his face thin and drawn, his eyes tired, his bones more prominent, yet he was only twenty-three years old! With his present prospects he could never marry Fay Jones. But, damn it! There must be a good time ahead, away from this bloody dungeon, with ma struggling to keep on good terms with that tyrannical old bitch! Scrubbing that damned long garden path that they were not allowed to use. It was medieval, like the attitude to Negroes in the States.

One sunrise Robby awoke only half covered with bedclothes. Douglas on the other side of Malcolm must have turned and yanked the clothes with him. His elder brother lay there with his eyes open.

'Bloody cold,' he murmured. There was no response.

'Aren't you cold?' he asked. Still no response. He lifted his head and stared at Malcolm. He was puzzled and vaguely afraid. He wasn't dead, was he? He looked like a corpse. Malcolm's irises and pupils had turned up in the normal way, and with the eyelids open, they were just visible and appeared to be staring at the ceiling. Malcolm was asleep with his eyes open! Robby lay back on his pillow. This was like somnambulism without action! The poor bugger must be so weary that he hadn't the energy to sleepwalk! Robby's interpretation was not far from the truth. In his boyhood days Malcolm had sleepwalked several times.

In her cookery class at college Margaret had made a macaroni cheese dish with cheese sauce, and proudly brought it home. Despite their hunger, none of the young people would eat it. The dish was placed on the bottom shelf of the Welsh dresser and left in frigid isolation for three days.

On the fourth day Malcolm came in, tall, hefty, thin faced, with huge hands and feet, his stomach having rumbled all the way from Fazakerley to Walton. He sat down wearily, and then caught sight of the macaroni cheese dish. He studied it thoughtfully for a moment, whistling in his quiet windy way, and then he slapped the table, startling his ma and Robby who were reading near the window.

'Oh, bugger it!' he shouted. 'Why not?' He jumped up, grabbed the macaroni cheese and devoured it from the dish.

'Well,' said Emma, 'that'll suit our Margaret, poor girl.'

* * *

The Blackburn House scholars always had an abundance of homework. Margaret found it almost impossible to do it in the gloom of lamplight, and it became a habit to go each homework evening with her ma to Flora's terraced house near Goodison Park. Seated at the end of Flora's dresser, she wrote her essays and exercises. Flora's became a haven for Emma and her children. Aunt Nellie was living there at that time and could be seen wandering around with a glass of hot water and bicarbonate of soda. Dole money was Jack Volant's income since the Moss Side Coal Company had mysteriously gone out of business.

After some weeks, Margaret believed that Flora must be getting tired of their regular visits for she always made them tea or cocoa and often provided food which she could ill afford. About eleven o'clock ma and Margaret reluctantly departed and trudged home through the night to their dreary little bedroom in the old witch's castle.

Occasionally Douglas was able to vary their routine when he received a more than ordinary amount of money in customers' tips, and he would give ma two shillings to take Margaret with her to a cinema.

Slowly pedalling around one day, Robby fainted and ran into the kerbstone on Walton Road. He came to be surrounded by faces and his shoulders held by a policeman.

'What happened, son?' the policeman asked.

'I must have fainted. I'm just hungry. I've never fainted in my life before.'

'Well you'd better get home son. Where do you live?'

He was about to answer 52 Sparrow Drive when he stopped short. That old witch, and Milly, and his ma. What a to-do there'd be! Especially if this copper went with him.

'Goodison Road,' he said.

'Well now, that's not far. Can you manage to walk home?'

'Yes thank you.'

'Get something to eat, lad, even if it's just an apple. And don't ride that bike, savvy. It's dangerous.'

Robby thanked the constable and struggled up. He picked up his cycle and pushed it slowly, his head feeling light and airy. When he reached Flora's he knocked at the door. Next second he had fallen again, against the door with his cycle across his legs. He recovered consciousness on Flora's front room sofa. His trousers were torn at the knee, his hands scarred and bleeding, and there were blood droplets from a wound in his forehead.

126

'Good God, lad!' Flora cried. 'What on earth's happened to you? You look like death.' He described what had happened, his voice weak and his breathing difficult. 'I thought the copper - was - was going to come with me when he - he asked my address. I gave him yours - didn't want him to go home.' 'Good God no!' said Flora. 'That old bitch would have had something to say. I shall have to stitch your trousers.'

Jack and Auntie Nellie sat with him while Flora went out to make a hot drink, cut some bread and make sandwiches.

'My God,' she murmured to herself, 'we've come to a pretty pass when one of us faints from hunger. God help us!'

*   *   *

In 1934 Angus wrote to tell his family that he was marrying Gwendoline Hanley and he wanted his ma and Margaret to come to the wedding. Malcolm and Douglas scraped together enough money for the train fares. Emma wore a dress she had bought from Jane Murphy's shop four years before, and wore one of her home-made hats; Margaret wore a dress Emma had bought from Paddy's Market for the elfish sum of 6d and a straw hat for a shilling. On the group photograph later, Emma and her younger daughter looked very smart, in spite of the low budget costs of their apparel. In Leyland they discovered that Mr Hanley had given a bedroom suite and a Persian carpet as a gift to the couple and Emma and Margaret were most impressed. At least, Emma thought sadly, Angus is getting some good luck.

October came and Malcolm, not to be left far behind, married Fay Jones as Robby had always known he would. When arrangements were being made, Fay came to Sparrow Drive and talked about her plans for the wedding. She had visited the dungeon several times and knew all about Mrs Helman's tyranny, and knew that the Fergusons were suffering and why people do not have to suffer such dire humiliation except when they are completely down and out!

Emma suggested that Margaret should be a bridesmaid. There was an immediate reaction of unmistakable hostility.

'YOU couldn't even afford to buy her a new dress,' Fay sneered. I've already made arrangements, Kate Clancy has promised. (Her voice held a note of triumph).

'Kate's a Roman Catholic,' Emma said, astounded.

'I know,' said Fay, irritably. 'She's agreed, so what's it matter?' Emma was deflated. Kate Clancy's sister lived with Esther and Jack Volant senior. To Fay they were the ideal guests - they had never been unemployed, were financially well-off, always bought splendid clothes at regular intervals, had good holidays, and always enjoyed at least one night a week at the theatre, and often at film premieres in town to see the latest films and pay inflated prices in consequence.

Fay had already considered, shrewdly, that there would be at least two worthwhile wedding gifts, one from Jack's sister, Esther, and one, or maybe two, from the Clancy girls. Perhaps Pa Volant might chip in, too, with a gift, but it was doubtful for he had a reputation of being careful with his money.

Emma attended the wedding, determinedly, despite the knowledge that Malcolm's income would now vanish. She wore the dress she had worn at Leyland, and her home-fashioned hat. Malcolm was her son and she had every right to be there. She guessed that Fay had refused Margaret as a bridesmaid because Angus and Gwen had not asked her. if Margaret was not good enough for Gwen's wedding in Leyland, then she certainly was not good enough for hers in Liverpool! No one was going to spoil her wedding with cheap clothes, and if those posh people in Leyland thought they were any better than her family, they were mistaken. Margaret as bridesmaid. Oh! That was OUT!

Emma travelled in the wedding car with the Important Guests and Margaret was left to travel to the church by tram.

As humble as it was, Flora's house was the venue for the reception. Magically, there was adequate food provided, and a barrel of beer in the scullery. Fay's family, relations and friends outnumbered Malcolm's by five to one! They were experts at enjoying themselves at other people's dos, and they entered into competition, it seemed to Malcolm, to see who could empty the beer barrel the fastest. The bridegroom held his own when it came to liquor, being his father's son, and was a little more sober than most, though affable in his role of Best of All Possible Worlds philosopher, guffawing loudly at the pranks and exhibitions, the beery blue jokes, the giggling sexy innuendoes, and as the time passed, he resigned himself to the euphemistic realisation that Fay's people were bluff, hearty, rough diamonds and stalwart Liverpudlians! This crowd, he thought, had originated in old Mrs Jones's womb - fifteen children all told! He could hardly imagine the extent of the offspring of such a brood, and wondered how many had not attended the wedding. He knew now he had burnt his boats!

*   *   *

Emma swept the backyard when the old gardener with the permanent dewdrop did not turn up. The Maltese daily help, the children's favourite because she cursed the old witch in her native tongue, did not touch the yard. There were three large plots built up in stone rectangles - three graves, Margaret said, in harmony with their environment, and from these, leaves and twigs and other debris blew in the wind and settled on the flagstones. Brushing up one day, Emma met Mrs Barker. They introduced themselves. Mrs Barker lived in the house whose back door faced that of Helman's.

Emma told all. Mrs Barker nodded her head wisely, and gave grim smiles here and there.

'Say no more, Mrs Stone. I know her well. Evil creature. And that granddaughter! Eh! I've never before seen such a creature. She waylaid my son one time in this very place. Wicked girl - mother and father divorced, father at sea, poor man, mother living with her fancy man in Tuebrook. What goings on!'

Emma liked the neighbour at once and they became

good friends, simply by talking together. Emma unloaded all her frustrations and Mrs Barker soon knew her predicament, with Malcolm gone.

Mrs Barker came boldly down the yard one day. Emma was washing dishes in the cellar scullery, a whitewashed room without windows, needing a light day and night. Emma had switched on the electric light. Damn it, if the old bitch complained she'd tell her a thing or two. I've had enough of her tyranny she told herself. Mrs Barker spoke quietly, fearing the ructions that would be aroused if the witch overheard.

'Mrs Stone, dear, I think I have a suggestion to make that might solve all your problems.'

Emma ceased washing up and dried her hands.

'If you can solve all my problems, Mrs Barker, love, you can work miracles.'

'Our Len's in the choir at St. Michael's and he's friendly with Ted Barnes, our young organist and choirmaster. He lives in Chepworth Street with his sister Georgina. The married couple housekeeping for them have gone. Ted found out that they were cooking the books. Would you take on the responsibility, dear?'

Emma did not think twice about such a golden proposition.

'I would be delighted, Mrs Barker, if they'll have us.'

'Oh, it's practically all arranged. Len's had a good talk to Ted and he's agreed.'

'Well, I must say, Mrs Barker, it was very kind of you to think of us like this. Good Lor' - I'll be overjoyed to leave this dungeon and live in a decent house. It's wonderful. I can't thank you enough.'

'Well, Mrs Stone, we've got to help each other in times of stress and hardship. Your children will be lovely companions for the two of them and they do need someone honest like you to look after them. Their mother is permanently in hospital - incurable disease I think.'

'Oh, dear dear! How sad! I will certainly do my best for the poor young things.'

'I know you will, Mrs Stone, dear. And we must keep in

touch, you know.'

When the Fergusons had moved, Milly had harsh words to say to her grandmother. She was a wicked old cow for driving them out. They had been the best boarders they had ever had - apart from the youngest son. Now who the hell was going to live in that cellar? There weren't many people like the Fergusons.

Mrs Helman was mightily puzzled that Emma and her brood had found another place. They were destitute, vulnerable, and with not a single prospect of improving their affairs. How had they managed to move and to where? They would have to furnish a new place, too. In bed that night she felt peeved that she had been out-manoeuvred by someone who had been under her miserable thumb. That basement would be another ten years lying empty. Damn them! That cheeky bitch, Milly, was right - people like the Fergusons were perfect victims for people with a spare cellar, they were met with only once in a blue moon.

*   *   *

Manny Dartman was a stocky man in his middle forties, with reddish hair and a fair skin with down on his cheeks that was easy to shave. He wore horn-rimmed glasses and frequently blew his nose one nostril at a time into spotless white handkerchiefs. One could tell he was wealthy from his well-cut suit and his car. He was the junior partner of Dartman Brothers, the Furnishers.

'Well, what can y' do?' he asked Robby in a snappy voice.

'I was an apprentice French polisher,' Robby said, 'but the firm closed its work-shops and started buying in furniture'

'Aye, lad, these are bad times. Are y'strong?'

'Yes, fairly strong.'

'See if you can lift that piano at one end.' Belying his recent starvation diet, Robby went into the window space and lifted the piano a foot from the ground.

'Good. Now then, say you were repolishin' some'at, what materials would you need?'

'Pure linseed oil, meths, French polish, white cloth, wadding, sandpaper and maybe a scraper if the damage is bad.'

'Right', Manny laughed. 'Well, young fella, we've got all those things - I was just testing you out, y'see. We have a French polisher at our Bootle branch; but there's no reason why you shouldn't do a bit here now and then. I can see y' an honest lad. Have y' got a bike?'

'Yer - it's outside there - bit of a boneshaker but it works.'

'Right now. You start on Monday at nine. OK? Fifteen shillings a week and we'll see how you go. First you'll be with our deliveryman, Dick, on the van. After deliveries y' come back here and work in the shop - have a chat with Miss Wilkins,' Bella. Just occasionally, I think, you'll go out polishin'. OK?'

'OK. Thank you Mr Dartman.'

Robby put his cap on his head and said goodbye. He had merely entered the shop and asked for the boss. The firm hadn't advertised. He had taken potluck, and Glory Be! He'd got a job at last. Wait till ma heard about it! He pedalled home in a glow of accomplishment.

*　*　*

As she came downstairs, Georgina saw Margaret through the open doorway, slim, pale, bespectacled and intelligent looking, doing her homework.

'Hello,' she greeted.

'Hello,' Margaret smiled, looking up, and Georgina went out, not foreseeing a future of enduring friendship. On her way to the theatre to see The Mikado, she hoped that at last she had found a sister. The newcomer was obviously younger than herself, being still at school. Her first reaction to her brother's announcement of a new housekeeper sent her heart sinking. Their experiences with housekeepers had been fraught with distrust. She hated the thought that more strangers were coming to live in their home. But Ted had added, grinning, there would be three teenagers, one a girl.

From the first day, Emma was called ma and Georgina liked her at once. It was a happy thought that there were three people of her own generation who could provide social interests as well. Georgina even began to enjoy helping Margaret with household chores. Emma had insisted from the beginning that the girls would share the work and the boys do all the heavier tasks.

Georgina's first impression of Robby was that he was quiet and kind, though she saw little of him because he worked late hours and went out at night. She never heard him raise his voice in anger and his unorthodox sense of humour made her shriek with alarm and laughter in that order - ridiculous actions they were like appearing to fall flat on his face, his hands outstretched at the last second to save himself; or suddenly jumping up to do something after sitting very quietly, and his sudden shout made everybody jump.

Douglas was very different. He made Georgina laugh by the derogatory attitude he adopted towards the girls; and his uncontrollable temper, sometimes put on, sent Georgina screeching with laughter. His mate, Tom Hurst, was often convulsed by Douglas's contempt or his fad for highly polished shoes, smart suit and perfect ties. The gods regarded Douglas as a carbon copy of the old rake, George Foulkes, now dead and gone to hell, - smart appearance and flaming temper.

'Hey, Doug,' Georgina remarked when she first met Tommy Hurst, 'your pal's quite a dish.'

'Ugh!' came Doug's answer, 'quite a dish! You're as bad as he is. He said the same about you two. Silly sod! Wouldn't walk twenty yards with either of you two.'

'We wouldn't give you the honour and pleasure,' Georgina retorted, 'thank you very much,' and Margaret added, 'I was about to say the same. Good for you Georgina.'

Over the months at Helman's hellspot, Douglas had

developed a vocabulary of swearwords and curses, even against inanimate things like tools and machines. With his cycle upturned in the kitchen on a winter's evening for him to mend a puncture or a chain link, the peace of the house would be blasted with explosions of furious language. Emma, reading one time in an adjacent room, could hear his impatience with inanimate objects that had suddenly become live creatures which refused to do his bidding - sods, bastards, stupid cows, buggering things, and stupid bloody pigs. Emma closed her book.

'I've had enough of you,' she shouted, 'you foul-mouthed creature. I'm going as far away from you as I can get!'

In summer she took refuge in the park, donning her hat and summer coat, taking her book and some chocolate, and sitting on a park bench reading her romance and eating her small blocks of chocolate. The girls laughed heartily when they heard how she combated her youngest son's temper.

Georgina would always remember one small incident that happened at that time - the Barnes's fox terrier had a serious complaint and the vet had declared it was incurable. Emma was of a different opinion. For three nights she sat up with the dog, feeding it warm milk and brandy by the spoonful, and Bobby made a complete recovery! This action convinced Georgina that ma had a strong, determined and very caring character.

The young ones' ages ascended in one-year periods Margaret, 14; Georgina, 15; Douglas 16; Edward 17; and Robby 18. Edward seemed the most responsible person next to ma, and Robby the most absent and dreamy. Angus's opinion that he was only less dreamy than Willis Cromwell appeared true.

The Chepworth Street house was not as large as the Sparrow Drive place, but it had plenty of rooms - sitting room, drawing room, dining room, living room, kitchen, scullery, and a utility room outside for doing the laundry. There were four bedrooms and a bathroom, and a large attic room. To the Ferguson family it was a comfortable, interesting abode, and they would always remember it with great affection, Douglas included. There was a very good over strung piano in the front room. Being organist and choirmaster, Edward practised the music he would be playing at choir practice on Wednesday evenings. He usually finished his recital by tinkling some popular tunes of the time. His music teacher had taught him the technique of organ playing for church services and also as a stand-in for the organist at Walton prison, a direful experience for a well-bred boy, the organ being pumped by an old lag. Edward always came home white and weary. When the prison's heavy wicket door closed behind him he breathed deeply like a released prisoner, and hoped, if there were passers-by, they would not think him to be just that, a released prisoner.

Emma admired Edward for his maturity and he in turn showed his appreciation of the way she had tackled the responsibilities of the family by organising himself and the others to contribute two shillings a week for dental treatment, and Emma very soon had a splendid denture of white teeth. The two Barnes' children were wholeheartedly taken with this little, lively woman, their saving attribute at a time when they had lost all faith in the people sent as housekeepers by the church, two couples, at least, having been dishonest in their household accounts.

Edward took Robby to a choir practice. It was the heathen being intrigued by this tall, thin fellow with his aquiline nose, white teeth, long, lean fingers, and his musical ability at so young an age. Robby sat in the pew and listened to the mixed choir of boys, men, and women as they practised an anthem. It was Robby's first experience of going into a church. Sometimes the two boys went by themselves, and with only the organ light on, the dark church seemed eerie and, to Robby, unfriendly. In time, the two boys, the younger leading the elder, became reasonably good friends; but there was always a barrier between them which neither understood.

*   *   *

'It's a bloody Scotch flat,' Dick, the driver, said, 'and a bleedin' ironframe Johanna!' When they arrived at the address, Robby saw that a Scotch flat consisted of a flat at street level, having a staircase up the side of it to a wide landing outside a similar flat upstairs.

'When we've got the bleedin' thing in,' said Dick, giving himself some comfort to look forward to, 'we'll go for some'at t'eat. OK?'

'Ok,' Robby agreed, secretly tickled by Dick's 'fedupness.' Dick pushed open the door to the staircase and shouted, 'Johanna missus.'

Dick ascended the stairs to verify the information that the customers had prepared a space for the piano. When he came down he was tut-tutting and shaking his head of crewcut, streak-browned blond hair.

'We'll strain our guts to giblets goin' up there,' he informed Robby. 'Climbin' a bleedin' wall wouldn't be much harder.'

Dick wore leather straps round his wrists and brown leather leggings buckled at top and bottom. The wristbands made him a heavyweight wrestler although he was only ten and a half stone. They moved the ironframed piano down to the tailboard and onto a two-wheeled bogie, and wheeled it to the kerb. Robby lifted one end of the piano for Dick to remove the bogie and replace it under the piano on the pavement, and then they wheeled the whole thing to the bottom of the stairs.

'You first or me?' Dick asked. He was always the gentleman.

'Please yourself,' Robby said.

'I'll go first then, bein' more experienced.'

Step by painful step they lifted the piano, holding on to its front leg and stout carrier bar at the back. Robby had the weight at the bottom. One careless moment and the hundredweights of musical strings, wires and iron would crash down onto him, sending him backwards down the stairs. He began to see what Dick had meant by being more experienced. After a long, grunting, sweaty time, they reached the landing. The mother and daughter stood there, anxious mouths open. When the piano was safe on the landing, they puffed and smiled.

'Ooh! You Are strong, you lads. I never t'ought y'd gerritup. It's a wonder yis 'aven' gorra nernia,' said the mother.

'Yer,' said Dick, 'can't y' see it bulgin'?' Dick breathed. The women laughed.

They carried the piano across the landing into the flat, and set by the wall where a space had been cleared. They rested for a moment.

'After a piano's moved,' said Robby, pedantically, as if advising Myra Hess before a concert, 'you should have it tuned.' He lifted the lid and played one or two chords.

'Hm,' he decided, fit's not too bad at all.'

'It sounds d' gear t' me,' said the mother. 'D' yis like it, our Cat'leen?'

'O'course a do. It's luvly.'

'Therey'are lads, a twoshillin' piece each. Ta very much. Y've bin great yis 'ave, an' God bless yis.'

'Thanks very much, madam,' said Dick. 'I hope yis 'ave lotsa good dos on the Johanna. Goodday ladies.'

Dick always called women Madam when they gave a tip and Missus or Ma when they didn't. Back inside the cab Robby asked him how such people could afford two-bob tips.

'She's a moneylender, mate, that's why,' said Dick, starting the engine. 'Some o' these ould dears are rollin' in it. Right, off to my favourite caff f' lunch.'

* * *

Margaret won her scholarship in 1936 at Blackburn House under the aegis of the Liverpool Education Committee and began her working career in August as a cashier in the restaurant of a large confectionery firm. For eighteen months she did the job conscientiously, never making a mistake in her money transactions and never allowing a diner to escape without paying the bill. Her prospects were slightly improved by a rise in wages to fourteen shillings and she left, believing she was grossly underpaid, and joined the staff of Littlewoods Mail Order firm in Old Hall street. Her wage leapt to 17/6d and by the time she left when the blitz had begun, she was earning 27/6d a week. The family was gradually crawling out of the quagmire of poverty.

Emma always accompanied the girls on their outings, with giggling acceptance by Georgina and irritation for Margaret. Robby said ma was acting as a chaperon. since the death of his grandfather he had learnt more about his ma's early years. Emma always remembered her half-sister, Lizzie, and what the innocent creature had suffered through her illegitimacy. Emma always said it was typical of folk to blame the wrong people. Bastards committed no sin; why were they always regarded with contempt and derision? The biggest bastard, ma said, was the father of the child, he being the one to indulge his lust, the dominant animal. There would be no bastards in her family and this also applied to Georgina who was now part of it. They were two attractive girls and Emma would never trust any man within ten yards of any attractive females if they were alone.

* * *

Edward had gone to a meeting. They were discussing the piano. Emma mentioned that their father had played the piano and had actually owned a grand at one time. It had stood in the big front room upstairs, in Kensington. When they left there he had sold the grand and had bought an upright over strung in its place.

'You used to play it,' Emma reminded Robby, 'until we had to sell it.'

Robby had forgotten those days at Miranda Road. He had watched Miss Jarret at school and his interest was aroused. He came home one afternoon, being in his eighth year, and picked out a hymn tune they had sung that morning. Within a few months he could play any simple tune he heard and learnt to put the left-hand accompaniment to it. Angus could also play but had little patience in trying to learn more. It became clear that both Angus and Robby had an ear for music. Angus had a mandolin at one time and could strum several tunes without completing any. He could play a banjo and a mouth organ was easy meat for him. But he never explored the instrument's possibilities. To get some money, Angus sold his mandolin. Robby progressed to more complicated school songs and could play a pleasant rendering of Early One Morning, including a simple left-hand harmony, when he was nine. In a more prosperous, fortunate household, the two boys would have been sent to a good teacher to develop their latent gifts. No such blessings were available to Angus or Robby - luxuries like developing talent were impossible where pennies had to be wrested with hard work. Later, hard times saw the piano carted away by a slick dealer for a comparatively paltry sum. Now, the Chepworth Street piano gave Robby a second chance to practise when maestro Edward was out, and to figure out the more difficult harmonies he heard on the radio, and learn the scales, the meaning of minor and major keys, and the best way to finger the notes. The fact that he could not read music failed to dishearten him - Art Tatum, famous jazz pianist, was blind, and many other jazz pianists could not read music. Charlie Kunz played every week on the radio and became popular nation-wide for his use of grace notes and the offbeat rhythm stress. Robby imitated him and could deceive people hearing him from a distance into thinking it was Kunz himself.

This ability to play by ear was scorned by most trained musicians. But how did music first come into being, Robby asked himself? The answer was obvious - by the sounds of the human voice. All music is played by ear at first and then noted so that other people could play it as the composer intended.

He was rearranging furniture in the shop window and Bella Wilkins was trying to sell a piano. The customer said he wished he could hear what it sounded like - neither he nor his wife could play. Bella apologised that she could not oblige them. Overhearing this conversation, Robby came out of the window.

'I'll give you a tune, if you like,' he offered. 'I'm no genius but I can give you some idea of the tone of the instrument.'

He sat down at the instrument and lifted the lid, opened the top and played a reasonably pleasant rendering of a Duke Ellington blues, following this with a quick rhythmic number, both in the style of Charlie Kunz.

Bella stood back, intrigued. This new chap was a dark horse!

'That was great,' the husband praised, 'thank you very much.'

'Yes,' his wife smiled, 'thank you very much Charlie Kunz.'

'Well, what would you do?' the man asked Robby. 'Would you go for that more modern-looking one over there or this one?'

'Is anyone going to learn to play?' Robby asked.

'Yes,' said the wife,'our daughter.'

'In that case you want a musical instrument and not a piece of furniture. I would buy this one any day - ironframe, over strung, lovely tone, and well worth the money.'

'That's good enough for me,' said the man 'What you say, Ingrid?'

'I think so too. This young man knows what he's talking about - I mean, we can't play a note. Is it in good condition?'

'Oh yes,' Robby said with complete honesty. 'All these pianos are reconditioned, repolished, and retuned, and, if necessary, re-wired before they are put up for sale. That modern one is about the same price as this, but here you have the real value - the sound.'

His disinterested honesty left them no further qualms.

'We'll have it,' said the man.

'Good,' said Bella, giving Robby a large-eyed, sweet smile. 'Will you come into the office please, and we can get things signed up.'

Robby stood up, closing both lids, and allowed the customers to wend their way out to the office. Looking up, he saw the crowd standing and looking and smiling - the secretary, Quilter, the chief clerk, a boy assistant, another of the office staff, and Manny himself. Robby's cheeks reddened and he smiled slightly at his boss. Manny grinned broadly and shouted, 'Come here, Charlie Kunz,' and Robby had the nickname for many weeks to come.

'Why didn't y' say y' could play the piano?' said Manny. 'Next time you're about when there's a piano sale, come down and play for 'em.' He winked. 'It sells 'em better when they hear them played properly.'

He felt well pleased with himself as he walked away from his boss. He was thankful that none of his listeners must have had a music sense if they believed him to be a real pianist. He was wrong. James Quilter, chief clerk, had been a drummer in his younger days at Blackpool Tower Ballroom, but he was also a proficient pianist. Why feel apologetic, Robby asked himself, about his not playing from music? How did Art Tatum manage without music? He was blind!

Next day the heavy iron framed piano was delivered to a council house in Fazakerley, at street level.

*   *   *

Ma declined Edward's invitation and said she would stay at home and prepare Sunday lunch. Church services, for Georgina, since her mother's departure, no longer had a meaningful reason for going and she and Margaret went out, as did Douglas and his mate. Edward went as usual to play the organ and Robby, being the sacrificial lamb, had already agreed to sing bass in the choir. As far as he knew, there was nothing special about the service except the choir singing to the high standards of Edward's expectations.

The Barnes's income was bolstered by a pension from their uncle whose partner their father had been in the prosperous firm of warehousemen that bore their name. You could see their warehouses from the Mersey. With such wealthy forebears the Barnes's children were financially sound, allowing Edward to take up various interests outside his church work.

Robby's first appearance in the choir was a ridiculous ordeal for him. He felt foolish dressing up in a cassock and surplice. He felt his alienation among the other choristers and tried to merge discreetly in the line of adults as they walked out singing the hymn. The congregation watched them coming in, their heads bobbing up and down from hymnbook to choir. Did he warrant the congregation's curiosity? Through the gossip news of sectarian groups, they knew that the Fergusons were living with the Barnes children. It was possible they weren't giving him a second thought!

The gods looked down and discussed his self-consciousness.

'He will learn,' they said. 'The congregation are interested in the new member of the choir, not because it is Robert Ferguson, but simply because he is new. Some of them are amused that the young choirmaster has managed to conscript a victim from the Ferguson family. Not everyone wants to join a choir.'

'But I'm sure the majority of them cannot guess the outcome of this boy's joining the choir,' said an elderly god. 'You know the old French saying - *He who is near the church is often far from God* - and I'm sure that most of you will see some truth in this saw. Robby has sown a seed, not of disbelief in God, but one of cynicism about sectarian religion. You will see. He will begin to think about dogmas and stories and the Bible itself, and that will affect his life.'

Yes, Robby secretly confessed to himself, gauche, shy, unsociable people were conceited. People were too concerned with their own affairs to bother themselves about others. That first morning in the choir he discovered a truth - reserve and reluctance to mix with others was stupid and vain. In future he would fight such reserve when it was necessary to mingle with unfamiliar groups. He even attempted in the days following to pass on his resolve to

Douglas, the colossus of self-consciousness.

Robby liked Evensong best. He found something moving in the words of the Nunc Dimittis with its perfect music. Psalm singing and prayers meant nothing to him and, it seemed, to the congregation who mouthed words like zombies looking around. Continuous repetition seemed to be the cause of lethargy. Words like *As it was in the beginning is now and ever shall be, world without end, amen,* had no meaning at all to him. His lack of things spiritual filled his brain with questions, what did the first six words mean? What was 'it'? What was *the beginning*? The beginning of the Universe The world? Christianity? The phrase *'Is now and ever shall be'* also puzzled him. Would present conditions last forever? If it meant that, then it was doubtful. In a thousand years' time the earth might be destroyed by meteorites, or overrun by rats or insects. The last four words, too, were questionable. Did they mean that the world would last forever and everyone should agree by saying Amen, so be it. Scientists knew this to be nonsense. The earth would not last in its present form forever, and, in any case, the point had already been made in the first line which meant the same as *World without end* so why say it? Did 'it' mean the beginning of the Universe - *as it was in the beginning?* This world was not as it was in the beginning. Everybody knew that in these educated days so why mumble them, every Sunday.

For all religious sects repetition seemed the kingpin of communication with God. Repeat a prayer, or praise God long enough and everything would be all right, prayers answered, wishes fulfilled, and the Almighty would look down kindly on the supplicant. If God needed constant reminders week after week throughout centuries, he must be either very deaf or absent-minded or very demanding. An Omnipotent Being, Creator of the Universe, already knew the fears, the hopes, the wishes, desires, qualities, characters, and greed of all people, without being told every Sunday morning and evening and during the week, too. If I were God, Robby thought, I'd be bored silly with all this tedious twaddle and I would refuse to listen any more. No wonder prayers were seldom answered!

Repetition could be explained in one conceivable way - people based the religion on fear. A good person was called 'God-fearing.' That was it. Fear God. The ancient Jews sacrificed lambs, doves and pigeons; the ancient Aztecs sacrificed humans; African tribes warded off evil spirits with sacrifices to appease the gods; in almost every kind of religion sacrifice was known.

His encyclopaedia had said the preaching of the prophets had been a constant protest against grosser forms of sacrifice, and after Christianity came, bloody sacrifices fell into disuse.

A saying, which was attributed by the Ebonites to Jesus, repeats the protest - 'I have come to abolish the sacrifices; and if ye do not cease from sacrificing, the wrath of God will not cease from you.'

After much thought, he decided that constant repetition of prayers, scriptures, psalms, and so forth, was no more than the modern equivalent of sacrifices - repetition warding off evil spirits and attempting to curry God's favours! Such claptrap today was ridiculous, making God an odd creature, greedy, and jealous, needing constant reassurances of faith! Jesus had been sacrificed to appease God and absolve the human race from sin. This was unacceptable to Robby. How was God a loving God if he did these things? There was no sense in naked faith,' yet he could understand the reassurance that came from a naive faith that was stubborn even in deep tragedy.

He thought of the Albert Hall as the universe, full of dust particles, some larger than others, one speck representing the earth. Imagine God as a Human Genius with the power to do what he liked with the dust particles. Might the Albert Hall be a speck of dust itself when compared with all the other buildings in the world? A sense of perspective came when you considered the Earth as a speck of dust and the universe as a larger speck. Would the Human Genius God in the Albert Hall concentrate his attention on one speck of dust simply because it happened to be Earth? The answer was No. Neither, then, would a true

God. It was arrogant of men to believe that Earth out of trillions and trillions of specks of dust at God-'s mercy would be selected by Him as special. Church religion was beyond credibility!

'He who is near the church,' said a Frenchman one time, 'is often far from God.' Since he had joined the choir, Robby had become an agnostic whereas before he had seldom given serious thought to church religion. And what about ma's Sunday School teacher? Because she had been beaten by her father, Emma had to kneel and pray for him. This illustrated a facet of church religion that was ludicrous in its knowledge of the reality of evil. The truth, too, that ma's father had been hated by his family was an anathema to the church; yet hate was a fact of human feeling given by God and without it love would be unrecognisable and valueless.

The meaningless nature of church faith was brought to light one morning after Robby's thoughtful blasphemies. The vicar began – 'Dearly beloved brethren, the scripture moveth us in sundry places' – and so on, down to - 'saying after me'; at which point the congregation comes in with the general Confession. But the vicar repeated - 'Dearly beloved brethren,' his mind wandering, and he recited, the whole ritual again, causing an uncomfortable stir among the people. The vicar had proved himself no more than a mere utterer of empty words, a doer of a monotonous job. It had always been like this in church religion - clerics with captive audiences mouthing meaningless phrases to earn a living in a little niche of power. Church religion was false, ludicrous in its dogma, and without a shred of real influence in the miseries and crimes of ordinary folk. Goodness in priests was the exception that proved the rule! Robby-'s cynicism of churchified religion remained with him for the rest of his life; but he could not guess at that time that he would gain a little benefit in his future career because of his attendance in the choir of St. Michael's Church!

CHAPTER 5

He was given a list one day of twelve names and addresses. When Manny had gone to lunch, Quilter confided in Robby that he had twelve hopeless cases.

'You'll get nothing from them so I've pushed in two or three possibles - John Bingham's clients. You might get some joy with those the rest, well, one of 'em's not paid for three years.'

'Three years?' Robby was aghast. 'How the hell does he expect ME to get anything from 'em?'

Quilter laughed. 'Take no notice. Do your best. He's thinking of making you a collector.'

'Oh, is he? I suppose I'll get a heap of rubbish?'

Quilter smiled and nodded his very baldhead. 'You can count on that, Robby. Come on, let's go up to the kitchen for a brew and a smoke.'

In the afternoon he went to a back street in a slum area, a stinking apartment house in a state of awful disrepair. Some half naked kids were playing around.

'Hey, you,' Robby called to a truant, 'does Mrs Larrigan live here?'

'Yer, mister - she's in d' front room at d' top o' d' stairs.'

The sky was overcast and the house dark inside. He ascended the black, bare stairs, trod on something soft and cursed. He went along the smoky landing to the front room. The door was ajar and he looked in. An old woman in a torn blouse and a skirt like a horse blanket was sitting on an orange box in the middle of the room. A narrow, black bedroom grate held a fire of half-burnt sticks, the blue smoke only half wreathing up the chimney. In the bay window space were blankets lay on the floorboards with a striped grey pillow, fat and wobbly.

He tapped on the door 'Mrs Larrigan?'

'Yer,' came a desolate reply. She did not turn her head but kept looking down at the bare boards of the floor.

'OK,' Robby answered, gently. 'Don't get up.' He turned and retreated downstairs. How did human beings get themselves into such a state? He remembered Sparrow Drive and knew the answer - ma and family had not been all that far away from this Larrigan destination! He looked at his list outside - 12.18s 6d. Last payment 12/3/32. Years ago! He would ask Quilter to close it as a bad debt.

'Hey, mister – y' gorralorra shit on y' boot.' It was the eight-year old truant. He looked down disgusted. By the lower step of the entrance was a rusty boot-scraper, a relic from when the houses belonged to humans with money. He scraped off the dirt then swished his boot in a mid-pavement puddle of water. He would carry a small torch in future.

He remounted his cycle and pedalled off up Everton Valley and reached Norris Green after a ten-minute ride. *The Wearin' o' the Green - They're hangin' men and women for the rent in Norris Green!*

The houses were in blocks of different styles, with gardens and trees and grass plots and bushes all landscaped by the builders. It was attractive - when the estates were built, highly praised by people who should know. Then the folk had moved in from the slums, some clean and respectable folk, happy at the prospect of living in such ideal, healthy surroundings, determined to keep up their standards of respectability. In two or three years these good type were a tiny minority with dwellings of exceptional worthiness. The majority had windows broken, cardboard filling the gaps; coal in ground-floor baths; small shops in back kitchens; greengrocers with cabbages and potatoes in stained baths; bags of faded apples in the pantry; hawkers with donkeys stabled in wash-houses, the animals' fodder being the weeds and grass in the gardens; hen-coops with chickens and hens scuffling around, pecking crumbs off the dining table; pigs in orange boxes covered with sacking; betting shops; cycle repair shops; tinkers; the kind of humanity that occupied Norris Green estates in those days, with few exceptions, could be housed in the Taj Mahal and end up in two years in a hovel not fit to breed cockroaches.

At the next call he managed to collect a shilling and wrote out the tiny receipt like Oliver Hardy, with gusto. He collected seven and sixpence all told. And back in the office

Manny said 'That's not much, Quilter, is it?'

'They were all hopeless cases,' Robby said. 'Mrs Larrigan only had an orange box and two blankets. I was lucky to get seven and six.'

'Look at it this way - it wouldn't stop us going bankrupt, would it, Quilter?' Manny smirked.

'I suppose not,' Quilter grinned.

They moved away and Quilter whispered, 'He seldom gives praise. You've done pretty well.'

'I'll say. You can close Mrs Larrigan's account as a bad debt.'

'I have done,' Quilter laughed.

When Robby first met Jonesey, the wireless engineer, in his den below stairs, he had learned a lot about the firm. The cellar workroom was a bright, warm little place with oscilloscope, voltameters, valves, soldering iron, condensers, and other things. Jonesey was small and stocky with horn-rimmed glasses, untidy hair and a permanent cigarette between his lips. Robby never discovered Jonesey's first name. Jonesey always grumbled with humour when one would expect gloom and despair.

'The last time I got a rise off Manny,' he told Robby, 'the twins were born. I'm asking him for a five-bob rise - I must buy them a wedding present - it's damned expensive, you know, a double wedding - two girls.'

The little man was engrossed in his work, a specialist radio-engineer, an elite occupation those days. He took an immediate liking to Robby and they smoked each other's cigarettes when the Dartman bosses were away. Some staff stayed to lunch and used the kitchen above Jonesey's cubbyhole. Shortly after his trial as a collector, Robby told Jonesey about Mrs Larrigan and what he had seen.

'Listen, Robby, start two people off with a small fortune each, in five years one of 'em will be a millionaire and the other a pauper. Mrs Larrigan belongs to the type that can't save money. They save nowt, invest nowt, they live day to day and have no future.'

'There's no hope for them?'

'Nah. No hope. You can't wonder at the rich having

contempt for the poor. Manny'd say that Mrs Larrigan deserves to be poor because she can't manage her own affairs. So where are you?'

'Some great misfortune may have struck her down, or something. How is it she's not on the streets? Why isn't she dead and buried? Where does she get food and rent?'

'She probably goes begging. And she doesn't pay rent. She'll be squatting. I bet the landlord still thinks he has a spare room to let.'

'How long will these things go on?'

'Things won't improve until we educate people properly or until we have a bloody revolution. Pour that boiling water on the tea, Robby, lad.'

Bella and Alma came up to join them. Alma was a happy, petite creature with a penchant for fun and games. Bella was tall, slim, and good-looking with her dark hair and large eyes, one of the highly sensible women who take responsibility in their stride and do everything efficiently. She told Robby she was not well paid. Quilter was her boyfriend's uncle. With Bella, Miss Morrison, secretary, Tom Lespargo, manager, and Quilter, chief clerk, the firm ran smoothly and they, among them, were responsible for every facet of the business; yet a misdemeanour of any kind would have meant their instant dismissal. Such conditions were normal then - the wealthy ruled, the workers worked long hours for little reward, and everyone seemed happy - except the wealthy rulers!

They were crowded into the small room. Jonesey offered to let Alma sit on his knee.

'Not on your life,' she giggled. 'I wouldn't be safe for a minute. I wouldn't mind sitting on Robby's knee.'

'What's the difference? You wouldn't be safe there, either.'

'Oh, I wouldn't mind that,' Alma laughed.

'You insulting little bitch,' Jonesey said, laughing incredulously. 'Just because he's younger than I am. I must admit, though, he's an answer to a maiden's prayer.'

On the second floor they kept the bedsteads and light furniture for easy carriage up and down. Robby and Alma worked together making up the beds for customers to see, fitting irons, adjusting springs, and lifting on the mattresses - an ideal setting for jolly romps with Alma. Innocent times they were. When Robby occasionally glimpsed Alma's thigh as she flopped onto the mattress he grabbed her suspender that held her silk stocking, and flicked it.

'Ooh!' she shrieked the first time. 'Robby! I didn't think you were a boy like that.'

Alma often rolled off the mattress and ran along the aisle between the furniture, he chasing her and catching her between two racks, she screaming faintly, he kissing her in he-man fashion.

'You're at my mercy up here, wench. There's no escape.' He would lift her and carry her back, kicking madly, to a made-up bed. Alma wriggling and giggling as he tickled her, and she showing a length of pink thigh between frilly knickers and silk stocking. The time always seemed ripe.

'Come down here, Charlie Kunz,' came Manny's voice one time. It was a piece of luck that Manny would not walk up the last flight of stairs if he could help it. 'What the hell you doin' up there?'

Robby's ardour subsided rapidly. Alma hastily adjusted her suspender and straightened her clothes. At nineteen she was a pretty little magnet for any promising lad. She had the quality of naturalness, without coquetry, without pretence, no mistrust of people she liked.

One collector, John Bingham, a canny Liverpudlian who had been at Mons, always greeted Robby and the girls with 'Up the workers!' He told Robby there'd come a time when touching forelocks, saluting officers, and licking boots would all be things of the past, like leprosy and the Black Plague. The working classes hadn't yet realised what potential power they held in their hands. He lent Robby *The Ragged Trousered Philanthropists*, the story of a group of house painters and their fight against established powers. Leftish critics had declared the book a little classic.

One month after his first experience of collecting, Robby and Manny signed a legal agreement, witnessed by

James Quilter, the bare bones of the contract being that Robert Ferguson would receive a fixed salary of £1.3s.2d. per week and would be paid 5% commission on all sums over £12 There was another clause about absence through illness or injury, the National Health Insurance Act being mentioned. Robby reckoned that at 5% he would be lucky to earn 25/- a week with the kind of clients he expected to get. Jonesey warned him that he would get a round that would be spread over Liverpool, with much cycling. The old collectors' experience gave them door-to-door collecting, persuading customers to collect their friends' money or their daughters' money, thus saving visits. They were experts at making things easy by reducing the amount of riding. But for Robby, it was as Jonesey had said, a scattered round, and he was unable to follow the example of the older men. Quilter told him he could gradually build up his round with new clients.

Robby discovered that he was covering an area of twenty square miles, from Sefton to Dingle. He organised them as conveniently as possible, certain days for certain districts, but it was a hard grind all the way, riding his bike in all kinds of weathers and whilst he was doing so, gaining nothing in financial returns.

Robby did not become really acquainted with Tom Lespargo, the manager, until later. Lespargo's great-grandfather, a Spaniard, had married an English governess. He was tall, good-looking, a sallow-faced fellow in a girl's pulp-magazine way, with curly black hair and a small black moustache. He had a ready wit and could talk himself out of any difficult situation. They gossiped that Tom Lespargo often chose the good-looking young clients because he could talk renewal accounts with them after he had spent time in bed with them when their husbands were at work. Robby doubted the rumour was true. He was to appreciate Lespargols diplomacy later.

* * *

One New Year's Eve, a house full of people, a visitor came to Flora's. Could she lay out her aged mother who had just died? It was most inconvenient but Flora immediately said she would. Had the neighbour got cotton wool and bandages, and some white hose? The woman said she had the first two items but needed white stockings. They were essential those days for the laying-out apparel, belonging to a past, mystic tradition. Margaret and Georgina volunteered to go to the draper's shop.

Nothing had been done at the neighbour's house, the corpse already showing signs of rigor mortis. The doctor had departed about fifteen minutes ago, said the woman.

'Take all the bedclothes off,' said Flora, 'and her nightdress. Some hot water, please, and soap, flannel and towel.'

The family members hurried around getting these things. Flora removed the old woman's dentures, closed her eyes, and placed damp pads over them. She straightened the limbs not without some difficulty, washed out the mouth when the water came, cleaned up the nostrils, then the face, replaced the dentures, and closed the mouth before giving it support with a wide bandage wrapped three times round the jaw and head. She then quickly washed the body, trimmed fingernails and toenails, inserted small plugs of cotton wool up the nostrils and in the ears, then, the most unpleasant tasks, packed the rectum and vagina with absorbent wool to prevent discharges. The wedding ring was removed and given to the daughter, and a clean nightdress put on the corpse.

'We'll tie the ankles when the girls come back,' Flora said. 'We need a clean, new sheet, if possible, and a clean pillowcase, and then we shall have to wait. In another half hour you must take the bandage off around the jaw because the mouth will stay closed then. And if I were you, Mrs Connelly, I would brush her hair and make her tidy.'

'God bless you, luv. You're an angel. I don't know how I'd have managed without you.'

'At times like these, Mrs Connelly, we should help one another,' said Flora.

It was not easy for the girls on New Year's Eve to find a shop that stocked white stockings precisely for performing the Last Offices. They entered several shops, explaining what they required and why. The last draper, an old-fashioned man in an old-fashioned shop, said he had the very thing they wanted.

Back at the neighbour's house Flora pulled on the pure white stockings over the old woman's scrawny legs and then, using a wide strip of bandaging made from a torn sheet, she placed the feet together and bound the ankles tightly. She placed the woman's wrinkled hands on her bosom one on top of the other.

'There you are, Mrs Connelly, the poor old soul is ready for the undertaker.'

The two young girls shivered within themselves. They could never do what Flora had done, fully realising that it needed a self-effacing nature and a deeply caring insight into people's grief and woe. The girls had never realised this aspect of Flora before.

*   *   *

After living in a house for some time an occupant's opinion may change from a first favourable impression to a more realistic one. From the females,' point of view, Chepworth Street house was not easy. There was plenty of washing to be done in the utility out-house and the girls had to do the ironing, and they grumbled at the number of shirts, Edward using a clean shirt every other day, Douglas twice a week, and Robby always maintained that one a week was enough as he didn't perspire very much. There were too numerous cubbyholes and rooms to be dusted each week; there were no fitted carpets, merely linoleum, carpet squares, and rugs. These loose pieces had to be lifted every time and taken into the backyard, thrown over the clothesline and beaten. The kitchen and scullery were quarry-tiled and had to be scrubbed. A coal-cellar down a flight of stone steps, a future refuge from bombs, was restocked with coal which the coal-dealer emptied down a round hole in the pavement outside the front door, its grid-cover removed and refastened by a chain once replaced. The coal was brought up in scuttles by the boys. Labour-saving devices were unknown to Emma. There was a fire-boiler in the washhouse, dolly tubs, a corrugated scrubbing board against which the clothes were rubbed vigorously, such a board having a happier life in later years as a percussion instrument in a skiffle group. The heavy, wood rollered mangle with a wrought-iron wheel as big as a bicycle wheel had a wooden handle used by Emma or the girls to squeeze out the water from the clothes. The ironing was done on old blankets folded and stretched across each end of a white deal table in the kitchen. Three flat irons were used, heated on the gas stove in the scullery, and the girls used them in turn as they cooled off.

Backache was Emma's regular problem. She had a prolapse of the womb but sought no medical help until years later. It was caused by her being on her feet much too soon after having her children, and by years of prolonged standing behind the counters of her shops.

Emma's feet were a ghastly sight, bunioned and crooktoed, with weak ankles and corns, the original cause of these painful conditions being a necessity in childhood to wear her sister's shoes and by outgrowing her own whilst waiting for Maggie to grow out of hers.

These chores and pains did not detract from Emma's gladness in living there for she knew it was a haven of good fortune. Yet her tolerance to pain could not override the irritation she sometimes felt at Edward's high-handed treatment of his sister. On one occasion Edward wished to invite some guests whom he wanted to impress. Emma agreed that a good impression should be made and that the meal should be served in the back parlour, an attractive, cosy, square room for privacy. Emma suggested that Georgina should be included in this little dinner-party. Edward declared coldly that the guests were not Georgina's friends, but his, rousing disgust and indignation in Emma's mind. On the night Edward enjoyed with his friends a first-class dinner, leaving his sister to eat in the kitchen with the Ferguson family.

'I'm very annoyed, Georgina,' Emma said. 'He has no need to put on airs and graces and refuse to let his only sister meet his friends.'

'Listen, ma,' said Georgina, earnestly, 'I don't WANT to be with them. I wouldn't go if he begged me. I'd much rather be here with you.'

Through the years Emma had bought all her clothes from Jane Murphy and she continued to do so. One time she bought an excellent bargain for Margaret of a good quality garment which had belonged to Jane's niece, a garment hardly worn more than three times by that fortunate young lady. With their living standards so much improved, the Fergusons were burgeoning out into a well-dressed, happy family. Most of the time harmony ruled their lives. On paydays Margaret called in at the sweetshop on the way home from Littlewoods Mail Order Firm and bought ma a quarter of sweets or chocolates. Then she handed over the rest of her pay and received back 2/6d pocket money and her daily train fare of 2½d to Exchange Station return.

Douglas was the occasional disruption to the peace and happiness. He always had highly polished shoes, carefully brushed hair, and clean nails. He hoarded his ties in a locked drawer to prevent Robby from borrowing them and turning them into pieces of twisted rags. Tommy Hurst, a regular visitor, was tall and giggly with his permanent expectations of comedy when in Douglas's company. Douglas's irate expressions of hates sent Tommy into chuckling convulsions.

The two of them could manage to go to a cinema twice a week and have an occasional supper after the show. They often went to the park, trying to click with the girls, and several times they took out a rowing boat for twopence to follow laughing girls in other boats in the middle of the lake.

Tommy was seated one evening waiting for his friend to get ready. Douglas's shoelace had over tied itself, or some such triviality, and his language assailed the ears of Margaret who was sitting on the edge of the kitchen table swinging her legs.

'Stop your filthy language,' she called to Douglas. 'It's all unnecessary.' Douglas came in and immediately brought his shoe down hard on Margaret's knee and she screamed out and started to cry. This was too much for Tommy. Doug had gone too far this time.

'Hey! Doug,' he shouted. 'That's not on! You've really hurt her this time.'

'She should keep her big mouth shut,' snarled Douglas.

Georgina put her arm around Margaret. 'You damned great bully!' she stormed. 'You wouldn't take on anybody your own size!'

'No, it's not on,' said Tommy. 'There was no call for that.'

'It's my business if I want to swear,' Douglas growled.

'And it's our business if we don't want to listen,' said Georgina. 'You're a bad-tempered devil, and no mistake.'

The gods, looking down, were very annoyed. 'That wretch has hurt his sister badly,' said a young god. 'Yes,' his elder agreed. 'I fear greatly that that youth has the ghost of old Foulkes writhing inside him, the wretched creature!'

'Come on you,' Douglas ordered Tommy, 'let's get out of this.'

'Terribly sorry, girls,' said Tommy as he went out, and they heard Douglas growl as they went down the hall, 'What the hell have you gotta be sorry about, you silly sod?'

In quieter moments the two boys discussed the girls they had been out with. The two girls did not believe they were as successful as they pretended.

*　　*　　*

Bella and Norris were going to the old Roan for lunch on Wednesday. Would he like to go? Robby said he would, knowing his ma would be shopping in town with Mrs Barker and he would be alone in the house. They took the bus from Aintree tram terminus and spent a friendly hour or so over beer and sandwiches. Norris got onto the subject of

his job as warder in Walton Prison. There were all kinds of
rackets going on, he said, and the hardened criminals in the
tough wings could teach first offenders - by contact during
exercise or by hearsay - more in six months than they could
learn in six years outside. Everybody kowtowed to the big
league criminals who had power inside and outside. No one
ever grassed on them because they were scared of
recriminations once they were released. Prisons always had
many types - homosexuals, petty thieves, thugs,
intellectuals, murderers, tramps, layabouts, drunks,
psychopaths, and many of them believed they were
victimised and were innocent.

'Prison's no answer to anything,' Norris maintained.

'You should know,' said Robby, 'but what else is
there?'

'I don't know,' said Norris.

Bella insisted that they talk about something more
pleasant, she had heard enough about prisons.

'She always says that,' Norris grinned. 'I can never put
the world to rights.'

'We haven't time to put the world to rights,' Bella said.
'Not even a bit of it.'

Norris had a boxer's nose but it was a natural flatness
owing nothing to the noble art. His smile consisted of two
creases running from the corners of his mouth to disappear
at the sides of his nostrils - the smile was a kind of sardonic
disbelief described without words. He was smiling now as
he said, 'I believe you play piano?'

'By ear,' Robby said, without enthusiasm. 'Let's talk of
something more pleasant.'

Bella laughed at the repetition of her words. 'I think he
plays well.'

'Chalk and cheese,' Robby said. 'When I hear and see a
real pianist I groan. I would have benefited from lessons
when young but we couldn't afford such a luxury.'

'Well, I'm no Solomon,' Norris tittered, 'but I can give
you a few tips when we get back to Bella's. She has a nice
piano, part of the furnished flat.'

'Oh? That's unusual,' Robby said.

'Yes,' Bella agreed. 'I left home under a cloud. Mother hates him, I'd have you know.' She nodded towards Norris.

'That is a mutual feeling,' he said, his smile more sardonic.

'After some scenes,' Bella continued, 'I got fed to the teeth,' found this flat within easy reach of work, packed my bags and I've lived there for three months now. It isn't a West End mews, but it suits me. I shan't go back home.'

Just before afternoon closing-time they left the inn and when they reached Bella's flat the first thing Norris said was, 'May I invite you, maestro, to play something?'

'No,' Robby declined, 'I'd rather not play in front of a musician of your stature.' Norris's crinkled smile was there again. He lit two cigarettes and gave one to Robby.

'Play the piano part for Rhapsody in Blue,' he grinned.

Bella had gone into the kitchen to make coffee. They heard her tinkle of laughter.

'Rhapsody in Blue?' Robby scorned. 'You're crazy. I can't play it without orchestra.'

'Play anything you like, I'll criticise,' said Norris.

'Obviously you're green with envy because Bella said I was good.'

'She knows nothing about music,' Norris said, very loud.

'I heard that,' Bella called. 'I took lessons as a child.'

'That's no criterion of whether you're musical or not.'

Robby reluctantly played Body and Soul in the way he had seen Edward playing it.

'That's pretty good,' Norris said, a flicker of amusement round his nose again. 'You should play the melody with your fingers more, not your thumb. I'll render you a piece - asunder.'

Robby let Norris sit down. Robby immediately recognised the difference in Norris's sound.

'I always sigh sick fully,' Robby laughed, 'when I hear music played properly. And disillusioned. I could spit.'

'Don't spit,' Norris grinned. 'Lots of jazz-men never learnt a note of music.'

'Like Art Tatum,' Robby suggested.

'Yer, marvellous,' Norris agreed.

Bella's sister arrived about four-thirty. She was tall and well built and pretty. Bella introduced her as her favourite sister, two others being married and older than Bella. Stella smiled shyly and after a while her attractive, placid, tentative nature appealed to Robby. She agreed to whatever Bella and Norris suggested. Looking through the newspaper Norris said King of Kings was showing locally. They'd go and see it. That was how Robby and Stella met and began to see each other regularly. That was why on one half-day closing Robby was invited to meet the parents, Mr and Mrs Wilkins. That was why there was much heart-searching and pain in years to come after the war. Stella Wilkins had fallen in love with her sister's friend on that first meeting. The sadness was that her sister's friend had not fallen in love with her!

*　　*　　*

Henry Wilkins was a chubby man with prominent eyes, pouched redly to match his cheeks.

'Collecting debts is a tough job,' Robby said.

'You've got a lot of bad'uns then?'

'Two-thirds are OK. I can't catch the rest of them.'

'Can't understand that - won't even pay when they have money. By the way'– Henry lowered his voice and glanced at the kitchen door - 'is our Bella happy?'

'Oh yes. Bella's always nice and pleasant. Seems to enjoy life.'

'D'y' think she'll marry Norris eventually?'

'I do. He's asked me to be his best man when the time comes.'

'I'd love to see her married - but I don't think mother would.'

'It'll be a morning wedding,' Robby told him. 'We've all got to be at work at nine.'

'Aye, I see,' said Henry, sighing. 'I wish I could be there.'

From the kitchen they could hear the scrape and tinkle of pans and plates and gravy sizzling, a muffled word or two between mother and daughter. When Florence Wilkins opened the door to pour off water from the potatoes down the drain, there came a scream from Stella's mother, and then a huge pup-hound, weighing a hundredweight, bounded in happily and leapt on Robby. His comfortable rocking chair was thrown back, his feet lurched into the air, and there was a crashing bump onto the wall at the back of him.

'God!' he gasped, struggling up.

'Get out! Get out! You darned nuisance!' Henry grabbed the dog's collar and dragged it out the way it had come.

'Mother, be more careful, love. He's just knocked Robby flying.'

'Oh?' said Mrs Wilkins, very annoyed. 'And whose fault is that? You should have locked him in the shed, shouldn't you? I can't do everything - make dinner and watch the dog.' Robby righted the rocking chair and sat down again. The stars were vanishing slowly. Stella, half smiling, came to the kitchen door and asked if he were all right. 'Yes, thank you,' he said, putting his hand to the back of his hand. It felt warm and wet. Stella went back into the kitchen. Henry returned and sat down.

'Sorry about that darned dog. He causes more trouble than he's worth. He's only a pup yet, that's why. He's always full of enthusiasm for strangers.'

'Hm,' Robby murmured, looking down at his red fingers.

'Are you all right?' Henry frowned, seeing the blood.

'Yer, I'm fine, thanks,' Robby murmured.

'D'you get every Wednesday afternoon off, then?' said Henry, resuming conversation.

'Yes, except when there's a soccer match.'

'They've got a team then?'

'Oh yes - and a pretty good one. I play right-half.'

'I never knew they had a football team.'

'We're top of the Wednesday league,' said Robby.

The back door opened again, Mrs Wilkins screeched

'No!' and the huge pup bulldozed its way through again, and leapt for the second time, all within two seconds. The chair crashed over, Robby's head hit the wall again and the dog stood over him licking his face where the blood began to trickle.

'Gerroff, you bloody great thing! Gerroff!' Robby shouted, pushing the dog savagely away. Mrs Wilkins's voice came, distantly through all the stars, 'Well! What language! Disgraceful!'

'Come here,' Henry roared, grabbed the dog, hit it twice and dragged it out again, this time locking it in the shed. It scratched and barked and whimpered all the time from then on. Blood poured down the side of Robby's face.

Fuming with rage, he got up dizzily and righted the chair. He loathed all bloody, stupid, slavering, stinking, untrained dogs! Stella came again, annoyed and horrified, too.

'Good heavens!' she gasped, 'you're bleeding!'

'Yer,' he said, unable to conceal his rage. 'They were two nasty bangs on the wall.'

'Mother,' Stella called, 'Robby's head's bleeding badly. Where's the first-aid?' Mrs Wilkins seemed more irritated this time. 'Oh - it's in the corner cupboard. I told you, Henry to lock the dog in the shed in the first place.'

Stella carefully moved the hair aside, washed away the blood, put ointment on the wound, and covered it with a plaster.

'Thanks,' Robby murmured, cooling down slightly. It isn't much. It was just the shock.'

'I know,' she whispered. 'Why she needs a big, rough thing like that - and he eats like a donkey. Are you feeling all right?'

'Yes, thanks. It's nothing serious.'

'Right, everybody - dinner is being served. Sit round,' came Mrs Wilkins' voice from the kitchen. She brought in the meat and vegetables and doled them out onto the plates. They all sat down without a word for a whole, stark, hostile minute.

Then Mrs Wilkins said, irritably, 'Well? Did you do it?'

'Yes,' Stella answered her 'There's a cut about two inches long. I put ointment on it to stop the bleeding, and a plaster.' There were no apologies. 'Oh well, it's not so bad. Everybody start else it will go cold.' She took her first mouthful and then looked up. She tutted furiously. 'Dear me! Just look at that wall!' They all turned and looked at the smear of blood behind the rocking chair. 'That will never wash off properly! I told you to put the dog in the shed.'

'Don't bother about it now, mother,' Stella said, embarrassed in front of her visitor.

They ate in silence for a while and then Mrs Wilkins said, harshly, 'Do you swear a lot?'

'What?' Robby asked, his thoughts far away in no-woman's land.

'Do you swear a lot?'

'Oh, mother,' Stella said, very annoyed. 'Of course he swore when the dog knocked him over twice. It was the shock. You'd swear if the dog knocked you over and made your head bleed.'

'I would never swear,' said Mrs Wilkins, vehemently.

'Now, mother,' said Henry, gently, 'I think you would, you know.'

'I would never swear,' Mrs Wilkins insisted, with venom. 'If a person can't control his temper and language, I don't think much of him!'

'And I don't think much of people who can't control their dogs, either,' said Robby, grim and angry. Stella almost choked on a forkful of potato as her laughter bubbled up.

'Do not laugh over the dinner-table,' her mother snapped, all twisted inside herself.

'Sorry,' said Stella, giving Robby an amused glance. He was eyeing her mother under his brows, his face red, his look full of intense dislike.

Norris was right - do good by stealth and hope to find it fame, was the way Norris had put it.

Tip-toeing to an invalid neighbour in early morning for the sake of anonymity when everybody would be getting ready for work and, she hoped, watching her through their

windows as she placed flowers or fruit on the doorstep and
hurried away afterwards in pseudo modesty; being told on
Friday evenings by Henry that he thinks he'll go a walk with
his two married sons, returning around ten-thirty, bleary-
eyed, and Mrs Wilkins enquiring, 'Did you have a nice
walk, boys? and Henry saying, 'Aye, mother, we did,' and
the sons keeping their mouths closed in case their mother
smelt their breaths the result of four or five pints of ale they
had swigged at a pub five miles away, in case the
neighbours might see them in a local and inform their
mother. Florence Wilkins knew they enjoyed their booze,
but like the Victorian women before her, she preferred to put
on an act of respectability and pretend a perfect decorum of
a saintly family.

Before leaving with Robby, Stella dutifully helped her
mother to clear away and wash dishes. Henry went to the
front door with them, and whispered to Robby, 'Let's hope
when you come next time, lad, it'll be more enjoyable.' If it
depends on me, Robby thought, there won't be a next time.

* * *

Bella's wedding took place at Walton parish church on
a dreary wet morning. Quilter gave Bella away, making
himself her uncle in the process. Robby was Best Man,
Stella and Alma the Bridesmaids, Jonesey and Miss
Morrison sat in the pews with two of the lads from
Dartman's.

'Hey, Robby, glance across the road,' Norris whispered
as they entered the church, 'it's the old ghoul noseying,
putting her curse on us.'

A casual, sidelong glance showed Robby Florence
Wilkins' stocky figure in a doorway, watching the
proceedings. Why on earth didn't the woman let bygones be
bygones and come to the wedding if she was so interested?

They all had to be at work after changing their clothes.
Stella to her branch post office, Norris to his prison, the rest
to Dartman's half a mile down the main road. It had been a

sparse wedding; a very unorthodox ceremony, no reception, no honeymoon, no frills, but bride and groom were working, with reasonable incomes, and these were the main considerations. As the months rolled away, the union of Bella and Norris was a success, and Florence Wilkins was peeved indeed!

*　*　*

Angus had now become an expert labourer in the rubber works. The wages were reasonably generous, compared with elsewhere, and on that account he suffered the unsavoury work willingly. Before synthetic rubber came into being, the mere smell from the open windows of the works in summer made some tender-bellied people feel sick. In those pioneer days synthetic rubbers were being experimentally used. Archie Dickson said that they had taken over in almost a hundred different products, though natural rubber had certain advantages, in Archie's opinion - it was resilient and elastic, resisted tears and cuts, it was good for processing, and could reasonably maintain its elasticity at low temperatures. But synthetics were superior, he said, in resisting deterioration by organic solvents and oils. They also resisted ageing and had a low permeability to liquids and gases.

'We don't call 'em synthetics,' Archie said. 'We call 'em Elastomers - it just means having rubbery properties.'

Angus was walking with his cousin one Sunday morning across Vicar's Fields.

'Synthetics make it a filthy job, Archie, I know that. I feel it's unhealthy.'

'I know, son, I've been there,' Archie laughed. 'Elastomers haven't made the job easier.'

'It's my ambition to get out - start on my own and be my own boss. That's my main goal,'

The job was difficult and hazardous. There were many powdered materials and pigments used as reinforcing agents to be blended in with the rubber, modifying its stiffness, strength, and resistance to abrasion. Carbon blacks, zinc oxides, clay, calcium silicate, and magnesium carbonate were used. Whiting and barium sulphates were used as fillers. Many of these became fugitive when moved, brushed and shovelled. Neither the industrialists nor their workers were aware that there might be a risk to health in the constant inhalations of these many varied toxic chemicals, especially carbon dusts, although Angus gave no signs that he was affected in any way. But Archie privately feared the possibility that they could be harmful. Apart from the toxic elements, the workers on calendars. extruders, and other heavy plant found the environment a Satan's palace.

Before Ronald was born it had been the weekend custom of Angus, Gwen, Willis, and Harriet, Gwen's elder sister, to go long walks into the country, Angus delighting in breathing the gloriously fresh country air of which he was deprived in his work. Such exercise and deep breathing kept him healthy. He continually exercised his brain, too, to conjure up ideas for releasing himself from his work. but nothing materialised. The coal business had failed and he was sometimes despondent in thinking that no other such openings would develop. Then, with the coming of his baby son, parental responsibilities forced an acceptance of his grim routine. But he lived in a modern house in healthy, pleasant surroundings. He had a young son and a pretty wife and good friends. These blessings when he compared them with his previous existence in Liverpool, were something to cling to and cherish. He believed he had taken one or two progressive steps up the ladder of social graces and he owned his own house, and these were accomplishments that his family had not achieved and probably never would!

*   *   *

Since Robby's employment at Dartman's had begun there were some frightening developments in world events - Hitler's rise, the Italians in Abyssinia, the Spanish Civil War, the abdication of the new king Edward VIII after only forty-six weeks and three days on the throne. But the poor have little sense of history and what seemed a disturbing event one month was forgotten the next. People were engrossed in living from day to day at a time when employment was a boon and the threat of unemployment the Sword of Damocles. Robby was to see the Sword hanging over his head once that disastrous year of 1936 had gone.

On a cold wet day in January 1937 Robby struggled on his bicycle against the elements, his waterproof cape sodden and no longer a shield against the bitter, lashing rain; and then the puncture away out in the wilds! The awful frustration and the cursing and the relentless despair, with his round of calls incomplete, and having to walk through the downpour, pushing his cycle to the nearest cycle shop. He cursed life and all its miseries. Those four miles were the most completely devastating miles he had ever experienced.

It was on closing time at the shop when he arrived, soaked to his entire body. He placed his cycle by the front door and walked, dripping to the office. Manny stood outside the door.

'Where the hell have you been, Ferguson?' Manny bawled. The employee was no longer Charlie Kunz, responsible for the sale of at least a dozen pianos.

'I had a puncture out in Netherton,' he said, loudly. 'I had to walk four miles to a bloody cycle shop. I'm soaked.'

'How much have you got in?'

'I don't know. I had to miss twenty calls.'

'Y' what?' Manny's eyes blazed. 'What the hell d'y' mean by that? How much did y' collect?'

'I said I didn't know - over twelve.'

'Twelve pounds? That's not bloody good enough, lad. D'y' want y' cards, eh?' Robby felt full to the throat. Jesus! The man could see what a state he was in! Tom Lespargo came out of the office, sensing something was amiss.

'If you can do any better,' Robby shouted, having reached the last straw of ignominy, 'go and bloody well do it and see if you like getting soaked to the bloody skin and on a worn out bike that doesn't belong to the firm!'

Manny roared. 'You what? Who the hell y' talking to? You insolent young bastard! Lespargo, get him out of here. Get his cards!' Manny stormed into his office, shaking the partitions by the way he slammed the door.

The gods were very sorry. They could see even from that distance that Dartman had no cause to behave in that inhumane way just because he had lost the argument this morning with Eli.

'Give us y' cash,' Lespargo whispered, 'and y' receipt book. Go upstairs and have a cuppa. I'll have a word with Mr M.' He hurried into the office after Manny.

Upstairs the other collectors were sitting around sipping tea. They all eyed him sadly. They could still hear Manny shouting from the office below their feet, 'I'm buggered if I will!' Occasionally Lespargo and Quilter said things they could not hear clearly.

'By Jesus, son, you've put the cat among the pigeons,' said John Bingham, the Marxist. 'Here, Arthur,' he told another ex-serviceman collector, 'wash my cup and get Robby some cha.' He eyed Robby up and down. 'You look soaked to the skin, lad.'

'Yer,' Robby sighed, shivering. He would be leaving all these decent fellows after Lespargo had settled his wages. And what would his poor ma say?

'Is it definitely the sack?' Arthur Biggs asked, seriously, coming back with the tea.

'Yer,' Robby murmured.

'There'll come a time,' Bingham said, 'when he won't dare talk to an employee like that. When workers realise that the fruit is ripe for plucking, then the sparks'll fly. And whose been financing that sod Hitler, eh? Not the Russians, that's for sure. Not the Japs or the Chinese - they've got their own war. Nor the French - and Germany was skint. I'll tell y' - WE have. OUR bloody Establishment have financed Hitler. And why? Because he's a bloody bulwark against the Communists. That's why. Eighty percent of ordinary folk know there'll be a war, the way Hitler's moving, but not Mr Bloody Chamberlain, nor the Daily Mail, nor the Express.'

Robby was half listening as he supped his tea. Each man in

that group felt deep pity for him and fear for themselves. Their turn might come next for they all knew that Manny had been in a fuming mood all day, only half knowing the reason for it. The mere whims of bosses were something to be

It was half an hour before anything happened, the front door having been locked by Bella. Tom Lespargo called upstairs, 'Robby, come down please.'

Robby met Bella at the bottom of the stairs. She smiled sadly and whispered, 'Robby, I'm terribly sorry.'

'Thanks,' he murmured, and went towards the office.

Lespargo put his arm round Robby's shoulder, confidentially, and entered the customer's office.

'I've had a word with Manny,' he whispered. 'He'll be in, in a sec. He demands a full apology. Mind what you say. Apologise first. He's agreed to overlook your remarks if you do.' Just then, Manny came in, a kind of incredulous smirk on his face.

'Well?' he growled.

'Mr M.,' Robby said, with a terrible effort of restraint, 'I'm very sorry for what I said. I was absolutely soaking wet - still am - I'd had a puncture and hadn't time to finish my round. I intended calling on them on Monday. I'm very sorry.'

'OK Never mind that now. Mr Lespargo and Mr Quilter have had a very serious word with me and this is what I propose to do for y' - at the end of the month you'll pack up collecting. You'll come into the office and look after the accounts - you'll be responsible to Mr Quilter.'

'Yes, thank you Mr M.'

'Never have I had people talk to me like that before - but - well, I realise now you were at the end of y' tether - we'll make allowances - the weather, the puncture - and listen, y' should carry an outfit, shouldn't y'? You forgot, didn't y'?'

'Yer. I forgot to get a new one.'

'Make sure you get to those clients on Monday first thing - OK?'

'Oh yes, I will.'

'So that's it then. We'll forget all about it. First o' February y' start in the office at thirty shillings a week all right?'

'Thank you Mr M.'

'Young Smart will take over from you.'

'OK Mr. M.'

'Right - get y' money and go home. Get those wet clothes off and have a hot bath.' Manny took out his white handkerchief and blew his nose loudly as he walked back into his office, sweetly, subdued, relaxed, and feeling that he had been magnanimous, which was true from his position.

'Thanks, Tom,' Robby said, taking Lespargo's hand, 'don't know how you did it, but thanks.' Lespargo laughed. 'Well, let's say, it wasn't easy. But you know what they say about me - I talked the tail of the Manx cat.'

The manager put his arm round Robby's shoulders again and guided him out of the office like a father. Robby received his wages and commission, said goodnight to all his friends, soberly mounted his cycle, and pedalled home, shivering all the way.

Well, he thought, as he lay soaking in a hot bath, he had escaped the miseries of the unemployment exchange, thanks to his friends, Lespargo and Quilter. What in hell had Lespargo said to Manny Dartman? That he would never know.

*   *   *

Malcolm was now working at his father's old firm, Grant's Granaries, where he would, during the blitz, join their fire-fighting service. Every time he moved another sack the rats came scuttling out. He detested rats. As he cleared the area of shiny, smooth floorboards and got nearer the wall, the grain spilled out more quickly, the larger holes becoming more evident in the sacks nearer the wall. He was used to the rodents now. They did not give him goose pimples as they used to do when he first came to Grant's. He never forgot that day on the S.S. Vestris when he had seen a rat streaking across the galley floor. He had stood for ten seconds cold and petrified. But he was young then.

Fay would be at ma's again this afternoon with the lads. Hope she gets home at a reasonable hour. She missed the last tram one time - probably more than once. The lads were going to bed much too late. It wasn't good for them. I must have a word with Fay. I'll have to go down to the storeroom and get some more bags. All rats should be exterminated, but the rat-catchers never seemed able to get rid of the horrible things. They do millions of pounds worth of damage throughout the country? Why didn't they get rid of them?

He came back with the sacks and started to shovel with the wooden spade all the grain the rats had freed out of the gnawed sacks. As he worked he whistled in his tuneless, windy way a number from The Broadway Follies, an old film they had seen when Fay's ma had looked after the kids – *'Talk about your Broadway dollies, that you don't see in the follies'* - and his mind, ignoring the tune, ranged over a series of memories that gave him no comfort.

It was a pity that business in Norris Green had not turned out as they'd expected. Given a fair chance they could have built up that business. The rent was too damned stiff and Fay having the kids, too. It had been difficult. Nothing was ever easy in this life. Remember that other shop opposite the presbytery - Fay and he getting ready to open, watching priests tucking in. Bottles of wine they had, great plates of meat and potatoes and veg, huge puddings in basins and great blue jugs of custard. The fathers fairly enjoyed their food! Yes, that shop had been ma's attempt, he appreciated, to help Fay and him.

Now he was down to this, labouring with Grant's Granaries. The wages were fairly good - that was the trouble really - the better the screw the fouler the work, like Angus in the rubber. If his adult life had been as good as his school days he'd be top of the world! If people stopped influencing him he could be a great success.

Angus was successful in a way because he was lucky.

Getting away to Leyland after that credit drapery fiasco, held escaped living with that bloody witch Helman. He was lucky getting that bedroom suite and all that other stuff from Gwen's father. Yes, Angus was always lucky. His ideas were always too big though, that was his trouble. His ideas were too big and he hadn't the patience to do things by degrees, or wait a bit, go step by step. And, by God, we used to fight in the old days, before I went to sea. Vicious fights they were, and poor old ma coming at us with the sweeping brush trying to separate us. Angus always wanted to dominate and I wouldn't let him. I was stronger than he was. He thought he was the main one after father died wanting to rule the roost all the bloody time, that was his trouble, and when Alec came Angus hated it because he wasn't the main one. Aye Alec destroyed the pecking order all right! He wasn't a bad old stick, really, and it was all rubbish the stories Angus told about Alec. Angus was like that - dirty anyone's name to get his own way. Never knew why ma always favoured Angus. You couldn't say he'd been especially good to her. It's always the case in families - the prodigal Son and all that. No sense in it, really.

Should be dinnertime soon. Good idea of Fay's to mix the sugar, condensed milk and tea like that, making a little block. When the whistle goes I'll get down to the kitchen for the hot water quick, and plop the block in the can before the water goes off the boil. I'm not eating in the canteen, although things have improved since father's day. I couldn't afford to pay for a meal every day, although they're pretty cheap.

But they can still think I don't go to the canteen because of father and the poisoning. I'm not telling them I can't afford it. I suppose, though, you could catch food poisoning anywhere, in a posh hotel sometimes. Remember those hoboes who came to do the washing-up in that big hotel in the States? They'd give anyone food poisoning. Dirty sods they were until the chef told them to take their coats off, leave 'em in the yard, and wash themselves. The hoboes hadn't liked that. The chef was all against employing hoboes. The management got the work cheap -a good meal

171

and a dollar a week. Some of them were lazy bastards. They'd always be out of work and on the roads, even with no depression. They were a stinking lot!

Ah, the whistle! Now for my slap-up meal of cheese and tomato sandwiches. The bloody rats will smell the cheese. I'll go for the water and sit with the other two lads. The rats'll steal the food from your mouth if you let them!

Will there be a war? I wouldn't mind joining if there was, if Fay'd let me. I don't think she would for a moment though. She'd be all against it. Let the younger ones go, she'd say. In any case, this job'll be reserved occupation - the boss more or less said so - feeding the troops and all that.

Angus's letter to ma said Baxter's Rubber works are making thousands of gas masks, just in case. God! It must be awful to be gassed! Uncle George used to talk about some pals of his who got gassed. Hitler's getting away with murder because we can't stop him. The world's always in a bloody state! That sod Mussolini and the poor bloody Ethiopians. If there is a war. Robby, Doug, and Ted Barnes'll be called up, poor little buggers. Hope they'll come through all right. None of our family ever joined anything. Ted Barnes should fit in well with army life, an officer in the Boys' Brigade and all that. He probably loves regimentation. He might even land a commission and our lads will have to salute him! That'd be damned funny. No, none of our family has had experience in anything like that. Angus would be hopeless in the army. He couldn't stand being ordered about.

Ma did well getting into Chepworth. Solved a lot of nasty problems. I felt guilty about leaving her and the kids, getting married that time, but Fay was insistent. Ma seems very happy at Chepworth. Georgina's a nice kid. She and Margaret make good friends. I hope my kids get some good friends when they grow up. They must make a success of life and not get all thwarted like their poor old dad. They may turn out to be like Archie Dickson. He's damned clever, getting a degree and all that. My lads could win scholarships. I must make 'em work real hard at school. I did well at school, but there weren't the chances those days that there are now. No one can ever say I haven't worked hard all my life - but I never seem to get anywhere. I'll make sure my lads get somewhere. You can never tell with kids. Sometimes you can show them the water but they may not want to drink.

This tea's good and strong - the cheese is a bit mouldy. No overtime tonight now they're changing everything. I did wonder why they're suddenly changing everything over, but I think I know now. There IS going to be a war. The poor bloody man in the street never knows what's going on apart from what he reads in the papers, and they vary all over the place, some say this and some say that. The Echo puts it straight there will be a war. That's good enough for me. Politics is the filthiest business in the world. Hiding the truth and telling lies is part and parcel of politics, damn 'em. If there is a war I could join the Merchant Navy. That would be great. I liked going to sea, away from it all, daily routine, fresh air when you're off duty, seeing foreign parts, having good mates like Peter Jackson. I wonder where he is now. That visit of his to Sleepers Hill was a great surprise. I wonder why he never kept in touch? Sleepers Hill wasn't a place you could be proud of inviting anybody to. It was better than Kirkdale but if Peter's family is like his cousins' people, they must be well off. He always said he was going to sea to get experience. I don't think he needed the money. I know why he didn't come again - we weren't posh enough for him! He didn't leave his address and obviously doesn't want to keep in touch. Ah, well! He was a good mate, old Peter.

*   *   *

Flora was pleased when Kathleen Clancy came to live with them. She was a nice young woman, Flora always thought, happy-natured and pleasant to be with, and less extrovert than her sister Sue. She always got on well with Jack which was more than you could say for Auntie Nell! It was a tremendous help when Kathleen insisted on paying much more for board and lodging than Flora had asked for. Jack was now managing a general store in a tough, Liverpool district. He had to mind himself when he brought home the money each night because the shop had no safe and the bank was always closed until next morning. There had been one or two break-ins there and it was not unusual for Jack to arrive home feeling disgruntled, a situation one could hardly imagine without horror if Auntie Nell had been there. Kate always greeted him cheerfully and soothed him down with a joke or two.

Kathleen was a good Catholic, hardly ever missing mass and always proving her genuine Christianity by deeds of kindness and generosity. Angus had fancied Kathleen at one time, when he had grown out of adolescence. She was red-haired, tall, curvaceous, had nice lips, an attractive smile, was always clean looking, and in Ireland she would have been accepted as a real, pretty colleen. She had earned the respect of all Emma's family and even of Ted and Georgina. Flora thought that Angus could have done a lot worse than taking Kathleen for wife.

It was because of Kathleen that Robby proved his efficiency in Dartman's office. One of the collectors he signed in early every evening, Robby had hardly seen before except first thing in the morning once or twice as the shop was being opened. Robby mentioned his name one night - Joe McGarrick - at Flora's and Kathleen had intervened at once.

'I used to know a Joe McGarrick,' Kathleen said. 'Dark -haired, thick-lipped, not very tall?'

'That's him,' Robby said. 'He never books in with the other chaps - always early. Unsociable type. Hardly ever speaks.'

'That's him all right.' Kathleen laughed. 'Lived next door at one time. Went to our school. He had a crush on me. Ooh! I hated him. He got done by the police one time for embezzling. How did he get a job at Dartman's dealing with money? I wouldn't trust him with our cat!'

'Oh?' Robby said, with great interest. 'Thanks Kathleen for that information. I'd better keep an eye on our friend if that's the kind of fellow he is.'

Robby remembered Kathleen's words some weeks later. Quilter mentioned that a certain client paid the correct instalment for three weeks and had then paid a shilling short ever since.

'Mrs Armstrong, Fazakerley - Joe McGarrick's client. She's a good client and it's most unlike her. She should be paying five bob a week and only pays four. It's strange.' Robby stopped work at once. 'Shall I pay her a visit and find out what's wrong?'

'No,' said Quilter. 'I don't think so. It might upset her. She's a long-standing client - her husband's a station-master.'

Robby thought it best not to press the matter. No accusations without proof.

On his free Wednesday afternoon he cycled out to the lady's address. Would she allow him to see her pay book receipts? Yes, there they were, regular receipts of five shillings a week.

'I'll show you my identity card,' he told the lady. 'I would like to take these books to the office. There is a discrepancy in the totals. Do you mind? I'll give you a receipt.'

'I don't mind at all,' Mrs Armstrong smiled. 'Give me your receipt.'

'Thank you, I'll post them back as soon as we've checked them through. One thing - please do not mention this to the collector.'

'I shan't' Mrs Armstrong agreed. 'Don't worry. He won't know anything about it.'

'Thank you,' said Robby, having a suspicion that Mrs Armstrong was guessing that there were funny goings-on and the collector was involved.

Next morning there was urgent discussion - Manny, Quilter and Robby knowing that a fraud had been perpetrated. It took an hour for Robby to discover the trick.

'I think I know what McGarrick does,' he told Manny. 'When he writes out the receipt, he uses a thick piece of card, same size as the page. The carbon copy goes through to the card - five bob. After leaving the client, he replaces the card with a bit of paper and rewrites the receipt on it with the carbon under it, but puts four instead of five. We get a series of amounts that are false. Mrs Armstrong gets her receipt for five bob but McGarrick's counterfoil shows four.'

Manny sneered. 'Smart Alec, eh, Quilter? But not smart enough for the Accounts' Department.' Quilter was honest. 'As a matter of fact, Mr M', it was Robby who cracked it.'

'Well,' Manny grinned, 'you've done a damn good job there, lad. How much has the bastard fiddled,' d'you think?'

'We can't tell at the moment, Mr M. We shall have to get his old books from the basement files - but I can estimate an approximate amount for his present clients. Looking through accounts, he apparently keeps to a rigid system, one shilling off every instalment over four bob - he doesn't touch smaller amounts. In this book of 500 receipts he has thirty clients who pay at five bob a week or over. The book lasts about four weeks - so he takes about five pounds a month. In eighteen months he's fiddled £108. From Mrs Armstrong he's fiddled seventy-eight shillings.'

That evening, Manny, Quilter, Lespargo, and Robby confronted McGarrick in the paying-in office. Manny outlined the evidence and told the collector that it was all up with him - they knew all about his fraud on the firm, and what was worse his fraud on the customer.

'I won't prosecute y' McGarrick, and y' can think y'self bloody lucky. Get y' cards and if I see your face around this area again I will prosecute you. Gerrout!'

On top of his previous conviction McGarrick would have received a severe sentence. He went off cursing, nonetheless, not recognising his luck and not blaming himself. He'd a right to bolster the paltry wages and commission he had been receiving.

After this confrontation, Manny gathered the collectors together an hour later, giving details, and praising the accounts' department. He assured them that any fiddling would soon come to light. McGarrick's round was shared out among them, according to the convenience of each address. The collectors spent about twenty minutes sorting out the allotment of clients, the outside addresses being given to young Sharp. It seemed to Robby that everyone gained except Quilter and himself - the collectors increased their income and Manny had one less man to pay!

Next morning the boss brought in a parcel. 'Here, Robby,' he ordered, 'deliver this parcel to this address.' Manny scribbled the address on a scrap of paper and folded it.

'Right, Mr M. I'll go straight away,' Robby said.

He took the parcel under his arm, removed his cycle from under the main staircase and wheeled it to the front. On the pavement he stood and unfolded the paper, wanting to know which direction he should take. On it was written 'Mr R. Ferguson, Chepworth Street.'

'God! What's all this about?' he murmured.

Emma was alone in the house. She asked him what he was doing home at that time. There was anxiety in her voice for it usually meant that anyone coming home too soon had been sacked! Robby untied the string and opened the paper and then the layer of tissue paper. Neatly folded were two beautiful suits, a grey and a brown. A tiny blemish on the grey sleeve and a bit of fading around the brown pocket, nothing more.

'Hey, just look at these suits ma. Manny has given them to me.' Emma came over and examined the suits, fingering the cloth and holding up the jackets.

'Good Lor!' Suits of this quality will have cost a small fortune, I bet. I'll get two coat hangers. Now you must look after them. It's not every day you get presents like these. And for heaven's sake don't forget to thank Manny Dartman.' Emma did not query the reason for the gifts!

Back at the office, Robby approached Manny's desk, ready to express his thanks. Immediately the boss put his finger to his lips, nodding his head towards Quilter who was making a telephone call.

'Well, did y' deliver that parcel, Robby?' Manny winked.

'Yes, sir,' Robby answered, smiling his delight and

mouthing 'Thank you.'

* * *

Stella had met Emma who had taken an immediate liking to her. Margaret and Georgina, too, had made friends and they gradually encouraged Stella to take part in all sorts of family social events. Soon everyone knew that Stella Wilkins was Going Out with Robby Ferguson. Stella especially liked the parties at Flora's place, and the humour of old pa Volant, Esther and the Clancy sisters. It was naturally assumed thenceforth that failing an earthquake, Robby and Stella would one day be married, and it played on Robby's mind on occasions.

The jackets of his new suits fitted perfectly but the trousers were a little short. Ma expertly unfastened the turn-ups, ironed out the creases and there they were, beautifully cut and smart-looking suits. Robby felt and looked very smart in them. He knew that Manny had presented him with the suits as an appreciation of his having discovered McGarrick's fraud.

By mid-1937 he had memorised about sixty telephone numbers at the office, knew the first name of many representatives from various firms, the names and addresses and circumstances of hundreds of clients, and could even use the typewriter efficiently. He enjoyed the office work away from the miseries of debt-collecting; and apart from these agreeable conditions, there was Enid. She was about eighteen, very slim and tall, and very pretty. She was a junior clerk, Canadian born, who had returned to England with her mother, her father having left them whilst they had been living in Canada.

A cyst had developed on Robby's left eyelid. Cysts grow from the inside, making a lump the size of a pea after a few months. He could no longer ignore it and Manny told him to have it cut off. For an eye specialist it was a trivial job - fold the eyelid back with tweezers to expose the growth area, pierce it, scrape out the semi-fluid secretion

and that was that - smarting for a few seconds, some eye
drops, a pad over the eye, and a bandage for a couple of
days. On the evening following this slight operation, Manny
had gone home and Quilter was upstairs drinking tea and
smoking a cigarette. Robby sat at his desk entering items in
a ledger.

His peripheral vision being blinded by the bandage,
Robby was suddenly shocked by Enid's arms around his
shoulders and her soft lips, hot and tender, over his with
such passion that he almost let his bandage slip down. He
recovered his breath and laughed.

'You little demon! Why did you do that?'

'Ooh!' she breathed in her husky voice. 'You stir me
like mad - that bandage! You're a handsome wounded
hero!'

He got up quickly and lifted her slim body onto his
desk. He put his lips to hers and she clasped him tightly to
her, enveloping him with her long thin arms, making his
head throb. Her lips seemed to draw him into her, her tongue
searching ecstatically. He remembered Maria at Aintree.

'By God, you're a beauty,' he said softly, after a while.

'You've certainly got It.'

'I hear Quilter,' she whispered. 'Let me up,'

She got down and returned to her desk.

'What about the movies tonight?' she whispered
urgently.

'Ramona at the Astoria?'

'That doesn't seem much,' he said.

'Supper late at our house – Momma's on nights at the
Infirmary.'

'OK,' he said. 'See you outside the Astoria for first
house.'

He went home that night and put on his best grey suit
and with sufficient money in his pocket, he took the tram to
the Astoria where she was waiting. The picture was all
romance but it caught Enid's attention at times and he had to
show some interest - but on the back row of the cinema what
is projected on the screen was hardly significant. Enid lived
near the cinema and they walked home towards the big

houses off Breck Road, huge rambling places converted into four flats where once the wealthy lived with servants paid £12 per annum with no beer. As they walked, Robby's senses vibrated under his bandage with anticipation of delights to come.

He was like a zombie in appearance yet full of life where it mattered, with this girl beside him a tall, slim gliding creature, a beautiful Siamese cat, mature in her understanding of the facts of life, and ready to let him share in her passion because her momma was on nights and they could have a free, private, intimate time of it alone; and he beside her, like a randy alley cat, all stirring inside with lust and desire. And she had had the sense to suggest supper first, like some society paramour of a General or Minister of Interior or Owner of some posh Night Club, not rushing into anything, doing everything with style, being civilised about it and lending zest to the whole procedure. His mind fashioned a detailed scenario for the evening - a light supper first, and gentle talk, friendly like, mature, with an occasional sophisticated, allusive remark to heighten the occasion. Then into the bedroom, she undressing slowly and saying in her sultry voice, 'Zip me down, please;' then he would follow her example, removing his suit carefully, no creasing, putting it on a coat hanger in the wardrobe; then removing his tie and shirt and vest and underpants, and they would stare at each other naked, both thrilled with what they saw, he hoped. He'd be enthralled with her shapeliness, her long slender legs with nice, round, full thighs slandering gently to those marvellously curved calves and slim ankles. Her breasts would be small, firm, healthy and round, delightful to kiss gently and touch with breathtaking care, and he would be drawn into her body and her soft, long, thin fingers would play over his muscles and stroke his body all over, tantalisingly, with her silken touch, making him wild with ecstasy; and kissing her all over and enveloping her all over with his strong, tall, muscular body and then the exquisite climax. He was in such a state he could hardly walk!

They came to the corner of the street where she lived. There was noise, a hubbub of people in the distance and a faint shout or two and when they turned the corner they saw the fire engine, the ambulance, and the police car, and a crowd of gawping people. The ambulance started off and came towards them, its bell tinkling and playing on his nerves.

'What the hell's going on?' Enid muttered, letting go of his hand. They ran to the house.

'What's happened?' she asked a bystander.

'Gas explosion,' he said. 'The old woman who owns the house was badly hurt, I believe. She's just been taken away in the ambulance. They reckon someone left the gas oven on, unlit.'

'It's not your flat, is it?' Robby whispered.

'No, it can't be - I didn't leave the gas on, unless momma did.' Enid's face was ashen, her eyes wide and ready to weep - like dripping pearls, he thought. When she made herself known to the Sergeant of police he took down details and then telephoned her mother, a sister at the Infirmary. The explosion had occurred in the old lady's kitchen, adjacent to momma's flat, and had blown a hole in the wall. Terribly scared and weeping, Enid was taken into a neighbour's flat and looked after. Robby recognised suddenly that Enid was a poor, young creature crying for her momma.

He departed at about half past eleven. He managed to run after an empty tram and leapt aboard it. He walked home from the depot and the theme song kept pestering his brains beneath the bandage - 'Ramona, I hear the mission bells above.'

Two elderly gods roared laughing. 'That poor devil,' gasped one, wiping his eyes with a gossamer handkerchief, 'nothing ever happens the way that dreamy brain of his imagines it will. He has the potential of that old rat-bag Foulkes who left that half dozen bastards in Furlongton and district. If that explosion had not occurred, if his thoughts are anything to go by, it would have been an orgy of huge delights!'

*   *   *

Georgina was working as an apprentice in a glove

factory, a job found for her by her girlhood friend, her cousin Eunice. The two brother proprietors thought highly of Eunice and Georgina gained much by having kinship with her. Georgina spent happy days in that workshop, making many friends. One of them was having her twenty-first birthday party on a Sunday and invited Georgina who could bring a friend, the girl said. Edward would not allow them to go. He took the scriptures of the church seriously and they told him that he should remember that thou keep holy the Sabbath Day. Six days shalt thou labour and do all that thou hast to do, but the Seventh is the Sabbath of the Lord thy God and thou shouldst eat thy meals and go forth and play the organ for the favoured of the Lord, praying reverently and letting the people of the Lord sing His praises.

So the maidens kept secret their unholy intent and lied unto the lord of the house, saying that they wouldst go f or a walk; and they gave heed to the lord of the house and did vow that they would come to the house by the appointed time.

And during the merry-making, verily Georgina looketh at her time-piece and lo, the time had passed unto ten seconds past ten of the clock; and the maidens went home in great haste, having not the wherewithal to use the tramway to the house of their lord. And they came to the house and were sore afraid when they heareth the chimes of the eleventh hour from the parish church clock.

And the door of the house of their lord was locked and the house was in darkness. And their hearts were filled with terror and Margaret sayeth unto Georgina, Let us go unto my sister's house so that we be reassured that ma is not there. And they hurried their steps unto the house of their good sister Flora; and the darkness surrounded them and they were sore afraid.

And it came to pass that the house of their sister Flora was in darkness; and they gathered unto themselves the gravel from the pavement and the gravel from the gutter and didst throw it at the windows of the house wherein the people did slumber. And there came no sound from within.

And they turned their backs on the house of Flora and

went with haste in their steps and came again to the house of their lord. And they knocked on the door of the house with mighty force and cries to those within. And the maidens were amazed greatly when they heard voices from within, and the laughter and giggling of the mischievous larks.

And the lord of the house opened wide the door and, behold, he did clip the maiden on her ear and they were admitted into the house with laughing reproach and a demand that their excuses be not described. And they noticed that the lord was with a person who was not believed to be a friend of his bosom, for it was he that blasphemeth and swore all the days of his life. And the maidens did not offend their lord for many days henceforth.

*   *   *

Many political commentators saw the sinister hand of Nazism as a definite threat to world peace, but there were others who maintained that Hitler was a great leader in having accomplished so much for his people. International tension had been growing as far back as Hitler's re-occupation of the Rhineland in 1936. Now, with Annexed Austria in the news, people were growing very alarmed. The agitation for autonomy by the German-speaking inhabitants of the Sudetan area of Czechoslovakia, under its leader, Henlein, pointed to that poor country as Hitler's next victim. John Bingham, Marxist, said that Henlein was Hitler's puppet and the agitation had been orchestrated by the Nazi gang. In 1937 France had already assured the Czechs that she would stand by her treaty of 1924 if their country were attacked. With this had come the Soviet pledge of immediate assistance in similar circumstances. Hitler smoothly reassured the Czechs that Germany would respect their integrity. But tension still grew. Contrary to Bingham's opinion, Chamberlain at that time could see no alternative to war.

Life proceeded smoothly, in spite of the machinations of dictators and politicians, and when Enid did not turn in next morning, Robby explained to Quilter what had happened the night before.

'Um! An explosion, eh? That must have shocked the life out of her! By the way - I thought you were going out with Bella's sister? What's happened?'

Robby felt a deep nudge of irritation.

'Nothing's happened,' he said. 'I'm still seeing Stella.

It's just that Enid asked me to go with her to the Astoria.'

Quilter smiled his disbelief. 'She's only a bit of a kid,' he said.

'She's not such a kid,' Robby laughed. 'She knows what's what.' Quilter went back to his desk, amusement on his face. What Robby did with his girl friends was none of his business, but Stella was a nice kid. Of course, they weren't engaged or anything, but according to Bella, her sister had been accepted into Robby's family circle.

Enid returned after a week's absence and Robby asked her about the explosion.

'Old Ma Wagner turned on the gas, apparently, found her matches were damp, and went to borrow some from the Parry's across the hall from us. The old girl's very forgetful. She stays talking to the Parry's and then goes back to her kitchen and strikes the match, and, Whoof! an explosion. Anyway, we're having the damage put right and having our meals with the Parry's for the time being.'

'How is the old lady?' Robby enquired.

'She had some burns and her hair was singed, but she's badly shocked. Momma says she's coming on OK though.'

'It could have been much worse,' Robby said.

'Yah - we could have been in there when it went off.'

'Are you glad we weren't?' Robby grinned. She looked at him with soft eyes. 'Yah - and no,' she said in her husky voice, and stroked his cheek as she moved away towards her desk.

*　　*　　*

At Chepworth Street that evening, Edward's pal, Barry, had called. They were talking in low voices and laughing derisively. He's in one of his denigatory moods, Robby thought, making lewd remarks about people. As Robby went through to the dining room, Georgina, apparently, had made some remark and Edward was demolishing her opinion with utter derision. Robby sat down to his evening meal and listened to the two friends murmuring together then sitting back and cackling their amusement.

After his meal, Robby got up and went through to the hall and as he passed the two boys, he overheard Edward's whispered, 'Hey, imagine him married to Stella!' They roared their amusement, Robby stopped in his tracks. Should he go back and challenge Edward? No, he decided, it was too trivial. His first reaction was that Edward was boosting his ego to a friend, showing off his superior wit. His second thought was - Why should they think that his marrying Stella was so funny? It was no less than an insult to both himself and Stella.

He had always regarded Edward as basically decent but inclined at times to be sardonic and superior. When his thin, pinkish face with its aquiline, aristocratic nose was set in a glum, introspective mood, you had to be prepared for some biting sarcasm. The fellow had had a very trying time at an early age - the death of his father, the strange illness of his mother, and all the accompanying problems, and Robby had always made allowances, at his ma's briefing, for those circumstances. Why Edward had picked on him as an object of derision he never discovered. There had never been great warmth of friendship between them, Robby realised, for Edward was not one to show emotions or sentiment. As long as he had remembered that, Robby knew, some sort of friendship had been possible. Like his ma, Robby was expert at riding humiliation.

For a week or two Edward's remark to Barry had rattled him from time to time. He saw no justification for it. Stella was a sweet, easy-going girl, as Flora had said, and Robby could not see why she, in particular, should be a subject for lewd discussion. He was puzzled.

In two years Edward would show another facet of his complex disposition - he would be turned down by the army, in which he had looked forward to becoming an officer, and would return home looking like an old man, haggard and pale; he had had rheumatic fever as a youngster and it had left him with a serious heart weakness; yet he would prove himself a hero by putting out an incendiary bomb on the roof of a bank. The bank had presented him with a gold medal for his bravery.

*　　*　　*

It was a strange quirk in the nature of the two Ferguson boys that neither thought about the future. Living from day to day was a learnt routine and planning for future success, or fulfilment of some ambition had been forbidden them by circumstances, and Robby's dreams excluded planning. The thought that if world events turned out for the worst, they would be called in the forces, never once entered their heads. They did not imagine wearing uniform, what army or navylife might be like, what the act of leaving home might mean. Even Robby's reading of the newspapers did not rouse him to surmise about his future, and Douglas did not read the newspapers. For Robby this disregard for future prospects included the marriage state, and when he did think of marriage he did so negatively. For so long his personal value as a desirable candidate for anything at all, marriage apart, never broke through the barrier of his accepted subconscious sense of unworthiness. Even at school, the process of being appointed a House Captain had amazed him for several days until he finally solved the mystery by remembering that Malcolm had blazed a trail before him and the headmaster was naturally making a favourite of him also.

Without knowing it, Robby was a fatalist - you could not influence your own life so you had to live as best you could from day to day, hoping that Fate might decree the success of any ambitions you had, and if it did not, there was nothing you could do about it. The old woman on her orange box, Mrs Larrigan, had made an indelible impression on his mind. Jonesey had said she had probably never saved a penny in her life. But ma had saved regularly when the young ones were at school. Where had that thrift got her? She had been MADE penniless! It seemed to Robby that if you were trying to influence the Fates to improve your future, you had to exclude from your plans the selfish wants and desires and assumptions of people like Angus. Ma was not like that Larrigan woman, ma had been misguided by others.

His income and prospects scared Robby from thinking of marriage. He was not tolerating, therefore, the subtle pressures of assumed responses from family and friends. They could assume what they liked - he would marry or not marry as he thought fit. To have one's future taken for granted was an assumption that riled him deeply. If he had believed that Stella was the right girl for him and he the man for her, his reaction to Edward's snide remark about their marriage would certainly have enraged him enough to retaliate strongly; as it was, he was merely irritated.

He had read eagerly since childhood - novels, essays, biographies, and some poetry, but he felt ignorant. Edward had always seemed more mature than he, always seemed better educated. Robby's occasional gaffes in conversation had given Edward huge entertainment. In those unforeseeable years to come he would live through many painful times when his ignorance would escape into the world about him. Yet he felt he had the potential to be a good scholar.

Ma was rooting through a box she always kept private, only she knowing the setting of its combination lock. She handed Robby a yellowing piece of paper folded. Had he ever seen it?

'No,' he answered at once, and began to read it, holding the four bits together carefully

It was a letter from Mr Beckett, the headmaster of his school, dated 7th September 1925. He proposed to Emma that Robby should be placed in a special class for boys of promise, and after the winter course, if he did well, he would be entered for the Scholarship or Free Place Examination next year.

'Why wasn't I ever told about this? I'm sure I could have gone on to Grammar school by passing that exam.'

Emma sighed. 'I know you could, but I'm sorry son, we just could not afford it. Look at that list at the bottom.'

Robby read the items on the counterfoil - English dictionary 1/-; Up-to-date Atlas 2/-; Exercise book 6d; School bag, pen, pencil, ruler, compass, encyclopaedia (state edition).

'You mean to say you couldn't afford these bits of things?' he asked, incredulously. 'I had the damned encyclopaedias already.'

'It wasn't that. You had to get a job. We were short of money coming in.'

'Margaret got her scholarship,' he pointed out.

'That was different. She was last in line.' Robby sighed deeply, folded the paper and handed it back to his ma.

'Eh, I don't want it, lad. Keep it as a souvenir.' Robby's laugh, tinged with bitterness, was not lost on ma.

'A souvenir of what?'

'Well, that you were capable of going to grammar school if things had been different.'

'Um,' he murmured bitterly - 'the story of my life, if things had been different. Something could have been worked out, surely?'

'You tell me what,' said Emma, defensively.

He said no more but thought about it as he went out of the room. A golden chance missed and irretrievable. It was too late - always too late. That was his lot - always too late!

*   *   *

On the evening of 27th September Chamberlain broadcast to the nation. In London, trenches were being dug in the parks as makeshift air raid shelters. Next day the fleet was mobilised and parliament returned from recess for an emergency meeting at which Chamberlain reported to the Commons about what he had done in negotiations, adding that he had telephoned Mussolini to ask him to intercede. Shortly after this point in his report, a message was handed to Chamberlain - it was an invitation to him and Deladier to meet Hitler and Mussolini at Munich next day. There were to be no Czech representatives at that infamous meeting; but the dismemberment of their country in accordance with Hitler's demands was confirmed by the four statesmen! Neville Chamberlain became a hero overnight when he brought back a document signed by himself and Hitler in which each agreed that any differences between Britain and Germany would be resolve by peaceful means.

Some days before these events Edward asked Robby to join him at the public hall to help distribute gasmasks and show people how to adjust them to their faces. After a brief instruction on how to fit their own, they worked into the night fitting the masks. Local social workers and nurses took charge of babies' masks and other officials helped the elderly.

The masks were stinking things, reminding Robby of the rubber works, and he had doubts that they would ever be used. A member of the choir saw Robby across the hall and came smiling towards him. She was a devout churchgoer and had very strict views.

'We must pray, Robert,' she said, 'that Mr Chamberlain succeeds with Hitler. I am saying special prayers every night and I think that if we all do the same, God will hear us and stop all this madness.'

Robby smiled pleasantly at the good woman and thought of a way of answering her without offence.

'Would you think that God already KNOWS we don't want war? In any case, you know,' he went on, dryly, 'Hitler won't know we are all praying and I'm sure he doesn't know God as we do.' The woman eyed him with a frown, not knowing what to make of this comment, then she walked away with a melancholic look in her eyes, to one of the women helpers to get her mask.

*   *   *

Angus came to Liverpool with Gwen and their young son, Ronald. Emma asked the boys to remove the sofa from the back parlour and take it upstairs to the front bedroom and place it alongside the double bed. On this they made a bed for the boy.

On the Sunday following Chamberlain's declaration of peace in our time, Angus joined Jack Volant and Robby for an outing to remember old times, Angus said - electric train to Aintree and a walk out into the countryside around Sefton. It was a warm, balmy October 2nd and the sky pale blue with ragged clouds here and there.

'Leyland Motors is building tanks like the clappers,' Angus told them. 'Doesn't say much for Chamberlain's efforts. I'd like to think he settled the trouble. There's all those bloody gasmasks, too. Complete waste of money. Someone's making a pile.'

'I don't think they're a waste, Angus,' Jack replied. 'We haven't finished with old Adolf and his mates yet. Everything's been made easy for him so far - he's got the French and Britain on a string, and the Czechs are the lambs to the slaughter.'

'I can't help but admire old Adolf, though,' said Angus. 'He knows what he wants and he goes right out to get it. I hope he just might keep that agreement with Chamberlain.'

'Why should he?' Robby broke in. 'They weren't supposed to re-arm in the first place.'

'The cause of all this trouble was the Versaille Treaty - it was so severe it was bound to make trouble in the future. You can't blame the Germans, can you?'

'The question is,' said Robby, recalling Bingham's remarks, 'who financed the Germans to get all these things built? We have - and probably the Yanks.'

Angus laughed. 'That's rubbish!'

'It's not so daft as you think,' Jack intervened.

'Someone must have backed the Germans. Who's got stakes in Krupps? Hitler's a damned good cushion against

Communism and the Government is hoping Adolf will stop it spreading.'

'I agree we don't want Communism,' Angus said, 'but I can't believe we financed Hitler. And what about peace in our Time? Neville must believe it.'

'He's the only one who does,' Jack laughed. 'They're calling up reservists, digging trenches putting up shelters, selling black-out cloth in the shops.'

They walked on in silence, Robby wondering why Angus was so keen to believe there would be no war. Maybe when you were married and had a son, you preferred to think like that against all the signs. They reached open country and Angus stopped to lean on a gate.

'Nothing's changed since I was here last. I remember that farmhouse. There was a kid taking some cows to pasture, trying to get them into that meadow over there. I made some cow talk and the herd fairly shifted through the gate. The lad grinned at me.'

'Funny,' said Jack, 'I don't remember that. I do remember, though, I was dying to go to the lav. We'd never been this way before. You told me the Gents was round the bend of the road. I asked you how you knew and you said you couldn't explain - you just knew. And round the bend, there it was, out in the wilds.'

'Yes, I remember,' said Angus. 'I also said the bus terminus was at the crossroads, too, and it was.'

'Well, how do you explain it?' Jack mused. 'A sixth sense, or extra-sensory stuff? What do you say, Robby?'

'Nobody seems to know much about it, so I keep an open mind. There are more things in heaven and earth, Horatio, etcetera.'

'The answer's usually quite sensible,' said Angus. 'I could have come this way to market with Farmer Voce.'

'You wouldn't come this way from Maghull,' said Robby. 'Voce would have gone to Ormskirk market. That would be the nearest.'

'Aye, you're quite right there. I really don't know.'

'How do you explain ghosts, then, Angus?'

'I don't believe in ghosts. When father died he was

taken to the Chapel of Rest. I went up to the bedroom and saw him lying there. He was so real, I spoke to him.'

'Get away,' said Jack. 'That must have been a bit of a shock?'

'I thought about it afterwards - when your mind's full of grief your imagination sometimes takes over. I IMAGINED he was lying there.'

'Imagination can play tricks with your brain,' said Jack.

'I agree,' said Robby, 'but I still believe old Shakespeare - more things in heaven and earth.'

The day was perfect for walking. They came to the road going north and when they reached the bend they saw the brick Ladies and Gents in the distance. Further along was the crossroad bus terminus of the Sefton Meadow bus. Robby felt strange sensations of unreality about the whole outing. They entered the urinal and relieved themselves before setting off back.

Another hour's walk brought them within sight of the great bulk of Walton prison where Norris was a warder. Despite its unpleasant connotations, the prison those days was a welcome sight for tired people with tired feet. They came to Hornby Road at last and within sight of the main road. They were puzzled by the sight that lay ahead - a crowd of people all staring up at the sky as if spellbound. Two tramcars had stopped opposite each other, one Aintree-bound, the other City-bound. Their drivers and conductors stood looking up like the rest of the pedestrians.

'They're looking at that cloud,' said Robby, 'it's the only thing they can be looking at. They hurried to the junction with the main road and looked up. In the midst of the pale blue sky was an immense cloud, perfectly shaped into the silhouette of a soldier - tin helmet, rifle over his shoulder on webbing, an arm bent with a thumb through the webbing, greatcoat, puttees and big boots in the position of marching. It was an amazing sight and everyone was awe-struck by it.

After a silent few seconds, Jack said, 'There's your sign, Angus, Robby - there's your sign. That's an omen if ever there was one!'

'Yer,' Robby breathed, fascinated by the unmistakable accuracy of the formation. The fixed attention of everybody proved that the strange phenomenon was not due to the imagination of anyone there playing tricks with the brain. All those people could not be wrong. Backed by the collective understanding, no one doubted the evidence of his senses. Chamberlain was wrong. There would be war!

'Let's go,' said Angus, 'its scares me.' They climbed the steps of the city-bound tram and when the great cloud broke into a non descript formation, the car started off and the people and the traffic and the Aintree-bound tram resumed their journeys, the witnesses thinking of how they would convince families and friend of what they had seen. There WERE more things in heaven and earth than were dreamed of!

*   *   *

It was Robby's turn to walk into one of the cubicles from the line of young men standing in Indian file as naked as they had been when the midwife had slapped their backsides. He felt like a bull calf being examined by the vet before an auction sale. The Medical Officer tested his heart, lungs, eyes, nose, ears, throat, head, body, penis, and said 'cough' as he held Robby' s testicles. He was told to turn round and bend down so that the M.O. could peer up his rectum.

'Right. You're OK. Get dressed Sonny Boy.' And that was it - blue eyes, fresh complexion, brown hair. 5ft 11ins, 150 lbs weight. He would be sent to North Wales to train as a wireless operator and do square-bashing.

Two weeks later in April his ma insisted on going down to the station with him. They got off the tram in Lime Street and walked into the smoky station.

'Do you want me to come on the platform with you?' ma asked.

'I'd rather you didn't,' said Robby. 'You'd need a platform ticket. Better say goodbye here.'

'If that's the way you want it,' said ma, and kissed him

with dry, tight lips. She watched him walk to the barrier and show his army papers, and when he had passed through, he turned and waved and she waved back. She watched him board the Welsh train, give a final wave, and go inside. Ma sighed, turned round wearily and hobbled out of the station, not even waiting to see the train depart, her corns and bunions points of agony as she walked. She got on the tram in Lime Street. There were no tears from ma.

Alone in the carriage as the train jerked off, Robby looked out of the window with melancholy thoughts and wanderings. He remembered the Bible Edward had presented him with that morning as he left the house. He opened his holdall and took out the little book. On the first end paper Edward had written – *'To Robby from EB. April 18th 1940. St John 14.'*

He turned to the New Testament and found the place.

Let not your heart be troubled, ye believe in God,

believe also in me. In my Father's house are many mansions:

if it were not so, I would have told you. I go to prepare a place for you.

He put the Bible back into his bag. What did it mean? There are many mansions in God's house?

If you were going to God's house it meant that you had to die first! The Disciples had put some questions to Jesus about it, hadn't they? If Jesus was preparing a place for him, Robby, and that meant Edward was expecting him to get shot! It was not an encouraging thought.

Poor Ted! How he'd longed to become an army officer. He could have had my place, Robby thought if there was a place being prepared for him somewhere. Still, Ted was being promoted to General Manager. He deserved it for working hard. When he and Douglas came back from the war, Edward would be a rich man! He'd still be rich if they didn't come back from the war!

*   *   *

194

Georgina sat with ma and Bobby, the dog, in the cellar. The bombs were dropping and the fox terrier was whimpering and ma soothing him. She switched on her torch. They could see some coal at the far end.

'What a terrible 21st birthday for you, love,' ma said.

'I don't know what I'll do, ma, when our Ted leaves. I'll be lost. I shall have to go alone to see mother, and there are some queer people in that hospital. I dread going without our Ted.'

'I'll go with you,' ma promised. 'We'll work something out - if the damned Germans will let us. The house is a morgue now, everybody gone and Edward living over the bank. If this bombing keeps on for much longer I shall have to join our Margaret in Leyland. You can come with me.'

'I don't know what to do, ma. I'm worried to death.'

Georgina's feelings of insecurity were relieved a week later. Fanny Thompson – 'Gran' Thompson to Georgina - the mother of Alf, one of Georgina's friends at the glove factory who had been called up, having been in the Territorial Army, invited Georgina to go and live in Southport. Alf senior, trying to help, suggested that she give up her job and find work in Southport. Within a few weeks all problems were solved. Edward had his furniture removed to Bedford, bravely saved the bank from being burnt down; ma travelled to Leyland and stayed at Angus's house with Margaret; Georgina moved to Southport and soon found employment and had no further need to travel through the blitz. It was all safely and sadly arranged - good friends saying goodbye and other good friends saying welcome. Three weeks later, Edward went down to Bedford with his future wife, leaving her aunt living over the bank, and Edward settled there as General Manager of his firm.

It was a few days before Georgina went into the W.A.A.F. that she was startled one Saturday morning to open the door to Douglas, neat and shiny in pressed uniform, gleaming boots, and smart cap.

'Gosh!' she gasped, her face pale. 'What are you doing here?' Douglas grinned. 'Don't faint - I've come to take you out to lunch.'

In a daze Georgina hurriedly dressed herself in her best clothes for this huge treat of having lunch with Douglas, the fellow who had sworn he would never walk down the street with her or his sister. It was beyond belief! The army must have the power to change people! And it turned out to be a very pleasant lunch and afterwards they went to a show. Georgina's deep feelings warmed her heart. Douglas could be nice. He was so shy and self-conscious that he just had to be aggressive all the time to cover his shyness. Yes, that was it - he was nice really. The army had worked the miracle of bringing forth his true nature. She saw him off on the train at Chapel Street, and as she walked from the station, she felt hot tears on her cheek!

The old god assembled his juniors and spoke to them. 'Look down on earth and see that the horrors of war are being brought into the homes of the populace. The civilian population will suffer the horrors before the fighting men will know of them. And yet you will see that the bombing and the terror by night and the long-suffering and the anxieties will engender among the populace great deeds of bravery and comradeship and love of their neighbours. It is a fact, my friends, that it is the old men, powerful and relentless, who declare war but it is the youth who fight it; if this were not so Earth would never know war. Old men know that to save their skins and their vested interests and their established powers, they must use the youth of the country to fight their wars, for the young men are inexperienced from generation to generation, and go blindfold into battle willingly as if the slaughter and destruction were great adventures of honour and glory and exciting deeds. Only when the war is ended does the truth emerge to sober their minds and make them old men before their time. But the brave deeds of ordinary civilians will not be brought to light as they should be; war brings out the worst and best of humankind. Take note of these people -

that elderly lady Nellie Cassells that good woman Flora Volant, that excellent woman Emma Stone, and that poor fellow Malcolm Ferguson who even now is fighting the flames of the enemy's destruction.'

At the outbreak of war Nellie Cassells, widow, aged 67 years, came at once to Leyland and was granted a council house. She was determined to release her brother, George, from the old hospital at Rochley, a one-time workhouse, and a depressing, gruesome Victorian pile. George was conveyed by ambulance to Nellie's home and was made comfortable in a single bed in the front room downstairs. His wife Charlotte was present when the ambulance arrived.

'Nellie, love, I shall visit as often as possible, you know. It's very good of you to do this for George. As you know there is no room in Henry's house, in fact there was a bit of a to-do with Eileen when I suggested I live with them. Henry insisted and just about managed to fit me in, what with the three grandchildren growing up and Arlene always ailing. I do a lot to help, cooking and looking after the children and so forth.'

Strangely, Nellie never complained about Charlotte's apparent neglect of her husband. Nellie had accomplished her aim and did her best to ease her brother's pain and feed him, making his life comfortable. George was grateful. He was so happy to be out of that workhouse, as he still called it, the workhouse that had given people in the past nightmares that one day they might end their lives in it. Here, in Nellie's warm front room, he could rest peacefully, take his pills and medicine, have a weekly visit from the doctor, eat as much as he needed, listen to the wireless and read his favourite books and pamphlets. Poor George! Huge cheekbones, hair thin and grey around his ears, his arms so thin that he could hardly lift a heavy book. When he gazed out of the window at the passing scene, his thoughts milled around in his huge dome of a head, and asked questions - why had his life been so hard and pitiless? Had the good Lord decreed that he would spend his life as a victim of poverty and pain? Was his pittance of a war pension the only recompense he deserved out of his days of misery and rats and water in the trenches? Was that all the people in authority thought his life was worth? Marx had overestimated the potential of the poor. The poor were poor in every respect; they could never rise above their status; their lives were cheap, their meagre wants were cheap, their ambitions were cheap, and their values to the community were cheap. The poor were disposable and no tears flowed when they breathed their last breath. For George, lying in his narrow bed, there was no future happiness that would come soon - the Church's mystic promise of a life hereafter! To George, that was dubious indeed!

*   *   *

Flora's eldest child, Jackie, and Keith, her youngest, were evacuated, the elder to Caenarvon where a couple had a sweatshop and he was happy, but little Keith to a farmhouse in Shropshire. He spent his solitude wandering round the farm and at night making his pillow wet with his tears. A pathetic little note settled what they had to do:

Dear Mum and Dad,

I am unhapy here an I keep cring an I want to go back to livpool I do not like the porig an I do not like the man cos he maks me go to bed at 8 oclok an get up at morng at 7 it is not nice here an please tak me hom.

Love keith.

Jack Volant set off one Sunday, early, to the railway station. He spent sixteen hours seeking the Shropshire farm and bringing Keith home. To the boy an air raid shelter with his parents by him with the bombs falling was much more preferable to sleeping in the attic of an old, remote farmhouse in solitary misery. Flora's second-born, Mary, was not evacuated, her health being delicate. And when the bombing ceased, Jackie, too, came home.

In May 1941 a fresh assault on Liverpool drove more folk from their homes. Flora's house was undamaged but she considered the time had come to flee, leaving her husband behind to arrange the cartage of their belongings. Kathleen, too, said a sad goodbye and went to live with her sister Susan, Esther, and Pa Volant.

The day before Flora was ready to move to Leyland, Jack's cousin, Michael O'Shea, came with a tale of woe - the previous night's raid had shattered all their windowpanes, despite the tape that reinforced them. Slivers of glass had sprayed all over, cutting into furniture and making especially dangerous all the soft furnishings like cushions and bedclothes.

'I'm going with the kids to Leyland,' Flora told Michael. 'We've had enough. Come with us if you like. Go back home and fetch everybody and any belongings you need. I'm sure they'll put us up at Leyland until we find somewhere to live. Margaret and ma have gone already.'

The O'Shea's were grateful. Michael returned home and brought his family and all they required for immediate use, leaving a good neighbour to keep an eye on his house.

Emma had moved with Margaret from Angus's house and now rented one belonging to a relation of Gwen's, the occupier having died. It was an eventful morning when the crowd of refugees from Liverpool arrived and surprised Emma. She readily welcomed them. Arriving home that evening Margaret was overwhelmed to be greeted by ten new occupants. That night they slept on mattresses and coats wherever they could find space. The elders used the upstairs rooms and the youngest the ones downstairs. Throughout the long, pleasant summer the O'Shea's enjoyed Emma's warm, crowded hospitality and they never forgot it. By Autumn they had found their own abode down an unmetalled country lane.

After a week at Emma's Flora was invited to live at Nellie's place, temporarily, and although Flora saw disadvantages in that the children would disturb Uncle George, she agreed, first warning her children to behave.

George was delighted that some young blood brought the house alive.

Examining respirators was not a stimulating occupation for Margaret at the Government depot. The day following the arrival of the refugees, she walked smartly into the manager's office.

She would like a job in the office.

'What makes you think you can do office work?' queried the manager.

'I have my school certificate, and I have always done office work.'

'I see. All right, I shall arrange it for you. Start in the office on Monday.'

She was much happier after that, doing work she enjoyed. In time she travelled to Blackheath in London to learn a new job, returning to Leyland to carry out the processes she had been taught, and her pay was raised from £2 to £2.5s.0d. But there came the time when, because of her age, she was called up for National Service. Although on Government work, her job was not a reserved occupation of national importance and she was faced with the prospect of munitions work, and she shuddered. The friendly manager, however, advised her to go to the Appointments Board and not attend the Labour Exchange, fruitful advice that resulted in her joining the Aeronautics Inspection Directorate, a department responsible for the ultimate safety of aircraft. She now used a micrometer and made spot checks on the work. She was satisfied that she was now using her abilities to the fullest advantage.

Left alone of all Emma's family, Malcolm lived with Fay and his two boys on the outskirts of Norris Green. Every night, during the blitzes, he donned fire helmet and oilskins and fought the flames. His tall, agile, big-boned physique gave him the ability to deal with dangerous situations, daring to rush in to save trapped mates among the flames, and when the holocaust ended, he and his family, too, escaped to Leyland. Malcolm doubled his income at the rubber works.

*   *   *

The Welsh holiday camp, recently finished by the contractors and hardly used for its main purpose, was dismantled for the troops. Army boots and clod-hopping soldiers threatened luxurious carpets, and army sleepers in the bunks in chalets had no need of quilts and sheets. All kinds of entertainment effects like swimming pool and monorail were taken down. But its comparative comfort pleased the troops. Its back lay onto the sand hills and its front gate opened onto the shore road.

The men were intrigued by the instruction period and lectures and worried themselves about the Morse Code, and they were convinced that they would never learn the difference between V and 4 and Q and Y, and many other similarities like the dots for E, I, S, and H. Then the operators' names for letters in speech communications by line had to be learnt - Ack, Beer, Charlie, Edward, Freddy, George, Harry, Ink, etc which in time would all be changed to suit the American forces when they, at last, entered the war.

After the square-bashing, Robby found he could march with the best of them. He managed route marches easily and was thrilled to be taught to drive a ten-ton truck. Map reading was an engrossing exercise and when he went out to camp overnight in his group of four, they learnt Orienteering and survival methods.

There were good comrades who were willing to go out and spend money on rip-roaring times, their philosophy being to have a good time now because they would never get the opportunities once they went abroad, so they believed.

Out of his 14/- pay, Robby had allotted seven to his Ma and found that his remaining shillings soon required, when the familiarity of friendship allowed, the borrowing of amounts to keep up with the more fortunate men. Charlie Brice, an ex-teacher, was a generous fellow. He suggested going to Dyserth for a drink or two.

'I've only got two bob,' Robby told him.

'Don't worry, I'll pay,' Charlie responded at once.

Charlie received a postal order each week and had no allotments, so he was, with his 14/- plus postal orders, a wealthy soldier those days.

On their way out through the gate they saw Rostron and Farley standing there.

'We're going over to Dyserth,' Robby told them. 'Are you coming?'

'Yer,' said Rostron, 'we'll tag along.'

The four climbed the steep road over the foothills behind the town, walking in their army boots which were now accepted footwear.

'Can you lend me five bob?' Robbie whispered.

'I can lend you half a dollar,' Charlie said. 'I'll be getting a postal order next week. I'll give you the rest then.'

'Thanks. At times, Charlie, your generosity staggers me.'

Charlie laughed and paused for a moment to take out half a crown.

'You shouldn't have told them we were going to Dyserth,' he whispered.

'Oh! Why not?'

'Rostron's a drunken bugger - always singing after a pint or two - a bloody noise! And Farley gets all morbid when he's had a few.'

Robby recalled the last time he had been out with Rostron - a sandy-haired, thin, pink-faced extrovert with large hands that gripped the pint glass instead of using the handle; someone who sweated profusely after drinking, with eyes that turned into slits, and his white teeth gleaming as he groaned out a song, his lips wet, and when the end of the evening came he could hardly stagger back to camp, and be giggling all the way. You never knew what would happen when Rostron was with you; but, Robby thought, he was a good, harmless sort and game for anything that caused a laugh.

Charlie did not like Rostron. In fact, Charlie did not like a lot of fellows. It was just after the Dunkirk turmoil that he suggested they go to visit his Aunt Chloe and her daughter Clara at Gronant. It was a fine May Day, Saturday afternoon as they walked off briskly, Charlie describing his relatives as they went.

'My cousin's a brilliant girl,' he said. 'About twenty-five, I think. Her painting and drawing makes me spit - I can't draw a straight line. And she plays piano like Myra Hess. Very well educated at a girls' private school then went on to university. She has an arts degree. Mind you, I think she could be a bit snobbish at times. Uncle Edgar was killed in Africa on safari some years back - Brigadier Edgar Brice, my uncle.'

'You're making me nervous,' Robby laughed. 'I feel inferior already.'

'Rubbish,' Charlie scorned. 'We're as good as they are. I wouldn't take anyone else to see them.'

Robby was now an acting unpaid lance corporal. His most important duty so far was to march the men down to meals every lunchtime and teatime, and occasionally send Morse to the class of thirty-two, a demanding task based on different exercises devised by the sergeant in charge.

They arrived at a large house surrounded by beautiful gardens. They walked down a curving path and around the back of the house. Robby felt out of his element - this was a very wealthy setting. Charlie's Aunt Chloe was there, frowning as she watched them approach.

'Hello, Charlie,' she greeted, none too warmly. 'What are you doing here?'

'We are stationed at the Signals' Camp, and I thought I'd bring my pal to meet you before we sail abroad.'

'Oh. Well - do come in, then. Sit down. I'll tell Clara.' She left the room, frowning.

'Don't think we're very welcome,' Robby whispered. Charlie's eyebrows raised in doubt.

They sat in two very loungeable chairs and looked around the room. In one corner there was a magnificent grand piano. The walls were hung with mementoes of Uncle Egar's adventures, African native work and objet d'art. The wide fireplace was fronted by a Bengal tiger rug from the Brigadier's Indian period. There were jades and carvings on table and shelves and an Indian carpet in front of a French window. To Robby it was the height of luxury and privilege. The aunt came back with her daughter, a tall, haughty, golden-haired beauty with long legs. As she entered the room she removed her glasses and placed them on a ledge near the door.

'I've taken the liberty of bringing my best friend,' said Charlie. 'Robby Ferguson.'

'Oh,' said Clara. 'How do you do?'

'How do you do,' Robby smiled.

'Would you care for some tea?' Charlie's aunt asked.

'Thank you,' Charlie said. 'We walked here and it's a warm day.' His aunt left the room.

'How are you liking the army?' Clara enquired, her voice soft and secret. Robby had a rude notion that she needed a shock, a ravishing or something to melt the ice in her superior disposition. When she looked at him, he felt toadish. Charlie said the army was OK so far.

'I wonder whether you would mind showing Robby some of your art work?' Charlie asked. Clara moved languidly to a chest of narrow, tray-like drawers and pulled one out. She extracted six or seven paintings. There was a still life of teacup and teapot, a box of cornflakes with the printing in perspective, teaspoons, and so on with the sunlight from a window touching them. The reality was fantastic. Clara showed several others and Robby was assured that the girl was a genius.

'They are all marvellous,' he said with awe in his voice.

'I thought you'd like 'em,' said Charlie. Robby was filled with a warm glow of admiration for the brilliant girl, and he thought it amazing how some people could be well over-endowed she was beautiful, well educated, tall, slim and had every exquisite gift. It was not fair of the Fates to give so much to so few.

Aunt Chloe came in after a while with the tea things and a small dish of biscuits. She poured out the tea and handed the cups round.

'There you are. Do have a biscuit.' Robby slowly and delicately nibbled a biscuit, crumbling it in his mouth, scared to make crunching sounds or spilling crumbs on the tiger rug.

'And how do you like the army?' Charlie's aunt asked.

Robby thought this must be a stock query for people who are not interested in the least about soldiers' welfare.

'I've enjoyed it so far,' Charlie said, 'especially the Morse. We're operators. Robby's pretty good. He sits in front and sends Morse to the class.'

'And you are a lance-corporal already?' said Charlie's aunt. 'Temporary unpaid,' Robby laughed.

'He plays piano, too,' said Charlie, ruining everything in four words.

'Charlie exaggerates,' Robby said. 'I'm an army busker.'

'Rubbish,' Charlie scorned. 'Would you mind if he had a go on your piano, Clara?'

'No thank you,' Robby intervened at once. 'I wouldn't dare.'

'You play a short item for our guests, Clare,' said Aunt Chloe.

'Yes, please,' said Robby, relieved to extricate himself from Charlie's idiocy.

Clara gave him a cold, shrewd glance and walked to the piano. She opened the lid and sat down gracefully. As soon as she began Robby's heart surged with delight. She played the very slow, sonorous prelude in C sharp by Chopin, not known to Robby. The tones of the marvellous grand filling the room and enveloping them in its huge sound. In later years Robby would remember that prelude and think of it as the most perfect short composition ever written - complete, haunting, with beautiful, subtle and heart-rending chords. Clara's playing brought tears behind his eyes. When the tea things had been removed, Charlie again asked Robby to play.

'Don't be silly, Charlie,' speaking seriously. 'After hearing this young lady play, I wouldn't dare.'

'Who's being silly, 'Charlie frowned, his voice like a nagging toothache. 'Clara's classic. You play jazz.'

The argument became ridiculous, making Robby feel coy as all three asked him to play. Charlie made him feel like some eccentric, reluctant genius, so ego-bound that he needed the extremes of persuasion to condescend.

'It would be sacrilege for me to touch that piano,' he said.

'Oh, come now,' said Aunt Chloe, her voice irritated, and contemptuous. 'You're being far too modest, surely.'

Sighing deeply, he got up nervously and went over to the piano. His brain sizzled with curses on Charlie and the two females. Why couldn't they have left him alone? As soon as he would start, Clara would weigh him up and agree that he was a busker, with no taste for the beautiful things in life. But her opinion would be untrue - he did appreciate beauty and genius and talent. For several minutes he hated Charlie.

'I'm warning you. You will regret the fuss,' he laughed. *Smoke Gets in Your Eyes*, he played, a likeable ballad with a quiet Jazz beat, soft and loud as he usually played it. The girl's scrutiny, cold and disdainful, unnerved him. He stood up, and that fool Charlie clapped and said 'Very Good'. Clara closed the lid at once.

About four o'clock Charlie said they would have to go back to camp. He said he would write and surprise them with an invitation shortly. Robby wondered what it was. They said goodbye and walked back down the garden path. Before they had reached the bend they heard Aunt Chloe's voice - 'Charles - a word before you go.'

'Shan't be a tic, Charlie murmured, and ran back to the house.

Robby stared at the plants and flowers as he lit a cigarette, relieved that the ordeal was over. He had just thrown the match away when he heard Charlie's voice, loud and clear - 'You bloody snobs.' He came stamping out, his dark eyes in furious anger. They hastened down the path.

'What's up?' Robby enquired. Charlie was too eaten up to answer.

'What's happened? You are in a fury, Charlie, boy.'

'Yer - and so would you be - bitches! Bloody snobs. Talk about bad manners!'

'Bad manners? That's the last thing I'd accuse them of.'

'Is it? Well, they said not to come any more with such uncouth friends. Uncouth, mind you. I've taught maths at a grammar school for five years. What bloody snobs they are!'

'It's me they're meaning, not you. Playing that bloody piano. You would persist.'

'Is it hell you, you daft bugger. Saying uncouth friends was just an excuse. They told me not to trouble them any more.'

'I don't believe that. Your cousin's a genius. She's quite entitled to be a snob.'

'Nobody's entitled to be a snob - especially an intellectual one - the worst snobs of all. I was going to invite them to the wedding when the special licence comes through. Now I'm buggered if I will.'

'What wedding?'

'Mine. Caroline is coming over next Saturday for two weeks. I should have a licence then. I want you to be my best man.'

'You what? Best man?' Robby gasped.

'Yer. Why not? You know what to do, don't you? There's nothing to it in registry office. You witness with the bridesmaid, and arrange for the breakfast and the room at the hotel, and all that.'

'Why don't you get leave and have a proper wedding?' Robby queried.

'Because I don't bloody want to. Caroline's family are all against it. She's bringing a friend as bridesmaid. That's all we need - you and her friend as witnesses.' Charlie was silent for a few seconds, thoughtfully studying the ground. 'You see, when it wasn't false modesty they were mad,' he said, suddenly.

'What the hell are you talking about?'

'I'm talking about Aunt Chloe and Clara. You didn't want to play because you were modest and they were damned annoyed because you were better than you said you were - and no expensive training. You knew your standard and were honest about it.'

'Thanks very much! That puts me at the bottom of the pile. Come on, Charlie, be honest - you're no brilliant judge of good or bad playing, are you? You're tone deaf - you said so yourself.'

'That's got bugger all to do with it. I know what I like.'

* * *

The troops from Dunkirk were all worn and tired, habituated to danger and cynicism. They watched the joskins with humour and disdain. They were unfriendly and blasé, lounging around the damp waiting for their leave. They made Robby feel silly and boyish because they knew it all, and he knew nothing.

The registry office wedding went off happily and the four people had the wedding breakfast in a local hotel where Robby had booked a so-called honeymoon suite for the happy couple. Charlie had contrived a few days' leave by permission of the Camp Commandant, and after the feast was over, the bridesmaid caught the train to Chester where she lived as near-neighbour to Caroline's family. Robby wandered back to camp feeling lonely and depressed. His friend was an idiot, he decided, getting married against the wishes of the bride's people, and before going abroad. A baby could be born without the father ever seeing it, if his name happened to be on a bullet, and the widowed mother would be hard put to manage. He should have waited until the war was over. Robby did not know that Charlie would not be sent abroad and would be able to see his wife fairly regularly throughout the war.

Then began their series of inoculations in May into June and July, against typhoid, paratyphoid and tetanus. Robby was surprised to see two or three men faint over from their jabs. Then there came the time when training had ended and names appeared on orders of men who were posted Charlie's name was not listed.

'I still owe you half-a-crown,' said Robby, as they were saying goodbye at the gate.

'Bugger it,' said Charlie, grumpily. 'You've been a good pal to me - being best man and all that. And Caroline thought the world of you.'

They gripped each other's hand tightly and Robby felt slightly embarrassed when he saw a glaze of tears around Charlie's dark eyes, and a frown dipping his heavy eyebrows.

'Hope to see you again some day, Robby,' Charlie said, his voice breaking with emotion.

'Yer, I hope so too,' Robby answered quietly, jerking his rifle more onto his shoulder.

'Thanks for everything,' said Charlie.

'Thank you, too. Damned sorry about that half-crown.'

'Sod the bloody half-crown,' Charlie said, with venom.

'You've got my address. Keep in touch. Cheerio, Robby.'

'Cheerio, mate,' Robby echoed softly. Charlie squeezed his friend's hand again tightly. Robby adjusted his pack and respirator, picked up his kitbag and walked over to the truck, climbed aboard and it moved off to Rhos-on-Sea, Robby waving and Charlie waving back and turning suddenly, head bent, to retrace his steps into the holiday camp. Charlie had been a good mate, generous in the extreme. Robby's naive acceptance of situations - such as the incident with Clara and Charlie's aunt - amused and touched Charlie. Unlike Clara, Caroline had warmed to Robby and had said, laughingly, that had Charlie not been on the scene, she would have fancied marrying Robby. She was no dumb blonde but had an attraction for men that promised the revelation of hidden depths. A week before the wedding they had been walking over the dunes, she and Robby behind Charlie and the bridesmaid.

'I think I could marry you if I hadn't met Charlie,' Caroline told him, laughing. It was her kind of coquetry, he thought.

'That would be daft. Charlie's a far better bet,' he laughed.

Her future husband and her friend disappeared into a hollow in the sands. She stopped in the hollow they had reached, took Robby's face in her hands and pressed her open lips against his with deep emotion and a thrillingly mysterious longing in the sigh she gave. Robby had a feeling that this girl came from some world alien to him.

'Hey!' he gulped, trying to come down to earth, 'You'll have Charlie striking me with his glove and we'll be down here tomorrow at five for the duel - and I hate getting up at four-thirty.' She giggled and took his hand again; and Charlie rising to the top of the dune with his companion, looked back and saw his future wife laughing, and the two of them hand-in-hand lurching through the soft sand like lovers. And Charlie was happy. He was a strange person, too.

In the truck going to Rhos-on-Sea, Rostron whispered into Robby's ear, 'Charlie'll cry his eyes out tonight, now you've left him, poor bugger. He worshipped you.'

Robby stared in amazement. 'Get away, you silly sod,' he laughed. 'You're crazy.'

* * *

With the utmost secrecy they left Rhos-on-Sea at two o'clock one morning in late November, marching to the station without any noise, said orders, to board a special troop train to an unknown destination.

The train jerked and stopped and moved and jerked and stopped and moved and went into a siding and waited, all in the dark hours, allowing the scheduled passenger trains to go through, then jerked off again, the soldiers wondering what the hell was going on, and swearing and wondering and tittering at lewd jokes about Fred Karno's army.

The station they arrived at was dim and dirty, running with water down its old brick-arched roof, all underground and un-swept since steam power was discovered. They sneaked out of their carriages, all orders *sotto voce*, and made devious routes from the filthy platform, like rats in a sewer, and came out up a flight of stone steps onto a landing-stage. Robby knew it was Liverpool.

A sickly November sun greeted them as it struggled

through far eastern clouds.

They lounged around in the cold winter wind, nobody telling them what to do, and after a short time the two men slithered off to a dockers' canteen that had red and white stripes.

'We'll have a cuppa,' said Rostron, 'and a wet Nelly each.'

'Roit, sor,' said the little man behind the counter.

He served them with an excellent, hot cup of tea and a wet Nellie sponge cake, and they stood slaking their thirst and giving a tiny promise to their famished stomachs.

'Yis are Signals, aren't y'?' the little man queried. 'Yis'll be sailin' on the ould Anselm.'

They eyed the man in amazement. Had the army written to him, explaining the whole situation? Had some general popped in to take tea that morning and divulged too much?

'Aye, we're Signals,' Rostron admitted, forgetting to think about walls with ears, and German spies under cocoa-room tables within easy reach of a radio transmitter.

'How big is the Anselm, then?' Rostron asked.

'Foiv t'ousand six hundrid tons - it's a bleedin' cork, wack, in stormy weather. When yis gerra t'ousand of yis aboard, yis woan' have room t' scratch y' balls. Now, the Ranjitiki's just foin f' the Brylcream laddoes - two t'ousand of them aboard and the Ranjitiki bein' t'irty t'ousand tons.'

'Thirty thousand tons? Get away,' said Rostron.

'It's true, wack, take me word forrit.'

'Well, I'll be buggered,' Rostron murmured.

They eyed one another and then roared with laughter. They thought of the strict secrecy that morning and suddenly it was all a farce.

It turned out as the little man had described - they were aboard a converted tub of 5,600 tons over a thousand men aboard, and the creaking old craft reacting like a cork in a full bath with the plug withdrawn; and their leader the great Ranjitiki, like a queen sailing down the river, followed by insignificant menials, like themselves, the most menial of the whole convoy. Then Christmas dinner, everybody except Robby, Rostron and two dozen or so more lads, as sick as a polecat; the old freighter at sea for two months, with the engines eventually conking out about a day's sail from Durban.

The convoy left them behind because they were doing only six knots, at the mercy of any German U-boat that happened along; and the escort Commander cursing the Anselm and its old salt skipper for holding them up, the lamp from the destroyer signalling and the Royal Signals men reading it - 'Make running repairs boiler. If not we must leave you.'

Three days ashore in Durban whilst the faulty boiler was put right.

Robby and Rostron with others were given leave ashore for three hours the first day and saw sights they had never dreamed possible - the differences between the white and coloured people before the beginning of Apartheid's miasmic publicity.

Their belief in army efficiency and secrecy withered away in that old tub, Anselm, and they remembered the pomposity in the assumptions of security and the infallibility of 'efficient' command: it was all a huge lark and they laughed as they talked to prevent themselves from crying.

*   *   *

The Lady Medical Officer at Wigan passed Georgina and the girl was astonished - she was like Douglas, Robby and Tommy Hurst, Douglas's mate - yes, she was AI now, after believing, that she would follow Edward's fate.

Then down to Gloucester to be kitted out and the lady officer asking her what she would like to be, as the lady read items from a list. At Georgina blank face the Ma'am decided, 'I'll put you down as an accumulator operator.' Georgina's face remained blank; but at the conclusion of her aptitude tests the Ma'am changed her original suggestion and wrote on her record - 'Training for Wireless Operator.' It was a coincidence that Robby teased Georgina with later. Georgina's letter to Edward telling him of her success in passing her six months course, astounded him and shivered his faith in his being a judge of character. He was astounded rather than surprised because one of his own reps had joined the RAF and had failed in his operators' course.

Georgina and her friends who had passed were proud the day they sewed on their Sparks and all went about thrusting forth their left arm - the whole community should see and take note: these girls are no dummies, so watch out! It was especially gratifying for Georgina who had suffered years of denigration at home.

Twelve months later she was in Jurby, Isle of Man. Her future husband Len Bronson worked in the signal section at the station that had been changed from an Airgunners' Training School to a Navigation School. At the former station Len had been a Tow Target Operator, a hair-raising position, going up in various two-seater craft like the Fairey Battle, Hawker Henley, Lysander, and Miles Martinets, from the trap door of which Len had the task of letting out the drogues to allow trainee gunners to practise shooting at the drogues with machine-guns. Georgina often marvelled that Len and his pilot friend had survived for all those months! Fortunately, the young gunners either shot or just missed the drogues and never shot or just missed the aircraft

Len and Georgina were married at war-end, Gran Thompson at Southport arranged everything and Edward, Coming Up Trumps, paid for everything.

* * *

Flora and Jack Volant rented a double-fronted property with a front garden on a road parallel with Emma's, a quarter of a mile away across fields with a footpath that joined the two thoroughfares and made a convenient way for the two households to keep in touch.

Flora went three times a week to Aunt Nellie's house to help with George and to do shopping. She also helped with all the other household chores. Nothing seemed a trouble to Flora. Family and friends commented on Flora's devotion to helping the old folk and all their hearts were warmed. Flora was the kind of woman who did the good deeds that are ideally preached about by clergymen, and there was nothing of the Florence Wilkins's sham about Flora's work. Each evening Jack came home by steam train to the tiny rural station, collected his cycle from the stationmaster's office and cycled home a mile or so through the lanes. Life in Liverpool was more stable now; only occasional bombers came up the Irish Sea, found Dublin's lights flaring over to the west, and turned east to Liverpool, but they had now to contend with a huge battle-ship in the Mersey and reinforcements of ack ack guns all round the area.

Flora wondered how the boys were faring, wherever they were, and often went to Emma's house to see if letters had come. She feared for the boys' safety and prayed each night at her bed. The first letter arrived in mid-1941. The censor had been busy with it.

Dear ma and folks,

So many things have happened since I left Blighty. We escaped from ---- safely and I am now finding life at an RAF station very restful. We are on shifts as wireless operators. It is a comfortable hut with Indian charpoy-beds, cross-woven hemp on stout wood frames. The army is generous with men on lonely desert outposts - tea five times a day, meat and veg four times a week, and small luxuries like cakes and pastries quite often. Three mates Joe, Pip, and Rick our corporal, are with me. I have been learning contract bridge, a great game, and we invite an RAF chap to be our fourth (one of us is always on duty). Weather is warm and we lie on our off-duty afternoons on our charpoys, reading, or writing letters. We borrow books from the RAF's small library. I am reading a book about Egypt, describing the pyramids and Shepheard's Hotel, a posh place in Cairo. We went on a tram marked 'pyramids' when we were there and although the journey took an hour the fare was only 7 milleums - 1¾done way. The tram is a terribly shaky old thing with a powerless trailer.

I was asked to play the piano at a pumping station half a mile from here. Pip told them I could play. A party of officers was passing through and the oil company staff wanted to put on some entertainment for them. All their wives have been evacuated and there was no one to play. I had little hope that the piano would be much good, this climate is no good for pianos and was wondering whether the officers would appreciate my busking. I was pleasantly surprised when I got there - they had a baby grand and it was rich and mellow in tone. The officers seemed delighted and three of them sang around the piano. Two senior officers bought me a whiskey each. I was there two hours, not playing all the time, and I had a meal in the oil company's dining room. The engineer in charge was pleased and said I played better than his wife.

So far the romance of the east has escaped me. Bazaars seem to be filthy places and I would never buy foodstuffs from them. Some of the lads have bought items of clothing or knickknacks but no food.

I see the war in --- will carry on because the armistice terms aren't acceptable to the --- --I have heard a rumour that we shall be moving shortly. Could it be to ---. Wherever it is I shall write from there.

Love to all

Robby.

They guessed that Greece would be the first censored word and the war in Syria the other references. Ma thought it was an interesting letter in that it gave reassurance that he was being properly fed, was in good company and not in danger. Angus declared, having read the letter, 'He seems to be having a damned good time.' And then he divulged his real reason for visiting, not to read letters but to enquire about the suits.

'Eh, no, you're not having them both,' Emma said, 'you can have one - I'll give the other to Malcolm. He needs a suit. I don't know what Robby will say when he comes home!'

'Oh, he won't be home for ages,' said Angus. 'Those suits are going to waste. When he gets home - he won't worry about suits - he'll be overjoyed at getting home safely.'

Emma went upstairs and brought down the two suits from the wardrobe. Angus chose the grey, saying that he would get someone to shorten the trousers. He would mention the other suit to Malcolm at work and tell him to come round. And so the two suits were disposed of to the elder brothers and the only person to think it something of an outrage was Flora. She told Jack one night.

'All I can say is - some people have a damned cheek. I only hope they make it up to Robby with extra coupons when he comes home.'

The ancient god, looking down, agreed with Flora. Angus was ruthless. 'He can well afford a suit. He's given Gwen his coupons for a dress when most women are making do with fashioning dresses out of old curtain material and bed-quilts. Robby should have followed Douglas's example and locked his things away.'

Robby wrote frequently, keeping his family informed of his progress through the war when the censor was kind enough to leave clues; but they seldom heard from Douglas in the RAMC who was in Herefordshire where there were wounded Dunkirk veterans needing medical attention. He could also come home on leave at times.

Emma sent off snapshots of family and friends and included Stella on one occasion as an esteemed member of the circle. With the restricted rail travel, as directed on Government posters, Stella journeyed twice to Leyland during the war, sufficient to keep the bond of friendship fresh, together with correspondence.

When the elder brothers were asked by friends how their younger brothers were faring, they usually answered, 'They seem to be having a whale of a time!' This was false. In war there are no good times. The constant ignorance of the troops as to their next destination gave them a continuous, smouldering anxiety and all the supposed good times were periods of forced relief - drunken sprees or a scratch game of soccer when off duty, and the only worthwhile happiness was found in the comradeship of common wartime insecurity, which enhanced what was good in life and shared the evils. But Robby made it plain that he thought himself fortunate in being a wireless operator. Fighting men in all services were being killed and maimed, or left to perish at sea. These tragedies gave substance to Angus's belief that Robby was enjoying himself - away from the firing line and doing something he enjoyed with no more risk than the people of London, Liverpool or Coventry. But the prolonged insecurity of the unknown factor - future dangers - was like a chronic disease when compared to a fatal accident; the fighting men, the pilots, the torpedoed seamen were those who suffered the latter, the subsidiary units like Signals and Medics the ones who suffered the chronic conditions. But later there were numerous occasions as the war progressed when the two conditions fused into one and all men were equal in the acute conditions of utmost danger.

* * *

The second letter indicated, with helpful guesses, the war against the Vichy French. Robby had written it under an apple tree and he described the scene and the old peasant who could speak English, having been in the States in President Wilson's time. They nicknamed him Al Capone because of the way he talked. Fuelling the flame of Angus's negative opinion, without knowing it, Robby finished with – 'The weather is so hot that we have the back of the truck open like an observation car. As I write I can look down over the valley with its winding road away in the distance like a seam on a coat of many colours. The smell of the pines all about us makes life worth living.'

Yes, Angus was convinced, Robby was seeing the world free and having a damned good holiday. None of the troops was suffering in the trenches like poor Uncle George had suffered. Robby and Douglas were damned lucky 'You've only to consider the rations they'll be getting compared with us at home,' he said.

* * *

Archie Dickson invited Angus and Gwen to the wedding and his mother, Maggie, invited her sister Emma. He and his girl were married at the Parish Church and the reception for the few guests was held in a small local hall. The wedding breakfast, meagre extras of Spam, and salads from Uncle Jack's allotment, was followed by the usual toasts and speeches and dancing afterwards to the music of gramophone records. Archie already knew that he was being transferred down to Surrey to do research work. Among the guests was a departmental manager, John Emerson. Angus considered this man to be marvellously well-dressed and a cut above everybody else. He was always pleased to talk to him on equal terms and always called him John.

'How's your brother going on abroad, Angus?' Emerson asked him as they stood apart from the dancers, drinking half a pint of beer each.

'He's coping very well, John. The Vichy French have signed the armistice at last. I think the lads abroad are having a better time than we are - what with German bombs falling and food rationing.'

'I know where I'd rather be, Angus. You can't say Leyland's been suffering! Two solitary bombs! Service abroad isn't pleasant. If your brother's letters give you the idea that he's having a good time, I bet the bits that are censored would tell a different story. That's what censorship is about. The folk at home must be kept happy about their lads abroad.'

'I thought censorship was to stop the enemy finding out things.'

'I hardly think the enemy can learn any more from soldiers' letters than they already know. Personally I read between the lines with our John's letters. No, censorship, honestly speaking, is to stop troops telling tales out of school. By the way, who IS that loud-mouthed woman over there - trying to be the soul of the party?'

Angus felt the nerves tingling in his neck. He was furious. 'I don't know,' he said. Why did she go shouting all over the place? If people didn't want to dance she should leave them alone! This wasn't a Liverpool do. He decided not to mention John's comment to Gwen - she already had an opinion about ma and he did not want to add fuel to the fire. He was relieved when John Emerson departed before the reception had really got under way.

'A typical Foulkesian denial,' said the elder god, disgustedly. 'If he denies his own mother he is not a Ferguson. And he is wearing that treasured suit of his younger brother's ignominious labours. That fellow will come to his senses one day and discover that the trivialities he bothers about are worthless. There is no difference between his ma and those more fortunate people, except that Emma is genuine.'

*   *   *

Jack Volant was now working happily in a grocery store in the area, having wearied of the persistent travelling to and from Liverpool. As assistant manager his salary was better than that of his managerial post had been in Liverpool. Apart from the absence of her two younger brothers, Flora believed this to be the happiest period in her life, Jack with a decent job, her children attending a good Catholic school and she managing to provide a variety of food, despite rationing. She could make a pudding from a cupful of flour, breadcrumbs, suet, mixed dried fruit and spices, grated raw carrot and potato. Carrots and potatoes were plentiful and things grown in their front garden richly helped the diet. Onion soup and carrot soup were good when you got used to them. Flour, baking powder, salt and milk, all mixed, made a fairly good scone or dumpling according to the amounts used. But despite all her work, she was determined to write to Robby to the address her ma had provided. Angus had written once, and it was usually Margaret or ma who did the regular correspondence. No one else bothered.

Dear Robby,

You will be surprised to hear from me. The address above is only a couple of fields away from ma's place and I can soon call in there and read your letters. Doug doesn't write as often as you because he can get leave at times. Jack is now working in Leyland, thank goodness, and doing fine. The kids are at school and everything is fine here, apart from the rationing and food shortages and such like. I am looking forward to the time when you will be home all safe and sound. The folks here are still talking about the two bombs that dropped. Believe me Son, they do not know they are born when compared with Liverpool. Archie Dickson got married and has gone down to Surrey to work in the labs there. He is a clever boy and I shall be very happy if any of my kids turn out as good as he did. Maggie is very proud of him, rightly so. Angus and Malcolm are still busy at the rubber and earning good money, working overtime very often.

The Motors are busy too. When Stella came she said she had written you once or twice. She is disappointed at not having a reply from you, although she may have written to the wrong address - the old one ma gave her some time ago. Anyway, write to her and tell her you have got them when you do, and put her mind at rest. She thinks the world of you and is looking forward, no doubt, to the end of the war and getting married.

Auntie Charlotte only comes once a fortnight to see George. I am still going there three times a week. Poor George is in a worst state now, even his pills do not help any more. Nellie is still troubled with indigestion and takes numerous aspirins and bicarb. I keep scolding her. Anyway, son, that is all for now. I hope to hear direct from you. Take care and such like.

Lots of love

Flora and Jack   XXX

When she took her brother's reply six weeks later to ma's house, she was pleasantly surprised to see Stella there. She and Margaret had arranged to go to Southport to see Georgina who had been granted leave.

'I received a letter yesterday,' Stella laughed. 'I did put the wrong address on, silly me. He received three of my letters all at once. Would you like to read it, Flora?'

'Ooh, no', said Flora. 'I don't want to read your private correspondence.'

Stella laughed again. 'There's nothing private in it, really.'

'Well, if you insist.'

'There is nothing private in it,' said Emma. 'I've read it.'

Flora opened the envelope and took out the letter. When she had read it she saw nothing more in it than had been in hers, except for one or two trivial items. It wasn't like Robby to be so cloddish, she thought.

Dear Stella,

Today I received three letters from you redirected by the Army P.O. Thank you for the news, especially about Bella and Morris's little son. Give them my congrats and I hope he grows into a fine, sturdy boy.

The armistice settled the war here and the Vichy have gone. We have had time to see the sights in Lebanon and have been relaxing after the campaign. We are camped near acres of vineyards and I must say that the lads have been decent in not harming the vines and the owner is happy. Mind you, the lads were warned about dysentery when they arrived.

I expect you know that I managed to escape from Greece. I was with the original advance party of a dozen

221

men from our section. Eleven of these were taken by the Germans. I was very lucky. Since then I have made more friends in this unit. One especially, Bernard Kelvin, was very interested in Margaret's photograph and would like to correspond with her.

If I get through this lot I shan't know what to do with my life afterwards. I have no real qualifications, only half trained as a French polisher, etc. The future looks grim to me and if I were you I would meet some nice young fellow with plenty of money and a reserved occupation and marry him immediately. I do not think I shall be able to afford you a very stable future. I do seriously ask you, Stella, to think carefully about the future and not to rely on me. Remember me to all our mutual friends and wish them well.

Kind regards

Robby   XXX.

'He seems terribly pessimistic about his future,' said Flora. 'Take no notice. Next time he writes he will be in a better mood, perhaps.'

'I hope so,' Stella laughed, nervously.

Emma saw more in her son's letter than had the good-minded Flora. Stella, too, had not taken serious consideration of it. She thought he was joking, knowing Robby's way of disparaging himself. A young man who is in love with a girl does not tell her, even in fun, to find someone else. She acknowledged that he was worried about his future after the war, his prospects being poor, but this was not the time to mention such things. The last war lasted four years and it was sensible to assume that this war would last as long if not longer.

On Sunday afternoon, in the house by herself, she sat down at the writing desk and wrote to her son, mentioning her anxieties and asking for a true explanation of his doubts about his future. He must be candid - did he intend to marry Stella after the war?

After posting the letter Emma felt better. She would soon know the state of things and she was glad she had been forthright with him. If Stella was going to be let down by Robby then she must not be left in the assurance that her wedding day was certain after the war ended. That would be cruel indeed!

Preparing tea for herself, her mind asked the question if men were influenced by joining the Forces and their natures changed? Robby had changed already, from the way he wrote. He was mature and less dreamy, which was a good thing. But would the army change his whole personality? That was the troublesome question.

* * *

In September 1940 Angus had joined the Home Guard, a mixed lot of local men and boys parading the countryside with improvised weapons, manning checkpoints and road-blocks and questioning strangers who had lost their way because all the signs had been painted out. The Channel Isles were occupied by the Germans and the chances of invasion seemed likely. They practised guerrilla tactics, how to deal with parachutists and how to make Molotov cocktails to throw at German tanks. They were required to do at least forty-eight hours of training each month. Angus wore a denim uniform which was too big, and the helmet sent Gwen into a choking frenzy of laughter, for Angus's head-size was 7 and no helmet wo uld fit his huge cranium.

On guard duties he often thought of his future. When the war was over he would leave the rubber works. He had opened an account at a local bank. His mortgage was almost paid off. If he could sell his house he would be able to buy a business. He knew he had few outlets - greengrocery, insurance agency, estate agency - but fish frying seemed the most sensible to begin with because he knew all about the business. They must plunge into something, otherwise he saw himself being in that rubber works all his life. Gwen's first reaction to his idea was astonishment.

'Oh, Angus! How can you think of such a business?

After all you've told me about it - how you hated it, and the smell of cooking and all that!'

'There's a damned sight worse smell at the rubber works. I don't want to be there after the war. It would kill me. We've got to be daring and take the plunge. We could sell this house and buy a run-down chip shop cheap and build it up, sell it and move into something else.'

'Well, Angus, if you feel that's what you want, I shan't stand in your way. But apart from Daddy's office, I've no idea about business.'

'Oh, I'll teach you. I think we could make a go of it. We'll never get rich working for someone else.'

They left the subject there, in limbo, and Angus continued to put away his weekly amount into a savings account at the bank. At last he felt he could see brighter prospects.

One of the gods who had been on duty, smiled cynically and reported what he had seen and heard. The old god said, 'you will see him work like a slave in the trade he despised when his ma needed help! And despite this, Emma will be pleased.'

* * *

Emma received another letter before getting a reply to hers. It was despondent and hardly likely to encourage Flora's belief that Robby's pessimism about his future had been a passing depression.

He had crossed the seas and they were in a terrible camp of damp, bedraggled marquees, the place crawling with livestock and rats running up the tents between the flysheets and the roofs. They were all under mosquito nets at night. All the men were despondent and suffering prickly heat rash. In the medical room when he went for lotion he had seen a big fellow with his shirt off and his back was a mass of blisters from shoulders to buttocks! The MO had told him not to sleep with the bedclothes off. Big beetles flew around and squirted acid. The man could have been blinded instead of blistered. Robby had covered his mosquito netting with newspapers after that. Everything steamed when the sun came out. The monsoon weather was continually drenching them as they worked outside then drying them in the fierce heat when the rain ceased. It was like living in purgatory. Morale was low. The filthy place had a stink all its own. With his rifle over his shoulder rubbing the rash, and midges to be warded off, the next day he had been thoroughly ill after his night on guard.

He had just finished a book by James Aldridge, aged 23, an Australian journalist. Its title, Signed with Their Honour. The story was about Greece and Crete and the Air force there - what little there was of it. The book had taken him back to those dark days of escaping from Greece. The REs were dynamiting down the road and each explosion gave the men hell because of their prickly rash. Fats Waller was playing on next-door's wireless, He wished he could play jazz like that.

The women were horrified at the description of rats and beetles and mosquitoes, and they wondered what worse things the censor had blacked out. Emma confided in Margaret that she had written to ask Robby about his intentions concerning Stella. Up till that time Margaret had had little doubt in her mind; but recalling Robby's letter to Stella, she began to see her ma's wisdom. The thought made her very sad.

The sadness was increased when Robby answered his ma's letter. He was as straightforward with her as she had been with him.

Dear Ma,

I have no intention now of marrying Stella. She is a nice girl and obviously takes after her genial father. But I am certainly not going to tie myself to a family ruled by a tyrannical old puritan. Stella was always good company and had a nice sense of humour, but that is not enough for marriage. But I shan't be harsh about it. I'll think very carefully and decide what to do.

I am in a field hospital in --- and I have tonsillitis and a number of other things. They say my prickly heat-rash is the worst case they've seen. They are kind and efficient here and I'm resting and feeling more relaxed. I have no appetite and I in spite of decent food, because of my sore throat I cannot taste anything properly. The medical orderly had given me a laxative and if it doesn't work I have to have an enema! This coming into dock, and there are a number of us here, is the result of that four months in that bloody horrible camp. It hadn't been in use for two years before we went into it. I have found out! I have lost a stone in weight.

Bernard and Trev came in today and said if I was out in time there would be a month's leave for us all. As I am due for discharge any day I may be travelling with them to Darjeeling where they propose to go. A month may seem a lot but we have had no leave since Blighty and Bernard has been out here longer than I have. I shall be quite flush for money because I have some back pay to come.

Love,

Robby.

When Margaret arrived home Emma told her, 'He doesn't intend marrying Stella. At the back of his mind I think he blames the family for pushing things, especially our Flora.'

'That's ridiculous,' Margaret protested, beginning to read the letter. 'Our Flora did nothing and I certainly didn't do any pushing. He met Stella at Bella's so he can't blame us for anything.'

'I don't know how to break it to the girl,' Emma tutted.

'I'll write to her,' Margaret promised. 'Leave it to me. Anyway, it's quite true what he said - he has no prospects, and he certainly doesn't want Florry Wilkins as a mother-in-law, the old tartar.'

'He wouldn't be marrying her, would he? I think he's still dreaming of being a writer, the fool. He thinks he must establish himself in something before he marries. But obviously Stella isn't the girl for him.'

'I dare say he could write a war book when the war's over,' said Margaret. Margaret did not foresee that if her words came true, Robby would join the spate of war book writers, one of hundreds who would write their little bits of history, and in Robby's next letter Margaret's thought did become a possibility.

Dear Ma and Margaret,

Darjeeling is 8,000 feet above sea level and our leave centre is 800 feet above the town. The air is glorious and flying insects nil. I made a sketch of Kinchinjunga and enclose it here. It is second only to Everest. Our view from the centre is the finest in the world, they say. We look down into deep valleys and up to a marvellous panorama of mountain ranges, with Kinchinjunga crowning all. There are snow clad peaks all around us yet the climate is not unlike a bright June in England, though we are in October now. It grows chilly at night.

The town is built on terraces which were made as protective works after landslides in 1899. They resemble promenades and you expect to see a flight of stairs leading down to the beach as you walk along.

We pony-trekked the other day with the guides taking us along safe mountain tracks. We met a colonel, his wife, daughter and young son. They invited us to tea at their bungalow. They were charming people. Today we went round the bazaars and saw the coppersmiths at work. We bought one or two bowls, hand-beaten with typical Indian designs in black, green and red. I bought a carpet further along and asked the dealer to send it to you. It is fairly expensive here so I think it would probably be beyond your means in England. The merchant reassured me that since the war started he has sent dozens of carpets to Blighty.

I have started to write notes for a war novel that I intend to write when I get home and I will include this place.

If James Aldridge can write Signed with Their Honour from his own experiences, I can write something about my experiences. Love to all, Robby.

Some weeks later Emma was delighted to receive a carpet as promised, a beautifully made pale blue and grey bedroom carpet with tassels. They carried it upstairs and when it was laid in the large bedroom, they thought it gave the room a luxurious appearance.

Following the delivery of this cherished gift, Bernard Kelvin wrote. Margaret and he had been corresponding regularly. He was due for repatriation. He promised to come post-haste once he had been home to see his parents. She was so thrilled that she decided to receive him with all pomp and circumstance.

* * *

Dear Ma and Folks,

It is over a month since Bernard left. I still feel forlorn. We reached our destination only to find that our section had moved up two weeks ago during our leave. Now we have to await transport. Trev and I occupy a tent in the jungle with a chap called Maxwell and two other section mates. I found a snake coiled up in my blankets the other evening. It was a shock. Roy Maxwell told me to make sure my mosquito net was tucked in under the blankets at the bottom. I knew this, of course, but had been careless.

The tango jealousy is blazing out from someone's American transmitter/receiver and it is a wonderful arrangement that gives me a warm feeling. These American sets have their own generators behind them on a trailer.

Roy has just come in from the canteen and said there's very heavy traffic - convoys going full-speed to Kohima. I hope everything goes well there for the poor devils trapped in the town.

Next Day:

This morning we went to the hospital to see John, Roy's brother-in-law who has had his arm amputated after a do when the Japs blew it to jelly.

He says he can still feel his fingers itching. Nerves are strange at times.

At the far end of the ward are some signals blokes from the heart of Burma. The Long Range Penetration Group (Wingate). I went to see them and found Jimmy Rostron - my mate from Prestatyn days. He looks ill. His legs are a mass of jungle sores. We had a long chat and when it was time to go I said I'd call on Saturday to take him some fags and chocolate. That's how things happen in the army - you meet all kinds of people you never expect to see again and suddenly you find the army is full of startling and unbelievable coincidences.

Goodbye for now and much love.

Robby.

That was the last letter the Fergusons received from Corporal Robert Ferguson and their anxiety stretched itself over three months of nervous suppositions.

One day the bus stopped outside Emma's small house and a soldier got down and looked around.

'That's the house you want,' said the conductor, and the soldier with his nut-brown tan and lean figure, came across the road and knocked at ma's door.

CHAPTER 6

1950
MAN OF LETTERS

The Ministry people were using a temporarily converted house in Wigan. Twenty-four applicants had arrived by ten o'clock and sat round on wooden forms in what had once been the drawing room. Robby saw they were a mixed lot, some under twenty, others about his own age, but each spruced up in his own particular way. A bald-headed man came in and counted them.

'Good. You are all here, gentlemen.' He handed out duplicated sheets. 'On this paper you will find twelve subjects. You are required to select one of them and write about it. When I think you have written enough, I shall return and collect the papers. You will find foolscap and pencils at the far end of the table there. Don't forget your full name at the top of the paper.'

He withdrew and closed the door quietly behind him.

They seated themselves, each with paper and pencil, around three trestle tables placed end to end, with long stools on each side. Robby felt his apprehension rise when he overheard their conversations: most of them were grammar school types. He didn't stand a dog's chance! And Angus had persuaded him to go in for it. He wrote his name and began immediately - THE ENGLISH CLIMATE - the first subject on the list.

Mark Twain wrote ~ There is no bad weather, only different kinds of good weather. This would seem nonsensical to many Lancashire people. The wisdom of the observation, however, is brought home to you when you are an Innocent Abroad. In the heat of the desert, your tongue raw with thirst, your eyes blinded with hot dust, your nostrils choked with sand, and your water bottle is empty and you could screech to the skies with the irritation of your prickly rash, then it is that you dream of rain lashing down on the flagstones of Manchester, swirling along the gutters, and rushing into drains. What a blessed picture this presents to you then! What delight to think of enjoying that wonderful, cool, refreshing weather that is so common in England!

When your body is drenched in sweat and you squirm beneath the tropical sun, you remember English springs and English autumns and the memory makes you sick with nostalgia. You think of green meadows on good summer days and fancy yourself lying in the grass under a sun that is not your arch enemy, with cool breezes fanning the grasses around your head.

Then you come down to earth: you are abroad and such luxuries cannot be enjoyed - there are snakes, scorpions, monster spiders and a multitude of insects to contend with, especially termites and ants that are native to most hot countries. The climate, too, generates its own vicious types of diseases that are unknown in England. You have all these secret longings about home, yet you suffer the irritations with stoicism because you are British: climate has bred in you great patience, great toleration, a sense of humour and its own gently moderating influences; and your long-suffering character receives confirmation of its qualities when you hear two foreigners screaming at one another over some trivial incident and you tell yourself you are superior to them because you are more stable by nature....'

'Hey! Chaps, look at this bloke! He's done a full page already!' It was a red-haired fellow sitting next to Robby. They all looked up and eyed Robby. They probably thought he was a bloody swot! A stout bespectacled youth at the far end of the table blinked down towards Robby's paper.

'I say, old chap,' he called. 'I shouldn't scribble if I were you. Your best handwriting is most important. That's what they're looking for, you know.'

One or two of the older men laughed and jeered at the youth.

'Balls!' Robby laughed. 'They're finding out if we're

literate or not.'

'Yer,' said one or two in agreement. Robby smiled at them and resumed his writing.

It occurred to him that if his theme was to agree with Mark Twain's observation, why was he complaining so vociferously about tropical weather? He put this right at once by pointing out that it is the frequency of kinds of weather that forms climate and weather itself is not bad; if, say, monsoons lasted three days instead of weeks and weeks, no one would grumble about them; if tropical heat lasted for two hours each day, no one would suffer from it. English climate was the best because of its great variety. The bald-headed man came in.

'Now, gentlemen, please pass down your papers and pencils. Would you please sort them?' This last was addressed to Robby. He was amazed to see that some of the papers had only half a page of writing and many of the essays were marked with crossings-out here and there. There were half a dozen respectable efforts, but the rest looked hopeless. Perhaps, he thought, he did stand a chance?

He remained at the top of the table and fell into a deep reverie, recalling his reception on the day he had come home, how his ma had linked arms with him and taken him across the fields and how Flora had thrown her arms around him and held him tightly, and he feeling her tears transferring themselves to his cheek.

On the Wednesday of the first week at home, he had travelled reluctantly to Liverpool and had taken a tram to Dingle, a mile or so from where George Foulkes had lived in those far- off days. He had found the red post office where Stella worked. He was sick at heart and pain filled his chest when he saw her face light up with great joy. A little pensioner was taking her money from the counter.

'Robby! Oh, Robby!' Stella had breathed, delightedly excited. He knew she loved him - the mere look on her face, animated and bright with sparkling eyes. He felt like a rat standing there waiting for the old woman to fumble her pension into her purse. He looked at Stella with a frown and shook his head. A letter would have saved all this misery for him. The old woman departed and he felt the utter desolation of being alone with Stella.

'Stella!' he said, sharply, his mouth dry, 'for God's sake don't look at me like that! I've come to say goodbye, that's all. I'm very very sorry - I say goodbye now and hope you find some decent fellow whom you will love. I tried to tell you in my letters. You should not have relied on me. I'm bitterly sorry, Stella.'

The sudden anguished dazzle of tears in her eyes made him feel sick. Her face was haggard and hurt, as if she had suffered a stab-wound.

'Your ma - Margaret - they tried to warn me - I didn't believe - I couldn't!'

With her handkerchief to her eyes she ran into the living quarters. He stood in the middle of the floor not knowing what to do. Then his cowardly self was relieved when an old man entered, clutching his pension book. The postmaster came out, frowning over his glasses.

'What have you done to the girl?' he demanded. 'Get out of this shop. Go on - get out. You bloody soldiers are all the same.'

That was it. He left the misery behind him and walked slowly to the bus stop and boarded a bus to Exchange Station. Once seated he felt the whole of his wretchedness surging back like a huge sore inside him of pity and sympathy and guilt. As the train stopped at each station, the various activities going on occupied his mind like a temporary balm. He had never known he could play the cad so well! He had suffered the ordeal because he felt he had been in a strange trance of determination to write FINIS to his association with Stella Wilkins. He never fully comprehended why he had behaved in that way, but he did not love her and a strong instinct told him that marriage with her would have been disastrous.

When the red-haired fellow had his name called and went into the interview room, Robby tried to squeeze from his mind the memory of that terrible meeting. He simply must go into that interview room looking bright and cheerful - a smiling face and confidence was the order of the day.

The big fellow was not long in. When he reappeared, cigarette packet in hand, the assembled youths looked at him expectantly. The stout one in glasses asked how he had gone on.

'Well, you blokes,' said red-hair, 'they ask three basic questions - among other things - Why do you want to be a teacher? What have you accomplished in your life so far? and Do you like children?' He took out a cigarette and lit it. 'I said I wanted a job with short hours and long holidays. I hadn't accomplished anything so far. And I hate kids.'

There came a spluttering of laughter at this cavalier attitude.

'So you know what to say, blokes - you want to civilise the world, you did mission work in Outer Mongolia, and you love all kiddiewinkies. Personally, I'm going back to my old man's workshop. I only came to please my mother.' He put on his coat, said cheerio, and left.

Robby was called just after noon. He had been there since nine-thirty. There were only three members of the panel behind a trestle table. He smiled and sat down. The bay window behind them showed a jungly garden with a bent tree in the corner. The bald man sat in the middle with a stoutish, jolly-faced woman in grey tweed suit, and on his left an elderly fellow with a hearing-aid. When the sun came out from a cloud, Robby was bathed in light, and the panel silhouettes.

'Mr Robert Ferguson?' Bald-head confirmed, and Robby said 'Yes sir,' respectfully.

'What a marvellous tan!' Tweedsuit burst forth in a jolly voice. Hearing-aid murmured 'hm!'

'We have read your essay, Mr Ferguson,' said Bald-head.

'Very good. I thought. What did you think. Miss Routledge?'

'Oh absolutely,' said Tweedsuit, 'and from personal experience of course. The references to Mark Twain fitted admirably - Innocents Abroad an' all that.'

'Yes, I thought that was neat,' Bald-head agreed. 'We have also read your application form and references. All excellent.'

'Why do you want to teach?' asked Hearing-aid – basic question number one.

'Well,' Robby sighed. 'As I have travelled the equivalent of twice round the world and have matured during that time. I have much to offer the children, not only in subjects like geography and history, but also in art and religious instruction, all of which I made notes on while abroad.'

'Good,' said Bald-head.

'Do you like children?' asked Hearing-aid. Number two.

'Yes. I do,' said Robby, honestly. 'I get on with them and they seem to like me.'

'Do you think that the experiences in the war give you a mature approach to teaching?' This was Bald-head asking leading questions.

'Yes, I think I have a lot more to give children than they would receive from young students straight from college.'

'Oh, I do agree,' said Tweedsuit. 'And what would you say you have achieved in your life?' Be honest, Robby warned himself.

'Not an amazing amount. I was promoted to corporal in the army and first-class operator. I had my first short story published when I was sixteen, and I have written a book about Burma.'

'Excellent!' said Tweedsuit, enthusiastically.

'I'm not saying that this book will be published...'

'Nonsense!' Tweedsuit intervened. 'Get it sent to a good publisher. Don't despair, m'boy.'

'Now, Mr Ferguson, I personally think you'd make a good teacher, and I must now ask my colleagues if they feel the same.'

'Absolutely!' Tweedsuit laughed, heartily. 'After some of this morning's...'

'Shush!' warned Bald-head. 'What about you Sedburgh?' Hearing-aid nodded his agreement and began to gather his papers.

'Good. There you are then, Mr Ferguson. In a few

weeks you will have a medical inspection, a cursory one - nothing to worry about - I presume you are A1?'

'Yes sir,' said Robby.

'Good. After that you will receive by post a list of Emergency Training Colleges for Teachers. You choose one and inform them and then you will be required to go there in time to take an entrance examination to decide what group you will be placed into. In your case, I think we all suggest English Literature and Art. You are, of course, proficient in maths - arithmetic if you like - having been an account's clerk. Very well, then, I have registered your name. We all hope you do well.'

'Thank you,' Robby said, stood up, smiled and said goodbye. As he left the room he heard Tweedsuit's hearty voice - 'A very engagin' young fella, by jove' and he felt like returning to kiss her on the cheek. These tweedy, horsey types were damned good at giving everyone around them complete confidence. He would get to work on that book again.

It was an amazing fact, he thought, that he had been accepted into the teaching profession. He would have to work like hell when the time came. He had passed honestly with only one trick - his first story published at sixteen. He travelled back on the stopping train from Manchester to Leyland with his heart singing and his future prospects brighter than they had ever been. He had forgotten all about Stella's misery!

*   *   *

Robby hurried through the yard past some outhouses, his eyes riveted on the rotting stake that held the dog's chain. Reaching the front door of the farmhouse he saw at once that it had not been used for years. Tufts of grass were rooted in the flagstones, the door firmly glued with the dirt and dust of ages. Timidly he edged his way round to the side door. At the corner of the house a mere foot or two separated him from the animal's slavering jaws! With his stick he made a swipe in mid-air towards the dog. The Alsatian slithered back from its lunge then pounced again with renewed fury. A great, heavy, vicious beast, Robby thought, and hurried to the porch of the side entrance. Watching him with a face like a gargoyle stood the farmer, Fitzwarren, a man of indeterminate age, with barrel paunch and heavy jowl and arms like oak roots. Robby was unaware that the man was probably his mother's illegitimate half - brother!

'Keep that stick t' y'self, mister,' he growled. 'The dog's tied up, aint it?' Robby's tan saved him from appearing white-faced and distraught. It took an effort to calm his jittering nerves and speak normally.

'Yes, he's tied up - but that stump's loose. I was warned at the office to bring a stick.'

'Oh, were y' now?' Fitzwarren sneered. 'Let's see what thee's got f' me?' Robby handed over the correspondence and turned to go.

'Hey! -'Owd on a bloody minute - Pendergast tells me y' does a bit o' sign-writin'?'

'I do,' said Robby, his spirits sinking.

'I want me name, address, and phone number on that there truck yonder - on t' door-panels. I've just finished paintin' 'em. It's on this 'ere card, look.'

Robby took the card and read, 'T Fitzwarren, Lane End Farm, Tel, Coppleton 423.'

'There's a good seven hours' work here. Three pounds.'

Fitzwarren guffawed. 'Thee's bloody jokin' fella. I wanna cheap job. I'll gi' thee thirty bob an' ten bob's-wuth of apples.'

'Apples? I don't want your bloody apples. Three pounds 'Thirty bob an' t' apples. If y' doesn't want bloody job some other bugger'll do it.'

'Not for apples he won't.'

'I con get a bleedin' expert f' three quid.'

'I am an expert,' Robby told him. He'd show this loud-mouthed bastard he couldn't tread on him. The bloody cheek of the sod!

'Then why are y' deliverin' bloody letters, fella?'

'This is a temporary job, mister - I'm going to college in January.'

'Orright - if y' doesn't want bloody job, bugger off.' Fitzwarren turned and re-entered the house.

As soon as Robby turned and came towards it, the dog reared up like a half-starved wolf and renewed its savagery. Robby raced across the yard, leapt over the gate, and mounted his cycle. He pedalled madly along the cart track, the Alsatian's insane roar growing fainter in his ears. At the end of the lane he dismounted and took out a cigarette. He lit it and drew deeply and thanked God the ordeal was over. There would come another time but held face that dread moment when it arrived. The fantastic cheek of the big, fat slob!

Robby began to doubt his gratitude to Jack Volant's cousin, Michael O'Shea - senior postman, for recommending him to the post master. Fitzwarren was a disgrace to the farming community - a lazy, sneaky disgrace.

One morning Fitzwarren saw him in the village. 'Hey, you!' the farmer shouted. Robby drew into the kerb and waited. 'What do you want?' Fitzwarren expected him to go over the road to him but he was damned if he would. The farmer came across.

'What about yon job? The truck's waitin' some spare parts. I'll gi' thee two pounds cash.'

'Three pounds,' Robby said. 'With that bloody dog of yours you should pay danger money.'

'Bloody dog won't 'arm thee,' Fitzwarren sneered. 'Orright, three pounds.'

'I'll come this afternoon to measure up,' Robby said, and pushed down on the pedal.

Fitzwarren returned to the greengrocers shop he had been about to enter.

Robby planned the job carefully, measuring the doors and outlining the job first, drawing out the name in an arc at the top, the farm straight across the middle, the telephone number centred neatly at the bottom. The dog's noise on his arrival, had drained the warmth from his face. There was some fat and a dirty bone near the kennel. Robby pitied the poor wild thing. All the villagers knew about it, some saying it should be put down, others saying that the RSPCA should be informed. Ignoring the animal he mixed the paint and started to work, dark blue letters against the pale blue background, knowing that the dark blue would help disguise the farmer's slap-dash painting. After two hours' careful painting, the first panel was completed. He examined it critically in toto and was delighted that he could find no fault.

He rested and lit a cigarette. He had not heard the dog for some time. A glance showed him the poor creature flat out on the flagstones, asleep in the warm sunshine. It wasn't a bad creature he thought. Its savagery had its origin in Fitzwarren's treatment of it.

Collecting his equipment he moved round to the other door. At once the dog was wide- awake, cursing him again in its canine bad language. Its glare and snarl unnerved him for a minute or two and he waited until his nerves settled down. He worked for another two hours and finished the job. Tomorrow he would bring clear varnish and cover the job with weatherproof gloss coats. Neither the farmer nor his wife had made an appearance. After cleaning his brushes and placing them in his box, he started to walk towards the gate. Once more the inevitable canine abuse. As he pedalled away he found that his opinion of the farmer had sunk even below the opinions of most of the postmen.

Next day when he had finished his work on the truck, he ignored the dog and knocked on the side door. In answer came Mrs Fitzwarren, small and sour, eyeing him sideways.

'Is Mr Fitzwarren in?'

'Nah,' she said.

'I've finished the job - sign-writing on the truck.'

'I doan know nothink about that,' she said.

'Will you tell him it's finished when he comes in?'

'Aye, I'll tell 'im.'

That was all. She went back into the den of a house and closed the door. He rode away down the track knowing he would be done, and his ears resounding to the dog's barking. Tomorrow he would ride to the farm and demand payment, letters or no letters.

*   *   *

The chill hour of four-thirty a.m. discouraged him as he stretched out an arm to switch off the alarm. Douglas groaned, then turned over. Robby longed each morning to lie back and relax. The days were all work, food and sleep. The strain was showing in hollow cheeks, and his continual yawning. Two rounds of toast and a cup of tea, then off through the morning mist to the sorting office. He sorted a letter for Lane End Farm one morning. His journey there to demand payment had been futile. The door was unlocked as usual but his enemy had been out and no sign of the wife. He had hardened himself to ignore the dog, despite the month that had elapsed since his last visit. Now with good reason to visit the farm he would demand payment there and then.

As he rode up the long cart track, he saw the blue truck in the distance and Fitzwarren opening the gate. He drew up, jumped from his cycle, leaned it against the gatepost, took out the letter, and approached. About to board the truck, Fitzwarren saw him and came to the gate.

'What 'ave thee got this mornin'?' he asked, breezily, like a cynical old friend.

'Official letter;' said Robby, his voice flat and unfriendly. The farmer's hairy-backed hand grabbed the letter.

'Right,' said Robby. 'You owe me three pounds. I want paying now.

'Oh? Thee does,' does thee? Well, thee's'all get thee money - don't worry.'

With terrifying suddenness the Alsatian appeared in the distance, coming round the corner of the house. Bellowing, it raced across the yard, its neck thick with a main of bristling hair. Foolishly dropping the stick, Robby turned, grabbed the cycle and mounted it. He began to pedal, crazily, with the fear in him almost paralysing his limbs. Fitzwarren guffawed. 'Come 'ere, Tiger,' he shouted. The dog ignored him. It was out for blood and it raced after Robby with ominous pants of fury.

Robby's foot jerked hard down and he knew immediately that the rear wheel hub had been tugged out of place by the force. The left side of the frame was being scraped by the wheel rim. The pace was reduced by two thirds as his legs pumped up and down and the wheel screaming 'Screak, Scrawk, Screak, Scrawk!' - a nightmare ride when all endeavour is to no avail and the doom you anticipate comes nearer and nearer and you wake up just in time to gasp relief that it's a dream; but this was no dream and there would be no awakening. The Alsatian caught up with him almost rabid, and leapt, its fangs showing. With a hard kick Robby struck its nose and it was thrown back momentarily, bellowing loudly. It came on again, half way along the track. Robby felt the hot sting of teeth above his anklebone and the warm flow of blood. 'You vicious bastard!' he roared, applied the brakes and jumped off. Taken unawares the dog hesitated for a fraction of a second and Robby ran to it and with full force of his boot kicked it beneath its snout. All his pent-up fury went into the kick. The dog was tossed back, snarling, its tongue suffering its own teeth bite. Robby kicked the rear wheel straight, and quickly tightened the wing nut. He remounted and rode off with speed. Tiger regained its impetus and sped after him, silently, licking its mouth, and reached the end of the track. It had vanquished its adversary from its territory. It loped back, feeling the hurt of its teeth on tongue and was rather subdued.

When Robby reached the main road, he sat on the grass verge and lit a cigarette. He turned up his trouser bottom and rolled down his sock. The blood was oozing out of the teeth marks and his sock was soaked. He would go straight home and his ma would attend to it.

As he pedalled home, uncomfortably, he tried to reassure himself that he was no more a coward than other people when it came to vicious dogs. Lots of people were scared of dogs. That time in Cairo when a mangy scavenger near Bab-el-Luk station had snarled at them, big Corporal

Trevitt had jumped to one side. He had confessed that mad
dogs scared him stiff, and no one would ever call Trev a
coward.

As soon as Emma saw the blood, she was furious.

'They should put that damned dog down! It's a menace
to the neighbourhood, everybody says. Suppose you know
who that Fitzwarren is?'

'No, I don't.'

'His mother was Molly Hickstead who was one of your
grandfather's so-called housekeepers. She left when I was
still at school and married old Tom Fitzwarren, poor devil -
farm-labourer. He was a good worker was Tom, and he
eventually married Molly, managed to improve himself and
get that farm. Of course, they said the birth was premature
when that fellow was born, but even as girls we knew she
was pregnant before she married Tom. Molly was one for
the men and at home we heard some awful goings-on. She
was supposed to look after us. Luckily she only stayed about
two months and then bamboozled poor Tom Fitzwarren into
marrying her. He didn't know so early on that she was
pregnant, of course. You take it from me that that farmer of
yours is my half brother, all right.'

'So that fat slob is your half-brother? My God! It makes
me sick to think about it!'

*　　*　　*

Robby cycled to Lincoln Meadows on a misty morning
in November. There were hordes of young men some with
old school ties and scarves. In the one-time GI's messroom,
a huge hall with fanlight in the ceiling, they all sat down and
were given three papers that would last three and a half
hours. Their future Vice-principal, a Cambridge man, acted
as the invigilator and a staff of lecturers gave out the papers.

Despite his initial nervousness, Robby quickly gained
confidence. A subconscious impetus lent his brain a clarity
and comprehension he had not thought possible; but he was
tired after weeks of early rising and late nights working on

his sign-writing. His concentration began to flag during the second paper and he found he could hardly keep awake, his initial nervous energy waning slowly, leaving him no reserves. He completed the General Knowledge paper and placed it with his English paper at the top of the desk. In the middle of the IQ paper he began to yawn, each yawn becoming deeper and longer until he was weary with opening his jaws. The men around him, irritated, frowned in his direction. Seconds later they too were yawning. In the space of three minutes the hall was a scene of yawning students! The invigilator mounted the rostrum.

'Right, gentlemen, stop now. Have a break for twenty minutes - and, incidentally, I advise you all to get to bed earlier. Tea and biscuits at the counter over there. You may smoke. When you come back you will fill in a form to show your specialist subjects. Leave your papers where they are - but just ensure that your name is on each paper.'

Robby bought some tea and biscuits and sat down at a corner table.

'I say, old man, you fairly started us all off - yawning like mad you were.' A large bony fellow sat down at Robby's table. 'I had to laugh when the old Vice-prince told us all to go to bed earlier.'

'I'm sorry. I haven't had much sleep lately,' said Robby. Another tall individual came over. The bony youth greeted him with 'Well, how goes it, Frank?'

'Not bad. How did you go on?'

'Oh, I made a mess of the General Knowledge things. I was just telling our friend here how we all caught the yawning disease. I'm Charlie Lowther, late of medics. This is Frank Stubbs, late Royal Corps of pigs.'

Robby's face brightened. 'I was in Pigs.'

'Were you? What a coincidence! What unit?'

'33 Corps - wireless op.'

'I was a line officer.'

'Once we get into this teaching lark,' said Lowther, 'We'll be the lowest educational pawns in the profession.'

'I don't see why,' Stubbs said, lighting a cigarette and handing one to Robby.

243

'Nor I,' said Robby. 'It's like the army - useless when it comes to full-scale war. This is an emergency and you call out the civilians.'

'Yer,' Stubbs agreed. 'Well put. And the conscripts were better than the regulars.'

'Every time,' Robby said. 'At least, we're not baby-faced kids straight from college.'

A bell sounded and they returned to their desks. When Robby had written Art and English on his form, his specialist subjects, he felt he had reached the point of no return. In January, said the Vice-Principal, they would assemble in this hall and would then be allocated to their various tutorial groups, depending on the results of the examination.

Robby rode home with mixed feelings. His English paper had been good, having had the attention of his earlier inspiration. He was dubious about the other two papers. Would he be placed in first-rate tutorial group or be left to struggle along in a group of mediocrities? By the time he reached home he was so tired in body and mind that he no longer cared. He went to bed and slept soundly for four hours.

* * *

The week before Christmas he worked full-time, sorting and delivering three times a day. There was only one letter for Lane End Farm and, apart from the dog, there had been no sign of life. Wages and tips and sign-writing money made a comparatively generous income which could be used to buy gifts for the womenfolk. His army gratuity had vanished long ago, the post office wage being a vital link between unemployment and teacher training for which he had been apportioned a student grant. Late Christmas Eve Jack Volant suggested going out for a drink at the *Pig and Whistle* to open the Festive Season. They dressed warmly against the bitter weather and walked into the village. Half an hour to closing time and they had difficulty in reaching the bar through the crush.

'Let's go outside,' Jack said, when they had their pints in their hands. 'We're well wrapped up.'

They pushed their way through the throng and came to the vestibule. Jack said, 'Cheers!' and Robby replied. They supped the beer slowly. Jack had never been a heavy drinker, but his brother-in-law felt he could easily have gone on a rip-roaring binge with some of his old army mates.

They chatted for a while about arrangements for Christmas and New Year. Robby said Bernard and Margaret were coming up from the Midlands on Boxing Day, and so forth. Idle chatter. Then the bar door opened and an elderly man came out. He stood for a while lighting his pipe. He had just thrown down the match when a burly fellow lurched out, bumping into the old man, knocking him against the wall. The drunk staggered across the threshold and over to a lorry in the car park.

'Hey! That's Fitzwarren,' Robby exclaimed.

'Clumsy bugger,' the old man shouted.

'So that's the swindling, loud-mouthed farmer you were telling us about?' Jack said. 'God! He must have had a gallon. Look at him! Just missed that darned gate post by an inch!'

'And he's got to drive to Coppleton, too,' said Robby.

The vehicle reversed sharply then roared away around the corner and along the main road, the three watchers seeing the rear lights swaying from side to side.

'Yon bugger'll kill hisself one o' these nights,' said the old man in disgust. 'An' a good job if he do, the useless bugger! 'Ow he gets back t' yon farm's a miracle!'

'He's a menace in more ways than one,' said Robby.

'Aye, he's that,' the old man agreed. 'Lazy good-for-nowt bugger. Th'on'y thing 'e can do is grow big taters. Goo' night t' y'

'Goodnight,' they called as the old fellow shambled off, puffing clouds of smoke onto the cold air. They took their empty glasses back to the bar and started back for home.

*   *   *

'A pity you weren't confirmed, Mr Ferguson,' the Rector said in his falsetto voice. 'We need loyal members of the Church in our schools.'

Robby did not answer. The Rector was a stumpy, hefty man with black eyebrows, bushy and threatening; sleek black hair all tight round his Germanic head and finishing in two short sideburns; the Rectorial lips had a permanent sneer, more developed now as he looked at Robby over his bull nose, and thinking that this ex-serviceman wasn't what he really wanted. He turned to the door of the huge rectory reception room muttering to himself about re-advertising for a suitable teacher for his 1839 boys' school.

Robby sighed. He could do with a soothing smoke but he dare not light up in that holy den of the black Rector. Why had the Authorities sent him here? He knew he had gone through his thirteen months at college and had come out with flying colours gaining a Distinction. He marvelled that he had done it!

The Rector's elderly housekeeper came in. She was used to all this. 'Come on, mister.'

When he entered the interview room he was faced with six members - a local butcher, two Parish Councillors, a retired mill-owner, the Rector, and a woman from the Education Authority.

'Please sit down Mr Ferguson,' the woman said. 'Your application form states that you were in the army six and a half years and reached the rank of corporal. I must say, you didn't advance very far, did you?' The woman's mouth smiled.

'I advanced as far as I wanted to go,' Robby said. 'I enjoyed operating. The war wasn't a career. Once you advanced beyond corporal you ceased to do operating and you became an administrator. Promotion would have meant splitting up from my friends, too.'

'Was that so important?' the Rector queried.

'Yes, it was important. Companions and operating were the only two good things to me in army life during the war.'

'Let's get on,' said the woman. 'I see you specialised in English and Art. Are you good at maths?'

'Yes - arithmetic I prefer to call it. I was accounts manager for a big Liverpool firm,' Robby lied. He had already written to Quilter.

For the first time the butcher intervened.

'Thar wouldn' taich abaht comoonism, wouldst tha?'

Robby turned his head to look at the fellow, a stout, blood-faced jelly of a man. Why was such a person on an interview board?

'No,' Robby assured him. 'I wouldn't teach any political isms.'

'Aye, we doan wan no commoonism,' said the butcher.

'Are you prepared to give up Saturday mornings to take inter-school games?' asked one councillor 'You are not expecting to take games during school hours, are you?'

Robby had a strong urge to say 'Why not?' but thought better of it and murmured, 'No, sir.'

'Good,' said the councillor. 'Schools waste far too much time messing about with games.' The mill-owner woke up to grunt 'hear hear!'

'Are you a regular church-goer, Mr Ferguson?' asked the second councillor, a sidesman.

'Not every week in the year,' Robby said, shifting in his seat. 'Since coming home from the war I haven't had time to join a church. I'm new to this part of the country. My mother and family came to live in Leyland while I was abroad. They were bombed out. I was a choir member at St Michael's in Liverpool.'

'Um,' said the woman, not impressed; but Robby saw the Rector making a note on his paper.

'You do realise, I hope,' sang the Rector, 'you'll be on probation for two years and you will have to attend evening lectures - all necessary in improving yourself?'

'Yes, I know that.'

'Are there any more questions?' The board of managers looked at the Rector and shook their heads. Robby relaxed. It was over!

'Very well, Mr Ferguson, we'll let you know,'

'Thank you,' Robby murmured and crept out of the room. As he walked to the bus station, smoking a cigarette thankfully, he imagined various kinds of derogatory remarks being made about him. To hell with the lot of them. If he didn't get a bloody job teaching, he would borrow some money and go into sign writing.

He paced the bus station for a while and when the big red bus came he went upstairs. It crawled past the rectory and he saw the Rector emerging wearing a black coat with black astrakhan collar, a black Homburg, and carrying a five foot stick, all shiny black except for the ornamental silver knob. The Rector walked with his shoulders back, looking at the ground over his prominent nose, and holding his stick about six inches from the top, winging it from side to side like a drum major on parade. The pavement was narrow and a young woman with a child in a go-chair had to wheel the thing off the pavement to let the black Rector pass.

'Arrogant bastard!' Robby muttered to the window glass. 'I wonder how purple his face would have been if I'd told him about Trev and me in Beirut with Dina and Necimya!' They were the experiences you never described when you wrote home!

*   *   *

'Please sir, con ah leave t' room wi' paper?' piped the twelve-year old Jobson.

Robby had a mental flash of wizened little Jobson on the bucket petty reading the Daily Mirror.

'What do you mean, lad - with paper?'

'Con ah tek paper wi' me t' wipe mesen?'

'Oh yes, I suppose you can. Where is it?'

Jobson leapt across to the wide window-ledge, groped behind the velvet curtain, and drew out a toilet roll. He tore off two pieces and placed the roll back in its hideout.

'I think you'd better take another piece, Jobson, for a polisher.' Forty-eight boys raised eyebrows and started to giggle, then roar with laughter, murmuring to each other

'A polisher!'

'What's all this about toilet rolls?' Robby asked. 'That big lad - sorry, I've forgotten your name.'

'Wilson, Sir. It gets pinched, sir, if it's left in the bog - and we're allowed only two pieces.'

'So that's it. Seems pretty mean, two pieces. Compare you, Wilson, with little Jobson. I'll let you have five pieces when you go.'

This roused more laughter, including Wilson whose face was a little pinkish. This new approach after years of stodgy school mastering was hilarious.

The headmaster, Walter Norris, came in, stick in hand. He was small, spare, sunburnt.

'What's all this noise, Mr Ferguson?' he whispered. 'Having difficulties?'

'No, no,' Robby told him confidently. 'They were laughing at a remark I made.' Norris sucked in a deep breath and blew out again through pouted lips. 'Dear me, I should never joke with them, whatever you do,' he advised, closing one eye as a secret warning. 'Keep 'em busy. Keep 'em busy.'

He hurried out, threatening the class with a few cane-prods in the air. Robby smiled at this performance and the boys in front smiled with him. This new fella was a bit of a card!

At lunchtime the three men were in the large classroom where Norris taught. Rogers, the third member of staff at St. Chad's, was a hefty fellow about sixty-three, with retirement occupying his mind. He was unqualified but a good, sound teacher, Robby had heard. Robby unwrapped his lunch, mixed sandwiches and an apple as dessert. Norris already had the kettle on the gas ring safely placed in the middle of a dirty old table, its brown dowels showing between leg and horizontal frame. The water boiled.

'Righto, then, Mr Ferguson, brew the tea please,' Norris said. He sat in his desk like a monkey god in a Chinese watercolour. The desk was an old throne with a square platform on castors, a sloping desk with lid, and a hinged seat.

Rogers was stirring his soup in a battered pan with which he had replaced the kettle on the gas ring. He never failed to bring his tin of soup the whole time Robby knew him.

'You've got to keep the little beggars down,' Rogers said, as he stirred, 'otherwise your life can be a misery.'

Robby wondered who the older man was talking to, but the headmaster broke in with 'Quite right, Jim.' Rogers went on stirring and Norris went on munching for about twenty seconds and then he said, as if he had never said it before, 'In all my years of teaching, Mr Ferguson, I have never known a teacher keep order who was too friendly with the kids.'

'I gave Curran three this morning,' Rogers said to the pan. 'He was blatantly copying in maths. If he could do maths as well as he can read, he'd be a real good'un.'

'He's been a real problem,' Norris added. 'Almost as bad as his elder brother. That lad was in the hands of the police on several occasions.'

'Oh? What did he get up to?' Robby asked.

'All sorts - breaking in derelict mills, stealing lead, borrowing bicycles without the owner's permission, breaking windows, et cetera. Real bad'un.'

'My class don't seem to be a bad lot,' Robby ventured. Immediately Norris tittered and Rogers guffawed. They weren't going to let him get away with that ridiculous statement!

'He's a lot to learn, eh, Jim?' Norris chuckled.

'Aye,' Rogers agreed his voice cracking as he said the word, the sound gradually fading with a finality that left no doubt about his opinion of this young upstart. Throughout the whole of the lunch-break of one and a half hours, not once did Jim Rogers look at his new colleague. Robby felt that he had trespassed into a secret society of boy-haters!

*   *   *

The probationary teachers were assembled in a classroom of a large secondary modern school. On the dais behind a desk sat Arthur Rudge, the School's headmaster, acting as chairman. Two colleagues sat one on either side of him. He stood up, his rotund body half hidden by a pile of new books, their dust covers shining. Robby wondered what they were.

'I have great pleasure in introducing to you probationary teachers His Majesty's District Inspector, Mr Gerald Corke.' Rudge indicated the great man on his left. Several young students clapped. Rudge put up his hand. 'We all feel honoured to have Mr Corke with us this evening, and it is very good of him to spare us some of his very busy schedule time.' Frank Stubbs who had become Robby's best friend at college, whispered, 'Doing us a bloody favour.'

Rudge next indicated his other friend. 'And this is a colleague of mine, Councillor Bates, Chairman of Education. Now, before I begin, I would like to mention this book.' He picked up one of the shiny books and fondled it lovingly. I feel strongly, gentlemen, that this book is a must in your reading. I will be selling these later and taking orders for more. It cost only ten shillings and sixpence and is worth every penny.' Rudge opened the book and read the blurb - 'The story concerns the visit of one of His Majesty's Inspectors to a small village school, how the school and its headmistress prepare for the visit, and how the visit affects the whole life of the village. It is written with a profound knowledge of children - and, I may say, of teachers.'

Rudge closed the book and placed it back on the pile. 'Gentlemen,' he declared, dramatically, 'I recommend it most heartily and, of course, as you may have guessed, it is written by our special guest tonight, Mr Gerald Corke!'

There was an outbreak of enthusiastic applause - but not from the ex-servicemen.

'Bloody racket,' Frank Stubbs whispered. 'He can't sell the rotten things and we're being blackmailed into buying them. Just look at that bloody crawler over there with his hand up, Pickering.'

'Yer, I see him. He works here. Rudge is his boss.'

'Yes, Mr Pickering?' Rudge questioned, smiling brightly.

'Mr Rudge, sir, I'd like two copies but I haven't sufficient money on me at the moment. Could I pay you in the morning?' Rudge smiled down at the Inspector.

'Yes, I think that can be arranged, Mr Pickering,' he reassured his trainee.

'Crawling sod!' Frank Stubbs repeated, and took out a packet of cigarettes, handing one to Robby. They lit up and waited.

'And now,' said Mr Rudge, 'Mr Corke will say a few words before he departs.' Corke stood up, a pleasant smile on his face.

'Well, thank you Mr Rudge for that splendid introduction and your mentioning my book. I shall be a millionaire in no time at all.' There was a murmur of forced laughter from the younger students. But the men on the platform did not fail to notice the dour, unimpressed reaction of the older men. 'You are all setting out, gentlemen,' Corke continued in his faraway southern speech; and then he noticed the two men smoking and glared at them icily. 'Would you mind not smoking at this time, gentlemen on the third row there?'

Robby and Frank pressed out their cigarettes on the floor.

'And before you leave this evening, would you mind brushing that ash away? A classroom is certainly not a place to smoke in, as you will soon learn.'

Robby knew at once that he and Frank had been the only ones smoking. A bad start, he told himself, remembering his family's expectations.

'As I was saying,' Corke continued, 'a great adventure, dealing with children, our future citizens and we should think deeply about that - it is a daunting responsibility.'

'Claptrap,' Frank whispered into Robby's ear. Then the substance of what Corke was there for came out.

'Life will not be easy for you during these probationary years and much will depend on how hard you work during these years as to whether you succeed in becoming qualified or not. The temporary certificates you are now holding will count for nothing if you fail these two years of trial. Three evenings a week you will be required to attend courses and lectures, and if you do not fulfil all the obligations, then, of course, you will not receive your teacher's certificate. Our organisers have developed schemes of work and later this evening you will receive duplicated sheets outlining these. My advice, then, is to work hard, be conscientious, remember that you have the lives of young children in your hands, and remember that you will be expected to be an example to them of good living, good social behaviour, and an inspiration to them. I wish you all good luck, gentlemen.'

The young students clapped their appreciation and then they all sat quietly and watched Corke and Rudge conversing in whispers. Rudge took out his cheque book, wrote a cheque and handed it to the Inspector. Corke shook hands with his two colleagues and departed with a slight wave to the assembly.

'How crawly can you get?' Frank Stubbs said in whispered contempt. 'I'd like to vomit over his bloody books. The bloody cheek of it! I'm buggered if I'm going to buy one even if they torture me into submission!'

Robby spluttered in a flurry of laughter and the two men gave them a quick glance.

When Rudge and Bates lit their pipes, Frank and Robby re-lit their cigarettes. Frank purred into Robby's ear again, 'God! The bloody arrogance of that book! It's on a par with the entry into Jerusalem.'

The remainder of the evening was taken up with the programme set out for the two-year probation of the student teachers. They each received a wad of duplicated sheets showing the various courses, lectures, and the meeting points they would tend each week. After two hours in the classroom, Rudge sold the stock of books he had paid for and had taken orders for more copies.

From the promotional and financial angle His Majesty's District Inspector had spent a very profitable twenty minutes of his precious time!

* * *

'After so long, boys, you become attached to a place,' said Jim Rogers, 'and I shall miss coming here each day. I shall miss your shining morning faces and the football matches. We've had our ups and downs, some of you boys and I, but deep down, I have loved you all.' There was moisture around his eyes and then a solitary tear trickled down his leathery old face. Jim blew his nose again and wiped away the moisture. There came an amused murmur from the tougher boys - this could not be true, old Jim Rogers with his large horny hands that could hurt like hell when you did wrong, actually LOVING them! It couldn't be true!

Robby knew he might never see the elderly gentleman again and he wondered, melancholically, how he would react when his time came to say goodbye to school life. But more than anything else, Rogers' departure was a snub - a fond farewell to the boys, a shake of the hand with his old friend and colleague, Walter Norris, thanking everyone once more for the leaving present, then the departure from the hall to collect his coat and hat, waving to the boys from the doorway and vanishing, just as if Robby Ferguson had not existed! He puzzled over this snub for a time. It was positively mystifying that Rogers could dislike him so intensely! Why? What had he done to alienate the old man? Why, over two years with Robby as a colleague, had he never spoken a word that was not forced by duty? Was the man jealous and if so of what? He had never been treated fairly by the Authority, had never been allowed leave of absence to become properly qualified, and he had, therefore, been underpaid and underprivileged. Such circumstances must have made him envious of the newcomer who had succeeded, because of some emergency scheme the like of which had never come the old man's way - and in a sour-grapes way Jim had believed the scheme to be inferior training - and he had gone on to the end unrecognised, quietly and reservedly teaching boys for many faithful days. Robby could only console himself with the thought that Jim Rogers would have disliked any newcomer. And three years later, it turned out, that they heard of Jim Rogers' death - a heart attack whilst he had been digging in his allotment! For a day or so Robby had honestly grieved for the man!

Angus's golden day had come. He had escaped from the rubber works! The proprietor of a fried fish shop died and her husband had put the place up for sale. Angus grasped the opportunity at once, having accumulated sufficient funds, together with the sale of his house, to buy the place outright. The shop was clean, fully tiled, and fairly modern with a cellar lit by neon light where all the preparations could be done well away from the living-quarters. There was promise of a very good trade, according to the books and the accounts, the premises being on the edge of a large estate. Emma had gone for a fortnight to give tuition to Gwen, and her son appreciated it. In the traditions of his ma's cooking abilities, Angus provided very tasty fare, free from the least excess of fat, perfectly cooked and always sold piping hot out of the electric boiler. He sold beans and peas but abandoned the variety that Emma had once sold. Within the month he knew he had been justified in taking the business. The previous owner had advised him to keep on with the suppliers of foodstuffs as they had been excellent, and the farmer recommended to him was Thomas Fitzwarren, Lane End Farm, Coppleton, five miles away. His potatoes were fine and large and grown in sandy soil. Angus was quite satisfied to take this advice, being new to the district thereabouts.

They lived over the shop in a well-planned three bed-roomed flat, its front room having a bay window. Gwen had qualms at first about moving from her comfortable home with its fine gardens back and front, and she was nervous about serving behind the counter, worrying about the smell of the cooking on her clothes,' and the possible embarrassment of meeting people she knew who came into the shop.

'Why feel embarrassed?' Angus frowned. 'We're not doing anything criminal or disreputable. We're just trying to make an honest living. We shan't be here for long. Just tell your friends I had to leave the rubber because I strained my back, or something. I know your mother hates it, but the days when folk frowned on Trade are gone forever. Don't worry about it.'

Ronald, now fifteen, was enthusiastic about the change and helped his father by loading the electric machine on Saturday mornings when his father prepared the fish on a large slab against the whitewashed cellar wall. Everything was clean and convenient and Ronald treated the business as a great adventure.

Angus began to rebuild his bank account and felt convinced that once he could build up the trade, he could sell the place at a very good profit and move on to greater things. He arranged with Malcolm and Fay, both experienced, to help on the busiest nights, and paid them well.

At a jumble sale Gwen bought the complete works of Charles Dickens and Angus spent his leisure hours reading through them with great enjoyment. On a rare occasion Robby visited them, Angus enthused over Dickens' stories. Dickens had done a lot for the poor, he said, brought to light injustices, and he was a great reformer. This was Robby's domain - English Literature.

'He brought to light injustices,' Robby agreed, 'but he didn't reform anything.'

'What makes you say that? You haven't read him, obviously,' Angus said.

'Of course I've read him!' Robby scorned. 'I took English Literature at college. All Dickens says in his books is that if all men were good the world would be a happier place. Everybody knows that already. He never suggests, for example, that there should be a redistribution of wealth. He writes about the Cheerybles and the Jellybys of this world. If they had given their money away all the time they wouldn't be rich. Dickens is a caricaturist. He exaggerates good and evil, but he never questions that there should be very rich men, he only pleads that they should be good and help the very poor.'

Gwen laughed and lowered her Sunday paper. 'What a

peculiar idea, Robby! A caricaturist?'

'It's not peculiar to me,' Robby said, quietly. 'Arnold Bennett was right when he said you can't describe characters completely, you'd have a book too tedious to read and impossible to write. You pick out characteristics and conventionalise them. That's what Dickens does.'

'But as a child he and his family did know poverty, surely? His father was only a.clerk or something,' said Gwen.

'Yes, comparatively. His father was the cause of their poverty - ten children and no plan in life to provide for them. His father was inadequate, always moving to escape his creditors, like Micawber. They lived in a kind of middle class poverty. Dickens himself, I think, was something of a snob. When David Copperfield has to work in the bottle factory - as Dickens did in a blacking factory - he thinks the work is beneath him. He doesn't say the work is beneath any of the other boys there. Dickens is probably in the top ten great writers of all time. What I'm saying is he has his limitations, and apart from bringing many evils to light - a good thing in itself, I admit - he did nothing to improve conditions and didn't even try to.'

Discussions of this kind irritated Robby. He felt he had to fight off Gwen's condescension and Angus's definitive opinions, which showed ignorance. Shortly after arriving home from the war, they had taken him to see Blithe Spirit. At times he had laughed out at scenes where Margaret Rutherford appeared, or in those sequences where Rex Harrison argues with his wife in ghost form. In one scene where Rex Harrison has his jacket off, Angus had leaned over and whispered 'just look how that waist-band fits the waist - perfect.' Mystified, Robby had asked himself, how could Angus be so trivial? And outside the cinema, when Robby had said he had enjoyed the film, Gwen had laughed.

'Oh Robby. What rubbish! All based on ghosts going and coming. It was so silly!'

'Hamlet was based on ghosts going and coming.'

'Oh Robby, how can you compare Shakespeare with

Noel Coward?'

'Easily. If you don't believe in ghosts going and coming, Hamlet becomes rubbish and the Bible and lots of other literature, including A Christmas Carol. And the Bible's full of supernatural appearances.'

'I didn't think much of it,' said Angus, putting an end to the discussion in his mind. 'I was most interested in Rex Harrison's clothes. I'd love a suit like that one he wore. I got a suit as good as that from Manny Dartman before the war,' Robby said dryly. And there was no response.

These trivial obsessions of his elder brother bored Robby. How could a sensible, intelligent man be consumed all his life with one idea of trying to raise his social status to such an extent that he could no longer enjoy a comedy by Noel Coward?

Neither of the younger brothers made a great effort to visit Angus. Douglas had not yet outlived even after three years, an incident when he was still in uniform on leave and went to see Angus and Gwen. She had picked a bouquet of flowers from her garden for her mother-in-law. Unknown to Douglas, Gwen's garden backed onto that of her parents. Douglas had fumed about carrying the flowers - did Gwen think he was a bloody fairy? Once out of sight around the corner,' he hurled the flowers over Mrs Hanley's high hedgerow. She had soon found them and taken them into Gwen who had recognised them at once. That evening Gwen had a few harsh words to say to Angus about his brother. The incident confirmed her belief that Angus's brothers, including Robby, were nothing less than uncouth. Ma had written a furious letter to Douglas and grieved that he seemed never to improve.

Douglas had found a job in the paint factory after the war, mixing paint samples and testing their colours for wear and fading. One weekend he brought home a smart girl about twenty, a secretary in the firm. Emma was not impressed and later her opinion of the girl collapsed to the nadir of contempt when she left her sanitary towel in the pan of the lavatory, unflushed. Just supposing the boys had seen it! Disgusting! She was a No Good and far too brazen for her family, the hussy. On his return, Douglas was attacked furiously about the incident. To Emma, talking about a sanitary towel was not as bad as actually seeing it where boys were concerned.

'That's nothing nowadays,' Douglas laughed. 'You don't bother about things like that.'

'Well, I do bother. And don't bring her here any more, the flighty madam!' Emma said, firmly.

Douglas's association with the girl ended when she became pregnant and married the father, much to Emma's satisfaction. She had been right, and Douglas, the fool, had learned a lesson.

Douglas was not such a fool. He had been in Germany during the war and after the Armistice, had seen the concentration camps and had helped with victims. He had been approached by three German boys, one of whom had a revolver. They were no more than twelve years old. Their leader, arrogant little bastard, Douglas said, had given the Nazi salute and had pointed the revolver at Douglas. Without a word Douglas had approached the boy who immediately pressed the trigger and there was a click. Douglas had wrenched the revolver away from the child and had given him a damned good thrashing. His mates came along, heard what had happened, and had dealt with the other little Nazis. Douglas maintained that there would always be Nazis in Germany. None of them believed the evidence of the concentration camps and their horrific cruelties, and they revered the memory of Adolf Hitler. When Douglas opened the revolver he had found three cartridges in the unused chambers!

*   *   *

Flora had been annoyed when Robby had broken off relations with Stella Wilkins. For a while there had been a coolness between brother and sister. Flora maintained that he had played a dirty trick on a lovable girl whom she highly esteemed.

'I don't think he did,' Jack Volant said. 'I wouldn't have a woman like that for a mother-in-law no matter how marvellous the daughter was.'

'That's what Margaret said. But he wouldn't be marrying Florrie Wilkins, would he? I think Robby's been hardened by the army. He's changed. He's become callous and selfish.'

'I don't think so. It's made him more mature, more like, like your Douglas, but what else can you expect? I'm sorry for Stella, but Robby never promised her anything.'

'It's all finished now,' Flora sighed. 'I thought a lot of that girl. I suppose we can do nothing about it.'

'What's more important - he wouldn't want you to,' Jack said, wisely.

It seemed to the family that Douglas and Robby were not keen to get married. Their work seemed to occupy them completely, especially Robby's requirements. There was a trio of lectures each week for which he had to write essays, homework that lasted two to three hours, all extra to the preparation of his school work.

After his routine had settled down, he remembered Miss Routledge at the Wigan interview and her jolly encouragement about his book. He brought down the work he had done on it, entitled *The Lions of Burma*, and spent an hour each night after his schoolwork, rejuvenating the text and reducing it to less than 90,000 words. After six weeks of revision with hope in his heart he posted the manuscript off to a reputable publisher.

*   *   *

When a semi-detached house came up for sale near Angus's shop, he considered Gwen's suggestion that they should move. He could see the possibility in taking the house on a mortgage to live in more congenial surroundings, let the flat above the shop, and walk to work each morning. But who would wish to live in a flat above a shop with all the bustle of customers every evening? The answer came when one of his customers, an elderly lady whose son and family had just returned from Australia, told him of her problem.

'I don't know where they can live somewhere near me,' she said. 'Since Tony died I've lived in my little house and I have no more room for two more adults and three small children. I know for a fact they can't afford a mortgage to buy a house.'

'I can help you,' said Angus, grasping this lucky chance. 'Why not let them live here? It's a fine flat upstairs and reasonable rent - entirely separate from the shop.'

The woman agreed happily, and Angus now had two properties, the rent on one paying a large portion of the mortgage on the other.

From a distance Malcolm watched his brother's schemes and he began to experience the restlessness that comes from feelings of inadequacy. He must move like Angus had done. He searched the small advertisements in the *Lancashire Evening Post* and there came an evening of good fortune - 'To Let, Fish and Chip shop, Blackpool. Living accommodation, three beds, bath, kitchen with dining area, and large utility room at the back.' Fay had no doubts.

They telephoned the landlord to arrange to see the shop tomorrow morning - he would stay off work for once. It all turned out well. Next day he gave notice to his own landlord and within a fortnight they were living in the bracing seaside resort of famous Blackpool! The shop, a mile from the front, excluded the patronage of holiday makers, but its surroundings were a busy shopping centre with many residential streets. They had made a good decision and Fay felt triumphant in that they were now independent and could soon be on a par with Gwen and Angus. Another bonus was that there was an excellent school close by for the boys.

Robby painted two notices for them on orange poster paper - UNDER ENTIRELY NEW MANAGEMENT - and Malcolm displayed them for a week in the front and side windows. Within a month the local population had taken to them, first because they were an attractive couple and second because their cooking was excellent and resembled home cooked foods. Emma's offer to help them get established was politely turned down by Fay.

'She can't say I didn't offer,' Emma told Douglas. 'That I favoured one and not the other.'

'You worry too much about what people say and don't say,' growled Douglas. 'To hell with 'em if they don't want help. Fay's experienced anyway, Gwen wasn't.'

Emma was seeing, not without a little pride, that her two older boys were finding the business they had so hated for many years now proving a good standby as a livelihood and she smiled with the irony of it. She knew catering was always a good trade and in those days there was a profit margin of 150%!

One evening Douglas reported that Benny Solomons had visited the paint works. He had seen him getting out of his Jag looking very smart, and had taken him into the office. Benny had two big paint shops in Liverpool, one of them in Kirkdale, the other managed by their old friend, Alfie Atkins. Douglas and Benny had chatted about old times. Benny's father and mother had died within a year of each other during the war, he himself had been wounded in the Desert, and his eldest brother, Joe, killed in the Ardennes. Douglas introduced Benny to the Sales Manager and the three of them had made a tour of the factory, Benny being especially interested in the new lines of wallpaper and colour charts for paints. Before leaving they had given each other their addresses and Benny promised to write and let them know next time he was coming to the works again. Then he would come to see them all. He had married a beautiful girl and had three children.

The news both excited and disturbed Robby for a while - there was Benny well established and prosperous and already the father of three children, whilst he, Robby, the same age, had no prospects of matrimony anywhere on the horizon. He sat down and wrote to Benny.

Dear Benny,

I was delighted to hear that Doug had seen you in the paint works. He said how prosperous you looked and how beautiful your wife was from the snapshot. And your three kids. You've done well. I always regretted I didn't keep in touch. The reason was that the family got into deep water and nearly drowned. Angus failed in business and came here to Leyland, leaving ma to fend with great difficulty because she had been his guarantor and she had to borrow money. I lost my job as apprentice French polisher which was another blow. So you see we weren't having a very good time. During the second blitz ma and Margaret came here and took this small house for rent.

I was very sorry to hear all the bad news about your family. How did Asher go on? Doug did not mention Asher. The war certainly dealt harshly with your family. I dare say Kirkdale received a battering from the bombs? I went into the Royal Signals as an operator and enjoyed the work. I was in Greece, on the Desert for a while, went on to Palestine, Iraq and Persia, then to India, Assam, and Burma. So I got around. I've written a book about the Burma do and I'm just waiting to see if they accept it.

I am teaching in a small school and have a temporary certificate until I pass through the probationary period which will be any time now. Then I hope to move on to better things. I am looking forward to seeing you again soon

All the best.

Fergy.

At least, Robby thought, he had a bit of good news to tell Benny, not such a success story as Benny's but good enough to show potential.

Robby called it Maunder Thursday. After assembly the hundred and twenty boys sat on the hall floor, when the head had left to go to his room, and Robby stood in front, prayer book in hand for the tiresome weekly dose of learning the Catechism. Rogers had conscientiously performed the chore at least twenty years and it was his legacy to Robby. The night before he had read through the Catechism, even the instructions to Clergy and he tutted his irritation with the utter nonsense of it all. Everyone hated learning the Catechism and Robby knew that without blatant hypocrisy he would never convince them that he had anything but contempt for the stupid rigmarole. He purposely missed out the first question 'What is your name?' It had the potential of complete chaos as they all shouted out.

'Who gave you this name?'

'My Godfathers and Godmother, in my baptism, wherein I was made a member of Christ, the child of God, and an inheritor of the Kingdom of Heaven,' said the boys.

'What did your Godfathers and Godmother then do for you?' The long weary chant came again - 'They did promise and vow three things in my name...'

Robby paraded up and down the margins of the hall. His thoughts were wandering.

'...and walk in the same all the days of my life.'

He saw Curran smiling up at him.

'Right, Curran, you're an excellent reader. Come to the front. You ask the questions.'

Curran almost leapt up, glad to be of service, enjoying the limelight. Curran seemed to discard his north-country dialect once he began reading aloud.

Robby stood near the screen that separated Walter Norris's room from the hall. Last year Walter would have rushed into the hall and advised strongly against using a boy to read the questions, but now he had resigned himself to the unaccustomed approach of his younger colleague.

The Curate always came on Wednesday morning to take assembly and afterwards do half an hour's Bible study. The Rector favoured the Girls' School down a narrow side lane. To the Rector all boys were an abomination. He enjoyed the peace of the girls' School which came under the strict domination of Miss Maggie Munroe. You could hear a feather floating in Crabby Maggie's department. Cecil, the Curate, had been assigned the dread task of trying to instil some moral sensibility into the minds of wilful boys. He loathed the task as much as Robby loathed the Catechism procedure. The poor, thin, ascetic Curate suffered from chronic catarrh and on occasions his air passages would block up and all speech cease. Robby as the disciplinarian, boiled with embarrassment on many occasions when this happened. The boys would wait - would the blocked up nose clear itself in time for the bell? Would the Curate's tight lips and bulging cheeks applying pressure succeed in clearing a passage?

Robby discovered later that a lottery was held each Wednesday about Cecil's catarrh. Big Wilson owned a good watch with a second hand. For a penny, a boy entered the lottery by guessing the number of seconds lost by catarrh. Wilson had the list of names that recorded each boy's guess, no two alike. Each Wednesday lunch time Wilson paid the winner and extracted sixpence commission.

Robby turned a blind eye for one reason - the lottery helped discipline, the punters were so engrossed with counting seconds that they listened to every word the Curate said!

A few weeks after the initial assault on the Catechism, Curran was caught stealing lead from a derelict mill, like his elder brother before him, and was put on probation. For two years he had been the chosen pupil to read the second lesson on Walking Day Sunday, a girl reading the first lesson. On the rehearsal morning before the Sunday procession, Robby accompanied the lad down to church. The entrance around the font was dark but the lights were on near the altar. In front were Miss Munroe with the Rector and two vergers sitting in the tenth pew from the front listening to a pretty girl reading from the Old Testament. Robby and the boy crept in and sat down in the gloom at the back. The girl read splendidly with loud and clear diction and well-modulated voice. The Rector and the two vergers stood up.

Miss Munroe went forward to the girl to take her back to school.

'Splendid! Splendid, Miss Munroe,' came the Rector's falsetto. 'Mary is an excellent reader.' The two females smiled and after a word or two with the men, they came down the aisle. Mary glanced at Robby with a coy smile and

Miss Munroe frowned her distaste when she saw Curran.

'Let's go down now,' Robby whispered.

One of the vergers saw them approaching and spoke to the Rector. He whipped round, his black eyebrows screwed in a fierce knot of anger. He threw up his arm dramatically.

'Out! Out thief!' he shrieked. 'I will not have a thief reading Holy Scripture in my church! Out, you villain!'

'Let's go.' Robby whispered, turning round. They retraced their steps hurriedly, hearing further remarks from the Black Rector about 'these teachers.' Robby was glad to get out into the fresh air.

Walter Norris's ire was raised several degrees when he had been given an accurate report on what had happened.

'You stay there, Curran,' he said, putting on his hat and coat. 'I'll go down to church and put this matter right. Don't you worry, lad.' The little man hurried out, puffing adrenal war paint.

The outcome of the Rector's rejection of Curran's gift of reading excellence was that the lad never again entered a church and in his adult years he was married in a registry office.

At lunchtime the headmaster outlined what had happened. He told the Rector his first duty was to welcome sinners in the church. It was not HIS Church, he was merely a servant of the community which helped to keep the church operating. He had warned the Rector that he would write a formal complaint to the Bishop. Meantime, the Rector could find his own reader for the second lesson and he would not see Walter this year in the march around the parish.

*   *   *

Jim Rogers had never considered entering the school team in the football league. The new board of managers now agreed that the bulge in the birth rate had given the school sufficient numbers from which to make two teams and have reserves as well. Robby appointed big Wilson, in his final year, as captain of the senior team. Robby soon knocked them into shape, insisting on their playing as a team and not keep the play confined to the best players, as had been their habit in the past. Passing of the ball should be decided by positions and not by the ability of players. After much practice before the season began, they had their first home fixture against a strong side from the market town of Bowminster. Their field was rented from a farmer, the ground rough and sloping to one corner. St. Chad's won 1 - 0.

'Wait till we get you on our own ground,' the Bowminster captain said. 'We'll murder you. We're not used to playing on a bloody dung-heap!'

The threat failed to upset Wilson, a huge, muscular lad who boxed and wrestled in his spare time.

'When we get you on a good pitch,' he boasted, 'we'll beat you five nil.' The visitors roared with laughter at this grotesque bravado. The Chad boys practised conscientiously each week, keen to show their new sports master that they had the skill to accomplish great things. As the season progressed they found they were just one point behind Bowminster. In two weeks' time they would have the return match with them to decide who would be top of the league. Bowminster were hell-bent to win, their only loss being against St. Chad's. There was one embarrassing aspect to mar the Chad boys' success - their worn-out football gear, especially shirts, many too small, lads like Wilson showing two or three inches of flesh between shorts and shirt.

'We need some new football gear,' he told Walter. 'The shirts are rotting away and the shorts coming adrift. They give the school a bad name.' His inspiration did not fail; he could not have made a more persuasive comment.

'Do they look so bad?' the head frowned. 'You should have mentioned it before.' Robby thought, he knows they've had this kit donkeys' years.

'My team looks bad, too,' said Allsop, the new teacher from college. Walter tittered. 'I hardly think we have enough funds for one team, let alone two, Mr Allsop.'

'We can raise the money,' Robby said, impulsively. He had thought about it during an away match. 'Raffles and

Jumble Sales. The lads can bring things from home and collect around the neighbourhood. I'll get some posters made.'

'Well, to be honest with you, Mr Ferguson, I don't like boys begging at doors; but I suppose I must agree with you that we shall never find the money otherwise.'

Robby produced twenty outlined Jumble Sale posters from a stencil and the boys carefully painted them in during art lessons.

'It's a pity we can't have the new kit in time for the Bowminster match,' Robby told Allsop.

'Well why don't we buy the kit and retrieve the money later from the sale? I'll pay half if you like. Can you manage the other half?'

'Yes, just about,' Robby grinned. 'It's a good idea. I hope the Jumble Sale works out.'

The result of this display of temporary altruism was that the Chad team ran out onto the Bowminster green and pleasant land like junior, professional players. Wilson threatened his team in the Bowminster School dressing room - 'We're going to beat 'em - by five if possible.'

Unknown to the Chad team, a situation verging on disaster had developed in the Bowninster sports department - two of their star players had broken into a bungalow which happened to be the home of a wealthy businessman, a governor of the school, a fact unknown to the culprits. The boys had been arrested by the police next day on evidence of neighbours. The Bowminster headmaster, punishing pupils where it most hurt, forbade them any further games that year and the two thieves were now awaiting their case to come up in juvenile court.

On the beautifully mown pitch, the Chad boys found it easier to practise their style of close passing and complete control of the ball, being able to dribble well, pass accurately and swerve without falling over tufts of grass. Against a demoralised side, they scored three goals by half time, and the final result was a win for St. Chad's 5 - 1, the Bowminster goal being a penalty. Wilson said it was an accident outside the penalty area!

For many years Walter had taken art with the senior boys. He had a cupboard packed with empty Vim cartons from the caretaker. Walter had pasted them round with coloured gummed paper, the top and bottom halves being in different colours and the sprinkle holes covered with coloured circles. Each week he placed three or four of them on a stool with a white card background and told the boys to 'Get on with it.' For an hour there was a monastic silence whilst Walter finished off the weekly administration chores without interruption. Occasionally he varied the routine by bringing a twig from his garden, placing it in a jam jar and the class drew this as the model. The boys were experts at drawing cylinders and twigs but nothing else.

The ultimate development of Walter's eccentric art lessons was that the adviser who came to release Robby from his probation, strongly advised the headmaster to rearrange the timetable to allow Robby to take art throughout the senior half of the school. Robby's opinion of advisers improved considerably.

'You boys are expert at drawing cylinders,' Robby said. 'You know how the light strikes the cylinder placed in various positions; you know how the eclipse at the top varies according to how high your eye-level is above it, and so on. But now we are moving on and we shall begin by looking at your fingers. They are cylinders, slightly flattened. All round you are cylinders - trees, telegraph poles, lamp posts, chimney pots, rope, arms, legs, bodies, and that gas pipe going up the wall there. Robby progressed to the boys' first attempt at painting a forest scene using their knowledge of cylindrical forms to paint trunks and branches. It was not long before the boys were able to tackle most art subjects using dozens of other basic shapes apart from the old, irksome cylinders, and they began to love their art lessons. Robby knew, of course, that he was not doing anything that Walter Norris would not have done had he the time to spare from the administrative work. And Walter was pleased that the new timetable was successful.

*　*　*

'You know, Mr Ferguson,' Walter said when dinners came, 'it really makes me sick to think of it - dinners in that hall, the smell, the food droppings all over the floor, the clearing away of dishes and tables, and the dinner duties we shall have to face. Every other trade and profession under the sun has its rightful time off for dinner, but not teachers.'

'The Infant's Head told me they could no longer cope at the centre, because of the bulge. Our hall's the biggest so they're sending the dinners here.'

'Yes, yes, I know all about that,' said Walter, testily. 'But I wouldn't put it past the Rector to have influenced the Authority in the first place. You won't believe this - to change the subject - I have been a sidesman at that church for twenty-seven years and the Rector never says my name. Every Sunday morning he says Good morning Councillor Burrows and then to me he says Good morning Mr - erm...'

'That sounds like a deliberate insult to me,' said Robby.

'It is, it is. That man is so full of his own importance he insults anyone he doesn't like. Of course, he dislikes me because I won't tolerate his high-handed attitude. He hasn't forgotten my reporting him to the Bishop about Curran that time. When he came to this parish years ago he started off by sending me a letter at the beginning of term outlining what religious instruction syllabus I should follow, and then demanded that I send six boys every month to be tested by him or his curate in their knowledge of the Creed and Catechism. I can tell you, I was down at that rectory in quick time. I said the teaching in this school is my business, not his, and in no circumstances would he be allowed to interfere. I told him to keep away. That's why he favours the Girls' school and Miss Munroe - although she doesn't allow him his own way, either, I must say that. When I retire, you'll see - HE will influence the managers in HIS choice of the next head, he'll make sure of that.'

Robby was on duty every ninth day, opening by saying grace then walking round the hall keeping order and admonishing children for bad table manners. Each time he caught the eye of a senior girl she smiled sweetly. They all seemed to be charming creatures one day the headmistress came in.

'Are any of my girls misbehaving themselves?' she asked.

'Certainly not, Miss Munroe. They are the nicest girls I've ever seen.' Miss Munroe cleaned her glasses and eyed him shrewdly, 'Are you being sincere?'

'I am indeed. They are beautiful girls.'

'Well, thank you. I shall tell them that. I am proud of my girls - although there are one or two exceptions. This is the first time I have had a word of praise from the boys' department.'

'Miss Munroe, Mr Norris thinks the same as I do.'

'Now I can't believe that for a moment,' she replied, acidly.

'It's quite true,' Robby insisted. 'He said your girls outshone all other girls' schools.' Robby leaned towards her and said, quietly, 'But I don't think he would acknowledge it to you.' Miss Munroe was enjoying the conversation. This Ferguson fellow was a charmer.

'You will always find peace in my school. Purvis, the inspector, told me the other day that my school was oppressively quiet, if you please. I told him that while I was head it would be quiet, oppressive or not. These people have no idea.' She looked thoughtful for a second or two 'I believe you type?' she asked, smiling.

'Yes. I have a machine at home.'

'I know I'm being rather cheeky - but would you be kind enough to type the minutes of the Soroptimist meetings for me? I'm appointed secretary and I can't type.'

'Certainly,' he smiled. 'I would be glad to.'

'That's most kind of you. They're confidential, of course. I'll pay expenses.'

'There'll be no expenses. I'll make a carbon copy as well.'

'Oh, excellent. You are kind. I'm glad we've had this little chat.'

Miss Munroe suddenly looked pleasant and human behind her gleaming glasses and they chatted on a little longer about Robby's war travels, much to the curiosity of the senior girls. Robby soon realised he had conquered the indomitable Crabby Maggie. A girl returned with the minutes, blushing as she handed him the papers. 'Miss Munroe says I have to tell you, thank you for being so kind,' said the girl with a shyness that was very attractive. As the weeks passed and the headmistress seemed to be mellowing, the senior girls all loved him for it. In a group, schoolgirls had a collective intuition that could size up a situation very shrewdly!

*　　*　　*

It was unusually hot before Whitsuntide. Robby counted and registered the school dinner money, a job Walter had delegated. It was Friday afternoon and all was quiet as middle school boys wrote their essays for the last of the internal examinations. Robby had allowed them to take off their jackets and drape them over their knees. The money totalled correctly and Robby stuffed it tightly into moneybags from the bank, and then sat watching the boys at work. Next week they would break up for the Whit holidays.

The desks were widespread to discourage copying. Robby looked up. One boy, Ian Curtis, in his solitary desk at the back of the room, looked flushed and strained. He was a tall, handsome, honest lad with a friendly personality, a member of a family that had left Liverpool during the blitz and had settled down locally. Robby thought the lad must have had stomach ache and was afraid to ask to leave the room because of the strict rules about examination procedure. Soundlessly, Robby moved slowly to the window ledge and quietly tore off three or four pieces of toilet roll, then crept towards Curtis's desk from behind so as not to disturb the class at work, all heads down, oblivious of anything else.

As Robby drew near, he saw that the boy's surreptitious movement beneath his jacket was not the result of stomach ache. The poor young devil had no idea that Robby was so close.

'Ian, here,' Robby whispered, 'go to the lavatory if you have stomach ache.' Burning red with awful embarrassment and holding his jacket in front of him, Curtis took the paper and fled out on tiptoe. He never forgot that afternoon until the day he died. And years later Robby remembered it, too.

Robby was thankful that the boy returned after a few minutes, for there was always the danger that his confusion might have driven him home in shame. Robby knew that the added phrase 'if you have stomach ache' had saved the situation. Curtis was pink-faced but brave enough to glance at his teacher and smile secretly, then sat down. As the bell sounded for break, Robby called Curtis over, the rest of the class leaving. Curtis approached sheepishly, eyes downcast cheeks pink, wondering what was about to happen, almost sure that Fergy knew!

'Well, Ian, feeling better?'

'Yes sir.'

'Not feeling guilty I hope?'

So, Fergy DID know. He murmured, 'Um.'

'Pass me a Bible from the cupboard, Ian.'

God! Fergy was going to make him swear on the Bible!

He nervously selected an un-torn Bible and handed it to his teacher.

'There we are, Ian, Chapter 38 Genesis. There is hardly any situation known to man that isn't dealt with in the Bible. I want you to read down to where it says *'And he slew him also.'*

When Ian Curtis had read the extract, Robby said, 'Now then, do you understand what all that is about?'

'I think so, sir,' Curtis frowned. Robby laughed. Honest Ian as always. 'I'll explain. God killed Er before he could produce children by Tamar, his wife. This was tragic to Judah, the father of the tribe and he ordered his younger son, Onan, to marry Tamar and have children by her. But Onan wanted his own family. Judah was telling Onan to have what was known as a Levirate marriage - marrying your brother's widow. You see, there was no male heir to the elder son and the Levirate marriage would allow Onan's offspring to be recognised as his dead brother's children. So Onan lets it drop on the ground. I suppose you know what IT is?' Despite his confusion, Ian Curtis had to laugh. 'Yes, I think so sir,' he giggled.

'So you see, Ian, although Onan's case doesn't exactly fit yours, you have no need to feel guilty. Everybody does what you were trying to do before I barged in. The boys, I myself, the Rector, Mr Norris - everybody at some time in his or her life does it - but not in the classroom...'

By this time the boy was choking with laughter, seeing a picture in his mind of Fergy, Norris, and funniest of all, the Rector, doing it in the classroom. Fergy was a scream at times!

'Onan had defied the laws of Moses, God's servant, you see, Ian,' Robby went on. 'He should have gone with Tamar properly, that is the point, and should not have withdrawn at the last moment. You see what I mean?'

'Yes sir,' Curtis tittered.

'In future Ian, if you feel a need to do it, take some paper and go to the lavatory. Just leave the room and don't worry about it. God won't smite you down. You are getting to adolescence now and according to the laws of nature - not Moses - you should be having sex with girls of your own age. Being civilised of course, most of us don't do that these days. The Stone Age people probably did, but they lived to be only thirty-five.'

Curtis was laughing again with a vision of Stone Age men and women wearing themselves out and dying precisely at midnight before their thirty-sixth birthday.

'And Ian,' Robby continued, 'I am NOT advising you to have sex with girls. I don't want to be attacked by mothers with umbrellas all shouting 'Why did you tell Ian Curtis to have sex with our daughters?' So, Ian, behave yourself and don't start wondering about girls just yet.'

'No sir' Curtis spluttered trying to control his mirth with his handkerchief to his mouth. Robby patted the boy on the head and told him to go now and not worry himself. When he reached the door, Curtis turned, quite seriously and earnestly, and called, 'Thank you sir. Thank you very much.' Robby breathed deeply and believed he had cleared away all the lad's feelings of guilt. It had been a sticky problem in more ways than one on that sticky afternoon!

*   *   *

The Lions of Burma would be published in the Autumn, Robby was informed by Congreve and Halsall, publishers of paperbacks. The book would be on the bookstalls in time for the Christmas trade. The printed agreement form showed typewritten insertions of £100 advance royalties and a royalty on each copy sold. Robby read through the agreement with the utmost care before he signed it and posted it back. One contingency clause that gave the publishers an option on any further work of the author pleased him most.

'Well,' Emma had the grace to admit, 'I was wrong years ago, lad. You've proved you can get somewhere at last. I must admit, I never believed you could. Let's hope it makes up for the disappointments of the past.'

She soon spread the news that her son was having a book published in the autumn. The family seemed impressed. Robby always guarded himself against family and acquaintances' reactions. Seeming was a good word for hiding jealousies.

One ally from a surprising quarter always pleased him - Harriet Cromwell, Gwen's elder sister. She was ten years older than Gwen, a thinnish, good-looking woman of intelligence and tolerance. In her quiet way she had taken a liking to Angus's brother for the way he had, she believed, Got On, remembering her visit to Liverpool with her sister years ago and seeing the living conditions of the family. On occasions when they met they had enjoyed discussions on various intellectual levels. They had discussed Biblical Prophecy one time, Robby putting forward opposing views on the validity of Revelations; they had talked about original

Sin; the supposed innocence of children; the declining standards of the nation's morals. Harriet had loved the arguments, especially when there was disagreement. She confessed to Emma one day that she liked all her family Harriet found them different from the folk she usually met.

'Why don't you go more to see Gwen and Angus?' Emma asked him. 'Tell them about your book. He's your eldest brother, after all. It was his idea that you went into teaching.'

'So he keeps telling everybody.'

'Now don't be sarcastic about it. He obviously had confidence in you to suggest it in first place. He's really proud of you, our Angus.'

'I doubt it. Angus must always be the Cock of the Walk. He wasn't enthusiastic about Fay and Malcolm opening in Blackpool.'

'What on earth has that to do with it?'

'A lot. He wouldn't like any of us to forge ahead and have more success than he has.'

'Don't be silly. I'm not enthusiastic about Fay and Malcolm either.'

'Why not? There's no reason why they can't make a success of it.'

'He hasn't got Angus's business sense, that's why.'

'I don't think Angus has any special claim on that. He made a holy mess of things in Liverpool and left you stranded.'

'I know all about that,' said Emma, testily. 'I'm not likely to forget it. But he's learnt a lot since those days. He paid off his mortgage before buying that shop. Malcolm couldn't do that because he was in rented accommodation. He was lucky to find a rented business in Blackpool, I can tell you. I admit it was a good move. The trouble is Malcolm doesn't OWN property, that's the difference. Angus does. That's business sense. He lives in a house which has a mortgage mostly paid by the rent from the flat over his shop. Malcolm should have taken out a mortgage during the war instead of renting. It was easier to rent, but it's a damned sight dearer in the long run. That's where Angus scores. He looks forward.'

Robby understood his ma's argument. That was why she still favoured Angus and conveniently forgot the past when she talked about him. She talked about the cruelties of her father but not the high-mindedness of her son. A mother, perhaps, cannot hate a son; a daughter can hate a father.

Robby received a letter from Benny Solomons typewritten on his business letterhead by his secretary, 'Our Ref, BS/MJ'. Robby smiled. Apart from the pleasure of receiving it, Robby could now use it as an excuse to visit Angus, the motive being a more modest one than to talk about his book.

Dear Fergy,

Thank you for your letter. Sorry I am late in replying. You certainly did well to get into teaching, though I am not surprised.

When the Da died a year after Momma, he left a surprisingly big amount and I was able with my share to take over this shop - paints and wallpapers, etc. Just before the war. Luckily the war didn't last long for me. I was wounded in the leg on the Desert and was invalided out. After discharge I immediately got hitched to Becky, a beauty as I think you will agree and my three kids take after her. Asher, by the way, has a jeweller's shop in Litherland and is doing well.

Kirkdale got a battering in the blitz. Your old shop and surrounding houses were blown sky high queer enough, though, the old pub on the corner and Jones's house next door were hardly touched, two of the twelve houses that were standing in Miranda Road when the war ended. There are still prefabs on the old park football pitches.

We were all very upset when Joe was killed in the Ardennes, especially Rose who thought the world of our Joe. I'd like you to come and see my shops one day. We must arrange something. I hope your Burma book gets published. War stories are all the rage now. I'll let you know exactly when I'll be coming to Leyland in July. Alfie sends his regards. He was unfit for the services and exempt from war

*work because of his invalid mother. That's how he came to
take over this shop when I got called up. When I came home
I bought another and Alfie manages that now.*

*He is married, by the way, and has a little boy. They live
with Alfie's ma. I'll be seeing y' soon.*

Shalom.

Benny.'

So Alfie hadn't turned out to become an engineer! Ideas
in young minds were fantasies. Yet Alf was the type that
could adapt to manual and technical work and would be
managing Benny's second shop very well, no doubt.

Reassuring his ma that he had no prejudice against
visiting his brother, Robby went the following Sunday
afternoon. Harriet was there, alone as usual, her husband
Willis not having accompanied her. Robby found this
strange behaviour. Angus once explained that apart from
being a tremendous bookworm, Willis also loved classical
music. Robby could see him now, his ear glued to the
loudspeaker, every Sunday afternoon, puffing soothingly on
his pipe. Willis was certainly a weird character!

'Benny Solomon wrote the other day,' Robby said as he
sat down.

'Oh? How did he know your address?' said Angus.

'Doug saw him at the paint works. Benny has two paint
shops now. Here, read his letter. It explains everything.'

'Well, poor old Joe,' Angus said, after he had read the
letter. 'I'm really sorry about that. He was a good pal. It's
strange, I never think of Jews doing anything silly like
fighting in somebody else's war and losing their lives.'

'It was their war as much as ours,' Robby said. 'They
would have been in a hellish mess if Hitler had won the war.
I think most of 'em were keen to fight. And their army now
is a spanking one.'

Gwen entered with coffee on a trolley with small
homemade cakes.

'Congratulations, Robby. When is your book coming

out? You've done very well.' For some reason Robby felt a huge glow of pleasure. At last! He thought. He had worn someone else down.

'I imagine it'll be out by late autumn,' he said.

'Why do you call it *Lions of Burma*?' Gwen asked, pouring coffee.

'It comes from the Chindit mythological beast outside Burmese pagodas. Fifteen feet or so high, they are, and like a griffin and lion combined. They looked like lions to me so I used that title. It's about the Chindits - the late Wingatels Long Range Penetration Group. About 3,000 of them behind Jap lines blowing up bridges and railway lines and harrying the Japs. They stopped the Japs starting their great offensive on India and proved that Indian and British troops were better than the Japs at jungle warfare.'

'How much will you be getting for the book?' Angus asked.

'An advance of £100 - paperback at 2/6d I'll get threepence a copy.'

'Um. You'll never make a fortune on those terms, will you?' said Angus.

'Won't that depend on sales?' Harriet laughed.

'Yes,' Robby agreed. 'Paperbacks sell in thousands, even with little known authors.' Angus was scribbling on some scrap paper.

'If you sell 10,000 you'll only make £125. That's not much.' Robby laughed.

'That's £125 more than I would have got if I hadn't written the book. I'm not aiming to make a fortune. I'm just a beginner and getting published counts most.'

'I do agree with you, Robby,' said Harriet. 'It's the satisfaction of creating something that must give you a wonderful feeling.'

'You'll never get rich thinking like that,' said Angus.

'I can see Robby's point,' said Gwen to his astonishment. 'I think too, that I would get more satisfaction from having a book published than worrying about money.'

Angus guffawed. 'You're a queer lot. You don't think like me.'

'We haven't your business sense,' said Robby. 'In any case, when you have an offer to publish, you don't bicker about the financial side of the contract.'

When he reached home, he told his ma what Angus had said and what the sisters had thought.

'Well,' said Emma, 'I suppose that if you are set on getting things published, the money isn't important. But you'll never earn a living from it if you go on like that. You'll always need an income from a regular job. I know what Angus means - to earn a living, making money must come first, otherwise you're a failure.'

'Yes, I understand that quite well. The point is, you've got to establish yourself first, the same as you do in a shop, build a reputation in other words.'

A visitor came next evening. She was having tea with Emma when Robby arrived.

She was about middle twenties, tall, slim, dark haired and with extraordinarily beautiful dark brown eyes, large and lovely.

'This young lady's come to see you,' said Emma. 'Harriet suggested she come round.'

'Hello,' Robby smiled. 'What can I do for you?'

'I'm Helen Bardsley,' she introduced herself. 'I live near the Cromwell's. Harriet told me about your book. She also told me you were expert at doing letters.'

'Well,' Robby laughed, 'I wouldn't say expert. I know something about lettering. Did you want some doing?'

'Oh no. I'd like to learn how to do it myself. I've started in the new junior school and I've got the job of doing all the signs for the school. Foolishly I told the head I was interested and she grabbed me - no one else volunteered. I need to do classroom numbers on square cards for the doors, directions for the mothers when they come. It's a big job.'

'Right. Bring a list tomorrow and we'll start.'

'Hold on!' Emma broke in. 'I'm thinking about Douglas. Tommy Hurst is coming tomorrow.'

'Oh? I didn't know they'd been in touch,' said Robby.

'Oh yes. Douglas wrote him before the war ended. He's been here before. I wonder, my dear, as your house is bigger than ours, would you be more private there?'

'Oh yes,' Helen smiled. 'We can use what used to be daddy's study before he died.'

Robby was excited at the prospect and gave his ma full marks for her suggestion, not realising that the wise Emma had sized up the girl, had liked her, and was already planning to buy a new dress for the wedding!

'We've heard a lot about you from Harriet,' Helen said.

'Oh?' Robby's eyebrows raised. Harriet was a great asset, too.

Next evening after he had eaten and had chatted with Tommy Hurst who had arrived before Douglas, Robby went to the bathroom, shaved, had a shower, put on his best suit and brushed his hair, and, his appearance at its best, he walked round to Helen Bardsley's house. It was old and double fronted and much bigger than the new semis surrounding it, one of which belonged to the Cromwells. Mrs Bardsley greeted him, a woman with pallid complexion, frown creases between her eyes and a strangely cautious attitude as she looked at him.

'Come in, please. I'll call Helen.' She turned her head and called up the passage.

'I won't say I'm an expert about lettering,' he told Mrs Bardsley, 'but I'm sure I can help her.'

'Well, you know more about it than she does at least,' Mrs Bardsley said. Helen, she shrieked, 'Mr Ferguson is here. Hurry.'

She came running out of the study at the back of the house, all excited and eager.

'Hello,' she greeted him, and gave a dazzling smile, and Robby told himself that Helen Bardsley was for him. 'We're using the study, mother.'

'All right. I suppose in an hour or so you'd like some coffee?'

'That would be fine,' Robby smiled, thinking the woman had suggested coffee in a very unusual way.

Helen took him down the corridor from the wide hall. It was a fine house, Robby thought, elegant and well furnished with good furniture like the pieces he had French polished one time long, long ago.

'This is the den, Mr Ferguson,' she said, throwing open the door.

'My name's Robby,' he laughed. 'Mr Ferguson is tiring on the voice-box.'

'Right, Robby,' she giggled, 'please come in.'

The study had a roll-top desk with its lid rolled up. On the desk were stacks of card of different shapes and measurements.

They worked for an hour before coffee was brought, and by that time each knew they were destined to be together.

✻ ✻ ✻

The family had always been vague about Angus's association with the church. Before coming from Liverpool they had heard that Angus was a regular churchgoer. They were all surprised. He had immersed himself in church life after his marriage and it had proved a bulwark against the early animosity of Mrs Hanley towards him. She had opposed her husband's amiable acceptance of their daughter's marriage. She did not like Angus's background, knowing that Angus had lived in one of the poor stone cottages on the main road, and Mrs Hanley looked down on people who lived there. This, with the occasional remarks made by her daughter in the past, assured her that Angus was no fit person to marry her daughter. Mr Hanley had been far more generous and understanding. Angus's persistence in his courting and his compliance with Gwen's advice to busy himself in church matters, had eventually worn down her mother's objections. His charm had attracted the attention of the vicar and they became good friends. As a sidesman, Angus had become known to many parishioners and they liked him, especially the female members. He had gone to the lengths of being confirmed early in his married life and had joined the Men's Bible Class for a few years. He was now a well-known character in church circles and his business had thrived. When his son Ronald had left school, Angus had been able to apprentice him to a friend, Jim Hart, a local printer. Angus remembered how he had squandered his own apprenticeship years ago. The boy ultimately developed into one of the best specialist printers in the county.

Angus had also made a friend of Willie Bretherton, a widower of sixty, who ran an estate agency with the help of a secretary. Angus was shrewd enough to learn much from Willie about the business. If Willie could earn enough to make a good living at the game, he, Angus, could do twice as good. You needed no qualifications except commonsense. Surveying could be done by the experts and valuations would be easy after a little practice. Angus was also aware that Willie was itching to retire and rest on the small fortune he had accumulated over the years.

Angus's next step was to sell his shop which he had improved beyond recognition. He placed the sale in the hands of Willie Bretherton.

'The problem is, Angus,' said Willie, 'no one will buy the place as a lockup - with those tenants upstairs. They'll expect accommodation that's for sure.'

'The answer's simple, Willie,' said Angus, having already rehearsed his say. 'Find my tenant alternative accommodation as near his mother's as possible.'

It was much easier than Willie had visualised. The tenants took a semi-detached house five hundred yards from the husband's mother's place and all was settled, Willie having arranged a very acceptable mortgage.

After the successful sale of the shop, Angus invited Willie to tea one Sunday, saying he wished to talk business. A partnership was signed a week later. Angus had bought a half share in the Estate Agency. Angus was lucky once more. The arrangement was the very thing Willie had been seeking for the past two or three years. Within six months, Angus had bought him out and Willie retired quite happy in his mind that he had left his agency in capable hands.

*   *   *

Robby visited Helen's house several times until all the required lettering had been finished and Helen now knew a lot about lettering that she had not visualised was so complicated. She was thrilled and excited that they had done so well together. When all the cards were finished, Helen rushed out of the den and Robby heard her enthusing to her mother. Mrs Bardsley's voice, which always carried far, unknown to her, said --- 'Yes, I suppose you COULD say they were professional. Tell Mr Ferguson how grateful you are and pay him what's due.'

'Of course,' came Helen's voice, almost in alarm, 'I'd forgotten the business side of it.'

She came back to an amused Robby.

'Rubbish,' he laughed. 'I won't hear of any payment. Good grief! In any case my price might be too high for you.'

'What do you mean?' she asked, frowning with a half smile.

'Well, I must confess - I've been mad about you since our first meeting. My price is that we become engaged to be married as soon as possible.'

She stared at him, her face a rosy pink, her lips apart, her eyebrows raised.

'Goodness! This is so very sudden.'

'I didn't mean to shock you,' he laughed. 'That's how I feel and that's my price.'

There was an awkward silence for a moment or two and then he laughed easily.

'If you don't solemnly promise to marry me,' he whispered, 'I'll squirt paint all over these cards.'

She laughed in relief 'Ooh! You wouldn't dare.'

'No,' he admitted, seriously. 'I wouldn't do that. But WILL you marry me, Helen?'

As he watched the expression on her pink face and in her glorious eyes, it suddenly came to him that he had been stupid to assume that this delightful creature would be free and not already inflaming some other fellow's heart.

Anxiously he asked himself if he could stand being told that there was some other man in her life. Surely for once in his life some good fortune in his longing for a woman who answered to all his dreams could bring fruition and lasting happiness. This was the moment, he decided, and dreaded her answer.

'There's someone else, isn't there?' he asked.

'Yes, there is,' she said, quietly. 'But we aren't engaged. He teaches at our place.'

Robby felt his heart sink as if punched by a sledgehammer. But all at once she came to him and he felt her arms around his neck and her lips mingling with his in a passionate kiss.

'Thank you for that lovely compliment,' she whispered. 'Please give me time to think about it. Please don't let mother have any inkling of what we say now.'

'I shan't,' he said, 'but God! I had lost all hope for a moment then! You nearly gave me heart failure! Be sure, I'll wait very patiently while you think about it. This is the very first time I've really loved anyone like this.'

She smiled and kissed him again, and he turned and left the house, waving as he closed the gate. Mrs Bardsley watched him depart and her brain puzzled over his delay in going.

*　　*　　*

In October Walter Norris confided in Robby that he was retiring at the end of the year. His wife's health had declined and he would be required at home. What he was about to say was confidential, he impressed on Robby.

'She hasn't long to live, Mr Ferguson. Cancer. She's been sent home from hospital. Her sister is with her at the moment.'

'I'm very sorry to hear that, Mr Norris, I am indeed.'

'Yes, it is tragic and I feel I must spend as much time with her as possible during her remaining years on earth.'

Robby felt the deepest sympathy for the little man and his poor wife. Walter was eccentric, no doubt, but the way he had always treated Robby, once familiarity had grafted their friendship, showed that his eccentricities were a rampart against the hardships of his shyness and nervousness, two qualities most ill-suited to a profession that needed the exact opposites of such dispositions. Walter had fought his way through and had reached as near the top as was possible in the profession, considering that his career had spanned only two schools.

That night Robby wrote out three applications for new posts. As he dropped the letters into the letterbox, he offered up a prayer to heaven, doubtfully, like a devout Catholic in a synagogue. He knew Michael Allsop was favoured by the Rector and would suffer no disturbance to his school life under a new headmaster. But the Black Rector had never liked Robby from the beginning and Robby thought him evil, arrogant and no Christian.

The first application for Head of Arts and Crafts was returned. He had not been placed on the short list. Disappointment's ghostly claw held his heart. His lack of a degree or diploma was always a sore spot, and he dreaded always being the underdog. Nobody had visualised how he had gone through agonies to control his nerves at college when lecturing to fellow students. Yet, balancing the scales, he had been successful, had an excellent certificate, and had been well liked by his student friends. What more could one ask?

The new issue of the Times Educational Supplement had nothing in it within easy travelling distance. Repeat entries for Surrey and Middlesex left him unmoved - he was determined he would not leave the district. His second rejection came a week later, references neatly stapled together and with a courteous note. He knew the last post was the worst - an assistant art master in a large Liverpool school. He called in at Flora's place.

'I don't know why you are so miserable,' she scolded him after his tale of woe. 'You were quite happy there. Does Mr Norris make all that difference?'

'Yes, he does. The Rector does not like me and without Walter's protection I'd have a dog's life with him. The Rector will make sure this time that he gets the kind of young fellow he wants, then he'll start coming into school and throwing his weight about, and the head won't be able to say Boo! An art job is more in my line. I know I can do it.'

'Well, I'm sorry, lad. You were so happy there.'

It had always been a habit of the younger children to confide in Flora because they had been brought up by her, and here he was, now, telling her all his troubles. His ma was all right discussing business matters but she tended to disparage the more subtle idiosyncrasies of her children.

*　　*　　*

The Deputy Director of Education eyed him over his spectacles.

'Well, Mr Ferguson, if you are willing to take the post, we are quite willing to appoint you.'

'Thank you sir,' Robby replied.

As he walked from the Municipal Buildings to Exchange Station, he wondered whether he had chosen wisely. He admitted to himself that teaching was not his true vocation. Now he had been appointed to a school of nine hundred mixed boys and girls in a rip-roaring district of Liverpool, by all accounts, and the school always changing its staff! But he had attained his object - to get out of Chad's before it was too late. No more Catechism rigmarole; no more bucket petties where the lads smoked; no miserable science lessons where he was one step ahead of the boys; no Rector's whims to threaten his future; no more walking days, Ash Wednesdays, Ascension Days and reading lessons in church. Now he would teach one subject, Art. The kids would be tough but he himself had been brought up in the slums and he knew the way their minds worked.

*　　*　　*

Despite the promise of a book to be published, he felt down and unsuccessful. He could not understand why depression had settled over him like a death pall. In his happier moments he knew there was little reason for pessimism. Instinct took over his mind occasionally and he imagined disasters to come. That had been an occasional phenomenon in his life - periods of black despair, especially after some happy occurrence, as if he could not sustain good fortune because he was suspicious of the Fates that would make him pay. He had often been too happy in his happiness, like Keats's Nightingale. After long hours of such moods he would strive to rouse himself to defeat the foe of inferiority. He had come through the war safely and with a good record; he had been well liked and loved by certain people; he had pulled himself up from the mire of younger years to gain a place in a respectable profession; he had been successful with that book; he had been befriended by two eccentric and unpopular heads; lots of people liked him - boys and girls, male and female colleagues, and he believed, Helen Bardsley loved him, otherwise that kiss had meant nothing but coquetry!

* * *

As he shook hands outside the church, Robby remembered those other term-end services; but this time the Rector was absent with flu and the new curate had taken the service of carols. Apart from some tiny regrets at leaving the ancient school, the occasion of the carols had been friendly and happy.

'Well, Mr Ferguson,' said Walter Norris, brusquely, hiding the melancholy of the parting of the ways, 'I hope you like your new post and do well, as I have no doubt you will. I have enjoyed working with you over these few years. I have another career ahead of me now - a sad one and one I wish to heaven I hadn't to do! My wife has declined over the past few weeks and I am not anticipating a happy Christmas. Nevertheless, I do wish you every happiness for the Christmas, and a prosperous future. And God bless you. Goodbye.'

Abruptly the little man turned and sped away, carrying his briefcase as he had done for thirty years. He boarded the bus that would take him to a sad and daunting future. Robby was sad too that he had not had time to say his piece. Perhaps it was better that way. What could he have said of any worth?

'Well, I'll be blowed!' came Allsop's voice from behind. 'Walked off without a word! He could have waited. I've just been talking to the curate.'

'He's a disturbed little man, Michael. You'll just have to excuse him. He'll have a very bleak Christmas - his wife's dying.'

'Oh!' Allsop was silent for a moment or two. 'I didn't know about it. I understand now why he's been so cantankerous lately.'

'He said, *'say goodbye to Mr Allsop for me'* so you see, he didn't forget you,' Robby lied.

'Did he say that? Well, I forgive the poor chap for his bad manners. I'm sorry about his wife. Someone should have told me.'

'He wanted it kept quiet. Anyway, it's too late now. He's gone out of our lives, Mike.'

'Yes,' Allsop sighed. 'He wasn't a bad old stick. He has my sympathy. I'm damned sorry you're going, too. We've had some good times together. I'll miss you. Anyway, I wish you all the best, mate. Hope you like your new job.'

'Thanks, Mike. Best wishes to you too. I'll see you around some time. Ah, there's my bus just come in. Look after those footballers Mike.'

'I will, Robby. Cheerio.'

'Goodbye.' Robby hurried away towards his bus. Sweet sorrow, he thought. How wisely described by the bard! That's exactly what it was.

'Sir! Sir!' Robby turned round. Ian Curtis was running towards him. He was wrapped up in a heavy coat and scarf for he, too, had been absent, another victim of the flu epidemic.

'Hello Ian. Feeling better?'

'Yes, thank you sir. I'm getting over it. I've brought you a present.' The boy handed over a parcel wrapped in festive paper.

'I say, that's very nice of you, Ian. Thank you very much - although you shouldn't have wasted your money on me.'

'I didn't waste it, sir. I wish I was leaving too. I've got to go until Easter.'

'That won't be long, Ian.'

'I came to say goodbye, sir.' Curtis stretched out his hand and Robby grasped it warmly.

'Goodbye Ian. I shall see you around. But you have my address - you must come and see me.'

'I will sir, thank you.'

'Don't forget - as scowsers in a foreign land we must keep in touch. I'm going to teach in Liverpool, by the way. Incidentally, I hope you achieve your ambition and get away to sea as you've always wanted.'

'Thank you sir. I'm looking forward to Easter, sir.'

'Well, Ian, a very Happy Christmas and the best of luck.'

'Same to you sir.'

Curtis suddenly turned away and hurried off. Robby boarded the bus and went upstairs to sit by himself at the back. He lit a cigarette. Those partings had been very touching. Apart from Walter's sorrowful farewell and Allsop's obvious regret, Curtis's sudden appearance had been a wrench, especially as his dark, intensely honest eyes had flooded uncontrollably with tears before he turned away!

*　　*　　*

Robby unwrapped the twelve free copies. His excitement increased as he saw the cover - three Chindit soldiers in jungle green crouched behind a clump of undergrowth and a distant bridge blown up, the yellow flames of the explosion and the debris flying through the air. The LIONS of BURMA in white letters breaking the dark greenery of the jungle scene; and lower down A Story of the Chindits. At the bottom Robert Ferguson, Price 3/-.

There was nothing more exhilarating than to see a book of one's own work done so beautifully! And he would receive 3.6d instead of 3d. On the inside title page was a line drawing of a pagoda behind a near view of a Chinthe, the fabulous beast's alternative name.

He placed two free copies in his bookcase. He would give one copy to each member of the family, one copy to Helen, and one copy to Harriet who had been so friendly to him. He would still have three free copies over and would hold on to for emergencies. He placed them in the bookcase drawer.

When he visited Helen she was delighted. Inside he had written 'To Mrs Bardsley and Helen, with kindest regards from Robby Ferguson.' How formal that sounded! He had wished to write more endearing words but Mrs Bardsley knew nothing of her daughter's kiss.

To most people a book is a book and that is the end of it. To a would-be writer, a book is a creation, a thrilling, beautiful work of art in which even the black print is gloriously attractive. Helen felt this thrill as she fondled the paperback.

'Robby, how thrilled you must be! And three shillings a copy, too?'

'Yes, I'll be getting 3.6d instead of threepence. It's too thick for half-a-crown.' Mrs Bardsley went to a small cocktail bar in the corner of the lounge and took out a bottle of sherry. 'I expect your mother and family are thrilled?' she said.

'Yes, they are,' said Robby. 'Ma is trying to wheedle my spare three copies for her friends and that's bad business as she well knows.'

They laughed at this as Mrs Bardsley poured the sherry.

'Here's to the great success of The Lions of Burma,' Helen said happily, and her mother murmured an echo as they all sat down to sip their drink.

An hour later, as he took his leave, Helen came to the

door with him.

'Robby,' she whispered, 'I've told John Parker that I'm being married. He was desolated. I felt very sorry for him. But on looking back I've never had any really deep feeling for him. But he's a very nice fellow.'

'And who do you propose to marry?' he asked, grinning.

'I propose to marry a famous writer with plenty of money and oodles of charm.'

'Is he buying a very expensive engagement ring, do you think?'

'No, he is not. I am telling him I don't need an engagement ring. It's a waste of money.'

'Well, he won't mind if he has oodles of money,' Robby laughed.

'I'm not marrying him for his money, I'll have you know.'

In the dark hallway she pressed her body against his, her warm arms around his neck, and her soft lips against his. 'I love you, Robby. I love you,' she whispered.

*　　*　　*

At weekend he went into Blackpool to visit Malcolm and Fay at their shop. He had a copy of the book in his overcoat pocket. He had written a greeting in the front of it. They were both delighted and genuinely pleased with his success, so much so that Fay kissed him impulsively.

'Go into Woolworths and Boots this morning,' she said. 'Your book's on the front counter at Woolworths. It says 'The Latest in War Books by a Lancashire Author.' It gave me a great thrill. I've been telling customers to buy it.'

'Thanks,' Robby laughed.

'We don't open till 11.30,' Malcolm said. 'Everything's ready. I'll run you down to the front, if you like. I have a second-hand Jag, you know.'

'A Jaguar? I didn't know.'

'Five years old but you can hardly hear the engine

running. It's in the garage at the back.'

'I'd love a ride in it,' Robby said. 'That's a turn up for the book. You're obviously doing well.'

'Best move we ever made,' said Fay. 'It's great. In summer we go down to the beach on Sundays. And Blackpool's a wonderful shopping centre.'

When they reached the sea front, it being wintertime, Malcolm found an easy parking space parallel to the tramlines. They crossed the shore road and entered Woolworths. There it was, opposite the front door on the book counter, artistically arranged on a triangular stand, about a dozen copies and a white card with the caption Fay had mentioned.

'It's great, isn't it?' Malcolm enthused. 'Think of all the people employed in producing that book!'

'Yer, and all getting their bit out of that three bob.'

It was a similar display in the Boots Chemists' book department. They were in time to see an elderly gentleman buying a copy. Yes, Robby thought, an exciting visit. There must be bookshops all over the country with different displays. And what about those other bookshops abroad? His mind buzzed with exuberance.

On the way back to the shop, Robby asked his brother how many miles to the gallon the car could do.

'Well about eighteen roughly,' Malcolm answered airily, as if the question was immaterial.

'You don't find it expensive?'

'Nah not really. I don't use it all that much. The furthest we've been so far is to Fay's people in Liverpool.'

'I'll be teaching in Liverpool after the holidays, by the way, specialising in art.'

'So you've left the little school? Doing art? That'll be great. You'll have to get a car now to go up and down to Liverpool.'

'One day I will,' said Robby. 'Meantime I'll use the train.'

When Christmas greetings had been exchanged, Robby departed to catch the bus back home. He didn't think for a moment that he would ever buy a Jaguar. He would never afford such a luxury. How did Malcolm manage to keep a monster like that?

* * *

Robby was not happy on the morning of his first day at the new school. The Deputy Head shook hands warmly and took him on a tour of the premises. Robby's first interest was the timetable stretched across a large portion of the staff room notice board.

'That looks damned complicated to me,' he laughed.

'Oh, it's quite simple when you get used to it, the Deputy Head chuckled in return.

They set off down the corridors as the children were coming in for registration. The Deputy gave a commentary as they went, describing the rooms and their subjects, filling Robby's head with a mass of information he could never remember. He was bewildered. Everything was so new with no resemblance to Chad's. He felt a sense of shabbiness and of being inadequately equipped for the job ahead of him, and the feeling was strengthened later when he met Frank Stubbs, his old friend from College, in the staffroom.

'Good grief! Robby Ferguson! So, you're joining our madhouse? What a great coincidence!' They gripped each other's hand warmly and with strength of deep feeling.

'What are you doing here?' Robby asked, all bemused.

'English, Robby, That's my domain. Still living in Leyland?'

'Yer. I'll be travelling by train until I can get a car.'

'I live at Ormskirk. I'll give you a lift to Ormskirk station.'

'That's decent of you, Frank. I'll give you something towards petrol.'

'You certainly will not, old son. I've gotta go that way. Save your money. Not married yet?'

'Not yet, Engaged.'

'So you're in the pipeline then? I've got two youngsters

and a marvellous wife.'

'I got a book published last Autumn. War story about the Chindits. *The Lions of Burma*. It's in all the main bookshops. Sells at three bob.'

'That's marvellous! I can afford three bob. This'll be a talking point in the English department, mate. I'll get a copy.'

'I'll bring you a free copy,' Robby said.

'No mate. You don't make money that way. I'll buy a copy and you can put your moniker on the inside' '*With love to Frank*' and some kisses.'

Robby laughed. Frank Stubbs was so out-going. Going home that afternoon through the Liverpool traffic, in his comfortable car, bought new, Robby recognised in his friend's bonhomie the mark of happy success. He bubbled with gusto and knew his worth, having no quarrels with the world.

Next morning Robby autographed Frank's copy of the book. In no time it was bruited about that the new member of staff in art was a writer. Robby knew this was not true - one swallow did not make a summer. But he was determined to make it true and already could foresee a time when he would be writing, possibly, crime stories when war stories fizzled out.

'What do you think of this place?' Frank asked him at lunchtime.

'Looks a nice place, as far as I can tell.'

'An architect's dream world, Robby. There should be a law that makes architects sit down with experienced teachers before they start designing anything. This school is already too small. Costs have been skimped and they didn't take account of the birth rate. There are new estates all round here. It's always a matter of economics. Crass idiocy! Rectifying omissions in building programmes is a damned sight more costly than paying out in the first place. Costs are always rising with inflation, and yet, skimping on essentials is balanced by stupid squandering - this school, you've noticed, has a foyer like a cinema with a mural that cost £4,000!'

'No! Well that's bloody stupid!'

'Architects get up my back. They use half the elevations by making 'em huge areas of glass which bake you in summer and freeze you in winter. The more glass you have the more gets broken. It cost Liverpool Authority last year £500 per school on average for re-glazing. Multiply that by the number of schools and it runs into millions. This school has four shower units,' two in lower school toilets and two in upper school. You know what? They've never been used and this school was built seven years ago. You enter them from the corridor and you can walk right through to the playground. No kid will stand naked in a shower that has no door or curtain round it when other kids are piddling in the urinals, plus icy blasts from the door to the play ground. Experienced teachers would have stamped out such ideas at once. A crass waste. They cost £5,000. There are flat roofs around the playground. The ball goes up and stays there. Kids climb the drainpipe. Drainpipe comes away. Kid goes to hospital. Fix new drainpipe £150. All roofs should be sloped around playgrounds. The stairs here lead from wide areas to narrow landings where the kids, waiting to enter the classroom, are crowded, and start pushing and squabbling. Chaos! Playing fields near language rooms and you can't hear yourself speak. Machine shops in the quietest area around the front gate. The list is endless.'

Frank Stubbs' disparagement of way-out ideas was scathing. And Robby agreed with him.

On the subject of courses for teachers he was even more scathing. A complete waste of time. You were pressed to attend lectures on *The psychological effects of corporal punishment*, or, *The Co-ordination of Personal Relationships*, subjects dreamed up by some grossly inadequate person with a generous salary trying to justify his existence in the scheme of things.

The ten per cent worthwhile courses were the practical ones where expert craftsmen showed teachers the techniques. All else was futile. To be frank the kind of people who attended airy-fairy lectures and courses, like that fellow Pickering who bought two novels from the inspector, were toadies, grovelling in order to Get On. And they did get on, simply because the kind of parasites that ran courses of this kind were also the people who sat on interview boards and they loved the crawlers who made their lives worthwhile. Without their toadies such personnel would be unemployed and unemployable when it came to running courses.

Flora argued with Robby about these slashing opinions. If kowtowing to the Authority was helping a person to Get On, why didn't Robby do it? It was no use ruining your chances of promotion because of a few silly principles. That fellow Stubbs might be wrong.

'He isn't wrong,' Robby said. 'A decent person has to live with himself. I refuse to grovel in order to get on. Teaching is the only profession in which the ambitious selfseeker wants to get out of it. Every other trade and profession has ambitious people, too, but the difference is that they wish to be better lawyers, better doctors, better joiners, better salesmen, and so on. The ambitious teacher wants to be a headmaster, or an organiser, or an inspector, away from teaching kids.'

'You do talk rubbish at times! If there were no ambitious teachers there would be no headmasters or any other kind of leader.'

Robby laughed. 'Flora, you've solved the problem! Let every school find its own leader naturally and not have one thrust on it by Authority who usually pick the wrong person seven out of ten times.'

'There's one thing certain,' Flora scorned, 'YOU will never be a leader. And what about your Walter Norris? You thought highly of him.'

'Walter was different - he is one of the three out of ten. He never attended a teachers' course in his life - and he was a damned good teacher. He was honest. He saw through all the sham and lip-service.'

'I'll believe you if thousands wouldn't,' Flora said, dryly.

*   *   *

'This week's model,' he said, stabbing his mark-book, 'is ahh! Our beautiful blonde, Sandra Nicholson.'

There was an immediate uproar of disbelief from the boys as Sandra walked out.

'I don't know why you boys are scoffing,' Robby laughed. All the girls in this form are pretty.' Again the boys murmured and made disparaging remarks, like MPs in opposition.

'Sit down comfortably, Sandra, and hold the magazine as if you are reading it. Now for a boy.'

He stabbed his finger again. 'Ah, come out Jimmy Clark.' A little red-haired boy with freckles, quiet and unnoticed and mothered by the girls, came out and shyly sat down, holding his magazine.

'Now then,' Robby said, the girls draw the boy and the boys draw the girl. If you are good still models you earn sixpence each.'

The class set to work quietly and after a time Robby went round. He enjoyed the Second Year 'A' form. His type of risqué humour suited this age when girl and boy attitudes had little consideration for sex appeal. The form confirmed his belief in streaming. Psychologists and Sociologists often frowned on streaming, saying that it tended to aggravate class structure. Robby compared the Chad conditions with these in Liverpool. The complaint by sociologists that the slow child was neglected and the brighter child received more attention from the teacher, seemed to him to favour the streaming system. Certain boys at Chad's had suffered, being unable to keep up with the brighter ones. A class of children of more or less equal abilities was a more satisfactory approach to teaching where slight differences in accomplishment had no harmful effects. The sociologists couldn't have it both ways.

To the teacher streaming had several drawbacks, also; a class of fifth-formers in the lower stream needed every ounce of the teacher's determination. Robby had such a form for a soul-burning eighty minutes one day a week. There were some tall, rangy lads and some hard, brazen girls. The hardest females were described by the cynical careers master as appropriate fodder for local brothels, and the boys thieves and future gaolbirds. Thomas Pepper was a handful of horror, graphically named by the careers master as a Bag of Rat's Vomit. Pepper's vocabulary consisted of about eighty words of which the main one was four-lettered and not found in the dictionary those days. Pepper often recounted his adventures of the night before with The Gang of which he seemed to be the Brigand in Chief. Robby dealt with them in their own language and strangely, the girls at least grew to like him. The form reinforced the truth that teaching is no career for softhearted people. Children were sadists and the general public were unaware of the cruelties suffered by teachers in classroom behaviour.

Pepper settled down after a time and puzzled teachers discovered that his grandfather had died, the only person, probably, who had shown him the least regard that could loosely be called love. But young memories are short and Pepper resumed his usual loutish attitude once his grandfather's death had become a dim memory.

It was just before the lunch-bell one day. Pepper had finished his work and was relating in his full flow of filthy language the happenings of the previous night. Every other word was 'Fucking'. Robby was marking the form's work and sitting by the front desk with several girls watching him, their arms folded in the manner of their buxom mas gossiping on the balconies of high-rise flats.

'Jus' listen to 'im sir,' one girl whispered. 'Carn y' stop 'is gob? The 'orrible sod!'

Robby's watch told him there were three minutes to go.

'Pepper,' he roared, making everybody jump, 'get your fucking paper and I'll fucking mark it!'

All mouths opened. Some boys started laughing. The girls gasped and one or two boys looked astonished, as tough as they were. Pepper's eyes stared wide, eyebrows raised, huge mouth agape. He went to his desk and brought his drawing.

'Ooh, sir,' said one of the girls, her senses wakening.

'Yes,' Robby shouted, 'it's awful, isn't it? I was in the army all through the war and I never once heard a man use that word as many times as Pepper's used it this morning. The word is meaningless, Pepper, you foul-mouthed scrawny creature. That foul language and all your talk is twaddle, lad. You never hit a policeman in all your mouldy life! They didn't send the Alsatian after you. You're all wind and water. None of those lads over there believes a word you say - you just fascinate them like a snake.' There was a bubble of laughter from the gang in the corner. To Robby's amazement Pepper was grinning down at his paper on the desk.

Some pupils who were not fond of Pepper were highly amused and excited. They had never heard a teacher deal with Pepper on his own terms. Other teachers talked with posh words and soft threats; some women teachers and younger men teachers seemed scared of Pepper because he gave them all the old buck you could think of.

Robby schemed for a few seconds - here was an opportunity, maybe to his own inconvenience, to smash Tom Pepper's clique of trouble makers and the idea arose from his study of Pepper's work.

'Well, Pepper,' he said, slowly and genially, 'in spite of everything, lad, you have talent. This is a very fine drawing, Thomas. You can join O-Level class next week - but you'll have to work - get that into your skull - you'll have to work.'

Pepper was still grinning, showing his big white teeth. Using that seven-letter word had amputated Pepper's feet of clay. It puzzled Pepper that a teacher could almost be one of the gang, with a knowledge of the vulgar usually ignored by teachers.

'Well, Thomas, what do you say?'

'Yer, if y' t'ink so - if am gud enough, like - yis arn pullin' me leg nor nothin'?' With a great show of indignation, Robby answered him, 'Do you think for one moment, Pepper, that I would BURDEN myself and the other kids in O-Level class with FOUR PERIODS of you if I didn't think it worthwhile?' They all saw the logic of this.

Pepper must have some talent; otherwise Fergy would never bother with him.

'OK then sir,' said Pepper subdued. He had not had such attention before 'is it We'nsdee all mornin', sir?'

'It is. I'll arrange with your year tutor to change your timetable. That'll be no problem, I'm quite sure about that.'

Pepper's trouble making was curbed at last and several teachers were grateful when they missed Pepper because he was busy with his art. Within months Robby made a friend of the lad. Any further use of the seven letter word Robby merely shouted, 'Pepper!' and Pepper usually answered 'sorry sir!'

The form went out when the bell rang, discussing the incident and giggling. The comical vulgarism had tickled them. Years hence they would recall the incident and tell friends and neighbours when talking about schooldays. But within two days their short-term memories had lost it among the other daily wrangles of school life.

CHAPTER 7

Benny Solomon's appearance belied Robby's remembrance of him. He was a prosperous man, tall, hefty, well fleshed, and smartly dressed in a grey suit of excellent cut.

'You're lookin' well, Fergy,' he greeted Robby, shaking hands.

'Not as well as you, Benny. You look a million - doesn't he, ma?'

'You certainly do, lad,' said Emma. 'You've obviously done well. And how is Rosie going on?'

'She's doin' fine, Mrs Ferguson. Livin' in New York. Married to a fella in insurance. They have two kids.'

'Remember pricing those Harmsworths, Benny? Quoting a shilling each, then letting me have 'em for half-crown. That was a shrewd ploy. You made 'em sound like a huge bargain.'

Benny laughed 'They WERE, mate, they were. I had some old stocks of wallpaper when I opened the new shop for Alfie. Old-fashioned design. Nobody'd buy 'em. I stained the tops of one or two ends with cold tea and we told customers we'd sell 'em half price if they bought six rolls. We got rid of 'em all right. They were so keen to get a bargain they thought a bit of staining was nowt and the old design didn't bother 'em.'

'Trick of the trade,' Emma laughed. 'Your father had none of those tricks.'

'No. The da was really too honest to be in business.'

'He still left you enough to buy a shop,' Robby laughed.

'I was sorry to hear about Joe,' Emma broke in. 'Poor Joe.

Such a big, handsome lad! What devilish things happen in war! How is that wound of yours, Benny?'

'It plays up now and then, Mrs Ferguson, but mainly in winter - an' I still limp a bit.'

'How did Asher go on in the war?' Robby asked.

302

'Sergeant navigator in the RAF. Got shot down over France. He and his mate baled out and wandered around for a bit until they managed t' get in touch with the French underground people. I told him it 'ud make a damn good yarn - but he was never any good at writin', our kid.'

Robby was alert at once. 'Listen Benny I'll give you a copy of my book about Burma. I've just finished another - The Moles of Paris - French Resistance. I'll be glad to write Asher's story if you like. Can you arrange it?'

'Yer. Great idea. He lives in Aintree near the station. Go and see him. You ARE coming to see my shops, aren't you? Alfie will be glad to see you, too.'

Robby used one of his three remaining copies, autographed it and gave it to his friend.

'Ta very much - this is an unexpected bonus for coming to Leyland. I'll call at our kids on the way home and show him this. I'll have a chinwag with him and tell him you'd want to take some notes. Is that OK?'

'Great! What's the best time to go?'

'Half day closing Wednesday - same as me. Go about two thirty, and then arrange another time with him.'

'I go back to school beginning September. Give me his address and warn him I'm coming.'

Benny arranged everything as he had promised and Robby travelled to Asher's place the following Wednesday. It was a beautiful home. Robby met the attractive wife and son, had tea, sat down and scribbled notes as Asher talked. He went again on Sunday afternoon and finished with fifty pages of notes.

'I'll make a good book out of this Asher. We'll share fifty-fifty.'

'No. You'll be doing all the work. If the book's accepted give me twenty-five pounds. I've done nothing, really, except talk. Any fool can do that. You'll have your work cut out making a full yarn out of it. Twenty-five pounds, Robby.'

'Well, Asher, our Mal always said you were a genuine, large hearted bloke.'

'He didn't know me,' Asher laughed. 'Anyway, when you want that wedding ring, come and see me.'

'Thanks, Asher. I'll take your card and give you a ring.'

As he sat in the train, Robby felt that everything was going his way. The two Solomon lads were useful to know, apart from having their friendship.

In April a cheque arrived from Congreve and Halsall with an accountant's certificate showing sales of 37,288 copies, giving a total of £559.6s.5d., a £100 of which he had already received as advance payment. He was astounded by the amount and remembered Angus's criticisms. This would show him! Yes, and it wasn't the end. Sales were ongoing and might do well during the holiday season. He was pleased that Angus, now established and confident, had been interested enough to introduce him to his bank manager when he had received his first pay-cheque from the Education Authority, for his salary to be paid straight into his bank account. Armed with this marvellous cheque from the publishers, he visited the bank and opened a deposit account.

April was a month of momentous occasions for him - an Easter marriage to Helen Maria Bardsley of this parish, with Bernard Kelvin as his Best Man, Douglas a groomsman, Margaret as Maid of Honour, and Asher's excellent wedding ring with a 33 % discount as a wedding gift . Nothing could have been more perfect than that wedding day and the night that followed it.

But the gods looked down and sighed very deeply!

* * *

Robby knew conditions would change when the baby came. There would be little time to write, to paint, to scheme about the detached house they were having built. The future promised to be exciting and challenging.

'We should have a good holiday this year,' he said. 'It may be the last chance for a while.' Helen laughed and shrugged. 'I'm perfectly happy without expensive holidays. I don't think we should waste our money. We have so many expenses to meet with the new house. We'll have a day here and a day there - that's what I like.'

'That's feasible,' Robby agreed, 'now we have the car.'

They were in the den, Helen seated at the table marking books and he lounging in the huge arm-chair with its soft cushions around him. He thought of the few months they had been together - she had been as near perfection as it was possible for a human to be. There had been a complete mental and physical harmony between them - except for the trouble with his mother-in-law. Helen had given delightful nuances to sexual relations, delicacy, gentleness and beauty. Her sense of household economics had always been wise. She had insisted that he should buy a new car, not some second-hand thing that might let them down in a year or two. You had to maintain certain standards that would gain respect. That was Helen - always an eye to their respect and pride.

He had not yet lost his feelings of pleasant surprise at the conditions in his new school. It had the benefit of a strong head and deputy head and there were few troublemakers. Most of the children had liked him from the beginning and with very few exceptions they enjoyed his lessons. His art club had been flourishing for three months, meeting once a week, and in warm weather they hired a coach and travelled to beauty spots, taking small desk easels and other equipment for painting outdoors. The pupils brought picnic lunches and enough money to pay for the coach hire. Helen packed sandwiches, flasks and crockery. Beside a brook, with the birds all around them, they sat and enjoyed their food and the friendship that existed between the children and themselves - until Mrs Bardsley accepted their invitation to go with them! It was a fine Saturday morning and the three adults went to Liverpool to meet the Third Year group at school. Robby parked his car in the school parking space, and they boarded the coach for their journey through the Mersey Tunnel, their destination, Eastham, across the river.

In the woods at Eastham the kids worked hard and quietly and when lunchtime came, they left their equipment on the grass and sat around eating their sandwiches, a prefect on hand to see that no litter was left lying around. After lunch a break for ten minutes when they could play games or visit the farm shop for ice cream or sweets. Robby and Helen were lying on a grass slope, listening to the squeals of excitement.

Helen's mother had gone off by herself to the farm shop to buy some honey. It was on her way back that she came upon Sandra Nicholson and a boy called Sean Magee.

From a distance they saw Mrs Bardsley speaking to the couple, then writing something on the wrapping around the honey jar.

'I wonder what your mother's doing?' Robby murmured. He got up and stretched. 'I'll restart them, otherwise the coach will be here before they're finished.' He walked off to see to it. When they had all started painting again he went round to each in turn.

Mrs Bardsley seemed a little out of breath when she came up to her daughter.

'I'll tell you what I've just seen,' she said. She stuffed the pot of honey into her bag. 'That boy Sean Magee, with Sandra Nicholson - behind a clump of bushes - and he actually had his hand up her clothes. Disgusting! I've taken their names and addresses and I shall write to their mothers when I get home.'

Helen's large eyes were even wider than usual in her amazement as she paused in the act of packing away utensils.

'Good Heavens, mother! You can't write to their parents. You report it to Robby. He'll deal with it.'

'Why should he deal with it any better than I can?'

'He will deal with it because he is in charge of these children. You will not write to the parents. I know how the school system works, you don't, mother.'

'We are not in school now,' Mrs Bardsley went on, stubbornly. 'It is Saturday. I saw what they were doing and I shall tell their mothers.'

'If you do, mother, I shall be very annoyed indeed.'

'Oh? You will be annoyed, will you? You are getting very bumptious lately. You would allow a boy to molest a girl and think it is not our concern?'

'It is not our concern. It is Robby's. He's responsible. I shall go over and tell him. Besides, the boy was not molesting the girl - she was probably enjoying it, more like, otherwise she would not willingly go behind the bushes with him.'

Mrs Bardsley looked at her daughter with a new, horrified light of incomprehension in her eyes.

'You're just like your father - to say such a disgusting and immoral thing about a young, innocent girl!'

'Mother, you're so old-fashioned. Adolescents have done that sort of thing for generations. Besides, they are more knowledgeable about things these days. That Sandra Nicholson could possibly tell you a thing or two.'

'How dare you,' her mother cried. 'If I were a teacher I would stamp out all that kind of filth, and no mistake.'

'But you aren't a teacher, mother. If you were you would have a different attitude. The innocence of children is a fallacy. They aren't as innocent as you were at their age.'

'My God! You have become hard and cynical - and I can guess who has influenced you, since reading that book of his. And what will HE do when that Magee boy is reported to him?'

'That is his affair and we mustn't interfere. He'll see to it on Monday, doubtless.'

'We can deal with it. If you tell him I shall never speak to you again.'

'Don't be silly, mother - I've got to report to him. He is responsible for these children. And he'll certainly not allow you to write to their parents.'

'Not allow...?' Mrs Bardsley was enraged. 'I'd like to see him stop me, indeed!'

'If anybody writes, he will write, not you. I keep telling you, it is not our concern.'

'Hmph!' Mrs Bardsley stumped off with pursed lips to the farm shop again.

The coach arrived about four and the children collected their equipment and lined up to go aboard. Helen recounted everything that had passed between herself and her mother. By the time she had finished speaking, all the children were on the coach.

'You are quite right,' Robby said. She mustn't get in touch with the parents in any way. I will deal with the matter. As you told her, it's not her concern.' Robby stepped up into the coach and Helen heard him say, 'After registration on Monday, I want Sean Magee and Sandra Nicholson to see me.'

He felt disgruntled and wondered why he had had the stupid notion of inviting the woman. She always interfered in their lives! 'Let's go and find her,' he said.

Through the window of the farm shop they saw her drinking the last of her coffee. She took her check to the pay-desk, paid her bill and came out in time to meet them. Ignoring her daughter she faced Robby.

'Well?' she demanded.

'Well what?' Robby said, deliberately.

'What are you doing about it - Sean Magee and Sandra Nicholson?'

'That is entirely my business, Mrs Bardsley, if you don't mind. I shall deal with it in the usual manner. I have already set things in operation. Please do not interfere.'

'Do not interfere? I saw what was happening - I actually saw the boy.'

'All right. All right,' Robby intervened, gruffly. 'Please get on the coach - he's waiting.' Feeling extremely insulted and snubbed, Mrs Bardsley boarded the coach and sat at the back, alone.

*　　*　　*

During the summer holidays he and Helen motored to Asher's house in Aintree and left a carbon copy of *Seventy-Seven Days*, Asher's story, then went on to Kirkdale to see Benny's shop. The premises were very old and stretched far back from the pavement. Robby introduced Helen and his friend responded with, 'You're just what I had expected.

Fergy always had very good taste in everything,' which remark Helen found most charming. He showed them around, taking them upstairs after asking Helen solicitously could she manage it, and they saw a well-stocked storeroom of paints, wallpapers, brushes, tools, ladders, cements, glues and dozens of other aids to decorating at home. Robby remembered Mrs Murphy's ironmongery at Croxteth and felt the same pleasure he had felt as a boy.

'By the way,' Benny remembered, as they came downstairs, 'I read your book. Very good, I thought. It was all new to me. I never got as far as India. I was only on the Desert during the war. I'll give you Alfred's shop's address and you can pop in there before you go back.'

Robby told him that their new house was almost finished and they would soon need materials.

'I'll call you on the phone. No old stock, mind, stained with cold tea,' he laughed. Helen looked very puzzled. Robby briefly outlined what Benny had told him. She giggled.

'Oh no, thank you. We want all the poshest, latest designs please.'

Alf looked much older than Benny, Robby thought, and they were of the same age. Alfie had probably had a more taxing life than had Benny. Alf had built all his own shelving for the shop and partitions for the storerooms and Robby remembered the woodwork centre where Alf had always been top boy. He remembered, too, Alf's carving.

'How is your mother now?' Robby enquired.

'She's not too good,' Alf sighed. 'We've had a difficult time. She needs constant attention and Sally, my wife, has been marvellous. It's not a good idea to live with parents.' Robby looked at Helen and she averted her eyes. To Robby these visits had been a soothing balm on the worsening conditions at home. Mrs Bardsley had been very difficult and was turning out to be a jealous old woman. They both guessed that she envied them their happiness together and she probably felt neglected. That was why he had invited her to go with them on occasions.

Quite by chance Harriet Cromwell met her friend,

Glynis Bardsley, on the market square and was astounded by outpourings of her feelings against Robby, influencing Helen against her own mother being arrogant and unpleasant. Harriet was bewildered. She tried to soothe her friend by saying that her daughter and son-in-law would be moving into their new home soon and then relationships would improve.

'Oh yes, relationships will improve,' said Mrs Bardsley, 'for them. They will leave me with that big house, on my own, a defenceless woman, with only my pensions to live on!' Loyalty prevented Harriet from saying more, for she knew Glynis Bardsley, ever since schooldays, could be very difficult when faced by any kind of dissension.

* * *

The first week in August Robby started to go to the new house to light fires to dry out the place. Each visit gave him a keen sense of possession and security. He owned this beautiful house, built to his own specifications – double fronted, three-bed roomed, dining-room, sitting-room, fitted kitchen, wash house and pantry, a cloakroom and tiled bathroom upstairs with a second lavatory.

The stair was of oak and needed no carpet. Outside was a brick-built garage and extra land if extensions to the house were needed later. He wrote to Dartman's ordering several pieces of furniture by description of trade names from the high quality manufacturers that he could remember, and fitted carpets. After a month of house warming, the furniture van arrived. Two carpet fitters had the whole house covered within four hours and they helped the deliverymen to position the furniture where it was required. Robby was sad to learn from the elderly driver that Dick, his mate at Dartman's, had been killed in the war on the destroyer in which he served. Robby's mind turned to his memory of Dick's nice wife and he wondered how she was faring as a widow with two children.

Helen was delighted with the high quality of the

furniture, despite her previous doubts about buying a pig in a poke, and within that one day in August, the cold, damp, new, mortar smelling house had been transformed into a gracious, sunny, comfortable home.

He continued to visit the house even after it was furnished, lighting fires as usual, and by 29th August, the water, gas, and electricity had been turned on and the telephone installed. They were ready to leave Mrs Bardsley's big, old house with its unpleasant atmosphere, and they decided on Saturday morning, the last day of August, for moving in.

On the Friday night, as they got into bed, he could feel with a gentle hand the foetal movement of the child in the womb, and a feeling of wonder filled his mind.

'Doctor Smollett said I had a very lively baby,' said Helen. 'Everything's as it should be. I told him I wasn't having any sickness now and he said that was normal - it usually ends by the fourth month. And I've informed the midwife of our new address, so that's in order. The doctor said I was very healthy and strong, so there.'

'He thinks you're a big, buxom wench,' Robby laughed.

Her small fist punched his thigh. 'I'm not buxom, you horrible thing, and I'm not a wench.' He leaned over on his elbow and kissed her. 'Of course not, my little goddess.'

'I suppose every mum's fussy about her first,' she said.

'You're not fussy. Everything will be fine, you'll see. Now let's get our beauty sleep, wench.'

She gave him another punch and turned over.

'Lie in tomorrow,' he said. 'I'll bring you a cuppa in bed.'

'No. I must get up. There are lots of things to do. We must tidy everything and dust round before we go, otherwise she will have things to say. Anyway, we'll play it by ear. I'm going to dream of how happy we shall be, the three of us.'

'And me,' he said, yawning. 'Goodnight my sweet.'
'Goodnight,' she murmured.

The gods turned their heads away from the earthly

scene and looked at one another.

* * *

As he dozed off he thought of his wife's character and what touched him most was her loyalty. It would not have surprised him if she had made excuses for her mother's recent behaviour, but, no, she knew that jealousy was motivating her mother's treatment of him. She had confessed to him one night that her father had not been the most fortunate of husbands when he married Glynis Braithwaite. He had been a lecturer at a large Polytechnic College and Glynis had been a secretary there. The greatest sadness in Helen's life had been the death of her father. In her relationship with him there had been a very disturbing, painful period when her mother had been morbidly jealous of her, without justification, and for several months had had a serious drink problem.

Helen had been given away at the wedding ceremony by her father's brother, Uncle John, and her Aunt May had presented them with a beautiful wedding gift of Wedgwood dinner plates. They seldom came to visit, having no great liking for their sister-in-law. This confirmed Robby's feeling that his wife was a good person and her mother a neurotic, and he understood why his first impression of Mrs Bardsley had been unfavourable. With this thought a touch of guilt seeped its way into his mind - wasn't this situation a replica of Stella and her mother, and hadn't his main objection to marrying Stella been the 'Tyrannical Puritan?' Surely this was different. He had fallen in love with Helen at first sight. It had to do with her sexual charisma that had instantly attracted him, together with a good humour and great intelligence.

It was in the early hours of morning that Helen heard the sound. She sat up in bed and he awoke.

'I heard a sound,' she said. 'Listen.'

Robby raised his head and they both listened intently. There it came again, a gasping, hoarse sound.

'It's mother,' she declared, and hastily got out of bed

and put on her dressing gown. He followed in a second and had thrust his arms into his dressing gown as he followed her into her mother's room. He switched on the night-light by the bedside. Mrs Bardsley was struggling for breath.

'It's a heart attack,' Helen breathed. 'Ring the doctor. I'll try to do something.'

He rushed downstairs to the telephone in the hall and dialled the emergency doctor's number. First-aid knowledge told Helen that her mother's asthmatic sounds were at least signs of cardiac asthma - suffocating, coughing, and showing froth round the lips as she wheezed and perspired profusely. When the coughing subsided a little she lay back exhausted and breathing faintly through her mouth. By the time the emergency doctor had arrived the onset had almost passed; but he had already arranged for an ambulance. It arrived a few seconds after he had completed his examination of the patient and had given an injection. The lady was carefully wrapped in warm blankets, carried down to the ambulance, and taken at speed to the hospital.

Visiting the patient soon became a routine after she had been transferred from the intensive care unit. She had a very serious heart disease. In time she was allowed two visitors for an hour twice a week. Despite her condition, she always received Robby with pan-faced coldness. They brought her grapes, Ribena, magazines, and so forth. She always said 'Thanks' in a flat voice. They asked how she was and she replied, 'Better.' When Harriet went with them and Robby had to stay outside, Mrs Bardsley showed the first signs of animation. Robby was always greeted with as much hostility as a sick person could show, after the first visit. She did not want him there. When Harriet went with them he stayed outside saying it would be better that way. Helen had the commonsense to agree with him and they found their reception by the patient much more accommodating. At one point, nonetheless, Mrs Bardsley started a tirade of abuse against her son-in-law and Helen threatened to leave.

'You go if you want to,' her mother retorted, 'Harriet will stay. You can always go back on the bus, Harriet.'

'No, Glynis,' Harriet had rejoined, forthrightly, 'I shan't

stay either if you keep on abusing Robby.'

Harriet saw the frustration in her friend's eyes.

'You are all against me, everyone of you,' she whimpered.

'Don't be silly, mother,' Helen said, softly. 'We are not against you and neither is Robby. Why you should hate him so I really don't know. He's done you no harm.'

Against this double opposition the patient had no rejoinder and remained glum and silent.

'Once you are discharged you will live with us,' Helen said after a time.

'What?' Mrs Bardsley squeaked. 'Live with you - and him?'

'Yes. Robby says you can't live by yourself in that big house.'

'Robby, Robby, Robby,' she sneered. 'He said, did he? Well, I don't believe you. He would never suggest such a thing. He's all for himself is that fellow and doesn't give a damn about anybody else!'

'Now, Glynis,' Harriet said, a touch of sternness in her voice, 'I heard him myself say so in the car. You can't live by yourself any more. You are not at all well.'

'I know how well I am,' Mrs Bardsley quivered, 'and I don't believe you about what he said.'

The truth was, of course, that she was right. Although he felt sorry for the woman, he did not want her living with them, an invalid with either himself or Helen at her beck and call. And if she had not recovered sufficiently by the time the baby was old enough for play-school or to be left with a minder, Helen would have to give up her teaching, and that was her greatest joy. But Robby could see no alternative; the situation had been thrust upon them. The problem was not new - it had vexed many a married couple and he cursed his luck that he was the husband of one of them.

*   *   *

The garden sloped with the lane and he had to level it off.

He had bought the basic tools - fork, spade, hoe, and wheelbarrow. He worked hard at weekends and in the evenings to dig the soil and transport it from one end to the other. Eventually he had made it fairly level and planned how he would arrange the garden. He drew a small plan and worked to it. His muscles ached and his back and thighs were stiff. He selected a large area f or a lawn and raked it level, removing as many stones as possible. He marked out an area for a rose garden, and another at the bottom for vegetables. On the eastern border he planted apple and pear trees. He sowed the grass seed and put paper scarecrows across on strings. Douglas came one Saturday and helped him concrete the paths he had marked on his plan. Harriet and Helen had been going to the hospital by bus and Robby never saw Mrs Bardsley alive after that had been normal procedure.

'Why not ask Alf Atkins to make you a garden shed?' Douglas suggested as he spread the cement. 'You'll certainly need a shed to keep your tools in. You're bound to get more tools later - then there'll be the lawn mower.'

'Yes,' Robby agreed. 'I'd forgotten all about the lawn mower. We shan't need one till spring though. It's a costly item, a garden. I'll give Alf a ring at his shop on Monday.'

And everything developed slowly over the weeks - the lawn had a faint green mist showing, the builder's debris had been moved by the dustmen and everything seemed ready for next Spring's magic touch.

*   *   *

'How is your mother now, love?' Flora asked Helen when they went to visit her.

'Much the same,' said Helen, sighing. 'Very depressed as usual. We knew she wouldn't be out for Christmas.'

'What a shame,' said Flora.

'Well,' said Helen, with a frankness that was endearing, 'I'm not so sure about that. She's daggers drawn with Robby, you know.'

'Oh?' said Flora, her voice rising in surprise. 'Why is

that, I wonder?'

'How has that come about, Robby?' Jack intervened. 'You did say you were getting along OK.'

'Well, I did at first,' Robby laughed. 'But something's happened to upset her since then, obviously, and I don't know what it is - apart from a little squabble we had one time.' Helen and Flora went out into the kitchen to make tea and a snack before the visitors went home.

'Flora,' Helen said, 'I think mother's going through the change. She's very, very moody. She's awfully jealous of Robby and me.'

'Jealous? Good Heavens! What on earth can she be jealous about?'

'I suppose she thinks I've deserted her. I can't give her the attention she needs at her time of life.'

'But you haven't deserted her,' Flora laughed. 'What a silly idea.'

'In a way, I know how she feels. I'm occupied with Robby and our new house, curtains and cushions and bed linen and so forth. There's the baby coming, She's bound to feel neglected and it's probably her hormone imbalance that makes everything worse for her.'

'Is she not thrilled at the idea of having a grandchild?'

'No, she doesn't seem to be. She has not mentioned the baby once.'

'How strange! Even I am quite excited at the prospect of being an auntie again.'

'Oh, I know you are,' said Helen, warmly, and kissed Flora on the cheek.

'Well, naturally,' Flora said, blushing slightly, 'all the family on both sides should be thrilled. I hope everything works out fine for you, Helen - easy birth and such like.'

'Thank you. I'm sure it will, Flora.'

When they had had some supper they put on their heavy coats and Jack and Flora went to the door with them. Jack opened it and the cold northern blast hit them in the face. The snow was already thick on the ground and the f all heavy and whirling diagonally so that they could hardly see across the road. It was a threatening moonless night and they shivered after the snugness of Flora's cottage.

'You go in,' Helen said. 'Don't catch cold.'

'God in heaven!' Jack said. 'Just look at it. I'll get you a piece of thick card, Robby, then you can scrape the snow from the windscreen.'

'Thanks,' Robby said, 'but don't stand waiting at the door.'

With the card Robby went all round the glassworks and scraped off the snow. Helen got into the passenger seat and shivered in the cold interior. Robby started the engine first time and set the windscreen wipers going.

'Drive carefully,' Flora shouted, words she would remember all her days.

'Don't worry, I will,' Robby shouted back. They both called Goodnight and Robby moved off gingerly, giving a final toot on the horn as a last farewell.

And the gods, looking down from beyond the snowstorm, sighed miserably and breathed their great pity and sympathy, knowing they were forbidden to help by the stern laws of the Goddesses of Fate.

* * *

CHAPTER 8

There was a pale yellow mist and a green misty forest below, and the sky above all white; and white drapes around him. He was lying on clouds, warm and soft with the flabby skins of water bottles around his body and they were far too hot. The nurse's young bosom suddenly loomed over him out of the clouds, near his face. He felt the clean, fresh-smelling hand on his head, cool, soft, gentle. Slim fingers sought his hand from the clouds below and she held his wrist. She peeped at the watch attached to her uniform then covered his arm again with the soft, billowy clouds, turning and vanishing into the yellow mist. He hoped the alarm wouldn't sound all at once and awake him from his dream. The clean smelling angel of mercy appeared again from the clouds and the yellow mist and another figure in white came and touched him through the clouds, felt him, lifted the edges of the close clouds near his head and turned to whisper to the angel.

Intriguing, all this. His inner brain laughed and said if that darned alarm goes off I'll be mad. What will happen next? Vivid dreams like this were rare, and this was very vivid in spite of the yellow mist and the green jungle beneath and the white sky and the clouds billowing all about. It was very warm in these clouds and where did all these water bottles come from? He could not remember having bought so many water bottles. They were dream water bottles, that was it.

Motionless, a mere heart beat from the grave, his mind with fragmentary stabs of the past with no meaning, no happiness, no reality, no future, no reason. Things came and vanished. He had not felt ill in a dream before. That was a strange thing, not feeling ill in a dream.

He turned his eyeballs first to the left and then to the right, like a cow in a field watching a train go by, and it was very painful. Left, a dark screen, right, green mist no - green - green canvas. That was it, green canvas and yellow wall above and white ceiling! No sounds. It was a hospital! Jungle sores were always painful like this and festering hot. They weren't water bottles, the heat was his festering hot legs. Was he in a marquee?

Three vague figures in white edging their way around the screen. One looks, sighs and shakes his baldhead. Poor devil! No visitors yet sister - careful nursing might save him now he's out of it - leave dressings for another day - call me if anything develops - pulse and temperature every half hour please. Consultant and house surgeon depart mumbling. Sister calls and the angel returns. Take over constant watch by the bedside. Check pulse and temperature every half hour, nurse.

The nurse seeks and finds his hand again, slim fingers take his wrist again. His eyes adjust with difficulty. Pretty angel. She looks up and catches his expression - a dull, blank, lost expression. Her face floods with pity and compassion fills her eyes. She is very intelligent efficient, but young. Why do things like this happen, she asks?

Frequent ramblings. A burning, half-drugged limbo. A brain leaping from one slight notion to another. A jumbled nonsense in a black background of intense, nagging sadness. The numbers plague his feelings of being utterly lost - twos and threes and fours - perhaps two hundred tons, or was it three hundred tons? In rare flashes of lucidity his conscious brain dismisses the numbers game which is wearying and not worth buying. It was nice playing bridge. Come on, old chap, tell us about Dina long legs and beautiful breasts. Young, clean cobber all bints clean cobber don't you worry cobber. Ask Brown the builder about that mat well. Don't dig the metal part of the brush into the paper lad! The house will soon be finished and Quilter's going to get some paint from Solomon Grundy born on a Monday. It worries your poor ma paying the money-lender and keeping down the bugs. We belong to the slums. They'll never publish anything when you haven't a decent suit to your back. Give it up three hundred and forty tons! The Black Rector is after you. Send for General Norris Green and pay the rent to the old witch. That poor old green tile with the face of Charles

Lawton in the middle of it. Drive through the tunnel before all the grapes go bad. I'll miss the bus with these two angels holding me down. The Germans are coming and we've got to open up to the Aussies who are all clean cobber. They are always left behind to clear up the mess after those two dogs at Bab-el-Luk station. They're dropping lots of mortar down the cavity walls, blast 'em, and they're dropping lots of mortar bombs. 2341265. Don't make fun of poor old Polonius - Laertes had no mummy. Not all artists cut their ears off! This bed's flooding. 2341265 - Corporal Ferguson SIR! Fancy saluting with his arm off, poor old John! 2341265 Corporal Ferguson SIR! Corporal of pigs, SIR! Little man dancing - little babies dancing. Poisons go all through you if you're not careful, corporal; Granddad's screaming from the grave with that dog pulling its chain and pulling up the roots and spilling the poisons. Don't scream like that you rotten old sod!

There came a period of some weeks when his comatose condition lessened and he began his period of reality - this was a hospital and it was not in the army, oh no. There were no MOs. This jungle clearing was a civvy dock. This wasn't dreaming and there would be no alarm clock. The nurses were all real. There were no bottles - the mysterious flabby sensation was a raw tender feeling that made body movement an anguish. There was something wrong with his legs! The mists were clearing. Why was he in a civvy dock? He'd had a terrible nightmare last night - weird things happening - grandfather screaming his head off!

When the nurses came to dress his wounds, he was sufficiently conscious to piece together vaguely what had happened - his head was wrapped in bandages; his legs and arms covered in dressings; there were tubes up his nose and intravenous feeding tubes taped to his wrist. The nurses were very gentle with him and when he tried to say something, his voice was guttural and faint and they pursed their lips and frowned and said Shush! very gently.

One day he was dimly relieved to have the tubes removed and the nurses began to feed him with a spoon.

They continued to give him injections from time to time and he rambled. The world of consciousness brought him agonising pain and he suffered the miseries and terrors of the unknown. When visitors were allowed in for a short time he could not understand what they were saying. There was a family with a teenage daughter and two sons. Their mother was large and cried a lot and their father held his hand. A small woman with very anxious, lined face murmured and sighed continually. There were self-conscious men and women who came and left grapes and bottles on his locker. They swallowed their spittle and went away looking sad and worried.

One day he heard what they were saying. He could pick out voices. There was a big fellow with dark hair who reminded him of someone and with him a timid, worried fellow who said, 'I've made your shed, old lad. You'll like it.' Another fellow said, 'I'm Frank Stubbs.' There was a bewildering mass of visitors with names he picked up in their conversations or when they stated who they were, knowing that his memory had failed. Some visitors would say, 'How are you today' and he answered in a whisper, 'Very well, thank you,' like a wrongly programmed robot. In a terrifyingly strange world he knew nobody.

There came a time weeks later when he vaguely formed a picture of schooldays, breaking through the barrier of his lost memory. He had always done well at school, he thought, regaining happy memories of the distant past. But he was not a schoolboy now because the nurses shaved him in the morning. An idea slipped into his mind one afternoon - could he be a schoolteacher. The idea was preposterous. At irregular intervals he became aware of the things around him and made out baskets of fruit with small Get Well cards from The Art Club Members and The Members of Form 4B. There were other gifts all signed with names he could not remember. He puzzled over them for a long time.

Months passed before he recognised Flora and Jack Volant for the first time. Flora broke down when she saw the recognition of them.

'There's nothing to cry about,' he whispered, when she

lowered her head.

The tears streamed down her cheeks when she thought of the reason for her grief. She turned away and took out her dainty handkerchief to blow her nose. Jack stepped closer to the bed and grasped his hand.

'Feeling better, Robby, lad?' he asked.

'Mending,' he answered, with a grimace for a smile showing where the dressings finished. 'I couldn't remember a thing last night and had all sorts of horrible dreams.' When Flora and Jack realised that the patient had compressed weeks and weeks of coma and nightmare into the two words 'last night' they moaned their misery and pity.

'Just you rest now, Robby, lad,' Jack soothed. 'When you're better we'll have a long chat.'

And then Robby asked, without knowing why, 'Where's Whatshername?'

'Shush!' Jack calmed him. Flora's anguish was too much. She gripped his hand for a second and went away, towards the exit.

'We'll come again, Robby,' said Jack. 'Tomorrow son. Go to sleep now.'

'Where's Whatshername?' Again the question came out from some dim recess of his mind. The sister, hovering near for just such a situation, called, 'Time now, please, I'm afraid. We mustn't tire him too much.'

Jack gripped his hand again and murmured 'Don't worry, Robby, lad. Everything will work out. Ta ta. See you tomorrow.'

He walked quickly to Flora at the entrance door, turned and waved, miserably, and disappeared leaving behind a very anxious, terrified patient.

Nobody would speak of what had happened. His mind had locked away a memory in a compartment of oblivion and he could not find the key. The haunting whispers of an unknown ghost called Whatshername hovered over his left shoulder. His subconscious mind decreed that it was a female ghost. Frank Stubbs, the fellow who had suffered torture for not buying a book, said he did not know what had happened. Flora came and wept all the time. Jack said,

'Doctor's orders, lad. You must get well and then we can sort things out, Robby. Don't worry. Just you get well and then we shall see, eh?' He recognised his ma who said, 'Shush! son. Not now, lad. You must get better.' He was constantly under sedation and frequently during those weary, frightening days, he lay half on his side and stared into space, his eyes blank, his brain racing and searching and building up one awful thought that fixed itself in his mind and became a brutish conviction. Whatshername had died in an accident! He had managed to survive. Whatshername was dead! The person whose ghost haunted him over his left shoulder had been killed in an accident, whoever she was!

During the fourth week of his fully conscious period, with temperature normal, and pain reduced to mere irritation, he was taken out of the ward to have his skull X-rayed. For months he had been in the same ward. As he was wheeled past the other wards he imagined that in one of them Whatshername would be sitting up feeding the baby. The thought was a mere flicker through his brain and was gone. He did not ask why he had visualised such a weird picture. Everything was bright outside the ward. His eyes had tired of green tiles and pale yellow tiles. The reds were now vivid, as a baby sees them, and the blues and browns radiated onto his brain like intoxicating drink. In the X-ray department the male nurse left him to take the medical history to the man in charge. Robby waited miserably, staring round the room. On a distant wall he saw a mirror. With great endeavour and some pain he pushed the wooden hand wheel fixed to the wheelchair and moved towards the mirror. How was he looking these days after so much misery and mystery?

In the mirror was a hideous sight! His pulses raced and the heat surged into his face. He saw a shaven head pierced with wounds, a skeletal face with big ears standing out with grotesque ugliness, a deep scar from the crown to the side of the face making a weird distortion of the whole side of the jaw.

'My GOD!' he murmured, his inside sick with horror. 'My GOD!'

The male nurse returned and wheeled him into the X-ray department, his patient staring ahead in numb dismay.

Three days later the surgeon came and sat on the edge of his bed.

'Now then,' he began, very gently, 'how do you feel today, Mr Ferguson?' Robby looked blankly ahead. What could one answer to that?

'Bit better.'

'Yes? You realise that your recovery has been something of a miracle? Many a person with less strong constitution would have died that first week. You are lucky to be alive.'

'Am I?' The surgeon heard the bitterness in the reply. 'That's very nice to know. I shall be happier when I know why this has happened to me. I know why Whatshername hasn't been allowed to see me - I look like a monster.'

The surgeon breathed deeply through his nose, his lips firmly together in a grim realisation of what was to come. He stood up and took one or two paces back and forth. What a task!

'I want you to call on all your reserves of strength and courage. To clear your mind of what has troubled it for weeks, I must now tell you what happened. Are you prepared?'

'Think so,' came the whispered reply.

'You had a car accident. It skidded one night - icy road, heavy snowfall, strong wind - icy patch and you finished in the ditch - petrol all over the place - caught alight. Your legs - one worse than the other - received secondary burns - head and face badly lacerated by glass. By some miracle you were thrown from the car so your body escaped the flames. I don't know how that could have happened. You were in coma and then for many weeks you were delirious. We gave you up.'

'You should have,' Robby murmured. He lay staring at the ceiling. Whose car had he been in? Who had been driving? His brain was frozen with the horror of it all.

'It's natural that you feel that way - but your recovery IS a miracle and we must hold on to that. You rest now. We shall talk again tomorrow.'

The surgeon whispered something to the nurse and left the ward, sighing as he walked down the corridor. He hadn't had the heart to say more, although he could have done and got it over with. But perhaps he had said enough for one day to someone with that chap's strangely diffused partial amnesia. And his patient lay all afternoon until his visitors came, wondering about what he had not been told and aggrieved that he had not had the courage to ask. And even the further disclosures next day did not help. The surgeon asked him who Helen was. Robby said he did not know.

'I'll tell you - brace yourself, Robert - I don't want to frighten you - Helen was your wife.'

'My WIFE?' My GOD! The nightmare was getting worse. After a little time looking up at the ceiling with wide, terrified eyes, he mumbled, 'I can't remember.'

'Helen was in the car and - you must be strong - she was trapped and burnt to death. You were unconscious and knew nothing of it. I have to tell you this dreadful news - you must not go out of here not knowing - the shock later would kill you - once your memory returned.'

The surgeon gently pressed his shoulder, turned and left. The patient lay in his bed like a corpse, his dull eyes unseeing.

*   *   *

It was several weeks later that it was deemed it would be safe for him to go home. Malcolm collected him at the hospital.

'Is this your car?' Robby asked, on the way home.

'Yer. It's the one you saw at Blackpool.'

'You live in Blackpool?'

'Of course,' Malcolm said, and knew he must remain silent from then on.

Robby had been in hospital for sixteen months, accepting in a weird, automatic, submissive way all the treatment doled out to him from medication to physiotherapy, with one idea in mind - to get out as soon as possible. His brain was suicidal.

On his first excursion outside, Flora was at Emma's and expressed her anxiety. Emma had told him that Uncle George had died, Mr Hanley had died, Mrs Bardsley had had another severe attack in hospital and had died. Robby did not know Hanley or Bardsley.

'He shouldn't go out alone,' Flora said. 'He hasn't used those crutches outside, except in the garden. I think I'd better go after him.'

'Yes I wish you would, I'd go but my feet are terrible this morning,' said Emma.

Flora hurried out and caught up with her brother.

'You shouldn't be out alone,' she told him. 'I'll walk with you, lad.'

'I'd rather go alone,' he growled, and hobbled off.

Flora said no more, understanding his mood - a mood that could flare up into frightening rage and screaming frustration. She followed him discreetly at a distance. He appeared to be going towards the village, she thought. He had forgotten his new house. He had even forgotten Helen!

Robby jerked along slowly, his brain obsessed with thoughts of suicide and misery and hopelessness. He remembered his days of delirium and his army number - 2341265 Corporal Ferguson SIR!

Army number? He had been demobbed years ago, so why should his army number come to mind? By God! He needed a cigarette to steady his nerves at this moment. Must find a tobacconist's shop. A cigarette? A spark from a cigarette? Perhaps he himself had been responsible for the fire! The horror remained at the back of his mind. He found a shop in the high street and bought a packet of cigarettes. He left the shop and pegged his way back home. He dared not trust himself to resume smoking in the street - he might feel dizzy and fall over, then someone would have to lift him up; in his chronic mood of bitterness he wanted no pity.

On the forecourt of the service station two cars were being filled with petrol, and through the gap between the pumps he glimpsed a blue truck; and then as he moved, a small part came into view. The sight stopped him in his fumbling tracks and left him with his heart pounding! He was breathless, almost on the point of swooning, his body ice cold. He gripped his crutches fiercely, containing himself with a tremendous effort. He closed his eyes tightly to prevent his reeling over. There came a raging torrent, thrashing with the memories flooding his brain, almost drowning his consciousness - through that small gap between the pumps he had seen it - ton 423!

That drunken, murdering bastard! His body shivered all over. Helen, Oh Helen! My lovely Helen! The tears gushed, blinding him. All was clear, he could visualise everything now. The light on the Damascus Road! He could not control the quivering, delirious terrible flash of complete comprehension. So that was it! Yes, that was it! Burning with black hate, he swore on oath - he would kill that fat, lazy, drunken, murdering lump of pig flesh! As all his memories returned, all his rambling thoughts from his hospital days, he knew complete remembrance of the accident. He and Helen at Flora.'s - just before Christmas - the Christmas before last it was. Snowstorm, as the surgeon had said. On the way home he had lit a cigarette.

Breaking into his reverie at that instant, Fitzwarren's truck creaked to a standstill in front of him, waiting for passing traffic on the main road. Robby saw the chain already dangling from the big petrol tank, although the boy assistant must have tried to put the cap on, at the end of the chain, swinging, with a circle of filthy rag around the inside of it. Yes that was it. That faulty petrol cap. That's how the petrol was splashed around his car. And the driver's door tied with string! Ignoring the speculations in his mind, he did know for certain that Fitzwarren had caused the accident. The headlights of his own car had picked out the end of the telephone number - CoppleTON 423! Yes, that was what had plagued him in the hospital bed. That was it - four hundred and twenty-three tons! It had not been his army number. He recalled the painting of that panel, the dog lying in the sunshine. Fitzwarren had swerved round the bend near the Pig and Whistle and had slid across the icy road towards them. Up to a certain point he could see every detail of the accident.

Crazily sniggering, with tears in his eyes, he confessed to himself his incapability of doing anything about it in his present condition. He stumped off. TON 423! The police would never believe him. By the time the boozers had rushed out of the Pig and Whistle, Fitzwarren's lorry would be well away, swaying drunkenly, far enough away not to be blamed. Anything that had to be done would have to be done by himself. The police would be useless. Fate had decreed this! Fate had held back his suicidal plans for this HAD to be - Fitzwarren would die, would burn, that was certain, and he Robby Ferguson would do it!

After some painful hobbling on his crutches he reached the new house. Despite mental and physical exhaustion, his brain was clear. Here was the house that they had planned together and had saved up to have built. He rested near the front gate and looked at the clean, new rustic bricks and the white mortar and the newness of everything - the grass growing freely and no sign of weeds. Who could have done this caring, this meticulous work of weeding? Weeks later he was told that Douglas had been going up there every other week.

Darling Helen! He whispered her name, quivering as he remembered those few meagre weeks together in their beautiful home. A few blessed weeks of happy memories that now knifed into his heart with deep wounds of anguish. Sobbing wretchedly, he hobbled to the front door and fumbled in his pockets for the key. He unlocked the door and stumbled over the threshold.

Flora waited outside, across the road. So he had remembered the house after all? But there was too much sadness here. She would ask Angus to put it up for sale. Yet, if she did this without asking their younger brother, there might be such a terrifying scene that she felt scared at the mere thought! It was all so strange - he could remember the house but not his wife, nor her mother, nor Mr Hanley, only his poor Uncle George! But it was no use prolonging misery. He must start thinking of his future. She began to wonder what he was doing in the house and half decided to go over and enter. She had had a duplicate set of keys made for the house, back and front. She had found the keys among the car embers, next to Helen's burnt-out purse. She shuddered at the memory.

Within the walls of their beautiful house, Robby felt the silence of death, a death that had crushed his soul and spirit into the dust. Several letters were piled on the wide ledge of the hall window. He ignored them and pushed open with his crutch the sitting-room door. For two or three minutes he wept excruciating tears, leaning on the doorjamb and remembering. 'Helen! Helen!' he moaned. He hobbled slowly into the room and slumped down in awful weariness onto the settee. Nothing more to live for, he thought. Gas was the easiest way out - you just dozed off into eternity if you had the courage. But he had a job to do first!

He lit a cigarette and inhaled. He felt dizzy and sick. He took more care, putting the cigarette down each time he puffed at it. The torturing memory of what had happened pieced itself together in a mental mosaic in which everything fitted - the sudden looming mass in front of them, Helen screaming, he spinning the wheel, the car screeching sideways on the impact of the lorry, the driver's door wrenched off the car, the icy skid towards the ditch, almost opposite the inn, the plunging into the ditch with Helen's terrified screams in his ears; his body thrown out through the door space, his legs trapped, the lorry's swaying open door striking him on the head; the splatter of glass everywhere, all over him, and then complete oblivion. But the car's faithful headlights, for a brief second, had identified the truck with that half number! His cigarette must have shot from his mouth and lighted the petrol. He had been mercifully unconscious of his wife's excruciating tragedy - trapped with the flames devouring her and their unborn child! If there was such a place as Hell, this was it, this memory, this piecing together of purgatory, this state of the damned! But there was one sure final thing - he would take that pig of a Foulkes bastard with him into that infernal life of the hereafter!

He lit another cigarette and stared at the empty grate, his power to remember fully restored, allowing him to hear her voice, see her smile and pout, picture her charm in the way she showed that lovable mock indignation, listening to her singing as she worked. She was so young and lovely and happy, with those large, dark eyes, in the prime of her beautiful life. Too good to live, people would say, trying to be kind.

With a hollow pain inside him, he struggled to his feet, took up his crutches and stumped from the room. He looked up the stairs and wondered if he would be able to reach the landing. He had had a bed downstairs at his ma's house and had not used the stairs. Leaving his crutches against the wall, he started to climb, using his less damaged knee, the right one, and his hands, and dragging his withered leg behind him, the one the flames had damaged most. In twenty gasping minutes he was in the box room, resting on a travelling case. Reaching over, he pulled down the lid of the bureau bookcase and there were the numbered cards she had practised on for Parents' Evening at school. The tears drenched his face as he blinked through them. Suddenly he heard her voice, distantly, like a spirit sound, - *'we've been lucky, my darling, having such a good builder. - I'm very happy here, my love. It's a lovely spot. - I hope you're right about Asher's book. I'm going to Manchester around the stores to see if it's for sale now. It'll be exciting to see it.'*

'You'll have to write another book soon. Dad's life was interesting. It would make a good story. I could give you the details and you being the expert, my love, could dramatise it.'

He had never been expert at anything save the naivety of trusting the world to appraise his efforts; he had been born with an innate impulse to do great things and it had all been beyond him: he was a miserable crippled nobody!

Thwarted all his life! He had had his ration of happiness, said Fate, and could expect no more - that ration of happiness that had lasted a few glorious months with his darling soul mate. In abysmal misery he made his way downstairs backwards. He could not endure this torture much longer.

For six weeks after the surgeon's gentle explanation of what had happened, and it had been vague, there being no witnesses only rescuers, he had lain in that hospital bed and it had been a ghastly torture cell of his own thoughts and speculations, amounting to a cruelty beyond his strength. Now the thought that his filthy smoking habit had been the cause of the burning of Helen and their child-to-be was too agonising to consider. In hospital only pills had kept him sane and made him sleep; and this present purgatory could be endured because his revenge would keep him sane.

He gathered his crutches and swung into the kitchen. He switched on the gas but there was no sound. Flora must have turned off the supply at the mains. He hobbled round and approached the gas meter cupboard under the stairs. He opened the door and looked inside - yes, everything had been switched off. How could he get down there to reach the gas tap in that narrow space and recover himself to stand upright again?

He heard a click of the key in the front door and Flora entered and stood watching him. She looked pale and anxious, having waited outside for a long time wondering whether or not to break in on his sorrow.

'What are you doing?' she enquired.

'I was going to switch on the gas.'

'What for? You don't need to. Come home, Robby lad. Don't crucify yourself. Sell this house and live with ma.'

'No,' he said, harshly. 'We built this house together.'

So, Flora thought, she had been right in guessing he had remembered everything by now. Again his voice broke and tears flooded his eyes. He adjusted his crutches and stumped quickly down the hall and out of the doorway, Flora following, sighing deeply, locking the door behind her.

* * *

By September he had become expert with his crutches. Often he would go out by himself, a lonely, forlorn figure, half crazed with a grief that would not diminish. He was angry for having to build up his courage to do away with himself. His hair had begun to grow again and some of the scars over his head were hidden, but he still hated the sight of himself at night when he saw in the mirror his evilly marked face and the ghastly deformed left leg with its almost toe-less foot 'Who cleft the Devil's foot?' He knew now. Fate, as payment for his happiness. He was a deformed wretch, eyed by small children with frowning fascination and by adults will ill -concealed pity.

He thought of his campaign of revenge. First there was the dog. Since Mrs Fitzwarren had died it was probable that the dog had not been fed properly and would be even more ravenously savage. His best plan would be to feed the animal and become its friend. It would take infinite patience over a long time. But there was something about the whole scheme that appealed to his twisted brain. This was a cause in the midst of a bereavement he could not bear any longer, and before he said goodbye to the world, he would right the horrific tragedy of Helen's death and rid the community of a drunken killer. Tinned dog meat was the answer. He would buy some and transfer the contents of the tin into a plastic bag perhaps, and take it to the dog. He knew Fitzwarren's habits well - the fellow would be away and Robby would have a free hand to befriend the Alsatian. Twice a day he would visit the dog. After its initial savagery it would become used to his visits and would not bark on the Saturday night when its master would fry in hell! Meat each time, with a little milk in warm water. When the dog had learned that he was its best friend, he would set it free before completing his plan. One dark night in the autumn when the old farmhouse would burn like matchwood following the warmth and dryness of summer, he would burn the place down and Fitzwarren would be lying in a drunken stupor. That would be his *lex talionis*.

When he reached the new house he put more coal on the fires. He had informed his ma that he was airing the place after its vacant days of stale air. He lit a cigarette and sank into a dark reverie. His life had been a series of half successes and thwarted expectations - the lost benefits of his schooling, his father's death the excuse; his sordid employment; his half learnt trade; his lowly wages in all the jobs he had tackled; his army life in which he had felt like an expert for once; his brief teaching career; his married happiness strangled at its outset! But this well-planned act of revenge would be his supreme achievement! It would not be hindered. The possibility of being discovered held no terrors for him and that was the main feature that deterred people from committing murder.

When he made the aching journey to the farm a mile and a half away on foot, because he wanted no one to see him on the bus, there was no loose stake and no dog, and a notice on the farm door said SALE BY AUCTION, Saturday 28th October 1957 at 10.30 am. Details from Bretherton and Ferguson. Estate Agents, Coppleton 918. God! Angus was selling the farm! There was no time to lose now. He had a month left. He had not reckoned that had the dog lived it would have been about 110 years of age in dog years!

At ten on a sunny morning he went out for what Emma now regarded as his daily outing, and reached the cart track. He stopped and surveyed the distant farm. The wagon was in the yard and the farmer pushing a wheelbarrow towards an outhouse.

'Blast it!' he muttered. He pushed himself through a gap in the hedgerow and fell onto the grass on the other side. Retrieving his crutches, he hobbled along to a thick part of the hedge and lay down. It was chill lying in the long grass, in spite of the warm sunshine. He was about to give up hope that the farmer would appear when he heard the self starter being turned and then the throaty roar of the ancient vehicle. He crouched low and waited. The blue lorry came groaning over the rough track. It passed him and turned onto the road at the top. Its sounds gradually diminished to nothing and he was safe. He climbed out of the field and over the ditch, using his right knee painfully. He pitched his crutches before him, using them to pull himself up, and then stumped along towards the farmhouse. He tried the door handle and it turned. He entered, closing the door after him.

The living-room was full of stale odours - fatty cooking smells, tobacco, ale, sweat and stagnant air - the bastard Foulkes pig was happy in his sty! Looking round the room he caught sight of a gun against the wall in the corner. He examined it. It had not been used for some time - a light, 20-bore double-barrelled weapon, the right barrel being cylinder, the left choke bored. It had one trigger for both barrels, a gun of Belgian design. With this weapon he could compensate for his disability, adding cream to the milk of his revenge. He could make known to his victim that he, the postman, was about to dispatch him to hell. There was less satisfaction in Fitzwarren dying in a fire, not knowing that he had been found out.

A dresser with two drawers stood near the gun - it seemed the most obvious place to keep the ammunition. Robby opened the first drawer and there it was, a box of cartridges and under it the gun licence. Impulsively he took out two cartridges and loaded the gun.

At home in bed that night he worried about the gun. Why had he loaded it? Would it not have been better to wait until Saturday? Fitzwarren might discover that the gun was loaded and remove the cartridges. He would then know that someone had been in the house! He would be put on his guard immediately. Without clues Fitzwarren would suspect nothing and continue his habitual careless ways. Yes, habitual careless ways - the pig wouldn't even look at the gun and if he did he would think he had loaded it himself and had forgotten. There were arguments to back this conjecture - the rough shooting had already begun and Fitzwarren had not used the gun and probably had no intention of doing so now that he was selling his place.

Despite the lack of fear about being discovered, Robby knew that safety had to be assured and he decided to examine the gun on his next visit. He needed the gun now, fully realising that he was disabled and no fit opponent if the big farmer attacked him. He would unload the gun and keep the cartridges for Saturday night.

The following morning he was relieved to find that the

door had been left in its usual unlocked state. He entered the house and went immediately to the gun. It had not been touched. He took out the cartridges and put them in his pocket, returning the gun to its place against the wall.

As he turned to come out of the house he heard the vehicle groaning up the track! Quickly, giving himself much pain, he crutched his way out of the house, closing the door, and hastily made his way into hiding behind the first outhouse that stood parallel to the dwelling house. The lorry squeaked to a halt. He heard two doors being slammed.

'I want t' get this place cleared out afore the buyers come along,' Robby heard the farmer say. 'I'm keen t' get out since the missus died. This side door is what I allus uses. Lock's broke. I got in t' 'abit o' not botherin' wi' it when I 'ad t' dog an' now it's too bloody late t'mend it. Come in Mr Ferguson. I'll mek us a cuppa tay afore startin' on t' surveyin'.'

So Angus was auctioning the farm? Of course, ma told him Bretherton had retired. And hadn't Fitzwarren supplied Angus's shop with potatoes? It was a horribly small world! Angus would make an estate agent's survey - measuring outhouses and looking at plans of the acreage for valuation purposes. The two of them might find him skulking behind that outhouse!

He turned, keeping himself hidden from the farmhouse windows, and hobbled across fifty yards of meadowland towards a clump of trees. On his right he saw the acres of potatoes, practically ready for harvesting. It reminded him to be wary of the casual labourers Fitzwarren employed at harvest time. As he staggered into the tiny wood and hid himself, he vaguely recalled that he had done all this before, without crutches - that time in Greece when they had hidden in some orchards waiting for sunset.

He saw Angus and the farmer come out. Fitzwarren swept his arm around to indicate the extent of his property. They moved round the outhouses and Robby could even see the white of his brother's notebook. Then he saw a strange sight - Angus looking through binoculars at the roof of the various buildings. That was a new one on him, Robby thought, and he was immediately on his guard - if Angus lowered those binoculars an inch or so, he could see Robby! He crouched down close to a tree and made himself as small as possible. So, Fitzwarren had decided to retire? On Saturday night, he, Robby Ferguson, would give him that pleasure - that fat beer swiller would retire from the face of the earth!

*   *   *

'What about your correspondence?' Emma asked him on Saturday morning. 'There may be all sort of things that are urgent and need answering.'

She was afraid to detail certain matters like insurances that would bring back terrible memories and arouse the very reactions she and her family had been fighting for months.

'I'll bring the letters next time I go to the house,' he said, quietly putting her off.

'Flora brought them,' Emma told him, and went to the drawer in the corner desk. She occupied herself thinking up ways and reasons for his not visiting the house. This time she was relieved that he was satisfied that Flora had brought them.

'I'm going to see a film this evening,' he said. 'It will take my mind off things.'

'Ask our Doug to go with you,' Emma suggested.

He restrained himself from a too hasty rejection.

'No. He has a date, hasn't he? He may not want to be put into an awkward position.'

'I'm sure he'll be delighted to go with you,' Emma said, which was untrue. 'However, if that's the way you want it … ' she faded out, content that he seemed gradually to be recovering his normality.

When Emma had gone out shopping, he made himself ready to go to the farm. He fingered the cartridges in his pocket. It would be safer to load the gun that night after the farmer had gone to bed. He made the journey to the farm a little quicker than on the last occasion. There was much less

pain in his legs. He went to the house and checked that the
gun was still there he could take no chances. Fitzwarren had
warned Angus that he intended to clear the place out very
soon. It seemed a futile journey for one with his handicaps,
but he felt he had to ensure that everything worked out
smoothly.

The most exciting items of correspondence were the
first payment of royalties for *The Moles of Paris* and the
good news that *Seventy-Seven Days* had been accepted. His
heart ached, in spite of all bitterness - if only Helen had been
there to share his success! It all meant nothing to him
without her. Before going tomorrow to oblivion, he would
write a little note to his ma and put it into an envelope with
his Last Will and Testament he had signed at the solicitor's
office with witnesses on the staff.

He practised going up and down the stairs. On the third
attempt he rested on Douglas's bed. There was the tallboy.
My God! Why hadn't he thought of it? That revolver that
Doug had brought home from the war was in there
somewhere. That was the very thing. Much easier to handle
than a shotgun. But what would happen? Once used it would
have to be thrown away somewhere and sooner or later
Doug would discover the loss. If he brought it back with a
bullet missing Doug would make a fuss, and even the police
might make a search for the revolver! No. He could not
inveigle Doug or anyone else in his plans.

He went to the new house and found three biscuits in
the larder and ate them. It was a damned nuisance with all
the power off. It was cold and he would like a cup of hot tea.
He went to the meter cupboard and struggled to get down to
switch on the gas. Then he reached over and put on the
electric mains switch. It took him ten minutes to regain his
standing position! He put the curtains over about five and
switched on the light. He boiled some water and made tea,
drinking it whilst he smoked another cigarette. When it was
time to go he switched off the light and looked round the
room. He whispered, 'I'm going now. Wish me luck.
Goodbye my love.'

His eyes moist with grief, he walked to Coppleton. Near

the farm he could see the blue truck under the open barn. The moonlight was brilliant as he limped along the track on his wooden legs. Everything was happening to plan. Fitzwarren was in bed because there was no light anywhere. Climbing those stairs would be a problem. His practice at ma's had been a help, but the operation was still a noisy one. He entered the house, took out his cartridges and loaded the breeches. Outside he checked that the bedroom was still dark. He hobbled to an outhouse, opened the door and saw the drum of kerosene. That would quicken the fire - and the can was there for pouring it out. He re-entered the house and moved steadily through the living room to the staircase, holding the shotgun under his arm. Leaving one crutch against the wall, he ascended, using the gun to support his other side. Three stairs without a sound, and then the sudden creaking of ill-fitting timbers! He held his breath to listen. There was no sound. He continued to climb, feeling easier whenever the stair creaked. On the landing he tried to orientate himself. He tentatively opened one door and looked in - a small box room piled with boxes and chairs and rolled carpets. He closed the door and tried the other side of the landing. A faint streak of moonlight outlined the farmer's stomach. The fellow's huge bulk, only half undressed, lolled across the bed. Robby boldly switched on the light. It must have been a 40-watt bulb because it cast a weird orange mirk which only half illuminated the room. He pointed the shotgun at the bed, his finger in the trigger guard all ready.

'Wake up, you bastard!' he shouted. He was startled at his own calm state of mind. 'Wake up!' His voice, loud and clear, had no effect. He shouted again and again but the figure lay there immovable. Robby was immediately struck by the fact that there was no snoring!

Holding the gun close to his side and his left arm over the crutch, he approached the bed with great caution, suspicion telling him that Fitzwarren might be up to some trick. No snoring might mean that he was awake! He might be tricked into going too near, then the farmer would pounce on him. In that case he would blow the fellow's face off. He was quite icy about it.

There was no sound of breathing, no noise except a slight high-pitched gurgling of gases from the big man's belly. What the hell was wrong with the man? Robby was losing patience. He felt the bed iron against his knee and looked down. He shrank back in horror, his heart thumping, his mouth dry. He was staring down at a ghastly, frightening, almost supernatural sight! The farmer's eyes were unnaturally wide, staring insanely with the whites all round the black pupils, his face a sickly green pallor, his mouth open showing bad teeth, the white-coated tongue lolling limply over the thick lower lip. Robby touched the face. It was cold and clammy.

Death by terror! Some stark horror had already sent the man to his doom!

Robby shivered violently. There was something appallingly ghoulish about a corpse with staring eyes, as if the man's last endeavour had been a struggle to understand the ghastly evidence of his senses before he died. Robby felt the streams of cold streaking through his body as he stared at the awful face. Then all the futility embittered him. The damned shotgun was a useless toy, his obsession with his revenge so stupid! The Fates had stepped in and robbed him of it! He had been kept alive for weeks on a false assumption that he could kill this creature lying on the bed, in revenge, to make him remember and suffer a death to fit the crime! Now all the fantasies had drained away and there was nothing left to live for. And Helen would never have approved of murder, no matter how guilty the victim. His life's purpose had withered and tomorrow he would finish it all. Tomorrow no one would stop him - it was his own useless life, and no one would stop him!

Now it would be stupid to burn the house down. The man was as dead as a doornail. What a banal phrase that was. He had heard it so often before. With more shivers of horror passing through him, he switched off the light and moved to the door. Why had the fellow died like that? Why the awful terror? He began slowly to descend the stairs backwards. He would look around downstairs for signs of an intruder. He was holding the gun by its barrels and at the bottom of the staircase he retrieved his second crutch, emptied the gun and put it where it belonged, replacing the cartridges in their box. There were no fingerprints because of his thick gloves that prevented blisters. He went outside and searched up and down the yard in the moonlight but could find nothing suspicious.

On the way home he looked at his watch beneath a lamp standard:quarter to twelve. Ma would be all anxious and ready to ask questions. He would think of something. He reached the road to Leyland through the fields.

Next morning, before lunch, he went to the new house. Inside he found writing paper and wrote his note to his ma. In a large envelope he enclosed the note and his Last Will and Testament. Before going out to post it, he prepared the kitchen, sealing doors, bringing cushions from the living-room to place by the gas oven door. Ma would send Doug to bring him home to lunch. Doug would find him, try to bring him back to life, fail, and then destroy all evidence of suicide. Next day the family would know the truth. When all was arranged, he collected his letter from the sitting room and went out to the door. He stood for a while looking round the hall and up the splendid stairs, remembering, remembering little things that crowded themselves into a fraction of time that had been the golden age of his life on earth!

* * *

Ian Curtis, now a bonny, clean-cut, dark-haired youth of nineteen, all bronzed from his life at sea, alighted from the bus and looked round for the road he was seeking. With help from a passer-by he reached the address and knocked at the door. A hefty man opened it, Ian recognised him as a relation of his former teacher, a brother, perhaps, stouter but with similar features 'I've come to call on Mr Robert Ferguson, my old teacher,' he explained.

'Oh, you've just missed him by about twenty minutes,'

Douglas said. 'He'll be at his new house. Go along this road for about half a mile until you come to the crossroads. Turn left then walk on until you come to a narrow lane off to the right, and the house is about five hundred yards down there. You can't miss it - it stands alone and it's all new.'

'Thank you sir,' Ian smiled, and set off.

'Who was that?' Emma called from the kitchen.

'Young fella - wanted Robby. I sent him to the new house.' Emma closed the oven door and came in. 'Why did you do that? He may have crossed the fields to our Flora's.'

'He's gone to the new house,' Douglas growled. 'I saw him start off.'

'I wish he wouldn't keep going to that new house. It makes him weep. He's a fool if he's gone there. But I doubt it.'

'If the young fella doesn't find him there, he'll come back here, won't he?' Emma sighed and went back to her cooking.

Ian felt guilty that he had not visited his teacher before this. When he had met his old head master, Mr Norris, in the library, he had heard the story of the tragedy. This had decided Ian to make a special effort to visit his teacher. Because of his time at sea he was a stranger to events.

As he drew near the new house, he saw a figure coming out of it. The man passed through the gateway, obviously crippled, and then came towards him. Well, it didn't look like Fergy but he supposed it must be. The accident had certainly made a mess of things. One leg was shorter than the other as it dangled, hardly bent, between the crutches.

'Hello sir,' Ian called as the figure drew near. Robby gasped and looked up with startled eyes, as if awakening from a brown study.

'Ian!' he exclaimed. 'Ian! What are you doing here?'

'I'm keeping my promise to visit you, sir. You invited me that Christmas you left Chad's.'

'Of course. So I did.'

It was difficult to re-adjust, Robby found. He felt cheated - how could he have taken into account such fortuitous a coincidence? This sudden confrontation

341

annoyed him. I must ask him to go, he thought. I can't talk to him. I'm in no fit state to talk to him. Despite the hostile thoughts, the words that he spoke were natural, controlled by a subconscious urge to do the right thing.

'I was just off to post a letter - but never mind it now. Come back with me, Ian.' Yes, he had been cheated again, but he felt some relief that his dreaded resolve to do away with himself had been delayed, and he cursed his inner frustration. He was using the excuse of this chance encounter. He was a coward and he had to fight it. When the boy had gone, he would carry through his resolve with determination, coward or no. As he opened the front door, he remembered he cushions and the towelling in the kitchen. MY God! If the lad caught a glimpse of those what would he think? They entered and Robby was careful to show him into the sitting-room.

'Sit down, Ian. I'll make some coffee.'

'I can do that, sir, and save you going to the trouble.'

'It's all right, Ian, thank you. I can manage. I've got used to these things.'

He went into the kitchen and began immediately to remove all evidence, hanging up the towelling and draught-killer cloths and taking the cushions to the dining room. He took some milk from the refrigerator and poured it into a saucepan and switched on the gas.

'I shall have to keep my eye on this milk, Ian,' he called. 'Shan't be long.'

When he had ground the coffee and made it, he put some scones on a plate with the cups and saucers and the coffee pot with sugar and cream, all set out on a tray.

'Do you mind carrying in the tray for me, Ian, please?' The young man was pleased to help his incapacitated friend and even poured the coffee and added the cream.

'I saw Mr Norris in the library,' Ian said as he passed the coffee to Robby. 'He told me about everything that happened, sir. I'm very sorry, sir. It was terrible.'

As they sipped their coffee and ate the crumbly buttered scones, Robby described what had happened, clinically, without emotion, not mentioning Fitzwarren, and despite his

342

determinedly impassive manner, he saw the compassion growing in the boy's deep blue eyes.

'Well, sir,' Ian sighed, 'I can't tell you how sorry I am. It was a cruel, terrible tragedy.'

Robby scrutinised his young friend carefully, seeing a different world all at once; perhaps an answer to all his anguish - youthful energy, the healthy glowing countenance, the obvious fitness and beauty and zest for life. Youth was a marvellous thing, a gift that was often unappreciated by those who possessed it. He had been like this at one time. Suddenly it came to him that life was a very precious thing, too precious to be destroyed wilfully, especially if there was still the potential to do good. He thought, whimsically, this boy has been sent out this particular day as an agent of the Fates to point out the error of his old friend's ways, unconscious of his task, merely by being there, as an incidental appearance of youth and charm.

The boy had passed no remark and yet his very presence had made Robby ashamed.

'Ian, would you ever consider suicide if some tragic thing happened to you?'

'No sir. Under no circumstances would I ever consider suicide.'

'What makes you so sure?'

'I'm sure of it because, firstly, it's wrong, secondly I see no sense in adding one tragedy to another. I think suicide is a negative idea and the coward's way out.'

'So you don't think it takes courage to commit suicide?'

'No sir. It doesn't take courage. I think people confuse courage with despair. A very desperate person commits suicide - as the coroner often says - while his mind is disturbed.'

Robby took up his cup and sipped the remainder of his coffee. Ian Curtis was making him feel even more ashamed and inadequate.

'Would you be surprised, Ian, if I told you I have been considering doing away with myself?'

'No sir. It would not surprise me at all. Such a terrible tragedy would make many people think of suicide. In a crisis people often think there is no other solution.'

'Well said, Ian. You have certainly thought about this matter. I don't know why, having the whole of life before you.'

'I have thought about it after having read something about it once.'

'The ever honest Ian,' Robby smiled for the first time in two years. 'You know, Ian, I appreciate this visit. I shan't tell you how near I got to suicidal tendencies. But don't worry, your very appearance today has opened my eyes. I shall never again think of suicide.' The visitor was silent for a while, sipping his coffee, selecting another scone and deep in thought.

'I think I'm a fatalist, sir,' he said at last. 'I was reading the other day about a well-known climber who had been up K2. He came to Wales on holiday, fell thirty feet and killed himself, down a gully. Another of his friends fell three hundred feet in India and lived. Such things don't make sense unless you believe in Fate - one man's time had come, the other's hadn't.'

'Perhaps Fate uses suicide sometimes, do you think?'

'I don't think so, sir. That's why suicide is a crime. I think Fate CAN be thwarted by unnatural behaviour - suicide, murder, and so forth - but it can't be thwarted any other way.'

'You seem to have given the matter a lot of thought, Ian?' The young man laughed. 'It may seem so, sir, but I'm not that clever. I've been reading that mountaineering book and there was a chapter on accidents. That's where I got these ideas.'

Robby found himself laughing again at the boy's patent honesty.

'Ian, you are the epitome of honesty. There aren't many honest people about these days. It's nice to meet someone like you. Why not come back to my mother's place for dinner?'

'I'm sorry, sir. I'm expected at home. I sail for South America tomorrow. I've got to pack.' He carried the tray and the coffee things out to the kitchen and without being asked washed the cups, saucers and plates in hot water. Robby found the deed deeply touching.

'Ian, you are a gentleman,' he declared. 'And I'm honoured to have you as a friend. When you come ashore next time, ring me on the phone and come again to see me, will you? Bring your girlfriend if you have one.'

'No girlfriend yet sir. Can I have your number, sir?' Robby called out the number and Ian entered it into his diary.

'I'll make it a point to come to see you sir,' he promised. 'I'm sorry I've been so long in coming.'

'Well Ian, you don't know how much pleasure you have given me today by calling. I was very down in the dumps. You've been a tonic.'

'I'm very glad, sir.'

They left the house and walked slowly back the way they had come, chatting all the way, Robby learning of places on the other side of the world that are known to sailors, and the peculiar incidents that happened there. And Robby shook hands outside his ma's place and sighed as he watched Ian Curtis walk off briskly, waving before he turned the corner out of sight. Ah, the certainty of youth was a marvellous gift!

* * *

The Monday Evening Post reported the death of Thomas Fitzwarren. His body had been discovered by a Mrs Mary Thompson who had called at the farm for the farmer's washing. On finding no one about she had gone upstairs as usual to change bedclothes and had found the body on the bed. She had telephoned the police and had sounded distraught. They found no suspicious circumstances to connect the death with any criminal act. The inquest would be held on Friday. Mrs Thompson had been treated for shock at Coppleton Hospital.

On Thursday there appeared on the scene, in response to a solicitor's letter, the only living relative of the farmer, his nephew Henry Fitzwarren, a man in his middle thirties. Angus would now have to deal with him in the matter of the auction sale.

The schools' half-term holiday saw the casual labourers with local schoolboys harvesting the potato crop, weighing them into bags and storing them in the closed barn. All these people would have to apply to the solicitor for payment.

Much to the disgruntlement of the nephew, his uncle had died intestate.

'It's typical of my uncle,' he grumbled. 'My dad used to say Uncle Tom ruined that farm. My granddad left him a mixed farm that was damned good in those days, but he got rid of livestock, sold some of the land, and he's been growing spuds ever since, and one or two other root crops. I don't know how he made a living.'

'I know how you feel,' the solicitor laughed. 'I warned him about selling off his assets. He used his truck for haulage as well, you know.'

'How much will the farm sell for?' Henry Fitzwarren asked Angus.

'The house is worth about two thousand pounds - needs a lot doing to it as regards decorating but it's solidly built. The remaining buildings and the land, the tools and machinery will probably bring a further ten thousand pounds. The truck isn't worth much - £50, possibly.'

'I suppose it'll have to go through probate?'

'Yes,' said the solicitor, 'but I shouldn't worry about that. You are the only living relative. I have all your Uncle's books in this office and I shall contact his customers and dispose of the potato crop. Leave everything to me. We have to wait for the results of the inquest before we can do anything. Then we shall have to see what the auction brings.'

'I suggest a reserve of £12,000,' Angus said. 'Are you agreeable?'

'Aye,' said the nephew. 'Get shut of the place. I'm an engineer. I can do nothing with it.'

*   *   *

Feeling calmer and resigned, Robby tried to settle down at home and resume his normal life. The dull ache of the tragedy lingered in the depths of him but he kept himself busy. He replied to all his correspondents, enclosing a cheque for £25 in Alf Atkins's letter for the shed. He paid Emma everything he owed her in insurance premiums and other items she had met during his stay in hospital. Within a fortnight he found himself once more on an even keel to take on his future. Robby had written to Benny Solomons and he came in true friendship, bringing several pattern books of wallpaper and some colour charts for paints. They went together in Benny's car to the new house and Benny took measurements, estimated the amount of paint required and the number of rolls of paper for all the rooms. Robby chose patterns and the following spring a reliable decorator known to both his ma and Flora, came and worked in the house for two weeks. With the interior completed, Flora insisted that she clean out the house and polish the furniture, and make everything ready for occupation.

'Can you afford a housekeeper?' she asked Robby.

'At this moment I can,' Robby said. 'But royalties don't last forever and I shall possibly be relying on my occupational pension eventually - unless I can settle down to write some more. The publisher has been a decent fellow and very co-operative since he heard of my accident.'

There was much to think about and he was pleased on that account. He placed the sale of Mrs Bardsley's big house into the hands of Angus. The house and all else had been left to Helen in her mother's will, despite their differences, and now everything came to Helen's widower husband. It was a deeply ironic and grievous situation, Robby thought. He wrote to Helen's Uncle John and Auntie May and received a sympathetic reply expressing great joy that he was recovering.

Robby bought a rich slab of oak, smoothed it, and painted in fine Roman lettering the name, 'New House' and when all was dry he French polished it with some old bottles of polish he had kept over the years. He carefully fastened it to the wall next to the front door and it gave some class to the entrance. He asked his ma would she come and live there with Douglas. She replied that she could not. Douglas was marrying soon and she was now seventy-six years old and did not fancy looking after Robby and that big house at her age. He should marry again or have a housekeeper who could live in. He dismissed his ma's first suggestion - no woman could possibly find him at all attractive as a husband with uncertain finances, and he decided to advertise for a living-in housekeeper.

He called at Angus's office one day and asked his advice on financial matters. He knew he had to invest something to put his money to profitable use. They discussed various schemes until Angus suggested he should go to see his accountant in Hough Lane.

'Mrs Bardsley's house should bring a goodish amount. Angus assured him. 'It's soundly built and the rates aren't all that high compared with the new property around it. I'll get in touch as soon as we make a deal.'

'Thanks,' Robby said. Angus was being very helpful, and as they went to the door of the office, Angus holding the door open for him, he said, 'I finished your first book. Great stuff. Keep at it, son. And by the way - that Farmer Fitzwarren - peculiar death, wasn't it? I had a funny sensation when I went to the farm one time to make a valuation. I always carry binoculars to see that the slates and whatnot are in good condition. I brought the glasses down one time, still looking, and I'm sure I saw someone in the small wood at the back. I thought it was you for a second. I looked closer but could see nobody. It was strange. I thought of what you'd said that time - 'More things in heaven and earth.'

'Yes, it was strange,' Robby said, quietly. As he crutched his way to the accountant's office he blew out his relief. That could have taken some long explanation if Angus had really thought it was him. But Angus's eyesight, binoculars or not, was very poor.

After the interview with Angus's accountant Robby was given some sound advice to do with savings and investments that would ensure him a reasonable income if his writing failed.

He had two more minor operations on his left leg and was assured by the surgeon that with physiotherapy and wearing a thick-soled shoe, he would be able to discard his crutches in time and use one walking stick if his progress continued. The surgeon advised him to contact a colleague of his for plastic surgery, which would do wonders for his face and might even vanquish the scars. This was encouraging and Robby began to believe, despite his sadness, that his chart of life's ups and downs was now recording a high peak.

*　　*　　*

When poor Lizzie died in her 86th year, Malcolm came from Blackpool and drove Emma and Aunt Charlotte, George's widow, to Glossop. The coffin had been left open and Malcolm told Robby that Lizzie had been a pathetic sight. There were deep marks of redness from the sores that had plagued her all her life, her poor ears large and crinkled from her stepfather's cruelties.

'She's now at rest, poor soul,' Emma had said.

Robby marvelled again at the stamina of his ma's brother and sisters, because Lizzie's longevity seemed to him to be a miracle. He had been a kindred soul with Aunt Lizzie for they had both stepped onto the brink of the suicide pit and had been saved by loving commonsense.

Malcolm had visited New House after his journey to Glossop.

'I had a bit of a snigger when ma and Charlotte went through Lizzie's belongings like two ghouls,' Malcolm laughed. 'We had to stay overnight for the funeral this morning. Lizzie had very little, poor soul. Her estate can't be worth more than £50!'

During their conversation Robby went into the kitchen to prepare refreshments. When he returned, his brother eyed him with sympathy. 'Not so good using those bloody crutches all the time, old son?'

'Well,' I've got used to 'em now, The surgeon said I'll be using a stick soon if all goes well. That'll be a great relief.'

'It will that,' said Malcolm. 'In your predicament - you know, being handicapped and everything, I hate to ask you this - could you help me out, d'you think?'

'Yer, if I can,' said Robby. 'What you want me to do? More posters?'

'No, I wish it were that simple. Fay and I received a final demand for tax. We've got one week to pay. It's four hundred and eighty pounds odd - Angus lent me £280.'

'Oh? That's good. But how can you pay back £480?'

'Well, I arranged with Angus to pay back monthly. Could I do the same with you - that's if you are going to lend me £200.'

'Yer, I'll lend you £200 and you pay it back as you've said.'

'Great,' Malcolm breathed. 'You've saved my life! I'll see that it's paid back, don't worry. Trade's on the upturn and we're doing quite well. It's just that at first it was bloody hard going.'

It occurred to Robby that Malcolm must have been desperate when Angus had limited his loan to £280, otherwise Malcolm would not have come to his brother who was unable to work because of his handicap. There had been remarks about Malcolm's big car from his ma, Douglas, and Angus, complaining of Malcolm's extravagance. But was it really fair to complain about the car? Robby thought. He hadn't complained when Malcolm had driven him home from hospital. Ma and Charlotte hadn't complained about going there and back to Glossop. If you were making snide remarks about someone's extravagance, then you had no right to take advantage of it.

'You know Mal,' he said, 'It's always best to keep on good terms with the Inland Revenue.'

'Aye, I know,' Malcolm agreed. 'In future I'm having a special account at the bank.'

The kettle whistled and Robby went out to make some tea. He set the tray again with cakes and biscuits and called his brother to carry it in. Like Ian, Malcolm was delighted to help, now that his financial troubles were over. As he poured the tea he took a chance and offered to pay interest.

'Rubbish!' Robby retorted at once. 'If you can't help family without charging interest, we've come to a damned pretty pass! Angus isn't charging interest, is he?'

'No, no. I did mention it but he refused.'

'Good. That's more like the family spirit. Will a cheque be convenient?'

'Absolutely. I've an account at the Midland in Blackpool.' They had two cups of tea each and some of the cakes and biscuits. Malcolm's sons were doing well - Stuart the younger was in the Scot's Guards and Frank in the police force.

'That's worked out very well,' Robby said.

Robby wrote a cheque for £200 and handed it to his brother. 'Damned generous of you,' said Malcolm. 'Ten pounds a month for twenty months? Will that be all right?'

'Certainly, if you can manage it.'

'Fay didn't like it when I phoned Angus. She said we should borrow the whole amount from you. I told her that wouldn't be fair.'

Robby laughed. 'Fay's a bit touchy - being beholden to Angus and I think she'd prefer Gwen not to know about all your business, do you think?'

'Oh aye,' Malcolm guffawed. 'You know what women are like.'

Shortly after tea Malcolm took his leave to drive back to Blackpool. Each month from that time forward, a cheque arrived regularly in the post for Robby, frequently the ten pounds that had been agreed, but far too often a cheque for five pounds with a note of apology, and on one or two occasions a cheque for £3! Robby had mixed feelings about Malcolm's foibles.

* * *

The housekeeper was a widow of fifty-five who had a married son living down south. She was living with her sister in Blackburn and the arrangement had not turned out to be very pleasant. This position with Robby would answer all her prayers. She was an excellent cook and good baker. She would be content with what Robby proposed to pay if she could live at New House. She was a motherly person, humble and peace-loving, and this, he imagined after the tale she had told, had been her downfall whilst living with an aggressive sister and family - the Cinderella story of the poor relation being put on. After hearing Robby's explanation of his disability, she wept and on her first day off she told her friend on the way to the cinema that she was determined to do her best for the poor gentleman. Her friend, being female, approved warmly. Once Mrs Hardcastle was established at New House, Emma decided to visit her son. Yes, she told him, he had chosen well. The food was excellent. After lunch she joined the new housekeeper in the kitchen and helped her dry the dishes. She chatted about her Blackburn days, once she knew that Mrs Hardcastle had come from there.

'Yes,' I worked at the Heller's for over four years,' she said. 'I met my future husband there, if you please. He was the father of my six children. I was happy there, but my father was the devil himself.'

She told her story of how she had absconded to Rochley and how her father had dragged her through Squires Clough at dead of night, and the place haunted, too, and how he had threatened to kill her as dead as a doornail, repeating it over and over again.

'Of course, you didn't believe he'd have killed you, surely, my dear?'

'Eh! I don't know about that, missus. Believe me, if he could have got away with it he would certainly have killed me. There's no doubt about that. He was a villain, a devil with a flaming temper!'

In the living room, within earshot of this oft-repeated tale, Robby sat transfixed in deep thought as he stared into the fire. Grandfather would have killed his mother if he could have got away with it. Well, He, Robby Ferguson, almost got away with killing someone. He had been just as guilty as anyone physically attacking old Grandfather's bastard child! He had killed Japs in the war, and all through those days of hate he had had a compulsive urge to kill the farmer, as if the ghost of his Grandfather was inside him, inciting him to murder, fulfilling his death threat at last so that Emma's son would perish by his own hand - he firmly believed now that the farmer had been the old devil's agent, the murderer of Helen, the would-be destroyer of Robert Ferguson, Emma's son. And the farmer's wide-eyed terror had been witness of what he had seen in that drab little bedroom before Robby arrived. Delirium Tremens, the coroner had pronounced - but Robby believed it had been something more than that, something evil, something wholly threatening, something grotesquely murderous, beyond Fitzwarren's understanding in this world! Someone, some THING, had visited that man!

Yes, he had killed before, several times, and had not been troubled; but none of those times had he premeditated crime, killing a man in cold blood and burning the body.

Now New House was peaceful, happy, like a rainbow over a black sky for he knew Helen's spirit would never desert their New House. As the tears moistened his eyes, the gods agreed among themselves that justice had been served without dire consequences and that Foulkes's influence from beyond the grave had been exorcised.